THIS ALMANAC BELONGS TO

_____

Sleepers Publishing Pty Ltd
PO Box 1204
Collingwood Victoria 3066
Australia
www.sleeperspublishing.com
sleepers@sleeperspublishing.com

The Sleepers Almanac No. 5
ISBN: 978-1-740667-32-6

Copyright of each piece belongs to its author.
This collection © Sleepers Publishing 2009.

The works in this *Almanac* are the authors' own and do not reflect the opinions or views of the publisher ('though they might).

All rights reserved.
No part of this publication may be reproduced, stored in a retrieval system or transmitted in any form or by any means electronic, photocopying, telepathy or otherwise, without the prior permission of Sleepers Publishing.

'Elvis, Husbands, and Other Men in Costumes: A Memoir' quotes from Ginsberg, Alan, 'America' in *Howl and Other Poems* (City Lights: San Francisco, 1956).
In 'Don't Smile Till Christmas', the Charlie Brown cartoon is from Schulz, Charles M, *Go Fly a Kite, Charlie Brown* (Holt, Rinehart & Winston: New York, 1960).

This *Almanac* was produced with the fabulous support of Arts Victoria. And this project has been assisted by the Australian Government through the Australia Council, its arts funding and advisory body.

Printed by McPherson's Printing Group, Maryborough, Victoria

Distributed by

Sleepers Publishing is a proud member of the Small Press Underground Networking Community (SPUNC)

the Sleepers almanac No. 5

Edited by Zoe Dattner and Louise Swinn
Sleepers Publishing, Australia

In memory of David Foster Wallace.

Contents

INTRODUCTION IX

Cameraman
Peta Murray 1

How to Talk to People at House Parties
Simon Cox 5

Don't Smile Till Christmas
Richard Lawson 7

Anatomy of a Story
Ryan O'Neill 23

Alex Gets a Job
Eleanor Elliott Thomas 29

Intermittent Red Flashes
Tim Richards 35

In Registry
JB Rawson 43

Salman Rushdie: The Complete Literary Endorsements
Andrew Weldon 47

My World
Andrew Hutchinson 49

In the Pines
Ella Holcombe 53

Elvis, Husbands, and Other Men in Costumes: A Memoir
Liza Monroy 55

God of All Things
Jo Bowers 81

The Day of the Hen
Tony Birch 85

The Etymology of Love
Daniel Ducrou 95

Hell is Other Parents
Jo Case 109

To Childhood
Todd Hearon 121

Attack of the Tiny Miracles
Max Barry 123

Missing
Kalinda Ashton 135

The Teaspoon and the Tolling Bell
Imogen Melgaard 147

Welcome to Romance Writing 1A
Rose Mulready 153

Haiku Angst
Oslo Davis 158

Kieslowski's Unlikely Comedy
Patrick Cullen 161

A Dark Place
Brendan Ryan 175

We Must Catch Up
Virginia Peters 177

Panic in Year Zero
Vinnie Wilhelm 195

The Honeyeaters
Myron Lysenko 209

The Love Quiz
Rosemary Jones 213

Pink
Leanne Hall 219

The Bible
Samuel Bartlett 232

Letter from Edinburgh Writers' Festival
Russell McGilton 233

off-white
Grace Yee 235

The Hungry Grass
Aaron Mannion 237

White Summer
Pierz Newton-John 249

Flight
Melissa Beit 259

Grief
Ian C Smith 269

Agapanthus
SJ Finn 275

THE BRIEF WONDROUS LIVES OF... 289

Hurrah!
Zoe and Louise gratefully acknowledge the time and assistance given by Kate Wyatt, Lucy Nelson and Ian See. Thanks also go to Fran and Emma at Hardie Grant, and to Arts Victoria and the Australia Council, for all their support.

Introduction by Zoe Dattner and Louise Swinn, eds

Walking through Fitzroy one afternoon, we came across a boy crouched over an injured bird. The boy was in the process of saving the bird, and we had faith that he would do everything in his power to give the bird life. He explained to us that he needed to go to his house for some soft gloves. We offered to wait with the bird until his return. When he came back a couple of minutes later, we talked as we gently placed the bird in his gloved hands; mainly our talk focused on the bird because we were all a bit infected with the tragedy of the situation. Just before he headed off we wanted to thank the boy – for the bird, mainly, but also for us, because then we weren't lumped with the responsibility, and also for the universe, which could always use more boys like him. We asked him his name so that we could thank him properly, and he looked at both of us with a little smile and said, 'Aviary'.

We've always collected stories. How could we not? The real ones – like Aviary – and the made up ones. Each year, reviewers and readers tell us which *Almanac* stories they like and which ones they don't, and here's the thing: they never agree. There is precious little logic to it, and it's almost impossible to discern any commonality of taste. If we tried to second-guess readers then we'd be stuck – we just couldn't – so we select the stories that appeal to us. We choose them because they move us, or they are well written, or they sound like nothing we've ever read before, or because they are funny or clever, or they feature a hugely appealing character. Perhaps they take us somewhere we have been some time in the past and want to return to, or perhaps they take us somewhere that we haven't been to and want, really want, to see what it would be like. Perhaps we like wearing other people's layers.

Do people who write stories need to believe, as Robert McKee puts it in *Story* (Harper Collins, 1997), that their 'vision can be expressed only through story, that characters can be more "real" than people, that the fictional world is more profound than the concrete'? We don't know. Do their publishers need to believe this? Definitely. And we do. It's a slice of the universe, and we believe in it. Real life is this good, because it contains stories. Here are just some of them…

Cameraman

Peta Murray

She wakes early, disturbed by a noise in the room. She rolls over, to see a pint-sized Batman beside the bed. He has a camcorder pressed to his mask. The tape is rolling.

'Where'd you come from?'
'Daddy brought me.'
'He's not supposed to bring you till tomorrow.'
'He had to go to Brisbane. On a air-o-plane.'
'Good of him to tell me.'

The kitchen is as she left it. There are the remains of her own dinner, a corner of a pie, aground in gravy. The ants have found it. She scrapes the plate and plunges it, ants and all, into scalding water. She pours milk for the cat and drowns a dozen more. The boy is there with his camera.

'Are you allowed to play with that?'
'Daddy borrowed it to me. This is a movie. You're in it.'
'Me. Dead ants. Anyone else?'
'Maybe.'
'Let me have a shower.'

She scrubs at her skin with the loofah. She's read that toxins come out through the pores. The water goes cold while there's soap in her hair. By the time she's dressed, the television is on, and he's filming the screen.

'Damon!'

'What?'

This is not the agreement. His father is not allowed to renege like this, returning the child early like a dull library book. She dials, and gives voicemail a piece of her mind. When she turns around, he's there again, his camera trained on her face.

'Did you film that?'

'Only the last bit.'

'Jesus.'

She slams the kitchen door and he knows better than to follow. She puts the kettle on and lets it boil, steaming up the room, as she flicks through the book she borrowed for her hermit's weekend. Someone has written all through it. There are pencil notes in the margin and whole paragraphs underlined.

The boy pads softly into the kitchen. She sets her book aside.

'Can we do something yet?'

'Soon.'

She ruffles his hair. He skates away in his socks.

She makes herself a coffee. On top of the fridge is her jar of cigarette butts. She's supposed to keep them for one year, on display, as a reminder. The pale pink filters look like babies' fingers in the ash. She stows the jar under the sink.

After lunch she goes into the garden with two oven mitts to kneel on. The weeds have grown up again, even where she sprayed them. She calls to the boy to get the fork.

'The digging thing. My digger.'

'What's it look like?'

'Never mind.'

She rummages in the tool shed for the fork. Something sharp slips under her thumbnail. She yelps. A line of blood forms under the throbbing nail, and wells over the sides.

She runs, dripping, to the laundry and thrusts her hand under a tap. Blood mingles with water, as it spirals down the hole.

'Damon! Get me a bandaid.'

He scurries off, camcorder perched on his shoulder like a pirate's parrot, returning with the bandaid and some antiseptic cream. He films as she unscrews the cap with her teeth and dresses the wound with her good hand.

'Don't help, will you?'

'How?'
'You're all I need, honestly. Cecil B DeMille. Christ.'
'What did I do?'
'For the last time, turn that fucking camera off.'

By three o'clock he's tired and irritable too. She sends him to his room for a sleep, and settles on the couch. She thumbs through the TV guide, looking at photos of the stars. She studies their teeth and hands for telltale stains. She holds up her own hands, examines her palms. Even in the afternoon light, lines are visible. She can see the lacework pattern of her own skin. Her knuckles are swollen and creased, and her index finger is flecked with brown. This is her right hand, her smoking hand. There's dirt under each nail, and the bandaid, like a little hat, on her thumb.

The phone rings. It's her sister, calling for sympathy. She's not in the mood to talk. She chews at the skin around her nails and tries to sound interested. She hears the pad of bare feet on the stairs. Like a periscope, the camera appears over the banister, its single eye zeroing in.

'Just a moment, Lou…'

She glowers at the boy. He turns and disappears.

She cooks their tea. He's one step ahead of her, hovering close to film her at the stove. He makes her sit and eat, for the camera. After dinner she plays Uno with him and lets him win. She takes him upstairs and helps him off with his Batman cape. He folds it carefully and slips it under his pillow.

'Don't be silly, Damon. Look at your pillow.'
'I've finished my movie.'
'Have you?'
'Watch it if you like.'
'How?'
'Just plug it in and play it in the telly.' He slides his hands under his pillow to feel his cape. 'I can sleep like this. Daddy lets me.'
'Well. I'm not Daddy.'
'I know. I know who you are.'
'Who am I?'
'You're Old Turkey.'
'Old who?'

'Turkey. I heard you on the phone. You said you stopped smoking and you're Old Turkey and that's why you're so grumpy. Aren't you?'

'Yes.' She kisses him and turns out the light.

She plugs the camera in to watch his movie. It's in and out of focus but it's all there, her hostile gaze, the floating ants, her open mouth and the three drops of blood on the steps. Even their watery dinner. It's all there in living colour, and over it all, for a soundtrack, her weary voice, sniping and snarling at the masked cameraman.

She goes for her purse. There's a ten-dollar note, and another five in change. More than enough for one last packet, and some sweets for the boy. Two more weeks, and then she'll try again. She leaves the television on, in case he should wake, and walks to the corner store.

How to Talk to People at House Parties

Simon Cox

I think the kid's name was Luka
and I'm not sure why his parents took him to the party
or what sort of *Jungle Book* bravery
steeled him against the Grown-Up throng,
but there he was, a five-year-old boy,
sitting on the linoleum floor playing paper
airplanes amongst a dense forest of adult legs,
oblivious to the drunken canopy of chatter above him,
throwing his crude origami aircraft this way and that,
a golden-haired chimp playing on the jungle floor.

I was getting a drink for my friend when
his plane's erratic flight ended at my feet,
and I imagined a hull full of panicky stick figures
emerging from the paper fuselage,
nursing finger-painted wounds and
escaping on spidery legs out into a wild night
already dissolving in a blur of
cigarette lighters, bottle openers and
names I would forget.

Luka (I didn't forget his name)
looked down at his aviation accident,
and then up at me with calm and expectant eyes,
and so I placed my drink on a table,
knelt down,
introduced myself,

and threw the plane back to him.

Ten minutes later my friend ventured inside,
wondering where I was with her drink,
and found me sitting on the floor,
a monk on a prayer mat,
throwing pieces of paper into folded freefall,
back and forth, back and forth,
with little Luka sitting on the linoleum.

She decided to join us, and
what we learnt there together she and I
– together the shortest edge of a Bermuda
Triangle that Luka's brave
vessel crossed again and again –
was that we were much happier on the floor,
floating on the calm waters of children's logic,
than we were out in the backyard rough
with cigarette smoke and beer breath and
the six-stringed freak waves of basement rock.
That we were happier sitting on the floor,
floating on the sea within the sea,
making airplane noises with our mouths. ('Wooosh!')

So much so that when Luka's
parents suddenly whisked him away,
and we were left sitting on the floor with
a mute piece of folded paper between us

there was a moment of shared indecision
in which we both, silently I think,
considered the possibility that
we might carry on regardless.

I said, 'what if we just sit here?'

You said, 'I think we should at least make a pretence
of not being socially retarded,'
and so we stepped out into the night.

Don't Smile Till Christmas

Richard Lawson

A red Fiat 500 is asking for trouble (from teenagers, not elephants). As the Bambino rims the fog-shrouded bay, Lou breathes deeply, incanting: '*I am not my past!*'

Bach pulses through the speakers. She turns left into a street speckled with weatherboards, passes the RSL where they had drinks for new teachers at the end of last term. She remembers the victory trill of the pokies, shudders.

It's first day, second term. Lou's about to start teaching history at Wy Wy High, on the Central Coast, north of Sydney. She expected a posting deep in Sydney's western suburbs, teaching poor kids waiting for their dole. The position at beachy Wy Wy sounded promising. At the very least it was an escape from Methodist School for Girls, the private college where she'd served her first year out. But her uni mate Myra, a Coastie herself, warned her not to get fanciful: 'Coasties, darl, are Westies who surf!'

For a second, Lou tries to hate Myra – for being right, and in Sydney. As the Fiat splutters into the school car park, she ejects Bach from the disc player, slips in Machine Gun Fellatio. She touches the five-cent splotch of psoriasis on her neck, manages not to scratch.

'*Nothing is more important than today!*'

Her affirmations have fogged the windscreen. She rubs a porthole with her sleeve, looks out at the dewy playing fields. Without people, the ugly buildings seem serene. Her watch says 7.32 a.m. but she can't see a soul. By now, the MSG car park would be full.

She has a flash of her poodle, Noodles, alone in their new unit. *How will I find a decent man up here?* Making her way to the staffroom, she remembers the men in the RSL last week, deletes 'decent'. She passes a beefy bloke in overalls, holding a trellis square up to the wall.

'Hey! I'm Lou – new history teacher!'

'Dunno.'

'Hey Danno!'

'Every fuckin' weekend, kids tear it down... every Mondee, I bung it back up!' he vents.

Danno's cranky hammer starts pounding. Lou opens her mouth, closes it, walks away.

The staffroom's locked. As she squats on the concrete, waiting, a year of MSG Mondays coagulates in her mind. She retrieves her diary from her briefcase, scrawls:

> Monday 28 April
> First day at Wy Wy. Flashbacks of MSG – that staffroom, me scurrying for my cubicle, past the menopausals, stooped over their desks like old nuns at prayer. (Could've ended up the same!) I can hear my 'Good morning' bouncing back at me, booby-trapped. Why did they dislike me so much? Why did I try so hard to please them?
>
> I can see my email box, bursting with deadlines, meetings, rosters for dances, debates, carnivals, musicals, meet-the-parent picnics... Who told them I was a soft touch with no life?
>
> I so remember every inch of the trudge to Pastoral Care, sniffing perfume from the flowers in the Principal's Cottage, taking in the sun-glazed hockey fields, marvelling how everything was Eden. (If he exists, God definitely sends his kids to MSG!) Jesus, how I yearned for demountables and squalor!
>
> And the stairwell, how I used to hide for a second in that niche near the janitor's closet, looking up at the whorl of pleated tartan, hearing the salve of adolescent bitching:
>
> 'Come on, ya gutlesh cunt – Mish Madishon never checshs the roll...'
>
> 'You didn't... O-MY-GOD... you-dirty-slut... Tell <u>all</u>...'
>
> Such a relief to hear those voices – so different from the ones that honeyed me all day with 'misses' – speaking as they

felt, not as they ought! If a moment could ever have been mystical in a place like MSG, that was it.

Picture myself again in the staffroom, in one of my 'frees' (ha!), taking out my aggro on the laptop (<u>their</u> laptop!) The stagnant quiet turns my fingers into mallets. Hilary Madison, one of the lifers, comes over, rests a barnacled hand on my shoulder: 'Why don't you join ush, Louish, for prayersh in the chapel at luntsh?'

7.57 a.m.
Lou watches Danno hammering below. *Not my type. Maybe he's single…?*

Two teachers arrive – a fifty-something bloke with a tawny beard, mad eyes; a woman, not much older than Lou, attractive. Perhaps they'll be friends. Lou scrambles to her feet.

'Jerry – Ancient History,' he says, unlocking the door.

'Lou – new—'

'Mod History teacher… Hey Lou.' A smile, mischievous, kind.

'Hello,' the girl says flatly, pushing inside.

'That's Stella,' says Jerry.

'Stella Coleman?'

Jerry nods. Lou's heart flutters. She and Stella are team-teaching Year 11 Modern History, beginning first up today.

She steps into the staffroom, inhales musty carpet. Jerry points out her desk.

'Early birds, eh!' chirps Lou.

Jerry guffaws, opens the window, pokes out his head. 'Jesus no! We got early classes, ma dear – timetable clash!'

'Oh! Um… Stella… Do you have a minute? Can we talk about Year 11…?'

'Nope.' Stella boots up the computer, starts playing solitaire.

Jerry opens the fridge, releasing a smell of rot. He removes a mouldy container, sniffs it, licking his lips.

'BRAWGHHH!'

His eyes flit dementedly from Lou to Stella, as he 'vomits' the sludge into the bin.

There's a knock at the door. A tanned boy pokes his head in.

'ONE more step, just ONE, you're on a card!' barks Stella.

Jerry motions him back.

'Emperor Tiberius, your minnows await in the grotto!' the boy announces, straight-faced.

'Presently, minion minnow! Presently!' declares Jerry, thrusting out his chin. When the door shuts, he makes a disgusting sound. Lou decides to like him.

Jerry and Stella go to their classes, leaving her free to take in the bedlam. Everything is so un-MSG. There are yellowing towers of handouts, never handed out; out-of-date schedules on the noticeboard; Teachers Federation posters in every corner, loud and proud. On the back of the door is a cartoon by Michael Leunig: a suicide hanging from a rope and pulley. The counterweight is a bucket under his feet, filling with his tears. Not much of a mission statement, but it tops the *Jesus Loves You!* posters at MSG.

Lou sits at her desk, unpacks her *Teachers Chronicle*, missing her laptop. The desk beside her is bookless. On the wall above there's a *Peanuts* cartoon:

> Lucy to Linus: You a doctor! Ha! That's a big laugh! You could never be a doctor! You know why? Because you don't love mankind, that's why!
> Linus to Lucy: I love mankind… It's people I can't stand!!

Lou smiles, just a little. The name on the roster next to the cartoon says 'Noel Henderson'. Maybe he's not too old.

She goes down to the common room, scything through strange faces with the welded smile she picked up at MSG. She empties her pigeonhole, hurries back to her desk, gets busy. Noel turns up, five minutes from the bell. He's fifty-something, bald, ugly.

'Welcome to Planet of the Apes,' he quips. His eyes are incendiaries. He paces the room like a speed fiend. Lou wants to ask questions, doesn't. She wonders where Arty Ainsworth, Head of History, is. He should be here to answer the questions she's afraid to ask Noel. She met Arty last week at the RSL – quiet to the point of strange, fifty-something, bald…

The first bars of 'Land of Hope and Glory' shudder through the school. It's the electronic chimes, the beginning of a teaching day. Stella appears just after a second wave of chimes. She picks up a pile of exams, nods for Lou to pick up the other.

'We'll start "Rise of Hitler" tomorrow. Today, we'll go over their exams from last term. Transparency, the principal calls it. Fucking window-dressing more like!'

Walking to E block, Stella briefs, Lou nods. 'This is the worst class in the entire school.' She stops, shoots Lou a glare. 'And in case the grapevine hasn't tickled you yet, this is the worst school in the entire state. There're thirty-three kids and they all have learning or behavioural difficulties… with eight IOs thrown in for fun.'

Lou raises an eyebrow.

'Intellectually moderate, as in mostly toilet-trained.'

'That doesn't sound too moderate to me!' says Lou.

'Wait till you see intellectually severe,' cuts Stella.

Lou doesn't ask. 'I don't really have special ed training,' she admits.

'Well, that's two of us. They cancelled special classes last year. "Integration" is their new codeword for "stop wasting money on morons". We're s'posed to have a special ed assistant once a cycle, but she's off on stress leave – indefinitely.'

E block is a dirty grey monolith, like all the others. Lou's heart starts misbehaving. She wants to touch her puffer, but can't let go of the exams. She studies the chewing gum scabs in the corridor carpet, thinking blackheads, rabid teenagers. They pass a line of buckets, half-filled with dirty water. Stella kicks one gently.

'They still haven't fixed the roof! In-fucking-credible! Don't s'pose you have too many leaks at that Sydney finishing school of yours…'

Stella stops. E13. Theirs. Lou hears caged thunder inside. Something heavy hits the frosted window near her head.

Stella sighs. 'Think of everything you've learned and forget it. Let the trouble find you. And *don't* try to save them. It's the only advantage of teaching in a zoo: no one seriously expects animals to read and write.' As her hand reaches for the doorknob, Stella turns for a final shot. 'You know what they say, toots – don't smile till Easter!'

Lou smiles. Stella frowns.

'Seeing you're starting second term, we'll make it Christmas.'

The classroom is thick with lanky, tanned, waxy-haired teenagers, slouching in clusters, spraying attitude. Lou draws in the pong of pubescent armpits, mouldy carpet. She notices with surprise a girl in hijab in the back row. Lou tries to find a stance that makes her look scary but cool. *Feel the fear, do it anyway!* A boy in the front row – good-looking, dangerous – winks. She remembers not to smile. The girl next to him is holding a doll in nappies upside down.

'EVERYONE BACK TO YOUR SEATS!' bellows Stella. Slowly, the kids dribble back to their chairs. Stella marks the roll.

'This is Miss Morrison. She'll be teaching with me from now on. Double the fun!'

Stella waits for quiet. And waits. Finally, she smacks a hand down on the exams.

'The principal's asked us to review your exams from last term.'

Blank stares. Stella ploughs on regardless.

'The topic – you might remember it – was World War I. Mayada topped the class with forty-eight per cent. No surprises there. After her, it's all downhill.'

Up the back, Mayada's headscarf quivers. Her eyes say *Wow! That's almost a pass!* A boy whispers something in her ear. Mayada punches him hard. Stella waits for the cheers to die, distributes papers.

'The multiple choice was atrocious! For the record, the Western Front wasn't in New Zealand. The empathy exercise was worse… how can a soldier write in his journal *after* he's had his head blown off? George gets a Logie for his effort. His Tommy had his fingers shot off by a sniper in paragraph one. After "Ouch, my fingers…" there's nothing but scribble. Nice try, mate!'

Whoops all round. A boy in the back eyeballs Lou while he picks his nose, rolls a snotball. He starts painting it with white-out. IO. Lou scans the class for others. Nearby's a mop of hair where a face should be, bobbing up and down, sans iPod. Eureka. Lou pats her puffer.

'At least those two showed a drip of originality,' Stella continues. 'The rest of *yooos* wrote nothing but rubbish. Everybody, get out your books! Write this down!' Most of the class don't have stationery. There's a melee of tearing paper, flying pens.

'Write this down, WRITE-THIS-DOWN: "I am never, NEVER again going to finish a writing exercise with the words 'AND THEN I WOKE UP'."'

Lou has playground duty at recess. She hovers round her area, hoping for peace. A few students come out of their sulks, stare at her briefly. Most ignore her. She sees smoke dribbling from the window of the girls' toilet, presses a hand to her chest, hurries inside.

A blond boy is leaning against the wall, chatting up two girls on the floor, smoking. He's one of her Year 11s. Lou spies another doll in nappies, face down on the wet concrete next to the girls.

'This is the girls' toilet! What do you think you're doing?' she wheezes at Blondie.

He draws on his cigarette, blows smoke in her face.

'Fuck off!'

The girls snicker.

Lou wonders what to do. She wonders too – pointlessly – about the psychology of it all. If she yells, he'll win, but how's she supposed to talk with a quiet voice, when there's no big stick, and he knows it?

'HOW DARE YOU! You're coming to the deputy NOW!'

Smoke seeps from his nostrils. 'Yeh? Hey girls, we're going to the deputy! How you gonna make me, Tox? Touch me and I'll sue ya!' He flicks his burning butt straight past her ear. 'You're a fuckin' joke!'

Tox? He's noticed her psoriasis. *How does a dumb kid hit bullseye without even trying?* Lou feigns tough, tells herself he doesn't know how much it hurts, but the girls' snickering cuts to the bone. She promises herself that tomorrow will be a mental health day, knowing it won't be. She has to find Ross, the deputy principal.

She leaves, but outside there must be twenty students milling. She pushes through them, Blondie at her side. The crowd shadows him, a swarm of blowies on the scent of dead meat.

Blondie starts up a chant: 'Hey Tox! Whatchagonnadonow? Whatchagonna...'

She tries to look purposeful, but it all falls apart when she can't find Ross's office. The mob howls. Lou bites her lip. If she cries, she'll lose cred forever.

Suddenly whispers shiver through the swarm. 'Roid! Roid! Roid!'

A muscle man in gym gear turns up.

'Is there a problem here, Miss?'

'This... this boy – I don't know his name – was smoking in the girls' toilets... he swore at me, refused to report to the deputy...'

Roid's eyes tenderise Blondie.

'You're in deep shit, Michael. Apologise immediately to Miss...'

'Morrison.' *Thanks for nothing Roid! Now they* know *I'm a nobody.*

'Sorry Miss Morrison.' Michael's meek as a bolloxed sheep.

'Report to the deputy's office, wait there till he turns up,' bawls Roid.

'Sir,' bleats Michael.

Why does Roid terrify Michael, when his stick's no bigger than mine? Why does a muscle man get respect for saying 'shit', when I'd just get into trouble?

In the staffroom at lunch, writing out her incident report, she waits for the heavens to fall, but no one says a thing. She recalls what Myra told her once: 'The world ain't against you, darl – it's far too busy playing with itself to care!'

Later, Lou asks Jerry about the dolls.

'Counsellor's idea, meant to make the girls think twice before getting knocked up. They have to take them everywhere. It's been a hit – the girls get to leave class to feed and change them.'

Noel ('Face' to the kids) tells them he's quit smoking. Arty, staring furiously at his computer, asks Lou if everything's okay. His eyes don't leave the screen. Lou guesses the question's rhetorical.

Jerry announces after-school drinks at the RSL.

'Ancient tradition, Lou. Attendance compulsory.'

Arty looks up, revs his throat. 'Not this arvo, mate. Off to the hospital. Val and I are getting hitched.'

Silence – the kind that roars. Jerry slaps Arty's back. Noel chews his fork. Stella plays solitaire on the computer. *Why would a man get married on the first day of term? In a hospital? Is his wife sick? Or a nurse? And why doesn't anyone say 'congrats'?*

Her last two classes are straight out of hell. At day's end, Jerry explains: even the teachable kids become vampires after lunch.

'Three words of advice, Lou: video booking sheet... but get in early...!'

She stuffs her briefcase, waits for the kids to disperse before escaping – a question of minutes. On the way out, she catches Noel smoking under the stairwell.

'Cigarette, love?' he says guiltily.

'No... I don't.' She can't quite manage a smile.

At her car, she freezes at the sight of green gobs splattered over her bonnet. *They must've seen me sneaking out for aspirin at lunchtime!* There's a note under the windscreen.

NO WARE U LIVE TOX

Lou pictures her Bambino parked outside her unit on Wy Wy's main drag. He probably does know where she lives. The tears come, just as Jerry and Stella turn up. Stella purses her lips, gets in her car. Jerry slaps Lou's back, just like he did with Arty. 'It's nothing personal, Lou... initiation rites and all.'

Stella screeches out of the car park.

Lou tells him about Michael, shows him the note.

'Ah, Michael's all fart and froth,' soothes Jerry. 'I didn't even know he could write. Come on, I'll drop you at the RSL, bring you back after.' He looks at her neck, frowns.

'Nasty rash there, Lou.'

Lou checks her neck in the side-view mirror. The five-cent piece is a ten.

Wednesday (hump day!) 30 April
No more oysters on my bonnet! Jerry's offered to pick me up in the mornings, drop me home after work. It'll mean coming in later and leaving on the bell. I can live with it.

Michael's back from suspension today. Stella was off on a sickie, so I had to fill in his conduct card. Wrote 'steady' for application (true!), 'improving' for behaviour. (The lies we tell!)

Monday 12 May
In the vortex, my constant is the staffroom.

Noel is intelligent, sardonic, angry, but less scary now he's back on the cigs.

Jerry is our (my?) harlequin, jesting to a court that's forgotten how to laugh, jesting anyway. (Could it be I've a teeny crush?)

Arty's hopeless... lights on, nobody home. All he does is stare at his computer, thinking maybe if he doesn't look up the world might disappear. Everyone treads on eggshells round him. No one twists the knife, not even Stella.

Stella's our Resident Bitch. Never does more than the statutory minimum. Always playing solitaire on the desktop, waiting for something to snarl at. She isn't <u>all</u> bad (I guess!) – Jerry says she keeps a box of cereal in her drawer, feeds one of her Year 8s in B17 every recess. The kid's malnourished (alkie parents).

Most of them can teach. Some might even admit they care (after a schooner or ten!)

Wednesday 14 May
Year 8 Parent–Teacher Night. Wheezing all day with the stress of it, worrying about what to say. Only had them three times, barely know who's who. All went well at first. (Hardly anyone turned up – that helped!) Then Alex Wilson's parents stormed out halfway through our interview, vowing carnage.

'I said he was doing fine. What's their problem?' I said to Jerry. He tried not to laugh. Alex is a she.

Sweet consolation: Tuesday afternoon sport with Jerry, taking the girls with period pain, the walking wounded, the forged-note brigade for walks on Wy Wy Beach. Here, sun on her cheek, sea at her ankles, Jerry's voice in her ear, the old wounds smart a little less.

Sometimes Jerry turns earnest, tells her about his other life – his rock garden, his wife, Eva, who teaches English at Central Coast Grammar, his son Tom, who's studying law in Sydney.

One day, he stops in his tracks, looks out at the waves, searching for something not there.

'It's a mug's game, Lou, this noble profession of ours. Was different when I started… smaller classes, kids muzzled, houses cheap. But it's all gone slowly to hell, and it's only getting worse. What's going to be left, when the likes of me go, and the likes of you realise they deserve better? What happens to the smart country when there aren't any decent teachers left to teach?'

Lou gouges sand with her toe.

'So why teaching? What's your excuse? You should get out, before you turn into Stella.' Jerry's voice is cruel and kind.

Lou's toe digs for China.

'She started out like you, you know. But you don't want to hear that. You're going to change the world. You're going to save them.'

Lou tries to meet his eye, squints in the glare. 'I thought I was at uni, in my essays, anyway. Now… I'm wondering how I'm going to save myself…'

'We're history teachers, Lou. We should know the bastards who want to save the world are always the ones who screw it.'

She keeps quiet, studies his life-bitten face, for the first time seeing an old man.

Lou's old wounds twinge. She wants to talk about somebody else's pain.

'Jerry, what's the story with Arty?'

'Arty! Used to be a live one, Lou! Dinkum! Union rep, footy coach, conshy teacher even. About ten years ago, his girl Sonya got into smack. One day she's sitting in the front row in D block, the next she's turning tricks in the Cross. Tore his marriage apart. He hired a private dick to find her, bribed her to go into rehab – some place in Sydney promising miracles, the kind Medicare doesn't cover, of course. Had to remortgage the house to pay for it. She's clean now, got a good fella, regular job, but it all meant Arty had to stay five years longer in this place.'

Lou watches kids dodging the surf. A few of the boys scoop up froth, spatter the girls' T-shirts. They squeal indignation, delight.

'Last year Arty met Val at an in-service. She teaches history at Gosford High. Nice bird. They weren't exactly fireworks, but there was a spark in Arty's eye – miracle enough. A month after Val moved in with him, the quacks told her she had bowel cancer, gave her six months if she fought it. One year tops.

'That's when Arty's spark died for good. He hasn't looked up from that computer since. Doesn't talk about it, no one asks, but Babs in the library has friends at Gosford High, keeps us posted. Val's been in and out of Gosford Hospital more times than I can count.'

One of the boys flings a used condom at the girls, with a stick.

'Desist, you horrible child!' Jerry roars. Lou takes in a lungful of sea air, as Jerry chases the kids along the beach. She watches the breakers crescendo and die on the sand, wave after wave after wave of them. *All that potential energy gone to waste...*

Friday 20 June
Feeling almost human, but soooo tired. Less work than MSG but much more stress! Daily bonfires have dwindled to spot fires. Psoriasis nearly gone. They still call me 'Tox' behind my back though. Learning the basics of animal handling. Jerry says the key is choosing your battles. Might have to cancel my trip to Myra's this weekend. SO MUCH MARKING!

Monday 23 June
Resolution: no more weekends marking, planning lessons. Noodles restless. Humping my dolls again. Squeezed his glands – better.

Monday 4 August
Scandal! The principal's banned the dolls. Counsellor Sue's in a tizz. One of her girls is preggers. Mother blames the dolls for making her clucky. Sue says the dolls have nothing to do with it, blames the government's $5,000 baby bonus. What next?

Wednesday 6 August
Drove the Bambino in today. First time since… Even left Bach in the disc player. (Fuck 'em!) Kids followed me to the staffroom, waving imaginary conductor sticks, but no gobs this arvo on the bonnet. Guess I'm a fixture!

Friday 19 September
Two miracles in a single day! Mayada got fifty-two in the exam, Michael came off his conduct card.

Early fourth term, Michael hails her when she is leaving one Friday. Normally, Friday arvo, anyone between Lou and the gate is road kill. But she stops, because it's Michael.

'I got this interview at Handyman's Heaven, Miss – full-time. If I get the job, it'll mean quitting school, but I reckon it's all good.'

Lou nods, flexes her knuckles round her briefcase handle.

'The dude on the phone said bring my résumé but. How do I get one of them, Miss?'

She puts down her briefcase.

'When's the interview?'

'Wednesday.'

Lou lets out a martyr's sigh.

'You'll have to write one yourself, Michael. But I'll help. Meet me in the computer room Monday, beginning of lunch. Don't forget.'

Come Monday lunch, staring at the blank screen, Michael hovering, she chooses her font, begins…

'What's your phone, Michael?'

'Don't 'ave one, Miss. We're povo.'

'Email?'
Michael beams.
'Got one of those!'
'Uh huh...'
'honeyglazedrentboy@hotmail.com' he notes proudly. 'Sick, eh!'
Somehow, by Tuesday, Michael has a finished résumé, replete with new email address, semi-honest job history, and a list of forewarned teachers as referees.

On his last day, he visits the staffroom to tell her he got the job. He invites her to a keg party Saturday evening on the beach. Lou can't make it (hot date in Sydney with Myra's flatmate!) but she's chuffed, lets him know it. This is as close to 'thank you' as she'll get in a place like this. Next day he's gone, unremarked, unmissed. For Lou, though, his face is one of the handful that'll stick.

Friday 10 October
Told Myra over the phone I can't make it to Sydney every weekend. She sounded hurt, but it's such a long way, and those Sunday evening bank-ups on the F3 really kill me!
   Friday night drinks at RSL. As usual. (Would be nice to have more social options than 'RSL or leagues club?') Five rounds half-listening to the old-timers banging on about the good old Whitlam days and their super. Everyone but me has an exit date. All they do is count the days.

Friday 17 October
Blurry night at RSL. Went home with Rob (Roid). Great pecs but... didn't stay after. (Know now why the kids call him Roid!)

Saturday 18 October
Bought Noodles a puppy – Kelpie cross. Saw him in the pet shop window, couldn't resist!

Friday 28 November (H -21)
Premier visited today. (Election time!) Had to sit in the hall, listening to him crap on how his history master inspired Present Greatness. After, he got a minder to hand the principal a giant cheque for the cameras. $5,000

towards a new roof. ($135,000 to go!) Kids didn't raise a boo, stunned, gawking, wondering what a premier was, hoping he wouldn't stop talking till they'd missed period four.

All the staff kept staring up at the rafters, praying for rain. No luck there, but Moira from Home Economics whipped up some homemade karma – let her IOs make the premier's morning tea.

Saturday 6 December (H -13)
I have to kill this diary. My head's so crowded. Thoughts keep changing colour before I can write them down. So many of my dreams are curdling into nightmares. Why record that? It's like that *Peanuts* cartoon above Noel's desk... I'm Linus upside down – hating humanity on principle, liking people by default. Mostly, after a seven-lesson day, I hate humanity *and* people, period! It scares me.

I just don't know how to end it. I hear the inner English teacher nagging: *you can't finish the story without a proper resolution...*

Monday 8 December (Last entry – positively!)
And then I woke up.

A whisker from the end, Stella finally blows a gasket with some kid refusing to pick up rubbish. She almost hits him, only Noel's there to pull her away. She goes on stress leave – indefinitely. With less than a week to go, the principal tells Lou to soldier on solo with Year 11 (now, God help them, Year 12!)

The final Monday. When Lou arrives, Danno's squatting next to the pathway, fixing trellis.

'Good weekend, mate?' she asks, not stopping.

'Dunno.'

The rain comes just as the chimes start. In E13, Lou positions the stand-by bucket under the leak next to her desk. Unacceptable! She accepts it. In five days she'll be free of this place for six weeks – no point bursting a vein.

She waits for the talking to cease. And waits. She never loses this battle, however long it takes. 'Never talk over them,' they told her on prac. 'It's thirty against one – how can you win?' She eyes the clock, working out how much she's earning (pre-tax) while they prattle. (Stella's trick!) She wears a twisted smile, suggesting she knows something they don't, which, of course, she doesn't. She remembers this is the worst class in the worst school in the entire state, and her favourite. She and they aren't exactly simpatico, but there's an understanding, perhaps even boundaries. They might be impossibly dumb, but they're never malicious. Lou, in spite of herself, in spite of her history books, trusts them.

Up the back Mayada shakes her head, smiling. All the boys are sitting in the first two rows. Something's planned.

'Hey Miss, your dress is hot! And ah mean hot, nowhaahm-sayin?' crows Aiden, the ringmaster.

'Ooooawwwwwrrrr!' On cue, the boys' desks rise up in a beautifully synched arc of tumescence. Lou knows that this warrants the Death Stare, but their choreography is fantastic. They must have rehearsed it. The girls go berko. Even Mayada claps. It isn't quite Christmas, but Lou flashes her pearlies, full frontal, bright as a summer sky.

Later, she sets a document study from the textbook, pretends to fill holes in her *Teachers Chronicle*, thinking of the journey they've travelled with her. Maybe there's a tear.

Plop, plop. Raindrops fall from the roof into the bucket beside her. Lou watches them shimmering outwards in sad little ripples. Up the back, Mayada asks a question. Lou wonders what she might have become, had she gone to MSG. *So many could-be prodigies dropping from heaven, no bucket to catch them beneath!*

At recess, Babs, the librarian, finds her on duty, tells her Val has died. Lou pangs for Arty, wishes Jerry wasn't on a sickie. When she comes into the staffroom, she can't believe her eyes. Arty's at his desk, staring into the computer, like nothing's happened, while Noel, who's known Arty for thirty years, sits, reading his Federation rag, not speaking as he feels, nor as he ought. Not speaking at all.

Lou digs inside for the courage to speak herself. She can't. The silence is too potent. She sinks into her desk, closes her eyes. All she hears is Arthur punching keys, Noel turning pages, and, outside, Dunno's hammer slaying wood.

Anatomy of a Story

Ryan O'Neill

Title: The Paper Cut.
Author: Emily Watt.
Pen names: Emily Foster, Emily Wye, EK Watt.
Alternative titles: 'Meet Mrs Write', 'The Write Stuff'.
Word count: 2,259 words.
Stories written before 'The Paper Cut': 'Mrs Smith's Romance' (1980, unpublished), 'The Love Doctor' (1989, unpublished), 'Teacher's Pet' (1990, unpublished), 'The Mystery of the Body in the Trunk' (1993, unpublished), 'The Canals of Mars' (1994, unpublished), 'The Ghost Lover' (1994, unpublished), 'Falling in Love' (1995, unpublished)
Author biography (23/06/01): Emily Watt has always wanted to be a writer. She is happily married to the adorable Michael, and has no children ('though not for lack of trying!) She lives in a beautiful house overlooking the Newcastle harbour, with her husband and three cats: Tom, Puss and Willow.
Genre: Romantic Fiction / Literary Fiction / Short Story.
Intended readership / target audience: Professional women aged between nineteen and fifty.
Number of hours spent on first draft: Eighty-seven (between 12/01/01 and 26/11/01).
Synopsis: Josephine Wright, a housewife and aspiring author, has a story accepted by *Australian Women's Weekly*. Her husband, Jason Wright, believes that the character of the foolish husband in the story is based on him, and is angry with Josephine. However, the couple reconcile when their neighbour, Margaret Chatters, reads the published story and can see no resemblance to any persons, living or dead.

Letter from *Heat* magazine (11/12/03): 'Dear Contributor, Thank you for your submission, but we are afraid that it is not suitable for our magazine. Please don't be disheartened – our judgement is well schooled, but inevitably subjective. You may like to subscribe to the magazine…'

Characters in story: Josephine Wright. Thirty-two years old. 174 cms tall. Long, blonde hair. Brown eyes. Lapsed Catholic.

Jason Wright. Josephine Wright's husband. Thirty-five years old. Surveyor. 201 cms tall. Prematurely balding. Lutheran.

Margaret Chatters. Josephine Wright's neighbour. Fifty-three years old. Housewife. 156 cms tall. Favourite food: lasagne.

Ian Chatters. Margaret's husband. Sixty-five years old. Retired chiropractor. Favourite colour: red.

Seamus Crawley. Jason Wright's boss. Forty-two years old. Irish. Bad habits include biting his toenails and eating fast food.

Alex Crumb. Jason Wright's friend. Thirty-three years old. Bricklayer. Has known Jason for twenty years and doesn't like Josephine. On rainy days he enjoys going for long walks.

Sheena Divers. Josephine Wright's best friend. Twenty-nine years old. Professional dancer. Does not like Jason Wright. Lesbian.

Lara Wright. Daughter of Josephine and Jason Wright. Fifteen months old. First word: Mama. Ambitions: unknown.

Mode of narration: Third person. Past simple.

Setting: A light blue, two-bedroom house in an unnamed Australian suburb. Also, the back garden of the house, the street outside the house, the next-door neighbour's house, and an anonymous office building a short train ride away.

Themes: Writing, Love, Marriage, Forgiveness, Comedy, Postmodernism.

Typeface: Keper IV New, Invented by Scotsman John Butler in 1946. This typeface has unusually long l's, t's and h's, so that many words resemble prison bars, and long sentences seem like fences.

Punctuation: 378 full stops, 300 commas, 183 quotation marks, twenty-four question marks, eight exclamation marks, five parentheses, three hyphens and one semicolon (incorrectly used).

Symbolism: Jason receives a paper cut on his thumb when reading his wife's story for the first time. By the end of the story, the cut has healed.

Jason scatters the pages of the story in the garden. Josephine and Margaret scrabble on their knees to retrieve them.

After their argument, Jason takes the train to work, and notices that on the map of the train station his neighbourhood has been blistered by a cigarette burn.

Jason and Josephine's books are kept in separate cabinets.

By the story's end, the couple are sitting on a couch reading Josephine's story together.

Author biography (19/12/02): Emily Watt is very happily married to her husband, Michael, a surveyor, and writes when he is away on his frequent long trips. Writing is the only thing that takes her mind off missing him. She lives in a lovely house in Newcastle, NSW, with her cats.

Letter from *Overland* magazine (22/11/03): 'Thank you for sending your story to *Overland*. We have received over 500 submissions for the current issue, and the standard of submissions has been very high. We are sorry we are unable to use your story this time, and hope you will submit to us again in the future. All the best…'

Metaphors: 'Slave words, dressed in pretty colours, were demeaned on display in the bookshop windows' (pg 2).

'Jason couldn't understand why his wife didn't like love poems, when she was a love poem' (pg 3).

'It was the fractured bone of fact through the thin skin of fiction' (pg 3).

Similes: 'Jason was all hard edges and harshness, like a sentence with all the vowels removed' (pg 1).

'Through the tears in her eyes she saw him, as if he were drowning in a mirage' (pg 2).

'She was shy of her beauty, as if it were a scar' (pg 4).

'It was as if her body was rotting, she felt her lips pull back in a death's-head grin' (pg 4).

'There was a thick red scab on his thumb, like wax waiting for a seal' (pg 5).

Timeframe: The action in the story occurs between 9 a.m. on Monday and 4 p.m. on Wednesday, sometime in the twenty-first century. The exact month and year are not given, and the season is vague, but it is most likely summer.

Literary influences: Ernest Hemingway, Colleen McCullough, Raymond Carver, John Cheever, Jackie Collins.

Funding: The author applied for funding from the Australia Council for the Arts and was refused.

Number of hours spent on second draft: Thirty-six (between 05/12/01 and 19/05/02).

Plagiarisms: Margaret Chatters' distinctive laugh is taken from a minor character in Muriel Spark's *The Prime of Miss Jean Brodie*. Jason Wright's hair and preoccupied frown are stolen from Captain Horatio Hornblower in CS Forester's *Flying Colours*. Josephine Wright's speech on pg 3 is copied almost verbatim from the last page of the Raymond Carver short story, 'Buffalo'. The reconciliation scene at the end of the story is lifted from Part 2, Chapter 3, of *Lanark* by Alasdair Gray.

Acknowledgements (27/11/01): The author wishes to make it known, if possible, that the preceding story could not have been completed without the tireless support, love and devotion of her husband, Michael.

Letter from *Meanjin* (05/01/04): 'Dear _____ Thank you for your submission, but unfortunately we cannot use it at the present time. Best wishes…'

Author biography (21/01/03): Emily Watt lives in a tiny flat fifty kilometres inland from Newcastle, NSW. She struggles to find time to write between twelve-hour shifts at the local meat factory. She loves cats, especially the three that her ex-husband kept after the divorce. She sometimes believes that writing, and the hope of publication, is all that keeps her going.

Dedication (27/11/01): For Michael.

Dedication (01/07/03): For me.

Spelling mistakes: 'heer' (pg 1), 'refrigderator' (pg 2), 'wokman' (pg 4), 'reconcilled' (pg 5).

Clichés: 'deaf as a post' (pg 1), 'cried like a baby' (pg 3), 'lifeless as a corpse' (pg 3), 'jumped back as if she had an electric shock' (pg 4).

Letter from *Westerly* (12/01/04): 'Many thanks for sending your story to *Westerly*, but I'm afraid that we are unable to publish it. Regards…'

Books consulted during writing of story: *Aspects of the Novel* by EM Forster, *Story* by Robert McKee, *How to Write a Great Short Story in One Week*! by Art Morrison, *The Elements of Grammar* by Prof. HJF Windsor-Colt.

Autobiographical details: Jason Wright has diabetes, as has Michael Watt, the writer's ex-husband. Jason and Josephine Wright live in a spacious blue house, as did Emily Watt at one time. Josephine Wright has a mole on her neck, as did Emily Watt, before the mole was removed in 2002.
Writing exercises used before commencing the first draft of the story: 'Write about a time you were afraid.' 'Look at this picture of a train. Write about it.'
Notes written in margin of first draft: 'Awful!' (pg 1), 'Why bother?' (pg 1), 'Michael is right; it's all a waste of time!' (pg 3).
Obscenities: 'arse' (pg 3), 'a load of crap' (pg 3).
Blasphemies: 'Christ' (pg 1), 'Oh God' (pg 5).
Critical opinion: 'So this is why you've been locking yourself away at night? This is why the house is a pigsty? This story? It's not that good, is it? I mean, really…' – Michael Watt, husband, on first draft.

'I liked it, but I think it needs a bit more sex, to, you know, spice it up.' – Susan Marsh, neighbour and friend, on second draft.

'Not a bad little effort, all things considered. I believe that you may have the makings of a writer. I'd like to offer you ten per cent off my book, *How to Write Creatively* (RRP $45) to help you take that difficult final step towards publication.' – Alan Howell, Howell's Manuscript Assessment Agency, on final draft.
Number of hours spent on final draft: 124 (between 11/05/03 to 12/06/03).
Note written in margin of final draft: 'Please God, let it be good enough!' (pg 4).
Letter from *Australian Women's Weekly* (01/02/04): 'Emily, whilst we enjoyed your story, we regret that we have a huge backlog of fiction at the moment, and will be unlikely to publish it in the near future. Best wishes…'

Author biography (12/06/03): Emily Watt is forty-nine and lives alone. She has always wanted to be a writer.
Stories written after 'The Paper Cut': None.
Final sentence of the story: 'And, of course, she lived happily ever after' (pg 6).

Alex Gets a Job

Eleanor Elliott Thomas

Dear Alex,

Oh, honey. I can see what you're thinking: it's two in the afternoon on a Tuesday, and you're wishing you could be at the bar. You wish you had the sour stain of cheap red wine on your chapped lips, that a cigarette was burning out between your fingers, that the air you breathed tasted of salt and ash and cheerful despair, and most of all, most of all, you wish that you were sitting amongst the kinds of people who are at a bar at 2 p.m. on a Tuesday. The drunken and the witty, the half-crazed, the down-at-heel, the charming, the lovelorn, the seditious and the addicted: you love those flawed people with their messy lives and uncertain incomes, those people who have never belonged to anything, or anyone. But you're not one of them, Alex, not these days you're not.

Your new life, Alex, is ordinary and regular, it pulses like a metronome and is coloured in with hushed, soothing greens and ergonomic off-whites. It's two in the afternoon and though you wish you were at the bar, the fact is that you're at work, and your new life is pretty easy, you know. But it doesn't make being you any easier.

Don't let it get you down, kiddo. You were excited to get this job, remember, and it's good work, the work you do, and worthwhile. The people you work with are bright, amusing and sophisticated; they're high achievers, they dress well, and they definitely don't spend Tuesday afternoons getting drunk and talking shit. We could fairly describe them as *sensible*, but these days 'sensible' is one of your least favourite words, right up there with 'overdue' and 'sober'; instead, let's curse your colleagues with a slightly less damning adjective – how about *worthy*? Because unlike those kids at the bar, your new coworkers do in fact appear to be *worthy human beings* who spend their days happily making a *genuine contribution to the common good.* Oh, it's enough to make you physically ill.

Of course, though your new job hurts, there's the rent to pay. But the payment you're worried about is not the nine hundred bucks you hand over each month to live in your artfully distressed, inner-northern rat's nest with cracks in the ceiling. No, the real payment which it grieves you to make is that right now it's 2 p.m. on a Tuesday, and no matter how much you want it, Alex my love, you don't get to be at the bar.

Dear Alex,
Today, a man walked past you in the park near your office, clutching the side of his face and screaming out wordless howls of pain. You were coming back from your lunch break, detouring slightly so you could spend a moment longer away from your desk, and you were thinking, vaguely, about whether you'd be happier if you were more of a loser. That's the sort of thing you think about when you're left to spend more than eight minutes on your own.

(You don't feel like a loser these days – not now you're a *professional*. You never imagined you'd be important enough to work in a building so tall that on particularly windy days the water in the toilet bowl slaps around like an ocean storm. But there you are, twenty-eight storeys up, in a building with a foyer which reminds you of the fucking Vatican. No, Alex, you're not a loser – not in the way you used to be.)

The screaming man in the park wore a beige sweater and jeans, and he didn't look nearly as crazy as he sounded. You had your earphones in, you were listening to Neil Young sing 'Needle and the Damage Done', and you had the volume turned up loud to block out the grey day around you (it was sunny, but it felt grey – is this how you figured out that you're depressed?), so you didn't notice the man's cries until he had almost passed you. You had, however, seen him approaching and thought, what with the clutching at the head and all, that there was something unsettled about him. You're observant like that. At any rate, when you did hear him, when you began to understand what was going on, your first thought about this screaming gentleman was: *I'm with you, buddy.*

When you realised that the man was in need of something, you stopped walking and took your earphones out, and you looked at him with an expression which you hoped conveyed sympathy and concern. You considered asking him whether he was okay – while he was plainly *not*, the question would at least show that you were willing to help. But despite the connection you felt between the two of you, the man looked so out of control that he frightened you, and for an instant, fear dragged your kindness back into the base of your throat. Then the moment had passed, and the man had marched on by, still screaming. You put your earphones back in and kept walking.

So, Alex, the question is this: would you be happier if you were more of a loser?

Dear Alex,
It would be fair to say that this week has not been a high point in your life. This week, you left work with a hollow buzzing in your head, a weakness in your legs and a deeply injured will to live. When you were at home, you sat slumped on the sofa, watching reality television, taking nothing in, your emotional state flickering unpredictably between desperation and resignation. When at work, you were just too wretchedly busy to even notice how bored you were.

Today, though, things have slowed down a little, and in the moments between finishing one mundane task and beginning another, you're sitting in your open-plan office with your teeth clamped tightly together, staring straight ahead. You're working hard to suppress a fierce urge which is building slowly in your guts, an urge to lift up a piece of office equipment like a weapon (keyboard? hole punch? ring binder? you're unsure which would be most effective) and use it to smash through the clear soundproof plastic which rises up from the grey wall of your cubicle, the plastic through which you watch your colleagues stroll past, chatting, laughing, wearing their demure suits and polished business shoes with a casual ease which leaves you frothing in incomprehension, all of them apparently impervious to the bleakness, the horror, the violation that is *this, this, this*.

Now and then someone will drop by to ask, *Hey schnooks, why the long face?*

Dear Alex,

Things are looking up, aren't they, Alex? There was a week or two, perhaps a month, where every task you took on, even the smallest chore, was accomplished with thundery anxiety. Could this really be your life? You felt justified in your melodrama. Christ, this couldn't seriously be the existence you had chosen for yourself.

As a child, you used to have such ambition. You wanted to speak five languages and play five instruments; you wanted to read every book ever written. You would be an artist, a diplomat, a spy, an explorer, and on the weekends, you would sweep into extravagantly cosmopolitan parties and enthral audiences with your wildly hilarious tales of adventure and your breathtaking good looks. Later, when you grew out of dreamy childhood and developed some degree of self-awareness, you decided that exploring and spying were kind of hard work, and instead, you fixed your sights on becoming a Dorothy Parker, or a Charles Bukowski – you wanted to be a person living on the *outside*. Whatever you ended up doing, you were Alex, and you believed it was your destiny to make your mark on the world.

As it turns out, your destiny is to hit the snooze button four times before tipping yourself out of bed on an arctic autumn morning, only to feel your left foot land, with a slight slide, in a pool of your cat's urine. Your destiny is to get up, mop the floor, and shower despondently before making yourself some toast, spread guiltily with your unsalted, fat-reduced peanut butter of choice. You'll feel fleeting despair at the filthy gluttony represented by your newly rounded belly, but your destiny is to be running perpetually late, so instead of exercising, you'll drive yourself to the train station. You'll still miss your train. Waiting on the platform, you'll squint nervously in the pasty glare of the morning sun, and before the 8.28 a.m. City Loop arrives, you'll have plenty of time to spot a new and unforeseen stain on your crinkled grey suit. Your marvellous destiny, Alex, is to stand forlornly on a train platform on a brittle Thursday morning in May, and to feel a quiet despair about the fact that, for the third week running, you have forgotten to collect your second suit from the drycleaners down at the plaza.

But hey, things aren't as bad as they were. Even as you squash yourself into the dense throng of fellow professionals on your overcrowded train carriage, you feel a sense of muted camaraderie wash over you. You're all in this together, you and the rest of the suits, and judging by the grim set of the faces surrounding you, you're not the only one who isn't exactly living the dream.

Dear Alex,
It's amazing what you can get used to. In the last few months, your hopes for yourself have been casually suffocated; your fantastic ideas about what you could be have faded slowly into a faint nostalgia for what you could have been. Today – all this – it's just an incidental slight.

You're a real person now, Alex, earning a real wage in a real job. Your job, in fact, could not be any *more* real, more daily, or more state-sanctioned, and there's a certain satisfaction in that. You're good at it, you're good at doing this adult thing of going to work every day, performing your tasks, engaging affably with your colleagues, reliably stacking stained teacups in the dysfunctional dishwasher in the staff kitchen. Alex, sweetie, it turns out that you're not the freak you wished you were.

Years ago, maybe three or four of them, you remember standing on a train platform, on your way to your first ever interview for a real job, and feeling small pools of salty damp building in your tear ducts, preparing to tread anxiously down your cheeks. You knew, already, that you wouldn't get that job, and you were right – you made inappropriate jokes in the interview and started laughing when they asked what you thought you could contribute to their organisation. You said: *that's a tough one, Eddie. Can I phone a friend?* You thought, back then, that no matter how hard you tried, you could not be a part of this universe, that you had no hope of being a worldly success. The thing is, back then, you didn't even want it, this *worldly success* – you wanted to be a drunken genius, a grand and brilliant and tragic *mess* – but you chased after it regardless with a ferocity you'd never realised you had in you. You studied, you photocopied, you interned and networked, and why? Because, you idiot, you wanted to prove you were real.

Well, sugar, here's the proof: you're sitting in your cubicle, and you're drinking instant coffee whilst typing up the kind of weekly task list which organised, competent people put together to guide them through something finicky and dull. And you're thinking about this morning, when your boss released you from his office with a pat on the shoulder and an exceptionally good performance review. Real life, it seems, is organised, competent, finicky and dull: it's been going on for months, and Alex, my darling, you have only just worked out that you're exceptionally good at it. So tell me, babydoll, how does it make you feel?

The answer might surprise even you. The answer is that you are beginning to feel that this adult existence – this plain, cottony way of life that you are nervously draping over your shoulders to see how it looks – this might actually be the costume you were meant to wear. For the first time in your life, you have found a cloak snug enough to fit around the smallness of your frame, and yes, of course you feel loss, and failure, and disappointment – but that isn't the whole of it. Come on, Alex, tell us what else it is that you feel.

Because nobody will blame you, cupcake. Nobody will blame you for this treacherous flavour that fills your mouth – this delicate taste of relief.

Intermittent Red Flashes

Tim Richards

Rant #1
The worst thing about this third-rate era we're consigned to is the way people are always inviting you to be impressed. Collie has a spot on MySpace where he invents axioms, publishes dog photos, and blogs on about fuck-all, and you're meant to be in awe of the ten thousand hits he had last month. Of course, he never actually says 'you should be impressed', but that's what's implied when someone acts laconic while they tell you shit.

Ten thousand hits is new-world impressive, and old-world success doesn't cut it anymore. Collie forgets that you used to work for television. No one saw your face, or knew your dog's name, but actors gave life to your words, and, some weeks, two million viewers tuned in. Television used to matter the way the net does now, but the trick was the same: to impress people without showing you need them to be impressed. To win respect without telling the world that you are a raving, fucked-up narcissist.

Stretching the Happiness Muscles
Doctor Long hates you because you call her 'Doctor' when a specialist wants to be addressed as 'Emma' or 'Miz'. But even with your libido nudging zero, which it has all this decade – the entire Howard era in fact – you still get the hots for Doctor Long. She has flaming red hair and says 'mmm' like a babe at the nipple, and her so-right glasses make her look like Solomon's wiser sister. She's smart enough to skip talk-cures and get you the stuff that's been jollying Swiss lab rats.

'Mellovex is stronger than the medications you've been taking, but it should have a pronounced impact on your wellbeing. My main concern at this time is to shift the chemical mix so that you can feel happier. Otherwise, your happiness muscles will go to waste.'

'Shit. I hadn't thought to worry about them.'

'You may notice a tendency to obsess about things, and to get a little... hyper.'

'Nothing that makes me ecstatic. I have to be able to write.'

'This should be fine for that. Make sure to read the instructions on the packet, and never take Mellovex in conjunction with alcohol. If it doesn't suit, let me know.'

Puzzling Responses
It usually takes a month to do a ten-thousand-piece jigsaw. When you started Bruegel's *Icarus*, you were going through a bad patch, and that took six weeks. But once the Mellovex kicks in, you have three puzzles on the go at the same time, taking eight days to finish a twenty-thousand-piece red and gold Rothko.

All the stuff you never notice suddenly becomes obvious, like the exact number of active pixels on your television screen, and the number of bricks that went into constructing your living room. When you're given the key to a world of amazement, you have to share that joy with people who matter, so you get Miranda on the blower and tell her how fucking immense the world is, and how you could go some rock'n'roll if she's up for it, which must come as a shock, given the way she stresses that you haven't seen her for twelve years. Not since Keating was PM.

'I'm on a new medication, and it's fantastic.'

'Sounds like you're on a new planet.'

'C'mon, a quick one for old times. I'll count your freckles.'

'No. When I wanted them counted, you weren't interested.'

Would You by Chance Have Some Spare Milk?
Work? You can't keep up with the words spilling from your head, and this new work is like nothing you've written before. All the old themes are there, but the sentences have rhythm and cadence, and you'd pause to admire them, only there's a new sentence waiting to be recorded.

You are so caught up in the novelty of being productive that you don't hear the movers at work in the neighbouring flat. But you hear the doorbell, and there you are – the unshaven, unwashed savant in a threadbare dressing-gown – opposite two stunning brunettes: voluptuous Liz, with eyes and lips to die for, and her even more exceptional daughter, Sian, nine tiny freckles on her left cheek, eight perfect flecks on the right.

'Would you by chance have some spare milk?'

'Your luck's in. In this shrine we worship long-life milk.'

Sian giggles, and if that's the last sound you hear before dying, you'll die a happy man.

An Everyday Use for Venn Diagrams

When Collie asks why you're always so determined to pursue the wrong woman, you tell him to poll the readers of his blog, but the cur has set you thinking about the women you once imagined to be right. A detailed statistical analysis might have something to offer.

Of the twenty-nine women you've seen/dated/romanced over the past thirty-one years, a disproportionately high number (thirteen) have French given names, but no obvious patterns emerge from hair shade, eye colour, or body type. You have certain abstract preferences, but when a woman with a pretty face and an interesting voice comes along, ideals vanish.

But statistics need to go deeper. So you come up with this new one about brothers. There's barely been one. Those twenty-nine women have had forty-five sisters (that is, seventy-four female offspring in their families) but just twenty-three brothers, and only eight of the women in question had an elder brother. That's got to mean something, but what? Are the women from these female-dominant families more likely to be hyper-feminine, or to have been nurtured as if male? Did they find you attractive because they didn't have older brothers to correct that tendency, or did they identify you as a man who might become a sister in a brotherly way? Having entered these affairs with eyes closed, you've now lost the chance to count freckles and hear what their skin has to say.

The Gingerbread Housing Initiative

'Maybe I should make another appointment. This stuff is too good. It's cocaine, heroin and Viagra in one punch. I'm floaty and priapic, and I've never written so much.'

'You sound happier.'

'Not sure. I'm working on stats to evaluate that.'

'There's no need to be frightened of bad stuff when you're only experiencing good things.'

'Doctor Long... Emma... What you just said sounds like the turning point in every German folk tale.'

Anxieties of Influence
You've read the instruction leaflet fifty times. It mentions the compulsions, the horniness and the inability to draw breath between sentences. In bold letters, it warns against combining Mellovex with alcohol, as if liquor could make you feel better than this Swiss pharmaceutical dynamite, but nowhere on that leaflet, above the text or below, does its author allude to the possibility of delusional thinking.

So when the spectacularly well curved Liz Barclay leans against the balcony, looks into your eyes, and reacts as if your every word was scripted by the Bard himself, it's feasible that it really is happening the way you see it.

'I met that big friend of yours the other day.'

'Collie?'

'He said you write for television.'

'Used to. I'm reinventing myself as a novelist.'

'You wrote *The Duckworth–Lewis Method*...'

'I was on the writing staff.'

'Wow,' she says, in a way reserved for Tarzan hot off the vine. 'That's incredible.'

When a woman like Liz sets her eyes on you in that way, it's no use saying that you hope those TV years won't be seen as the high point of your professional life. She doesn't want to hear it.

'You should come in and hear Sian sing.'

You tell her you've heard Sian sing, and that her daughter has a pretty voice, though that's only partly true. When Sian goes through her scales, you put the headphones on, and you haven't heard her sing anything that could be called a song.

'She has an amazing voice. She needs to be on television. That's the only way singers get the attention of record producers.'

'I don't know anyone that does variety.'

'You must know heaps of people... Your friend said you wrote with Doug Stebbings.'

'Occasionally. We weren't close. Doug's a hard man to get close to.'

'Singers would do anything to get on his show.'

You want to tell her no way, you hate Doug – the man goosed you every way but south. He could've offered you a gig on his show if he had the wit to know real comedy from the shit he gets away with. Nothing, but nothing, will persuade you to ask Doug for a favour. This is what you intend to say, but Liz's lips are bulging, and her eyes are licking you from head to toe, and you remember Sian's giggle, and in those circumstances – those exact circumstances – you know that you have no right to deny the world access to Sian's giggle. Besides, what are the odds on someone having exactly the same number of lashes on her left eye as on her right, the way Liz does?

'It would mean so much to us. There's nothing I wouldn't do to see Sian get the break she deserves.'

Blame is the Name of the Game

People don't want to hear the father-shit you cart around, but they're going to hear it anyway, because you live in a century where every ear is an Oprah crowd hungry for candour and causality.

Dad was no poor woodcutter. As a big-time lawyer, he prosecuted famous criminals. Dad was a hard-hearted optimist – the world was going to get better, but to do that, it needed to become more efficient. Since the life we knew attracted too many of 'the wrong sort of people', it would have to be replaced with something more exclusive. This meant culling the unfit, and Dad's notion of fitness focused on those unfit to make money.

Mum never contradicted him. He was the oracle so far as she and sister Barb were concerned. If Dad had told them he was draining the family fortune to establish the Tyrants with Gout Party, they would have been first to sign up. A day never went by when you weren't told how physically and mentally superior you were, and it's easy to believe that shit when you want to believe it, especially when the world's most confident man tells you to in a way that would sway a cynical jury.

Fleas seldom cut down big, sonnet-quoting bastards, but a flea got in Dad's ear. When a friend of Mum's told him she'd seen a man who looked exactly like him riding the number eight tram down Toorak Road the previous day, a band snapped. Dad gave up everything to look for that man, as if he'd always known he had an identical twin, and that there was a warmer, more inclusive dad who had to be slain if his dreams weren't to be thwarted.

So the man who always disparaged 'the losers who ride trams' became the most touched of all those losers, and though Mum immediately saw reality, and treated him as someone who deserved compassion whenever he ambled home, the transformation totally arseholed your sister Barb, who began fucking junkies like there was a bounty payable to junkie-fuckers. Though you and Barb were reasonably close, you couldn't speak, and it was like watching someone be eaten alive from the inside.

All of us have experiences that we assume to be unique, but starting out in television, you found yourself working in a team of writers where no fewer than six had scagged-up sisters, while four had dads who might have been the doppelganger your old man was seeking on the number eight tram.

On her twenty-first birthday, Sally Quinn's dad confessed that he'd met her mum when she 'acted' in the pornographic film he was directing for her maternal grandparents. So it was Sally who mentioned Doctor Long when told that you were looking for a shrink who put pharmacy before prattle. Chemical optimism couldn't be worse than the quasi-optimistic crap Dad inflicted on you when he was still someone to be reckoned with.

The Way of the World
'Are you on something?'
'Why do you say that?'
'You're talking so fast, and you've just told me it was good to hear my voice three times in a minute.'

There's history here. You told Sally you'd stay in touch, and you haven't. This largely because she took a job with that filthy shit Doug Stebbings – the moral equivalent of distributing how-to-vote cards for Howard. Worse, the reason you liked Sal in the first place was her ability to cut through to the truth. So it's with some unease that you tell her you've met this girl with a sensational voice and terrific looks who will be a real winner given the chance. Doug's people could do worse than call her in for an audition.

'I'm just a writer. Call the talent co-ordinator.'
'They'd listen if it came from you.'
'You must want to fuck this girl badly.'
'Jesus, Sal.'

'Richard, television's fucked because it's full of people who got here the way you'd like this girl Sian to get here.'

Speaking the truth doesn't give you the right to be offensive, so it's at this point you tell Sal she only got that job because Doug likes the way she fills a sweater. It's not as if you don't already know what burnt bridges smell like. It was a small fucking favour to ask.

Reflection
Having spent your life thinking about Hansel and Gretel, you know that one's meant to see Gretel's heroism as an expression of her sublimated desire to vanquish her stepmother and win back her father, but you tend to fixate on the practicalities of constructing a gingerbread house in a forest.

You figure that the H–G story is about loyalty and the forces that subvert loyalty, and about the various ways you can be led astray when you've gone hungry for a long time. If sister Barb had looked out for you the way Gretel looks out for Hansel, things wouldn't have deteriorated to a point where Swiss chemistry was required. And there's one other thing to be said about this fucked-up third-rate era. Once upon a time there was just the odd witch or wolf to look out for; now whole industries are devoted to separating the confused and helpless from the flock.

Worry Merchants
The machine's never been so fascinating. You've always liked counting the red flashes more than answering and erasing messages, but now the red has a special lustre, and the recorded voices are displaced, like speeches removed from an excavated time capsule.

'Richard, about those delusions. I've seen new research about Mellovex, and we need to consider alternatives. DB 2312 might be worth a try.'

On the machine, Doctor Long's 'Richard' is indistinguishable from 'wretched', but after you've heard Emma say it forty, forty-five times, 'wretched' sounds fine. You can live with being Wretched.

An Environmentally Friendly Gingerbread House
Of all bog-common sexual fantasies, mother–daughter is never one that's excited you too much. Three's a crowd, they say. But hear this: you haven't known gratitude till you've known intergenera-

tional gratitude, and it's not as if you're breaking new ground with this pair.

'When did she say they'd call?'

'Not soon. The show's fully booked for singers this series, and then it depends what internationals come through. But when I told them Sian had a rare gift, they knew I wouldn't say that about just anyone.'

In this situation you ought to be paying attention to the way Liz's hands explore her daughter, but you're obsessed with the freckles on the girl's shoulders, and annoyed that Liz keeps talking while you're trying to count.

'You'll have to think of some way we can repay you for what you've done,' she says, without hint of irony.

And now you know there are exactly 161 brown flecks on the girl's shoulders, and you'd seize this moment to speak of Sian's perfection, and the pride you'll feel when she's a superstar, but the kid's swigging from a glass of Chablis, and, when her fingers part your lips to empty wine from her mouth into yours, there's no gainsaying this witchery.

The First Red after Pillar-Box Red

No sooner do you slot the last piece in the blue-on-blue Franz Klein puzzle than you find yourself in Toorak Road, boarding the number eight tram just before it turns into Park Street. There, you are unsurprised to find your grubby father sitting across the way, scanning the compartment with wide eyes. You try to tell him how offering false hope to a needy mother and daughter has unlocked the door to optimism, and that from here on, it will be happy days, but the old man doesn't want to know. You must have him confused with the demented lawyer who has been chasing him for years. And now the barely clad Liz and Sian push past to tell this bum what a huge help you've been to Sian, how you've promised to make this girl a great star, and how, with his dark spell lifted, he can give the trams away.

None of this stops you necking their bottle of wine, though your head's splitting, and the throbbing red on the St Kilda Road stoplight is no common red, but answering machine red, each flash signalling a call that must now go unanswered.

In Registry

JB Rawson

'Did I tell you about the time everyone on my train was reading the same book?' I said, but Steve wasn't listening.

'I said,' I said, and he told me he heard what I said but that there was never a time when everyone on my train was reading the same book, and he was sick of hearing about my imaginary stories.

'Can you just pass me the next pile of letters,' he said, 'and shut up for a second?'

But I couldn't.

'We could talk about footy,' I said.

And he said, 'Alright, what about it?'

'I wrote to the AFL,' I said, 'with some of my ideas.'

'What now?' He wanted to know. 'And this had better not be some stupid thing you just made up.' It was, so I sat quiet instead.

'What?' said Steve.

'Nuthin'.' I licked another envelope and put it on the pile.

'You are such an idiot,' he told me. And he was right, but I wanted to tell him that on Anzac Day when the third quarter starts I think there should be a machine gunner, maybe up high behind the back pocket, one on each side, and three and a half minutes in they should start to fire. An old-fashioned machine gun. Authentic. For Anzac Day. And that I wrote to tell the AFL that, but they didn't write back.

And there were the other things I wrote about too, but I didn't tell him those either – that I wrote to a professor at Melbourne Uni and asked him if there was ever anyone who studied prehistoric smells and other smells from the French Revolution or the Spanish Inquisition or when Cortés first stepped off his boat and put his foot down in the place they'd call Mexico. I asked because I wanted to know when there were the most smells because I was guessing that it would be about 1780. Don't you think? I asked my mum this once and she said she thought with all the artificial smells they make now for air fresheners and so on that it would be now, but I think she's wrong. Anyway, so I wrote to ask this professor and I really wanted an answer, I wanted there to be some person who studied smells. Mostly that was because I was hoping the TAB would open a book on it and I could put down maybe $20 and if I was right get about $12,000 back, but I needed some kind of official answer to prove I was right. He didn't write back either.

Or about the time I wrote a letter to the priest to ask him if when we died and we were good we went to heaven, which I thought was probably the case, but that if it *was* the case, what happened on Judgement Day – wasn't everyone already either in heaven or hell? And he said – because he did write back – that everyone just hangs around being dead until Judgement Day, but we don't know about it because we're dead, and then on Judgement Day we come back to life and God says either 'heaven' or 'hell' and then that's where we go. And so I wanted to know how come at my auntie's funeral they said her pain is over now and she's with God in heaven when really – according to him – she was dead in the ground, and that time he didn't write back.

There are things you can't google. That's one of them, and also questions about whether there were more smells before or after 1780, or whether if you measure the average speed of things now it will be faster or slower than when there were dinosaurs. Sometimes it makes me mad. I told a cat on the street the other night about how angry it sometimes makes me. I told him, 'You can all fucking die for all I care!' – I said it out loud – and then I asked him if he thought maybe in my last life I was a Lithuanian Jew and all my family got rounded up and killed, because sometimes I feel so angry and I just don't have any reason to feel like that.

'Steve,' I say.

'What?'

'Do you want a cup of coffee?'

'Are you going over the road?' he asks me. And I tell him, no, I'm just going up to the kitchen for a Nescafé.

'No way, I don't want that,' he says, and he asks me: 'How can you drink that shit?'

And I want to ask how he can pay $3 just for a cup of coffee. I don't. I just get up out of my chair and walk to the kitchen. I put two teaspoons of Nescafé and three teaspoons of sugar in my cup and I fill it up with water out of the tap almost to the top with room for just a little bit of milk, which I put in, then put the cup in the microwave. I press 'one minute' then I watch it turn and wait for the cockroach that lives inside to run in front of the lit up clock so I can tap the glass and see if he hears me.

You want to hear about a program I wrote? I'm not asking Steve now, I'm asking you. He won't listen to what I say anymore. It's a program for Facebook – you know that website? Yeah. So it's a program that you run and it updates your status reports and your profile every few days, adds pictures of holidays and friends' babies and that kind of stuff for you every couple of weeks. You run it, right, and all your friends think your life is going really well. And then you can just go, you know. Just leave. No one would even guess.

When I say 'I wrote it' – it's more I thought of it. I don't know how to write a computer program yet. Besides, I only have one friend on Facebook – my mum. She won't talk to me in real life anymore, though.

'Anyway,' says Steve, when I get back with my cup of coffee, 'you should spend more time thinking about filing the mail properly and not so much about ways to get Nicole Roxon to have dinner with you.'

'Her name is Nicola,' I tell him.

'Whatever,' he says. 'Because before Mr Bruce was down here and he said things have "gone astray" and we need to "lift our game".'

He put his fingers up in the air while he was telling me, to let me know Mr Bruce had said those things, not him.

I just shrug. Sometimes I unstick the envelopes when they come in and take out the pension forms and write in the boxes they haven't filled in D O N T W O R R Y T H E J U D G E M E N T W O N T B E T I L L L A T E R A N D Y O U C A N T F E E L W H E N Y O U A R E D E A D and then stick the envelope back up and write RETURN TO SENDER on the front. So that's probably what Mr Bruce means about 'gone astray', but I don't see what I can do about it.

Steve asked me once how come if I worked all day in Registry, which I do; I wasn't sick of letters. Like how come I was always writing them to the AFL and to Nicola Roxon MP, who is my local representative in federal parliament, and to Andrew Bolt, when all I do all day is open letters and close letters and send letters and take letters to all the other people who work upstairs with their computers. And Steve doesn't even know about most of the letters I send.

There is a lot to talk about, I don't say to him. There is all the world of time: a *lot* to find out about, and I'm sitting here licking envelopes while you tell me about what happened last night on *Motorway Patrol* and that tonight when you get home you are going to jerk off and eat Doritos.

Do you want to know what I'm going to do tonight when I get home, Steve? I know you don't, but here it is anyway. I'm going down by Stony Creek backwash. I'm going to lie on my back down on the pier and I'm going to listen to the birds' feet sucking in the mud and have my eyes fill up with all the lights bright orange on the cranes along the docks. And while I'm lying there this girl will come sliding from the mud and she'll crouch just past the creek edge, her fingers still tangled in all those weeds that stretch their roots into the water, finger ends all pointed from digging out the eyes of fish. She'll be slick with mud, her mouth lined with it, feeling grains of gravel, probing them from between her teeth with her mud-coated tongue and chewing on grains of gravel. She'll spit one into her hand and then she'll wipe her hand on the damp grass, get up from the creek and untangle her fingers from the rushes, lick the cuts that had opened where she clung too tight, and coat them all with mud from her tongue. I'll see her coming and I'll close my eyes, and then I'll feel her lick the water from beside my eyeball, where the wind stung me and made me cry. She'll lie down next to me on the tumbled wooden pier and she'll mutter to me, she'll tell me that under the mud down there, in the mud under the river where the bridge's pylons drive deep into the river's guts, she can hear everything the earth ever knew. 'It's all still there,' she'll say to me. 'Dive down with me,' she'll say to me. 'Squeeze your head full of it, nostrils and ears and down your throat. Breathe your lungs full of river mud.' But I won't tell you about it, Steve. I'll just tell you about how I had to go get a kebab because there wasn't anything in the house worth eating. Which will be true, because after I open my eyes and the girl is gone I probably will walk down to Spotswood and get a kebab.

ADVERTISEMENT

SALMAN RUSHDIE

NEW IN HARDBACK

THE COMPLETE LITERARY ENDORSEMENTS

Over 15,000 jacket quotes from this literary master, beautifully presented in three sturdy leather-bound volumes.

"Absolutely engrossing"
— MICHAEL ONDAATJE

My World

Andrew Hutchinson

It seems to me that when you are regularly awake to see the clock switch over to 4 a.m. that you are a different breed of person. It seems that it's a whole different world you enter, when daylight dissolves. This world is more mine than at any other time. Because no one else wants it. And the colours are different, either brighter under a streetlight or gone into outlines and shades. In my world. You can walk along a road and only hear yourself. Your feet echoing, as if your steps are much grander than really they are. Your breath hanging and curling in the night air.

Sometimes I walk to the petrol station that's eternally open, like a bug attracted to the buzzing lights. The man says hi and asks if I'm coming from work tonight, probably because I'm wearing a suit. I say no and give him exact change for a Coke and some breath mints. Always exact, because that's the way it happened. Tonight, I shake three mints into my palm and flick them to the back of my throat like tablets I used to take for tonsillitis. Feel them track down to my stomach.

It's here that I first met the guy who always says, 'Hey how you doin'?'

He walks in just as I'm about to leave, the fluoro lights sucking any colour from his skin, making him look like paper.

'Hey, how you doin'?' His hand comes out from his jacket and taps my shoulder. He tells me about how he went down and got that sail he was talking about. I can barely remember his sail, only vaguely as a thought of my own, ambling home one night wondering what he wanted a sail for.

'That sail, y'know? I got one, you should come see it.'

'Do you have a boat?'

'Yeah, and now a sail, big white one, even got some numbers, ship identification code or something.'

We wander along the streetlights, me making sure I don't step on a crack in the pavement. He asks generic questions that seem so much hollower as they echo off the trees and the bitumen. A car flashes by, shines us into life for a moment.

'Hey you were wearing that suit last time I saw you.' He points as if alerting me to this.

'Yes.'

'You comin' home from work?'

'No.'

'So why the suit?'

'It's the best clothes I have. It looks okay?'

'It's definitely you.'

We walk onto the road at an intersection, balance on the white lines, and we try to make the traffic lights change. He jumps on the tar-covered ground, trying to find the sensor and, with no one else around to notice, he makes the red go yellow, then green.

'Mine's green,' he yells across at me, waving. My skin bright under the red beams, shining from above.

'So, did I ask you about the suit?' He points at me. He kicks my empty can along in front of himself.

'Yeah, you did already.'

'Hey, why is it that you do this?'

'Do what?'

'Hang out at 4 a.m?'

I stop walking, let him go ahead for a few steps. I look down at my shining shoes, right at the edge of a crack.

'I'm looking for something,' I tell him. 'And it's easier this way, less hassles.' He thinks over my answer, his eyes looking up into his skull, then he continues kicking the can, switches between his right and left foot.

'Wait,' I say. 'Can we go down here, just a minute?'

Across from us there are forgotten trucks and rusted cranes. The white trails of spider webs across every angle. Huge metal arms reaching towards the sky, arms that used to work on buildings and dreams, now dormant and overgrown. Wind is pushing the long grass up against the fence that we're staring through. A drive-in screen looms across the empty car park, speaker posts poking like a war cemetery.

He stares at the screen as if imagining the film that could be playing, gets the best view he can through the wire. His fingers gripped over like a prisoner.

'This is where she was last,' I say to him, my eyes searching between the posts.

'Who?'

'A girl.'

'Your girl?' he asks, and I laugh just once, keep my mouth closed.

'She was for that night.'

'What happened?'

'We came here, and it was a beautiful night. I wore my suit, because I wanted a good impression, y'know?' He nods, eyes focused on me. 'Her fingers slid into mine like they were made to fit together. And she was like an angel. I spent more time watching her watch the film than, y'know? And when the time came we kissed and we said goodnight. And I slid my nose gently along her cheek and felt her lips brush across my skin. Then she closed her eyes, a few loose hairs trailing across her face in the night breeze. She opened them again, smiled, then she walked away.'

'Where is she now then?' The wind rattles the grass against my leg.

'I don't know. We had such a good night though.'

'She didn't want to see you again?' He frowns.

'I don't know.'

'Did you call her?'

'No.'

'Why?' he asks, astounded.

'I couldn't. That was… It wouldn't be the same.' I link my fingers over the mesh. He goes to ask something more, but catches my eyes and stops himself. He nods, forces a smile.

His house is along a main road, cars whispering beneath the streetlights. He leads me through the living room, all messed with empty video cases and newspapers and magazines. He's left the TV on, nothing's on though. He walks up a staircase of buzzing fluorescent light, lifts open a door and the breeze chills through my clothes.

On the concrete rooftop is moonlight. The cars down on the road reduced to a soft hum as they pass, one by one. He walks on ahead, leads the way towards a boat, rested up on stacks of old tyres and bricks. It's a small wooden boat, a two-person sized, weather-damaged vessel. Paint falling away in flakes. A sail is wrapped around the mast.

I stand back as he releases the sail into the wind, and it's like when my dad used to flick a sheet over my bed and I'd run under; let it fall over me like a cloud. I climb into my side of the boat, which echoes at the touch of my shoe.

'Lie back,' he says, staring across the night sky. 'And then you've got to look straight up.' He points towards the moon. I rest my head onto the wooden floor, watch the sail playing in the air above me. We lay alongside each other, the sides looming over us and the noise, hollow and creaking.

'Now we're floating away,' he tells me. 'See, the sky looks like it's moving, right? But it's not.' He pauses. The moon highlights halos around the edges of clouds. 'Really, we are moving. Floating across the ocean.' The sail flaps, straightens itself out across the stars. 'On a cloudy night you go a little bit faster.'

A bird tilts along the breeze, its feathers flickering.

'And we're going away,' he says, 'to anywhere you want.' He pauses again and the cars going by sound like waves, washing beneath us.

'You could take that girl with you,' he says.

'Yeah.' I smile, floating along the water. 'That'd be nice.'

In the Pines

Ella Holcombe

As kids we were told not to stand underneath the powerlines. We were told that their magnetic pull would scramble our brains. We rode our bikes to the powerlines in secret, lay under them and listened to that restless hum of electricity. Lines stretched out like track marks against the sky. At night in the back seat of the car on the way home we sent our tiny dreams hurtling down those wires to the city. When we shut our eyes we could see the lights flickering on in buildings like hundreds of eyes opening. Our house had no curtains. When it stormed the lightning tore down the passageway and into the bedrooms. And the rain at night on the tin roof. From our beds we could see the city far away through the trees. One winter a brother and sister killed themselves in the pine plantation up the road. They left a note on the kitchen table. It said that they were leaving to be with Kurt Cobain. In the pines, where the sun don't ever shine. At dinner Dad made us put down our knives and forks and listen. He said nothing, nothing, is ever so bad that it has to come to that. I was eleven. My brothers were nine. We ate the rest of our dinner in silence. The next day we rode our bikes up to the pine plantation. A policeman stopped us on the road, told us to go home. We rode back towards home. We sat for a long time under the powerlines, watching the city, watching the dark start to creep across the sky.

Elvis, Husbands, and Other Men in Costumes: A Memoir

Liza Monroy

1. WEST HOLLYWOOD – LAS VEGAS, NOVEMBER 2001

Big Day!
I wake up hazy in Razi's apartment to the buzzing of his cell phone alarm, my head pounding. I push my free airline sleep mask up my forehead, reach for the phone on the nightstand. The display reads Saturday, 17 November, 7.30 a.m. Razi is already stirring in the kitchen, sautéing up thinly sliced breakfast potatoes and poaching some organic, locally produced eggs. I'm about to yell for him to at least bring me some Advil and peach iced tea when a wave of nausea hits me and I remember: today is the day.

We're driving out to Vegas. The ceremony happens this evening.

No wonder I drank so much last night.

This whole thing could blow up in my face.

I dart upright, catching a glimpse of myself in the mirror hanging over the dresser on the other side of the room. I've got hair sticking up all over and black mascara racooning my puffy eyes. I flop back onto the mattress and pull the sleep mask back over my eyelids. Darkness, a delicacy.

Razi's airy ground-floor two-bedroom has floor-to-ceiling windows and shiny hardwood floors. The front door opens out onto a courtyard, a pool at its centre catching the morning sun. Unlike my room a few blocks east on Hayworth Street, it is organised, clean and spacious.

It's been over a year since we moved – quixotic, twenty-one – to finish college a semester early at our East Coast school's outpost in Los Angeles. All the film majors flocked here, Razi and I among them. My two closest girlfriends, Jen and Kate, native Bostonians, had dropped out and driven to LA to start new lives as California transplants. They've since moved back home. I've had the apartment we formerly shared to myself for a couple of weeks.

I, too, had at first refused to accept that the culture here could be as image-obsessed as its stereotypes claim. Now I worry the city itself is to blame for my dissipation. I've become a person who buys fat-free cheese even though it tastes like eraser. I have a membership at a 24-hour gym and sometimes I go at two in the morning after three cocktails. In my work as a freelance production assistant, I have driven all over the city seeking millennium-edition glass Evian bottles to decorate a bathtub scene in a Toni Braxton music video. I am a five-foot-two, 110-pound girl who drives a camera truck the size of a semi for two hundred dollars a day. This is actually a great rate for someone barely twenty-two years old, of my standing on the Hollywood ladder – approximately one or two rungs below zero.

One of my recent jobs introduced me to one of the most bizarre places I've ever seen, the Gallery of Mansions. The Gallery of Mansions is a cordoned-off community in the midst of hilly, arid landscape in the Valley, where each McMansion is different from the next: Tudor style, French chateau, Gothic, Palladian, Tuscan villa. People own these homes and live there, but they exist to be rented out for film shoots. I joked to another production assistant that this whole place was a parody of a metaphor and he looked at me as if I was crazy.

People say this is what you do to break into the entertainment industry. Get a foot in the door. In this company town, I overanalyse the commonplace, searching for meaning where there is none to be found. What happens to the rest of your body? Is it still attached to the foot or, pressing down on the accelerator of a 28-foot camera truck, does the foot take on a life of its own, leaving the rest of you in limbo?

Eleven months ago, December 2000, I was graduating from college in the middle of a heatwave. Florida was recounting votes, then no longer counting, then recounting some more. I was flip-flopping, too, deciding to stay in LA instead of following through with my plan of moving to New York to live with my then-fiancé. There had been an election, a too-close-to-call extravaganza, and a tallying of votes, then, suddenly, there was no president-elect. There had been a marriage proposal, a sparkling diamond ring, and a yes, and then, suddenly, no fiancé. I got the apartment on Hayworth Street with Jen and Kate, since Razi had already settled into this place with a room mate, an architect from Beirut who has since moved in with his boyfriend.

With Jen and Kate gone and the lease ending soon, my plan is to stay with Razi until we, too, go east, to New York City. It's been only about two months since the terrorist attacks but I haven't changed my mind about the move. I am going to drive across the country and commence our apartment hunt, along with my own personal venture to get my ex-fiancé back. I never would have guessed that at twenty-two I'd already have been engaged – twice.

Razi will stay behind, sell furniture and other unbringable belongings and meet me in Manhattan. West Hollywood made a great hiding place, a place to pretend to have fun until I forgot that I started out pretending. Los Angeles is a lot like Italy – my estranged father's homeland – its sunny exterior concealing darker realities.

And yet, I exist in a perpetual state of nostalgia. As soon as I leave somewhere, I long for what has passed. I will miss the other LA, the golden place. Driving up Highway 1 to Malibu for early morning surfing on a work-free weekday. Hangover dim sum in Chinatown on Sundays, running through the streets afterwards shooting bubble-tea tapioca balls out of oversized straws, the tapioca balls hurtling across Chinatown sidewalks like bullets, Razi and I giggling like mischievous children, which in a way we are. The thrift stores and red-lit hole-in-the-wall dive bars on the Eastside. Hiking in Runyon Canyon and reaching that final peak where the whole city is spread out all the way to the Pacific Ocean. From there, Los Angeles is majestic, quiet and still as a mirage on a side road in the desert towards Nevada. Where, in less than twenty-four hours, we'll be pulling off our greatest stunt yet.

'Cheerio, sweetie!' Razi calls from the living room in a fake British accent.

My five minutes are up. I toss the sleep mask on to the nightstand and reach for the glass of water, glad I at least had the foresight to leave it there the night before.

'Morning sunshine! Hurry up and get ready! We have a long drive ahead!'

Razi patters over and sticks his head through the door. I'm sitting up on the bed again, clutching my stomach. With his curly black hair gelled into perfect corkscrews and his white button-down shirt right out of its 'We ♥ Our Customers' wrapper, Razi looks fresh, bright-eyed, and not even slightly hung-over. His smile is as bright as the sunlight pouring into the room and he has a dancer's body. He barely even works out and sometimes I catch myself feeling jealous that his thighs are slimmer than mine.

I remain sprawled on the bed like a chalk outline on pavement. It hurts even to move my eyeballs but I peek up to meet Razi's gaze. When his dark eyes lock with mine, my irritation at his cheerfulness dissolves.

'Feeling ready?' he asks.

'I feel like crap,' I announce.

'I'm boiling water for coffee. Aren't you glad you packed yesterday?'

'I can barely lift my head right now, much less that suitcase.'

I tilt my head towards the overstuffed bag in the corner of the room.

'Don't you worry about a thing, sweets. I've got it all under control.'

He dashes back out into the living room. I reach into my bag on the floor and put on my dark sunglasses. I wear them indoors on days when the sun is just too much or whenever I get an eczema attack around my eyes, which is often, given my fifteen-hour days on commercial and music video sets run by panicked people on budgets and deadlines. My life in Los Angeles is superficial and I have a chronic skin affliction, both of which may or may not conceal something festering beneath the surface. I don't handle stress well and there's no cure for eczema. Medical researchers have more significant conditions to discover antidotes for.

I wrap the blanket around me like a burqa. The sunglasses, their lenses the size of two saucers, temper the sunlight streaming in through the blinds. I'm ready to traverse the desert, or at least emerge from the bedroom. Razi stands in front of the stove in the open kitchen, moving a spatula around as a pot of water reaches boiling point. I open the front door, step outside, take a breath.

Even after over a year here I marvel at these ethereal surroundings. Sunlight dances across the azure pool. Palm fronds rustle in the warm Santa Ana. People in Los Angeles claim these winds create seismic shifts in everyday consciousness, making people act crazy and do irrational things. Maybe, if Razi and I get caught, I will blame the whole thing on a particularly strong bout of the Santa Anas.

I walk back in, sit down at the kitchen table, and drop the blanket around my shoulders, leaving my sunglasses on. Razi slides a plate of scrambled eggs in front of me. I drown them in ketchup and eat. He hands me a cup of the vile instant coffee he makes because that's coffee in Beirut. In need of caffeine, I choke it down anyway.

After breakfast, I shower, dress and shuffle about to double-check for toothpaste, shampoo and other cosmetic necessities as Razi rattles off our road trip sustenance list.

'Let's see,' he says. 'We have water, Gatorade, sour cream and onion chips, and I made a few sandwiches: peanut butter and banana in honour of you-know-who, and some tuna with pickles and cheddar since you like salty more than sweet.'

Razi carries our bags down to the garage and piles them into the boot of his cranky blue 82 Nissan Sentra.

It's early and Santa Monica Boulevard is still empty. In a few hours, there will be lines on the sidewalk for eggs Benedict and cappuccinos, valet parking for Jaguars and Beemers, West Hollywood boys in tank tops and sneakers en route to the gym. We will be closing in on Vegas by then.

Part of me still doesn't believe this is really happening. I never thought I would actually go through with it and neither did he. But Sin City here we come. I tell myself it will all work out. It'll be fine.

'It'll be fine, right?' I ask.

'Having second thoughts?' he shoots back. Razi's hands tighten around the wheel as he speaks on. 'Because we can still turn around...'

'No. No I'm not,' I say, though privately I wonder whether this time I've taken free-spiritedness and what I thought was a healthy disregard for authority too far.

'I'm nervous, too,' he says.

'Really?'

He nods. For some reason it has not occurred to me that Razi might be anxious as well, even though I'm not the only one making sacrifices for this marriage.

'Sweetie, if you aren't into the Elvis package, maybe it's not too late to switch to the pirate theme…'

'No pirates. Elvis is great. It'll be fun.'

The little tin clunker of a car accelerates up the on-ramp to the 10 East. Blur of palms, steel, concrete. This is either the fourth or fifth time I've made this trip. One night on the Strip some months before, I lost a hundred dollars at the tables and left my friends to wander around the city alone at daybreak, hung over and miserable, squinting into the sunrise. I didn't buy groceries or go out for a week after that so I could still make rent. A hundred dollars is a lot of money at this life stage. Razi's father, Mohammad, wired us two thousand dollars as a wedding present — a thousand each for gambling. It's more than I have in my checking and savings accounts combined. This time around, I will play high stakes.

Father-in-Law

Razi's prominent businessman father might normally hate the idea of his only boy — who was supposed to be a Muslim — marrying a Jewish American girl, but in this case he is overjoyed even though I am both of the above — plus he's never even met me. If Razi came out to Mohammad, he would be disowned or worse. So his father is thousands of miles away in Beirut, praying that I will bear his grandchildren. Razi has told Mohammad repeatedly that he and I are only good friends, and good friends we'll remain. Yet, each time, these words fall on ears of denial. Mohammad hopes his son and I will fall in love along the course of this immigration journey.

You Ain't Seen Nothin', Carrie Bradshaw

With LA well behind us, Razi pulls over at a rest stop and says he wants to introduce me to a show called *Sex and the City*. Before I have a chance to protest he pops the Season One disc into his state-of-the-art laptop and passes it to me. He steers back onto the freeway.

I close the laptop.

'You know I don't watch TV,' I say.

Our friends joke we're like Will and Grace, but I've never seen that either.

'Sweetie, this show is different,' he says.

'Thanks, but I'd rather read.'

'You'll become nauseous if you read in the car.'

Razi squints at the freeway and gets quiet. He's hurt, as if my rejection of the show means I'm somehow rejecting him. I understand; I'm oversensitive, too. I open the laptop, press 'play', and the *Sex and the City* theme music begins. The first episode takes my mind off my apprehension. The air whips hot through the car windows like gusts from a blow-dryer. Monochromatic desert surroundings off the freeway fly by outside. I could just as easily have been born here, living in one of those box clone houses.

'Are you watching? The *best* scene is coming up,' Razi says, never shifting his gaze from the road. My eyes dart back to the computer screen. As I listen to Carrie's puns about crossing the line between professional girlfriend and just plain professional, all I can think is I am about to become a professional wife.

What Happens Here Stays Here

The next time I look up, the open road is gone, replaced by casinos, strip clubs and billboards advertising magic shows. We pass Circus Circus and the Bellagio, Versace and Prada storefronts, then steer off the Strip and pull into Motel 6 – largest one in the US of A, West Tropicana Avenue, exit 37, right across from the MGM Grand – and check-in to our sparse, generic room.

It is dusk now, the sky an orange, pink and midnight-blue layer cake, desert haze in the air disappearing into the sunset. My phone shows 7.20 p.m., forty minutes to go until chapel time. I wriggle into a hot pink slip dress, the dress a synecdoche for our approach to the whole event: maintain a sense of humour no matter what. But alone in the bathroom of a shabby motel room at nightfall, the wrong part of me feels light: not my heart but my head. Moths flutter around the lamplight and inside my stomach.

There will be no white gown, no reception and only one guest: Razi's friend, Sonar, a self-described flaming queen who wears eyeliner and had liposuction to further tighten his naturally firm stomach. He drove in earlier and awaits us in the lobby. Not your classic matrimonial sojourner, Sonar is a most appropriate witness for this sideshow circus of a ceremony. The dingy motel and Elvis-themed wedding make this experience a dire yet amusing opposite of any little-girl fantasies of veils and beaded dresses, bouquet tossing and toasting champagne, to love, to forever, that I might have had.

My mother the Foreign Service Officer is stationed in Greece, knows nothing about this wedding and would be furious that I would defy her this way. My mother works for a living to prevent the very thing that Razi and I are about to do, which he calls the very definition of irony. Earlier this month, the Immigration and Naturalization Service awarded my mother a certificate of appreciation 'in recognition of your contribution in the fight against illegal immigration'. She would never approve of her daughter marrying a gay foreigner to help him stay in the United States, even though she knows and likes Razi, and wouldn't understand I was doing it out of love. It may not have been romantic love, but this was my most important relationship. Razi was forever, anyway, unlike the straight men in my life. My ex-fiancé dumped me over the phone and hasn't spoken to me since, and I haven't heard from my father in almost four years. My mother told me he had moved from Seattle, where he'd lived for over twenty years, back to his hometown of Genoa, without telling anyone.

Familiar Consequences
My mother, Penny, began her State Department career in the visa section of the US consulate in Guadalajara. My high school summer job had been in the visa section of the embassy in Mexico City, where Penny was Chief of Citizen Services. I did data entry and laminated the cards, studying each person's face and name and silently wishing them a better life. Because of this I was aware of Razi's one-year post-graduation chance of getting his F-1 student visa turned into an H-1B residency one. First step: get hired by a company willing to sponsor him. It costs an organisation thousands of dollars to do this, but the employee pays it back through their earnings. But it turns out entertainment companies don't sponsor foreigners for entry-level clerical assistant positions. There are plenty of US citizens eager to have staplers tossed at them by manic studio executives for twenty thousand dollars a year.

A wave of nausea washes over me as I apply burgundy lipstick under the fluorescent overhead light. I wish I could attribute it to my earlier hangover but the realities of the situation are setting in: I am marrying a man I will never be in love with, cementing my future as a divorcee before even tying the knot. It's either the perfect practice run or an exercise in despair; I can't be sure. Sometimes my questions end in periods, just like relationships. Full stop. Move on. What if. Forget. Repeat.

Emotions aside, the potential legal consequences are frightening. From an article in the journal *Legal Affairs:*

> Though sham marriages that lead to green cards have been used as comedic Hollywood tropes (see, for instance, the Gérard Depardieu romp, *Green Card*), CIS officials say the job of sizing up immigrants is always serious business. 'This is not just a matter of someone pulling one over on us. This is a matter of national security,' said Shawn Saucier, a spokesman for CIS, which was formerly part of the Immigration and Naturalization Service and is now an arm of the Department of Homeland Security. The penalties for trying to dupe immigration officials are stiff. An alien accused by authorities of marriage fraud can be deported and barred from ever obtaining a green card. And a person who knowingly marries to evade immigration laws can face five years in jail.[1]

Deportation. Fraud. Jail. Mohammad. Mom. The government is serious, my mother is serious, everyone is serious but me.[2] All I really know is I am going through with this. I've given my word. I can't let him go. Razi needs the green card, and I need him. Maybe Razi and I can adopt an entourage of international children after we're successful screenwriters with a Tribeca loft and a country house upstate.

I've had constant adventure and travel, but beneath it, a life of rootlessness moving from country to country with my unmarried mother while I was growing up. It was only the two of us, no siblings, no other family around. My father has always been mysteri-

---

1 Burke, Melissa N 2006, 'To have and hold a green card', *Legal Affairs*, January/February, www.legalaffairs.org accessed 11 November 2008.
2 With apologies to Allen Ginsberg, another gay love of mine, whose poem 'America' I committed to memory in high school. Its opening line still haunts me, especially in this context: 'America I've given you all and now I'm nothing.'

ous, a man with a daughter he doesn't call or visit. I don't know if it's his drinking or if he just doesn't want to talk. I long for answers in silence, fearing the second possibility: that he has actually abandoned me. I wonder if he fears I've abandoned him. Are we just afraid of each other? My father doesn't even know who I am, who I've become, and when I think about this I become depressed, so I don't think about it, except, as with most things you try to push out of your mind, it surfaces involuntarily and manifests itself through your actions. And so, here—

I am moments away from dashing out into the taxi that will take us to the chapel on the Strip. I have so many fears: is this right? Will I end up jailed? Will Razi get deported? Am I out of my fucking mind? And if so, why does it feel as though I'm absolutely not? I don't think of our marriage as a sham. But would the government? Where, exactly, is the line between love and law? I pick up my liquid eyeliner from the edge of the sink and lean in close to the mirror, attempting to draw a straight black line across my left eyelid and failing. Any bride gets jitters – every women's magazine I've read says it's healthy, a natural reaction to change. I am doing an important favour for a friend, something a true love couldn't grant him. If our roles were reversed, I know he would do the same for me. People move in and out of the permeable membrane of my world. Razi is the exception.

In the city of imported palm trees, I have brief love affairs and casual friendships. Razi is not Los Angeles. He is my gay best friend, my brother, my partner in crime. Soon to be literally. But I do and will argue with anyone who says we're engaging in unlawful behaviour. Razi sort of resembles a real husband already: we're inseparable, he loves me no matter how flawed I am, and we don't have sex. One of my exes, a 42-year-old movie producer, used to say I should quit the business and become a lawyer. He found me skilled in rationalising and rhetoric, which is probably why I'm in this situation in the first place. I reasoned my way into it. I'm having major doubts, yes, but I know, I simply know, that I'm doing the right thing. I'm doing this for Razi. I'm doing it for me.

'The taxi's here!' the groom shouts from outside the bathroom door, his tone verging on panicked.

'Alright, I'm almost ready,' I shout back.

Even though I can't see him from in here, I can picture his slender frame in his dress-casual wedding outfit of khakis, button-down shirt and brown leather jacket. I can see the concerned expression on his face. He's always been beyond uncomfortable running late for anything from class to meeting friends for brunch.

I clasp in my second earring and take a final glimpse in the mirror. One of my film school professors said: *always push your story to a place of extremes. When it's verging on unbelievable, that's when you've nailed it.* He was talking about screenwriting, but I'd gone and applied his words to my life.

My lipstick shade suddenly seems all wrong. I wipe it off and reach for another, leaning in towards my reflection.

2. ATHENS, NOVEMBER 2001

On Ceremonies
Across the Atlantic, my mother receives her appreciation award from the INS for 'interagency co-operation'. This is right around the same day that Razi and I are driving through the desert to Vegas. My mother moved to Athens, Greece, when I went to college, and for a year 'home' was a place I'd never been.

She clasps in gold earrings and smooths her knee-length red dress, looking in the mirror. She is petite with shoulder-length highlighted hair, a small, rounded nose, sparkling eyes and a smile worth using to sell toothpaste.

The ambassador calls her up to the podium. He shakes her hand, gives her a medal and certificate. Someone snaps a photo. The INS thanks her. Her daughter would smear her good name, her professional reputation, turn everything she's worked so hard for to shit.

Elvis will call me up to the stage. The room will be empty. Sonar will snap a photo and we will have to show it to an INS agent one day. They will look through our photographs, evidence of our shared life. They will ask questions. They will seek proof that our marriage is not for immigration purposes. I have other ideas: if I don't marry him, he will have to go; I don't want him to go. That's a love marriage, to me.

My mother won many awards from the Department of State: meritorious honour, superior honour, even one from the CIA, though they would only write 'From Your Friends at the Embassy' on the certificate. She won't tell me what that one is for. She was nominated for a Barbara M Watson Award for Consular Excellence, one of the highest honours in her field. There were five-year, ten-year, fifteen-year and twenty-year service awards, and she's received them all.

The day she married my father, she had one quick ceremony all her own. I trace the fault lines in official versions of family stories, trying to crack open the earth, get at the core. In Italian, the word *storia* means both history and story. A *storia* can be a tale of true life or made up entirely. The word itself makes no distinction. History and fiction – you'd never know which category *una storia* fell into unless you asked. My mother says it's more like a Truffaut film: my father's father worked in a laundry in Brooklyn as a POW during World War II, the same time as my mother's mother lived on Eastern Parkway, a Jewish neighbourhood, also in Brooklyn. Generations circled each other.

I learned Italian right alongside English, but I never considered *storia*. Then I found out that my parents' marriage also originated with an innocent lie – a true love that began with a fiction. Their *storia* fascinated me. They were actually in love, but what my mother told my grandparents about my father seemed to be pulled straight from an Italian history textbook.

Convertible

Before my mother became a bureaucratic heroine, there was her other life, the one that ended with me. When the girl who would become the woman who would become my mother was twelve, doctors discovered thyroid cancer, and once her thyroid was taken out, the chubby brown-haired girl metamorphosed into a teenage swan. Because my grandparents were so relieved that their daughter had survived, they gave her everything she wanted for the rest of her youth.

I exist because of one of those things – an MGB convertible.

My mother owned what its advertisements called 'The Great Escape Car' in Rochester, New York, in the early seventies, when she made her own great escape to Italy. She had moved to Rochester with a man, but the relationship didn't work out. She entered a PhD program that would send her back to the country she first fell in love with at sixteen, when she was on a high school study abroad program, The Experiment in International Living. My mother was drawn to Italy, a lively country where more negative realities, both personal and political, are swept under the rug, unacknowledged. She spoke Italian fluently, majoring in Romance languages at Stanford, and then at the University of Washington, where she had transferred to finish college a semester early.

My mother wanted to keep her Great Escape Car, the orange convertible. She decided to put it on the SS *Leonardo da Vinci*, a ship bound from New York to Genoa. Instead of flying to Florence, she would drive down the Italian coast. It was the first of many seemingly simple decisions that altered the course of things in unimaginable ways. She met my father, a maître d' on the ship. After a three-month courtship, she called her parents in Seattle and told them to send her birth certificate – she was going to marry the Marchese di Monferrato, a man from an Italian royal family.

The Marchese di Monferrato was not an invention of my mother's imagination.

My grandparents had no idea their new son-in-law was not a Marchese at all.

They also didn't know that the real Marchese Giovanni I wrested control of Monferrato from Matteo I Visconti, Lord of Milan, and his occupiers, in 1303. Giovanni II, Marchese di Monferrato, defeated the Queen of Naples's troops in Gamenario in 1345. In 1378, Giovanni III took over Marchese di Monferrato–hood. None of these men were my father. The Giovanni my mother married was a waiter from a family of farmers who strapped him to a board when he was born so his spine would grow straight.

Penny and Giovanni lived in a ranch-style house on Lake Washington Boulevard with a pool, a small wood and fruit trees. Even from an ocean and a continent away, Italy played a starring role in their lives. My father worked in Italian restaurants and my mother found a job at the Italian consulate. In 1979, after five years of marriage, my mother then approaching her twenty-ninth birthday, I was born.

The large glassed-in solarium in the back of the house became my playroom. During summers, we visited my father's mother, who I called Nonna (Italian for 'grandma'), in Genoa, and I played with my little cousin, Chiara, daughter of my father's brother, Uncle Mario, who was ten years younger than Giovanni. The brothers had little in common, but now that Giovanni had a family of his own, we were brought together.

The rest of the year, my mother, having quit the consulate, stayed home with me. When I was four, she enrolled me in a Montessori school, where I quickly took to reading and writing, bringing home the little storybooks I made for my parents. But what had started out as a privileged American life didn't last long. My father started drinking too much after his shifts and coming home past midnight; one night he burst into the bedroom where I slept, smashing a wire-and-clay sculpture I'd made at school against the wall and screaming in Italian while I hid under the covers.

Oh, the Places You'll Go
When my father moved back to Seattle, it was never an option that I would go with him. I belonged to my mother. I would live around the world with her, attending private international schools for which the US government covered tuition. The summer before fifth grade, we moved to Rome, where we remained for four years, the longest I had ever lived in one place. For high school, it was off to Mexico City.

My mother had always wanted an exotic life, an adventurous life, a different life. She hated the idea of the workaday nine-to-five, stopping-at-the-grocery-store, coming-home-and-watching-TV type of existence. I believe she must have thought the Foreign Service would grant her the chance to live abroad in romantic locales, to have adventures, to break her parents' traditional mould.

My mother and I travelled constantly, venturing off to medieval Italian towns, spending a Thanksgiving in London, taking a jaunt to Djerba, and a road trip to see castles in the French countryside. Staying home for a lazy Sunday was forbidden. My homework came with me, and I did math problems on beds in Tuscan villages, wrote my English class essays on airplanes, studied for tests in the car on our way to wherever we were going while my mother talked to me. We were together, a vibrant, centre-of-attention, extroverted diplomat and her quiet offspring who loved to read, write, and live in an inner world of imagination and words. All I wanted was to stand still for a moment. My mother could never be still. And I was hers.

The highly unpredictable volcano Mount Etna, located in Sicily, erupted in 1992, when I was twelve. Hot lava barrelled down towards Zafferana, a town of seven thousand. My mother took me to the volcano. At the time, the Italian military had cordoned off the area and was using controlled explosions to divert the flow of the lava. After our journey to the base, all we could see was snow, no lava to be found. My mother spotted a TV journalist with curly grey hair and ice blue eyes giving a report. She somehow convinced him to allow us into his news helicopter when he was headed to give a report from farms being destroyed by hot red lava, on the other, forbidden side of the volcano. I went over with them and walked around as his cameraman filmed crying, screaming farmers. The lava slowly inched, bit by stony bit, over their land. The molten heat burned up through the rubber bottoms of my white Keds.

The Marchese di Monferrato
Over summer vacations, I went back to Seattle for a few weeks, always staying with my grandmother across the lake in Bellevue, where Bill Gates's house would eventually go up, nestled behind trees down by the water. My grandparents had divorced in the same period as my parents, the mid-eighties. My grandfather had been having an affair with one of his patients for years; my grandmother saw his car parked by the apartment building the woman lived in at the time. He had said he was going to the hospital, but her instinct knew otherwise. She sent him away. He remarried the other woman and lived with her in a smaller house near the university.

My mother took me to the first Starbucks down by Pioneer Square in Seattle as a child. She'd buy bags of whole beans while I stuck my face in the plastic tubs with scoopers attached, just like they had in the candy store. My father had moved to Capitol Hill and I wasn't allowed to stay there, even after he moved from a basement to a nicer apartment with clean carpets and an island kitchen. He worked unpredictable shifts, days and nights, drank more than he should, and lived in an area hospitable to street punks with multicoloured hair and floor-length leather coats. On Wednesdays and Sundays, my father's days off from serving pasta to the business-lunch crowd, my grandmother would drive me to visit him at his Republican Street studio. It was the quintessential bachelor pad, with a Murphy bed and an enormous entertainment system as centrepieces. There was an enormous black-and-white photographic portrait of his parents in the foyer. There were no books.

My father sent cards on my birthday and on holidays. He never called or came to visit me even though he and my mother remained on cordial terms. When I saw him in Seattle, I asked him every now and then.

'I will call you,' he'd say.

He never did.

The last time I saw him before he disappeared, I was seventeen. I was visiting Seattle in between moving from Mexico City to film school at Emerson College in Boston.

He met me in the hallway and I noticed his body swaying as we walked towards his door. It was eleven in the morning, and I knew he was drunk.

Back inside his apartment, my father fixed his gaze on me.

'Why are you looking at me like that?' he asked.

'Um, I'm not,' I said.

I walked over to the fridge, took out a Coke, cracked it open. We were going to have a normal day at the beach.

We took the bus down to the lake, and I swam while he lay in the sun, occasionally sipping from an aluminium thermos. Back at the apartment, I'd seen him pour vodka in it, followed by juice.

'I'm leaving Il Terrazzo soon,' he said as I flopped down on my towel. 'Some people are opening a new restaurant. They want me as a partner.'

'For real?'

I heard this story every so often.

'At the least, I'll move into management.'

While unpacking our picnic lunch, my father realised he'd forgotten silverware. He rustled around in the picnic basket and said he'd go buy some plastic forks and knives. Then, quietly, he began to cry. It was as if the silverware were the last straw, his final failure in a life that didn't play out as he had hoped. I stared out over Lake Washington, not knowing what to say. 'It's okay, Daddy,' was all that came out when I finally spoke.

'*Sono finito con queste genti*,' I heard him mutter as my grandmother's pale blue Toyota pulled up in front of his building to pick me up – that's Italian for 'I'm done with these people'.

Sometime after that, I called his apartment and the phone rang and rang. He never had an answering machine. After this became the norm rather than a deviation from it, I brought it up with my mother.

'Maybe he went to visit Nonna in Genoa,' she said.

Nobody knew for sure where he'd gone, but no one seemed to be trying very hard to find him. Myself included. Wherever he was, the green card didn't get him very far.

My mother told me he never had ambition.

'He was a fish out of water,' my grandmother liked to say.

In the Hollywood ending, I would have followed my original plan, gone back to Seattle after high school, studied forestry at the University of Washington, and been able to save my father. But most times, I have read, a drowning man will pull his would-be saviour under.

If it hadn't been for Penny and her MGB convertible, Gioacchino Giovanni Gennatiempo (sounds like royalty, doesn't it) would have married a provincial girl and settled into small-town life in Northern Italy. It's what he should have done, but then of course I wouldn't exist and there would be no documentarian for these events that wouldn't ever have happened.

Yes, that is where he went, I told myself, Northern Italy. I convinced myself of this so I could get on with my life. Underneath, though, I was always suspicious of a family secret, some buried thing that would eventually become unearthed. It nagged at me, the mystery of my father, a longing for something I never quite knew, to cease being so constantly adrift. The daughter of two expatriates, I wanted to find somewhere to belong.

At the School of the Arts at Emerson College, we were all outsiders: punks, gays, film geeks. Here, we had our own little world where we were encouraged to be creative and thrive in our eccentricities. I grounded myself in this everyday existence in Boston: sipping too-sweet white wine from plastic cups on docks by the Charles River with my girlfriends Jen, a dark-haired, Italian–Irish writing major, and blonde, sea-glass-eyed Kate, who was getting her BFA in dance. I took courses in film history, theory, and production, dated acting majors, and got a job waitressing at a dark jazz restaurant in the financial district. But I always felt that there was something missing. This hole was either within me, or else it followed me around like a shadow, as if I could slip and fall in at any moment. I didn't know for sure, about that and many other things, one of them being the culture shock I would experience on coming back to my own homeland. My family was fractured, fragmented, elsewhere.

My father had wanted to be a filmmaker instead of a waiter. We were sitting in his tidy studio apartment in Seattle one summer afternoon when I was twelve or thirteen, when he told me he'd once had an old Bolex and imagined himself a Fellini, directing in Cinecittà during Italy's golden age of auteurs in the fifties and sixties. By the time I was applying to film school myself I had forgotten all of this.

'Your father really loved movies,' my mother told me. 'He didn't really need people. He could watch them all day.'

3. WEST HOLLYWOOD, SEPTEMBER 2001

Still 72 and Sunny
The morning was a strange one in Hollywood. Thousands of miles removed from the chaos, madness and horror of the World Trade Center attacks, I watched the news in total shock. I'd woken up to the girl downstairs pounding on my door and yelling for me to turn on the television. The start date of the independent movie I was about to begin working on as an art assistant was pushed back another week.

Not knowing what to do with ourselves that day, Razi and I drove north-east to the strip of Franklin Boulevard with the newsstand, Bourgeois Pig coffee shop, and a sushi restaurant. I was surprised the restaurant was even open, but we sat outside and ordered. The World Trade Center was burning and in LA we were eating tuna rolls.

'Now I'm never going to get sponsored,' Razi said. 'Those terrorist assholes were all Middle Eastern. Who will hire me now?'

'I feel sick about eating,' I said.

Razi was still waiting for me to answer his question.

'I said I'd marry you. I will.'

'They're going to see my name on my résumé and never call me for interviews.'

'People aren't that prejudiced.'
'They will be now.'
'Look, just tell me if you want to do it, and we'll do it.'
There was still some naive part of me that believed Razi would find another means by which to stay.
But he was right.
Nothing changed.

Razi wanted to work and be in love and, eventually, have a family, too. He didn't want to go back home and face intolerance. If the only conduit for him to attain what I considered basic human rights was through marriage to a woman who loved him, I could find no reason not to move forward.

The visa's expiration date neared. Over drinks at the Abbey, Razi told me it was almost all over.

I gulped my cocktail, hopped off the barstool and dropped down on one knee.

'Lose an earring?' Razi asked.

'Let's do it. Let's get married,' I said.

Razi's eyes darted back up to meet mine. For a moment he didn't speak.

'I don't know,' he said. 'What if you regret it? What if you meet someone sooner than you expect?'

'It's clear that a normal marriage wouldn't work for me,' I rationalised. 'I lack the template. I'd be putting my ability to marry towards a worthy cause – you. Besides, this will be like an automatic filter for boyfriends. Any guy who disapproves of our situation is out.'

Razi laughed.

'Think of it as a shortcut towards me finding the right guy. The right guy is *so* going to get what this is about.'

He nudged me in the ribs. 'Then I'd be helping you in a way, too?'

He was the brother I never had. Becoming family almost made sense.

'Exactly,' I agreed.

'In that case, I'd be honoured to be the envy of straight men everywhere,' he said.

'Straight men?' I looked around. 'Where?'

We laughed and hugged some more. I told him I didn't have a ring because I hadn't planned on proposing tonight. We decided not to wear rings anyway.

Onlookers stared. It wasn't every day they witnessed one of their kind accept a marriage proposal from a female at the Abbey.

'So, Vegas?' Razi asked.

We agreed on an Elvis theme. He pulled his pocket organiser from the backpack at his feet.

'How about November 17th? Five days after your birthday.'

'Okay,' I said.

Never one to keep a schedule, this was my standard response to invitations. Luckily, Razi's brain worked like a Blackberry.

'There's just one thing I ask in return,' I said.

'What's that?'

'Move to New York?'

He said yes.

Engagement Party
We threw a pre-wedding get-together at the Abbey. Razi handed me a martini with buoying berries as we stood in the outdoor courtyard. Next to him, his boyfriend, Adam, a fresh-faced blond, sipped a Tom Collins. Razi and Adam had met at the gay Starbucks on Santa Monica some time ago, but our unpredictable film industry schedules (Adam was a prop master) kept the two of us from ever meeting before tonight.

'Razi's told me so much about you, Lisa,' Adam shouted over the throbbing bass of West Hollywood gay bar music.

I was not offended. This happened all the time.

'Liza,' I corrected. 'With a Z.'

'Oh my *god*, *right*,' he said apologetically. 'Like Minnelli! How could I mess that one up?'

My grandmother named me Liza. It's not short for Elizabeth and she swears it had nothing to do with Liza Minnelli, though the record *Liza with a 'Z'* was a staple of early childhood singalongs with my mother on the brown shag rug of my parents' house in Seattle. It wasn't until I came across an *Artforum* article that stated Liza Minnelli is 'a representation of polymorphous sexuality, cosmopolitan pleasures, and their interrelated political ramifications'[3] that I wondered if being her namesake, whether purposeful or not, had anything to do with my love of all things gay. Liza Minnelli married gay men, too, albeit not in order to be a one-woman asylum-granting nonprofit.

'Here you go,' Razi said. He was handing me another cocktail – Adam was in the middle of telling a story and I hadn't even noticed that my glass was empty. Great-Uncle Walt and Great-Uncle Richard were the most stable couple in my family and there I was, marrying a gay man as if it were the most normal thing for a young twentysomething girl to do. For me, I guess it was.

And so.

A bathroom mirror. White rabbits. Our very own Mad Hatter's tea party. Alice, through the looking glass, coming out the other side.

4. LAS VEGAS, NOVEMBER 2001

'Hurry Üp!'
Razi yells, pounding on the bathroom door. 'The taxi's been waiting forever!'

I'm stalling, applying and reapplying different shades of lipstick to justify staying in there so long. Crushed Grape it shall be.

'We're going to miss our own wedding!'

'I'm here!' I fling open the door.

Razi smiles when he sees me.

'You look beautiful,' he says.

The doors of the Motel 6 slide open and we float out into the warm Vegas night. Vegas, that neon-lit strip in vast desert, a place that looks like it could crumble at any moment, as in relationships, or cities built on fault lines.

Sonar, the witness, turns around in the front seat as I scoot into the back seat beside Razi. Sonar's eyebrows are plucked perfect and he is wearing eyeliner.

'Hello you two! Happy wedding night,' he says.

'Hey Sonar, how was gambling?' I ask.

'I lost money but I got two phone numbers,' he says.

---

3 Hainley, Bruce 2006, 'Just say yes: Bruce Hainley on *Liza with a "Z"*, *Artforum International*, vol. 44, no. 7, pp. 107–8.

'Well at least one person might hook up at this wedding,' Razi jokes.

'Why aren't any of your friends here?' Sonar asks as the taxi speeds towards the Little White Wedding Chapel.

'My only really close friends in LA besides Razi were my room mates but they moved back to Boston a few weeks ago. I asked another girlfriend but her sister talked her out of coming. Her sister's convinced that this is an illegal green card marriage and she could be implicated.'

'Well isn't it?' Sonar asks.

'No, it's not,' I argue, 'and I'll tell you why: Razi isn't paying me other than in measures of love and devotion. I'm doing it because I can't stand to lose him. Isn't that why anyone gets married? The only difference is that we are going to be able to date and sleep with whomever we want, and we have our own rooms. There are plenty of stranger arrangements in some straight marriages, don't you think? Besides, I've been out there. There's no one for me, or at least I can't find him, or I've lost faith. So I'd rather marry Razi here and date some fun, intelligent, nice, straight guys, but save that all-important commitment of who's going to take care of you when you're sick, who's going to help pay your bills when you're broke, who's going to comfort you when you're depressed, hold your hair back when you throw up from drinking too much or some stomach bug, to someone I know I can count on. You know?'

I know I'm rambling. I chalk it up to anxiety.

Razi says, 'Honey, let's stop for some champagne. Your nerves need calming.'

'It's that obvious?'

'Uh-huh.'

At a roadside liquor store, Sonar springs for a celebratory bottle of Veuve. We drink it out of a paper bag in the car. The driver doesn't seem to care. It's Vegas, after all. The bottle is empty by the time we arrive at the chapel.

Trouble in Paradise

'They're ready for you,' says the heavily mascaraed, blue-eyed receptionist. 'Just give me your receipt and the marriage licence, please.'

'The what?' Razi and I say in unison.

'The marriage licence?' repeats the bubble-haired receptionist, in a tone typically reserved for five-year-olds.

'Do you have that?' I ask Razi, who in turn stares at the floor.

I wonder if it's a sign. I don't think I can leave Vegas and then come back and do this again. Reason and good judgement might set in, in the interim.

'Minister Frank?' the receptionist squawks into an intercom. 'Can you come out here please? Bit of a problem with these next ones.'

This place is a factory. A gentle-seeming older man strides out of the main chapel. Gelled thinning white hair, jeans and cowboy boots.

'What seems to be the matter? Commitment jitters? We offer premarital counselling for only a small additional fee—'

'They forgot to get a licence,' the receptionist says.

The minister looks at his watch.

'Is there any way Elvis can wait?' I ask. 'We could run and get it—'

'Gonna be crowded down there on a Saturday night,' the receptionist says.

'I can pay for an extra hour or something,' Razi says.

'Don't worry,' the minister says. 'We'll switch the order of the evening.' He turns to the receptionist. 'Put the Mafia wedding in front of them and tell Joe to hold off on changing into the Elvis outfit, give him a beer or something.'

'Where do we go?' Razi asks.

The receptionist gives us directions downtown to the wedding licensing office, which, fittingly for Vegas, is open until midnight. The three of us run out of the chapel and jump into a taxi on the Strip again, Sonar in the front seat, Razi and I in the back.

'Marriage licence place, please,' Sonar says to the driver.

'Shit, shit, shit!' Razi says.

'This is insane,' I say. 'Do you think it's a sign?'

'Calm down guys,' Sonar chimes in. 'We'll go there, get the licence, and everything will be just fine.'

I never thought I would be so grateful for the presence of a man in eyeliner.

'And *you* are fabulous,' he continued, turning around in the front seat and looking at me. 'I mean, in that dress, honey, no one would ever know you didn't have a totally flat stomach.'

Or then again.

Standing in line under the fluorescent lights of that bureaucratic office, a sense of reality that's absent while in a Vegas Elvis chapel sets in. Couples line the wall at the entrance in front of us. I wonder if any of them are doing this for green card purposes, wonder who is eloping to avoid over-involved relatives, who just met at the craps tables earlier tonight, who will get an annulment in the morning. The blonde lady with the Mexican in a Dodgers cap? The Goth kids who don't look a day older than eighteen? The dowdy pregnant brunette with the reluctant-looking man who's missing one front tooth? The little Asian couple excitedly chattering in Japanese and snapping photos?

Maybe Razi and I fit right in. Razi jokes with me in the line and I feel like a patient in a hospital waiting room preparing for surgery, squeamish about being put under.

'Are you nervous?' Sonar asks me.

'No. Well, maybe.'

'I am definitely nervous,' Razi says.

'I keep forgetting how much this affects you, too,' I tell him.

'Of course, sweetie,' Razi says. 'Do you think I *want* to do this? I love you to pieces, you're my best friend, but is this something I would do for *fun*?'

We get the licence and climb back into the cab that Sonar had instructed to wait for us.

'Alright, back to the Little White Wedding Chapel!' our witness commands.

Wedding, Take Two

We catch the end of the gangster ceremony. A rotund couple who look like figures out of a Botero painting say their vows to an old actor dressed in a Mafioso suit. The *Godfather* theme music cranks up as they make their way, smiling and rosy-faced, back up the aisle after the you-may-kiss portion of the vows.

They look happy.

I wonder what I am.

'I'm in love… I'm all shook up,' our costumed Elvis sings. There is bad fake foliage and drapery behind him. This is our cue. Razi and I dance our way down the aisle. Elvis wears a bad wig and a shiny red fake-silk button-down. He gyrates his hips, a painful exaggeration of the original King's moves.

'I think the minister's gay,' Razi whispers, gesturing over at the older man.

'Act straighter,' I whisper.

Razi adjusts his tie and puffs up his chest like a football player, and we both crack up.

'Not quite like that,' I say.

'Whatever, sweetie. It's our wedding. Twirl, twirl!'

We dance to the ridiculous music in the shanty building on the Vegas Strip. My nervousness evaporates. I feel free for the first time in a year. I will consider this my initiation rite into a more fun version of young adulthood.

'Do you promise to polish each other's blue suede shoes?' Elvis asks. I beam at my almost-husband.

'I do.'

'Do you promise to walk each other's hound dogs?'

'Of course,' Razi says.

'I'm more of a cat person,' I say. Razi nudges me in the ribs. 'But sure.'

'Yes, yes to everything, Elvis,' he says.

'In that case, I now pronounce you husband and wife. You may kiss the bride.'

ICK! I think as Razi and I lean in.

It is an awkward peck but no one seems to care.

It's gross and incestuous in the same way as kissing my brother would be, if I had a brother. Now I sort of do. Don't call it marriage; call it adoption. Latent activism. Rebellion against a senseless system. DIY unconventional family-making.

Razi, Sonar and I catch a cab as Elvis, the minister and the receptionist wave and throw rice and throw rice and wave. It may have been a fake wedding, but nobody could say our love wasn't genuine. It would have been more genuine if Razi could have been standing next to his boyfriend up there at the altar. But given the state of things, a man would not have been able to help Razi the way his best girlfriend could.

We run out into the chaos of the Vegas Strip and head to the Stratosphere, a Space Needle–shaped hotel casino with 'THE WORLD'S HIGHEST THRILL RIDE!', the Big Shot, on top, 921 feet above the Strip. It shoots you up at the speed of a rocket launch, and then you fall at zero Gs over the concentrated lights, which from up there resemble a neon huddle of fireflies in the vast desert emptiness. I scream out into the blackness as the speed and altitude overwhelm my senses. Everything is so different all of a sudden, yet so much the same. My new life will be one where the men are gay, the nights are late, and the word 'settle' means sleeping with people you don't consider attractive, not down payments and giving up birth control.

Back down on earth, Sonar goes to search for a gay club. Razi and I hit casinos, ending up at the Hard Rock. After fake Paris and the hideous Luxor pyramid, I like it in here. Multiplicitous dings and singsong beeps and flashing lights on slot machines blend in a cacophony, a symphony with financial stakes. We are down a few hundred dollars after the blackjack tables, but we don't care. Mohammad's money is taking us a long way. On our way out, I drop a quarter into a Jefferson Airplane-themed slot machine called White Rabbit, just for fun, and keep walking.

Dingdingdingdingdingdingdingding

We spin around. Three white rabbits. One thousand dollars!

'It's our lucky night,' Razi says.

We scurry to collect the quarters in giant plastic cups.

The guy who walked away right before we got there will never know he missed the jackpot by just one turn.

We leave with more money than we went in with.

Married life seems promising, for once.

God of All Things

Jo Bowers

They had stripped down to their jeans and were lying, side-by-side, on his high, wide bed, like a pair of beached canoes. Their hands touched in the territory between them and she was giggling, still, at the things he had said as he'd removed his top and then hers. As they'd orientated themselves around each other. They were supposed to be making love but instead he was making her laugh.

Making her laugh. She realised, with a riveting shiver, that she wasn't laughing out of politeness, or to flatter him, or to try to kid herself of anything. There was no controlling any of it.

She sighed and rolled over to look at his profile, a definite thing in the shadowy, half-lit room.

'This is big, isn't it?' she said to his gladiatorial nose.

'What is?' he said to the ceiling. He moved his hand to his face.

'This. All of it. Us.' She kept her eyes on him as she said it.

He let his hand drop down again before turning his face toward her. He was all seriousness now. 'It looks like it could be heading that way.'

His eyes were pewter, like some unconquerable part of the ocean – sometimes so much like it that it frightened her. Moving through them was his life: a dark ship stacked high with solid, square containers, loaded with things about which it wasn't her business to know. She was a recreational vessel, all colours and stripes, bobbing about and loosely moored. Her sails were transparent in the sunlight.

Who had strayed into whose waters? How would she stay afloat in his wake? How would she?

She thought to pull her hand away and bring it to her side, but instead she reached into his big palm with her fingers. He took them to his chest and turned away, carrying her arm across his shoulder as he rolled. She put her other hand against his back. Her pink fingernails were small, joyous things against the broad reach of his skin. She saw strength there. She felt it in her hands.

They slept like that, side by side, on his bed. She clung to him in the night, boats on a sea that would carry them to some safe shore.

In the morning he brought her the papers. She propped up on one elbow, the rest of her hidden beneath a swathe of sheets.

'I've got to go and watch my son play cricket,' he said. 'Stay here? There's coffee and food in the kitchen. I should be back in a couple of hours.'

She nodded and wondered what was happening to her. Wasn't this the guy she'd refused to wait for when they'd first met several months ago? He was going through a hard time. He'd asked for her understanding, but she wouldn't compromise. 'Listen,' she'd said back then, 'I don't care if you need to spend time with your friends. None of this has anything to do with me. So why don't you just stop calling until you're over it?' She'd hung up the phone in disgust. The 'it' was the divorce he was going through.

Now he was through it, more or less, though he was still shaking in his sleep, something he'd not been aware of until she'd told him. 'It was like trying to sleep with the aftershocks of an earthquake,' she said, remembering the year she'd spent in California.

'I don't know what's wrong with me. Maybe there's a fault line in my soul.' But they both knew. Things were shifting seismically.

So she was waiting, still outside his world although inside his bedroom. Funny how you could be intimate with someone in the night and still not exist for them in a daily sense. What he would do tomorrow, next week, was none of her business. Going into his kitchen felt like a trespass. There were photos on the fridge, bills on the table. There was poetry on the walls. She looked for coffee. Had he left it out for her?

Her eyes fell on a ruthlessly dog-eared Bible, one of the modern translations that tried to make Jesus cool.

Definitely a Christian, she thought. She'd seen signs of it: a reference to one of the saints on his website; a not-quite-kitsch crucifix on the mantelpiece. Some white gospel in the CD stack she'd rifled through last night, while he was in the bathroom after their return from the restaurant. She'd edited out the evidence as she went along, not wanting to believe – not now that they were getting on so well – that anything could come between them. And *God* of all things! It was unimaginable. She'd think about that one later, once she'd figured out what kind of Christian he was.

The kind that believes in sex before, during and after marriage, she thought shrewdly, picking up the Bible and turning it over in her hands. When she'd first met him, a friend had emailed to her a poem of his, found on the internet. There was a reference to semen. 'Watch out,' the friend had warned, 'he doesn't practise safe sex.'

The Bible fell open at a worn groove.

You're blessed when you care. At the moment of being care-full, you find yourselves cared for.

She closed it quickly and put it back on the table, resuming her permitted search for breakfast items. She scanned the pantry, a shelf crammed with canisters, a benchtop bearing a same-brand team of stainless steel appliances. The kind you buy all together in a box if you need to set up house in a hurry.

When was the last time she'd really cared about anyone?

She opened a cupboard above the sink, exposing a jar of dark coffee grinds and a plunger. She clasped her hands together. Now I'm ready to sail, she thought.

The Day of the Hen

Tony Birch

What Sonny Macris had explained to me as a choice when I'd spoken to him on the phone earlier that morning I took as a clear ultimatum. Get the money to him by six that night, he'd said more than once, or I'd be getting a visitor. I was to drop the money at the suburban cafe where he kept a more or less legitimate business out the front while running a highly lucrative card game from the back door. I knew the establishment well enough, and it was not a place I had fond memories of, having lost a brick there more than once; one time too many as it had turned out.

Four hundred dollars was not an amount that Sonny would normally bother chasing himself. It was little more than pocket money. But collecting it had become a matter of principle, he'd made a point of reminding me more than once.

It was not only the conviction in his voice on the other end of the line that persuaded me to take the threat seriously. I'd seen the results of Sonny's handiwork before. He had a habit of insisting that accumulated interest be compensated for in pain and suffering.

He was particularly unhappy that I'd been seen out and about at a nightclub the week before, throwing around the winnings that I'd won on a bet on a title fight. It happened to be a nightclub that he had an interest in, and one where enough loose-mouthed patrons knew I was in his debt. They couldn't wait to crawl back to Sonny and report my misdemeanour to him.

I left the house around eight that morning with some urgency. I had a lot of running around to do and no wheels to get me from A to B or beyond. I'd been driving a 76 Charger for a few months but had sold it back to the yard at less than half the price I paid for it when I was desperate to get my hands on some cash in a hurry; cash that I should have passed on to Sonny to clear the ledger. It had been my intention to do so but unfortunately I got waylaid along the way, found myself at the casino and walked out with nothing.

Getting my hands on the money did not turn out to be as difficult as I thought it might have been. I managed to scrounge the lot by four o'clock that afternoon. I started well by collecting on a hundred-dollar debt that Latimer, three doors down the street from me, had owed me for weeks. He'd knocked at my door one Thursday morning and more or less begged the money out of me, telling me he was broke and desperate to get his hands on the cash to pay for an ampoule of super juice so he could spike his greyhound, Flashdance.

The dog was set to run in a big race at Sandown that night, but would need some extra pep in her step if she was to get anywhere near the bunny. Latimer outlined his plan with such enthusiasm that I not only lent him the hundred, I gave him another fifty to put on the dog for me.

It turned out to be a total fuck-up on my part. I don't know what vet Latimer uses, but I wouldn't send my mum's budgie to him for as much as a check-up. I had held the dog down while Latimer injected her before putting her in the car and driving across town to the track. When he got there she was laid out across the back seat, sleeping like a baby. Latimer couldn't rouse her and Flashdance did not come good until around lunchtime the next day.

I also picked up an advance of two hundred and fifty from a milk bar owner in Richmond who I regularly supply with a delivery of cigarettes. The only catch being I had to throw in a couple of extra cartons with my next drop – a reasonable price to pay, I thought, considering his financial risk.

I negotiated the final fifty with a pawnbroker in Russell Street over a watch I had been holding for a colleague in the trade. It would have been worth twice that on the street, but I didn't have the time to tout around the pubs for a buyer. As soon as I passed the watch across the glass-top counter I knew I would have some serious explaining to do later on, but this was not the time to think about it.

After leaving the pawnshop I headed for the train station with the four hundred dollars stuffed into one of my socks. The last words Sonny had said to me before slamming the phone down in my ear was, 'don't be fucking late, son, don't be late.' Although he said it slowly and very quietly, in his distinctive gravelled voice, the message came down the line like the screech of a demented chainsaw mixed with a barking-mad pit bull.

The words of Sonny Macris haunted me all the way to the station.

When I got there I realised I did not have the additional $3.30 I needed for the train ticket and the validation stalls leading to the platforms were all manned, not only by regular station assistants, but an army of railway police, suited up, badged and ready to interrogate anyone without a ticket.

I looked up at the timetable. I had just three minutes to get on the next train for St Albans if I were to meet the deadline. But I also had a more immediate problem to deal with. The automatic ticketing machines do not accept fifty-dollar notes and the queue snaking away from the only open ticket box was going nowhere.

Even if I'd had the time to buy a ticket Sonny would not be happy with me pulling up short. The amount was an insult really, likely to upset him more than if I were, say, fifty dollars light, which would at least be worthy of negotiation. Whereas $3.30 would be understood for what it was: a mark of disrespect.

As I wrestled with my limited options I was saved by a teenage kid wearing a baseball cap and expensive sneakers, who at that moment decided to take a suicidal run at one of the stalls, straddle it and baulk around the patrolling attendants on the other side.

Although the kid hurdled the gate with room to spare, unfortunately he landed awkwardly and slipped on the tiled concourse, where he was quickly set upon by a half-dozen railway police. On the positive side his misfortune was my good luck. As he was being slammed into the tiles for the third time I slipped through the unmanned gate, walked calmly down the ramp to my train and closed the door behind me just as it was leaving the platform.

The train was crowded, mostly with teenagers in school uniform. At North Melbourne station the first factory workers who were just knocking off work for the day joined us. I would have found a seat had I been quick enough, but I was preoccupied with thoughts of the train breaking down between stations and me not getting to the cafe by the required time, where I imagined Sonny seated at a table in the back corner playing with a set of boltcutters.

I should not have worried myself sick over being just a few minutes late. It's the money that counts, right? But Sonny had never been a predictable type, nor entirely reasonable, so I could not be sure what he might do if I was late.

Sonny had many nasty habits. One of them was that he liked to make an example of anyone guilty of untidiness or disrespect. 'Incentive tales,' Sonny liked to call them. Whether they were true or not, his clientele, his business partners, and sworn enemies alike, had all heard the story about the car boot permanently lined with black plastic, and the supply gaffer tape, a shovel and the box of crude tools of the trade that he kept on hand.

We crossed the river and pulled in at Footscray. Although the carriage was already full, more schoolkids and afternoon market shoppers forced their way onto the train, along with their bags and makeshift trolleys stuffed full with fruit and vegetables and meats.

By the time more factory workers got on the train at Tottenham we were packed in like sheep on our way to the slaughterhouse, with every square foot of the carriage occupied. Luckily, when we pulled in at Sunshine around half of the passengers got off the train. I quickly grabbed a seat before anyone could take it from me, sitting next to a bloke wearing a dirty boilersuit. Looking at him covered in grease from head to foot, half asleep and worn out by hard labour, I was reminded of the many reasons I had managed to shy away from a proper job for all these years.

An old man struggled onto the train just as the doors were closing, pushing an old pram jammed full with crushed aluminium cans. He had a heavy canvas bag under one arm, also overflowing with crushed cans. He off-loaded the bag and dragged it across the floor with him as he guided the pram with the other hand, crashing into punters as he did. It was only when he stopped in front of my seat that I noticed he also had a bird with him, in a cage balanced on top of the pram.

It was a beautiful looking hen.

The bird tilted its head to one side and looked out through the wire, directly at the worker sitting next to me, who stared back at the bird as he nudged me in the ribs. 'What do you reckon it is, the bird? Is it a rooster or what?'

To be honest I don't know a lot about birds, let alone the poultry family, which I guessed this bird belonged to. The bird was no rooster, but it did not look like an ordinary hen either. Its feathers were a rich brown colour and it had a white speckled necklace of feathers around its neck.

I leaned forward and studied the bird more closely. I tapped on the wire frame to get its attention. Whether it was the cage it was cooped up in, or maybe the crowd around the cage, the bird was clearly unhappy about its situation. My travelling companion again asked if I had any idea of what sort of bird we were observing.

'I dunno mate. I'm not sure what it is, but it's not a rooster. It hasn't got one of those things on its head. You know, those red things. It's most likely some sort of chicken.'

He sat up a little straighter so that he could give the bird his full attention. 'You're right. It's not a rooster, but it's no chicken either. Can't be. A chicken's just a baby bird, isn't it? This is fully grown.' And then he added, almost as an afterthought, 'But it's not only roosters that have that red thing on their head.'

He made a 'click click' sound with his tongue, trying to catch the attention of the bird. It was a poor attempt at any sort of bird-song. The hen turned her back on him in disgust.

'What do you think it does then, the bird?' he asked.

I had no idea what he meant, but then I didn't really give a fuck. I was still worrying about what Sonny might do to me if I were late. 'What do you mean, mate, what does it do?'

'The bird. What does it do? You know, some birds can talk. Others have a nice whistle. I had a mate who used to live in a block of flats in Yarraville. And he used to have this cockatoo, this pet cockatoo that used to fly down to the clothesline from the balcony and thieve all the pegs off the line and bring them back to him. And not his pegs. Never. Only knocked off the pegs that belonged to the other tenants.'

I watched the bird in the cage while he told his story of the cockatoo. I didn't say so, but the whole thing sounded like bullshit to me. Any cockatoo that could fly down to the clothesline could also fly away from a miserable life in a block of flats in Yarraville. I was sure that it would have headed for the nearest gum tree with its first opportunity for freedom, unless it was some type of homing cocky, and I was confident that there was no such breed.

I leaned over and tapped at the wire again. Although the old man gave me a look of discouragement I kept on knocking away at the cage. 'It lays eggs, I suppose. That's why people keep them, isn't it?' I pointed to the bird's owner, who had been listening to our conversation but had not said a word. 'Ask him.'

So he did. 'The bird, mate? You've just bought the fella, have you?'

The old man looked a little offended. 'She's not a fella, mate. And I've had her for years.' He then put a finger through the wire. As he did so the bird moved across the cage and let the man gently stroke her neck as he whispered to her, 'Maggie, my baby girl, Maggie.'

'Why's she on the train with you?' the factory worker asked him. 'You moving house or something?'

'No. I've been out doing me work.' He grabbed the handle of the canvas bag and shook it like mad. The rattling of cans could be heard the length of the carriage. 'She don't like staying at home on her own since the telly broke down. She gets all anxious.'

If the other passengers weren't unhappy enough about the precious space taken up by the hen and the old man's collection of scrap metal they were really pissed off when the bird suddenly moved to the back of the cage, and in one swift movement stuck its beak through the wire and pecked viciously at the bodies now pressing against the side of the cage.

A piercing scream actually shook the carriage windows when the bird stabbed its beak into a schoolgirl's fleshy thigh. Several of her schoolfriends joined in with a series of high-pitched squeals of their own, sending the poor bird into further panic. Having been locked up myself on more than one occasion I had a fair idea how the bird was feeling.

A woman somewhere in her late sixties, if she was lucky, sporting a blast-from-the-past B52 hairdo and carrying an old-fashioned string bag bursting with oranges, was knocked off her feet. As she landed on top of me she winked and said, 'It's your lucky day, love,' before struggling to her feet again.

The bird started knocking its head against the top of the cage. The worried old man lifted the lid a little to give the bird some room. My companion waved a warning hand towards the old man. 'Wouldn't do that if I were you mate. Wouldn't do that.'

But it was too late. As the old man lifted the lid of the cage the bird escaped and flew into the air.

As the old man lunged forward the bird frantically flapped her wings about and fly-hopped her way to the other end of the carriage, briefly touching down on the bald scalp of a middle-aged man, then the gelled flattop of a teenage boy, and finally the head of a pigtailed schoolgirl.

As passengers joined in the chase the bird made her way back to our end of the carriage. She eventually perched herself on the luggage rack above my seat. My weary worker friend looked up at the bird, pointed to it and put his finger to his lips. 'Shhh.'

As the carriage went quiet with anticipation he jumped up from his seat and grabbed the bird in both hands – just for a moment. Maybe it was the grease and oil all over his hands? I was not sure. But just when I was sure he had secured her, the bird slipped out of his grasp, flew into the air again and disappeared into the crowd.

Bodies spread and feathers flew. Somehow the bird popped into the air again. I was just as shocked as the bird herself when she landed in my lap. I instinctively wrapped my arms around her and held on as tightly as I could. As I felt the bird gradually calm down I relaxed my grip on her neck, worried that I might otherwise choke her to death.

The crowd parted. The old man walked towards me. As I passed the bird to him he whispered, 'Thank you.'

He looked a little embarrassed about the scene Maggie had just caused. He then bowed his head and actually kissed the bird on the neck, whispering something to her before returning her to the security of the cage.

The train pulled into St Albans station. I looked down at my watch. I had just a few minutes to spare. I filed out of the train behind the old man and the bird. She was staring at me from the cage. Was it a look of gratitude for rescuing her from the crowd, or was the bird angry that I was largely responsible for her being incarcerated for a second time? Who could really say?

I looked along the platform. Being a commuter without a ticket, I decided that my easiest escape route would be to jump down from the platform and cross the tracks at the far end of the station where I could hurdle a low cyclone wire fence and cross an empty paddock to the main street and the cafe.

It was not until I was about to hop down from the platform that I noticed there was no station attendant on duty to collect the tickets. I could have simply walked out through the gate with the other passengers, but as I was already on my way I kept going.

As I was jumping the fence I noticed two men approaching me. They were both wearing jeans and T-shirts, and looked like refugees from the Sunday morning fundraising barrels I used to front up to with a sledgehammer hangover. One of them was a little shorter than me and built like a welterweight, lean and all muscle. The other one was heavier built and clumsy-looking. He was at least half a foot taller than me and twice as wide.

It looked as if Sonny had sent a forward posse to escort me to the cafe; unnecessary, I thought to myself, but a good piece of theatre for a suburban gangster trying to create an impression amongst the bib boys, I suppose. I was sure that I was really in trouble when the taller of the two men reached into his back pocket. Fuck, I thought, not a gun? All because of a lazy four hundred dollars?

'Stop there. Transit Authority,' he called out to me, as he pulled a badge from his pocket and stuck it in my face. 'Do you have a valid ticket for travel on this train?

Playing for time that I didn't have, I thought it would be best to plead ignorance. 'A ticket?'

'Yeah, a ticket. Are you deaf or what? Your ticket. You can't travel on a train for free. We're not in Communist Russia.'

His offsider felt an immediate need to correct him. 'There is no Communist Russia, Dave. It's been over for them for years now. They're a market economy these days.'

Dave ignored him. 'You got ID on you?'

I looked down at my watch. I had about one minute to spare if I was to get to the cafe on time. I did not know what I should do next. If I tried to run I might get past Dave but his athletically built deputy would grab me for sure.

As I contemplated the embarrassment of getting done for the major crime of fare evasion I heard a combination of a 'squeak squeak', 'rattle rattle' and 'squawk squawk' heading in our direction. It was the old man and his pram, loaded with his treasure trove of crushed cans and one very angry bird. She was obviously still unhappy over the incident on the train.

The old man stopped on the footpath, parked the pram and bird and walked across the paddock. The further away he got from her the louder her squawking got. She was obviously a pet that fretted for her owner. It now made perfect sense as to why he would take her with him when he went out collecting cans. She would have sent the neighbours crazy if he'd left her at home on her own.

As he walked towards me I saw that the old man was holding something in his hand. He waved it at me. 'Your ticket, son. You dropped your ticket on the platform.' He was desperate for me to take it. 'Your ticket. You lost it back there.'

When what he was trying to do finally clicked with me I grabbed the ticket out of his hand. 'Thank you. That's real considerate of you, mate.'

I studied the ticket like a foreign object before handing it over to Dave. 'This is what you want. My ticket.'

Dave looked doubtful. He poked a finger at the old man. 'His ticket? You sure? Where's your own ticket, then?'

The old man nodded over his shoulder. 'Back there, in the bin at the station. I don't like to litter.'

As Dave sniffed at the air trying to locate the rat he could smell, the old man turned around and trundled back to his pram. He picked up his canvas bag, slung it over his shoulder and continued pushing the pram along the footpath. The hen poked its beak through the wire and continued her complaint to the world.

While Dave inspected my ticket his mate watched as the old man and the bird toddled away.

'Hey Dave. Did you see that bird the old fella's got with him? I've seen a lot of chickens before. My brother, Ed, used to run an egg farm out the back of Laverton, but fuck, I've never seen a chicken like that before.'

By the time Dave had looked up from my ticket the old man and the bird had disappeared around the corner. 'It wasn't no chicken. I didn't see it, but by the sound of it, it was an adult bird, for sure. All baby birds are chickens. A chicken is not a breed, Charlie. A chicken is just a fucking chicken.'

I tapped the toe of my right shoe against my left ankle, checking that the roll of money was where I had planted it. I again looked down at my watch. 'Excuse me. Dave is it? Dave, can I take off now, mate? It's just that I have a meeting that I need to be at and I'm running late.'

The Etymology of Love

Daniel Ducrou

I heard Lucinda before I saw her. She tripped and fell in the audio books section, knocking over an entire display shelf and sending a tremendous crash and clatter through the library. There was a stunned silence and a few muffled laughs, and for whatever reason, the people seated nearby hesitated a moment too long before moving to help her. By the time I reached the toppled stand, she was hurrying towards the door, head down and red in the face. One of the other staff called after her, but she disappeared without turning back. Cleaning up, I found a small snap-top purse amongst all the splayed audio books. Once I'd finished re-shelving everything, I took the purse back to the service desk and searched through it. I found her library card and scanned it.

Lucinda Maria Llewellyn. What a wonderful name. I marvelled at it.

I dug into my backpack for my name origins book. Lucinda, a feminine form of Lucius, from the Latin for light, bringer of light, first light. Maria, Hebrew, meaning bitterness, or sea of bitterness. I searched for Llewellyn, but it wasn't there. I looked around to make sure the other staff weren't looking, took a hit of vodka from my hipflask, then dialled her number. It rang for a long time before she answered.

'Hi,' I said. 'This is umm… I'm calling from the library. Are you okay?'

'Yes,' she replied, after some time, her voice almost a whisper. 'Just embarrassed.'

'You didn't hurt yourself?'

'No.'

'Umm... I found your purse. You must have dropped it when you fell. I can leave it here at the service desk until you're ready to come and pick it up, if you'd like.'

'Is there any chance you could bring it to me?'

'Excuse me?'

'Can you bring it to me? I'm too embarrassed to come back.'

'No, I'm sorry. I can't.'

'You can't?'

'I'm working.'

'But you could come after you finish, couldn't you?'

I thought about that a moment and was about to reply when she cut me off.

'I'll pay you,' she said. 'A hundred dollars. Is that enough?'

'No, that really won't be necessary.'

There was a long pause before she replied.

'Good, so it's settled then?'

I was impressed.

'I guess so.'

'Oh, you didn't tell me your name.'

'Dwayne,' I said.

She hesitated and I sensed her disappointment; it was a disappointing name. She cleared her throat.

'So, when do you think you'll get here, Dwayne?'

'About six.'

She told me her address, and I let her, even though I was staring at it on the screen, then she thanked me again and said goodbye.

The neighbour's dog started barking the moment I pushed open her front gate. I took a nip of vodka from my flask and rang the doorbell. The front light was off, so I had to wait in the dark, feeling like a prowler. I was turning to leave when Lucinda burst through the door.

'My God! Shut up!'

The dog stopped barking and Lucinda smiled at me, blinking, her eyes magnified by thick glasses.

'Sorry,' she said.

She was wearing a cable-knit woollen jumper, tracksuit pants and ugg boots, and her hair was tied back slightly skew-whiff.

'You must be Dwayne.'

'Yes,' I said. 'From the library.'
I handed her the purse.
'Thanks,' she said. 'I appreciate it.'

She unsnapped the clasp, withdrew two notes and held them out to me. They were twenties, not fifties. I took them, and immediately wished I hadn't. I wondered if there was some way I could give them back without making things uncomfortable. A heavy silence fell between us.

'You have a wonderful, wonderful name, by the way,' I blurted. 'Really quite musical.'

'Oh.'

'You know Lucinda means light, or first light, really – from the Latin, Lucius. I hope you don't mind, I looked it up. Maria, means bitterness, or sea of bitterness, which is unfortunate, but, at least sounds lovely. I'm interested in name meanings, word origins and that kind of thing. Onomastics. Etymology. I looked up "Llewellyn" too but it wasn't there. Well, not in my book, anyway.'

'It means lion-like. It's Welsh.'

'It's a wonderful name. You really are very lucky. You're a light-filled lion. A lioness.'

She considered that for a moment before looking up at me.

'What does Dwayne mean? If you don't mind my asking.'

'Nothing special. It means dark, or dark-headed one. It's Irish.'

She studied me for a moment, then gave a nervous laugh.

'I'm sorry, would you like to come in for a tea? Irish tea perhaps?'

'Do you have Irish whiskey?'

'No, I have brandy, but it's not Irish. It's St Agnes. I don't know where it's from.'

'Renmark, South Australia.'

'How do you know that?'

I shrugged. 'It says on the bottle.'

'Oh.'

She opened the door and I followed her inside. All the lights were on. Ceiling lights, floor lights and lamps. I wondered about her electricity bill. I wondered about the environmental impact. I wondered about being invited into Lucinda Llewellyn's house.

I took a seat at the circular table and looked around. It was an old kitchen with wall-to-wall cupboards from floor to ceiling along one side, an electric stove, and bright, art deco prints Blu-tacked here and there. There were pot plants on top of the fridge and along the windowsill. As far as I could tell, she lived by herself.

Lucinda burnt herself making tea, but not badly. She ran her hand under cold water and dried it with a tea towel.

'My eyesight's not so good,' she said, almost apologetically.

I watched her carefully as she adjusted her glasses.

'I don't remember you wearing glasses at the library today.'

'Well, that was the problem. I wouldn't have tripped if I'd been wearing them.'

'I'm glad you weren't wearing them. I mean, not that they don't suit you. I mean: this is nice.'

She poured herself tea, and mixed me a brandy and dry. The wall clock ticked through the silence.

'You must have had a wonderful life with a name like yours,' I said.

She looked at me bewildered, 'Not necessarily.'

'You see, your name is your starting point. Everything flows from there. And if there's a certain music, or in my case, lack of, in the name you're given, it affects the way you grow.'

'You sound pretty certain about that.'

'I've thought about it a lot. I mean, your name is drummed into you from the day you're born all through your formative years. All through your life. Sixty, eighty, ninety years. Like a mantra. It's got to have an impact. If you're given an off-key monosyllabic slur like mine—'

'My God, you're really hung up on this, aren't you? And Dwayne's such a nice name. What's your surname?'

'Strang.'

She hesitated.

'It's not so bad.'

'Not so bad? Dwayne Strang? You can't even say it out of your mouth. It comes out your nose. What kind of name comes out of your nose?'

She started laughing.

'And where's the life in it? Where's the pop and bounce? It's just two lonely twangs of disappointment. Discordant and lopsided. Can you imagine hearing your whole life: Dwayne Strang, stop scowling. Don't look so disappointed, Dwayne. Don't be sarcastic, Dwayne.

My God! What chance did I have? My parents had to be fucking kidding. They didn't think about music or meaning. They might as well have just picked a name out of a hat. I mean Strang is bad enough; it's almost "strange" but not quite, which is stranger if you think about it. But that's inherited, so I guess there was nothing they could do about that. But Dwayne, the dark-headed one. I mean, c'mon! I don't even have dark hair. It's light brown, and falling out. I'm sure a new hair falls out every time someone says my name.'

'It's really not so bad,' she said, laughing more now.

'And, I mean, think about it… There have never been any kings or prophets or gods called Dwayne. I'd give anything to have a name with some kind of mythological power or potential glory. A name that I could grow into. I'm sure I would have been less ugly if my parents had only given me another name. Adonis Strang would have been fine. I'd look completely different. My God, I'd be beautiful. And muscular. A name is your starting point. You're ruined if you get a bad one.'

Lucinda was now breathless with laughter, but she stopped suddenly with a little squeak, glanced at me and crossed her legs. I leant towards her and raised my eyebrows, and she looked around the room, pursing her lips and trying not to smile. Our eyes met for a moment, and her cheeks coloured slightly.

'But surely you have a middle name?' she said. 'Something that might offset the discord?'

I shook my head. 'I was robbed. My parents didn't even think of it. I mean something like Bernado – Dwayne Bernado Strang would have been fine.'

'Have you thought about changing it by deed poll?'

'Yeah, I've thought about it. But there's something creepy about people who change their name.'

'Mmm… I guess so.'

She smiled and poured me another brandy, half spilling some on the table.

'Sometimes good things come out of bad things though.'

'Like what?'

'Well, your passion for language. You may not have developed it if your parents had given you a more musical name. You would have just taken it for granted the way I've always taken my name for granted. I've always thought it quite ordinary.'

I drained my second brandy and slammed down the glass.

'But Lucinda Maria Llewellyn! That's fantastic! I fizz up every time I say it.'

'You're half drunk.'

'I know, I know. But Lucinda! Lucinda! Now that's a first name!'

'I don't understand why you like it so much.'

'Well, it's got light in it. It's got hop, skip and jump! It's a gleaming tri-syllable. And it's linked to the stars, to the celestial bodies. Who knows, it's probably got mythological roots. Mythological roots give you the power for transformation. You could become anything with a name like that!'

'Anything?'

'Anything!'

She smiled and sat back in her chair.

'Do you mind if I take some photos?' she asked.

'Of what?'

'Of you.'

'What for?'

'I don't know. I like taking photos.'

I poured myself another brandy.

'I'm ugly, though. I mean, it's not my fault, but I am. I've got bad skin, crooked teeth, thinning hair.'

'You're not so bad.'

'Really?'

She looked at me with her huge eyes and nodded.

'Yeah, really.'

I let her take photos. We looked at them afterwards on the small digital screen. She'd cut off the top of my head in most of them. She really couldn't see very well. But that was okay. I preferred it that way.

I woke on the couch with a sleeping bag over me and sat up, dazed. Lucinda was asleep on the adjacent couch, buried beneath a huge doona, her glasses folded beside her. It almost looked like she was smiling. I must have drunk myself to sleep. It was just after nine, which meant I was late for work. I got up quietly, grabbed my things and was just about to leave when I remembered the money. I placed it on the coffee table, let myself out and hurried up the street.

Lucinda called me at the library less than an hour later.

'You forgot your money,' she said.

'I didn't forget it.'

'And, well… I wasn't trying to short-change you or anything. It's just—'

'It's fine. I'm embarrassed I took the money in the first place.'

'My vision's usually worse in the evenings when my eyes are tired.' She hesitated. 'I have a condition called glaucoma.'

'Sorry?'

'Glaucoma. It's a build-up of pressure behind the optic nerve.'

'Oh, well, that's no good.'

'No, it's not. But I was thinking.'

'Yes?'

'I'm meant to do regular cardiovascular exercise – it's meant to help regulate the pressure. But I find it stressful doing it alone.'

'What kind of exercise?'

'I don't know. Walking, swimming, dancing. Those kinds of things.'

'I could take you for a walk, if you'd like.'

'How about tonight?'

'What? Tonight-tonight?'

'Yes! Tonight-tonight! And I could cook you dinner to say thanks. If you'd like?'

I didn't answer straightaway and it must have unsettled her.

'Unless of course you're busy or have other plans? I mean if you don't want to—'

'No – I mean yes – I'd like to.'

'So it's settled, then? You'll come?'

'I'd love to.'

I fell hard for Lucinda and she fell hard for me. We both fell the way Lucinda fell in the library. Suddenly, unexpectedly and violently. Except for our brief nightly walks, we rarely went out. We stayed at home and riffed conversation. She called me D, or Dwae or Dwayney. She called me Dirty Dwayne, Delicious Dwayne, Drunken Dwayne. I called her Lucid Lucy, Lucy Lovelock, Lucinda Lou Lou, Lucinda Lucinda.

Everything seemed to fit. The light and dark of our names. The fine and coarse of our bodies. Her beauty, my ugliness. She made me forget the loneliness of my old life. She looped around me in conversation. She stalked me like a lioness, and I rose up lion-like to meet her. She paced and pounced on me. She ripped into me and tore at me like I was her life source. Lucinda was lewd and rude. She shoved my face between her legs and demanded her pleasure. She said it helped her vision.

Lucinda sang in the shower, she sang velvety blues, wonky and perfect. She sang jazz lines up and down the hall. She hummed tense little songs on the toilet. She strummed air guitar, screwed up her face and danced around the living room to Joy Division, and I screwed up my face terrified of what she might knock into.

At night, she clung to my great, hulking weight like I was life itself. I loved feeling needed; I loved being depended upon. We'd go walking in the streets together and I'd keep her close to me so she didn't trip or stumble. Over time, we went out less and less. We stayed in and talked. I drank. We made love. We watched movies. On sunny days, we lay in the backyard and stared at the blue sky. The sheer blue enormity of it. Lucinda took photos. I read books aloud to her when her eyes were too tired.

I realised I was in love with her and she was in love with me. We shined each other senseless. It made everything else okay. I suddenly understood all those dumb love songs on the radio. More than that, I sang along with them. I sang the way Lucinda sang – out of sheer joy in the mundane particulars of everyday life. But unlike Lucinda, I sang completely out of key and off the beat. I blamed my name.

There were only a couple of things on which Lucinda and I clashed, and one of them was her clumsiness. Like most annoying things, the more I tried not to let it get to me, the more it got to me. Lucinda broke things; she injured herself, she injured me. We knocked heads when we were making love.

One night, she spilt coffee on me while we were watching a movie. I leapt to my feet, cursing, and knocked over my own drink in the process.

'Jesus, Lucinda!'

'That wasn't my fault – you bumped me.'

'I didn't bump you!'

I brushed at the steaming wet patch, grabbed the DVD control and hit 'pause'.

'Did you know that the word clumsy,' I said, 'comes from the Swedish word, *klummsen*, to be benumbed with cold?'

'Are you calling me cold?'

'No, I'm calling you clumsy.'

She fixed her enormous eyes on me.

'Well, I hate to say it, but you're pretty clumsy yourself.'

'What? I'm clumsy, am I?'

'Yes! You're clumsy when you're drunk, and you're drunk right now – so I don't know, you do the maths.'

'Okay, here's the equation: even if I am drunk this evening, in the morning I'll be sober, and you'll still be *klummsen*.'

'You'll be sober in the morning but you'll be *klummsen* by lunchtime.'

'What are you saying?'

She regarded me through her thick spectacles. 'I think you might have a problem.'

'What are you talking about?'

'You need to cut back your drinking. You don't make sense, you repeat yourself, you can't get it up, you fall asleep, you bore me.'

'Well I think you're being hysterical. Hysterical, from the Latin *hystera* for uterus, from when physicians believed that women released gases from their wombs that made them go crazy at certain times of the month.'

'You're a lunatic, from the Latin *lunar* for moon, meaning moonstruck psycho.'

'You're being a bitch, bitch from the medieval, *biche*, from the Old English *bicce* from the Icelandic *bikkja*, for dog.'

'God, you curse like a *bikkja*! You use word origins like a passive aggressive nut case. Passive, from the Latin, *passivus*, incapable of feeling, as in not capable. And aggressive, from the Latin cunt.'

She fixed me with a cold glare and I stood there stunned by her ferocity.

'The reason I'm *klummsen*, Dwayne, the reason I trip over and knock into things, the reason I keep the lights on all day, the reason I don't care that you're apparently so goddamned ugly is that my glaucoma is getting worse. I didn't want to tell you but the treatment isn't working.'

'What do you mean?'

'I mean: I'm going blind.'

'What?'

'Blind, from the Old English blind, from the Greek, blind, meaning blind. Meaning unable to see.'

'You can't be going blind. What about all our exercise? The new eye drops? The oral pleasure? I thought we had it under control.'
'I was lying.'
'But why would you lie?'
'Because I'm scared you'll leave me.'

I left Lucinda the following week. I didn't give a reason; I just stopped visiting her and avoided her phone calls. After a couple of weeks, I called to check she was alright, but she hung up on me. I called again a week later and she did the same thing so I stopped calling altogether. I worked, I went home, I drank myself senseless. The other library staff looked at me in dismay when I arrived each morning, but none of them had the guts or the interest to ask me if I was okay.

I entered a great period of darkness. I was depressed. And afraid. My drinking was out of control. Lucinda was the best thing I'd ever had. Blind or not. Without her my life was barren. She was my life, my light, my lioness.

I paced back and forth by her front door, raised my hand and hesitated. I turned to leave, took a shot of vodka, then turned back and rang the doorbell. The neighbour's dog started barking. It took a long time for Lucinda to answer, and when she did, she opened the door very slowly. It was wonderful to see her; no one had eyes as big as hers. She frowned. She didn't shout at the dog.
'What do you want?'
'Can I come in?'
'No.'
The dog continued barking.
'Why not?' I asked.
'I can smell vodka on your breath, for a start.'
'I was nervous about coming. I really need to talk to you.'
She sighed, opened the door wider and motioned me inside. All the lights were blazing and it gave me hope, but as I followed her down the hallway, I noticed that she was moving very carefully, with a quiet nervousness.
As we sat down at the kitchen, I realised how much her sight had worsened; she was blinking more and she didn't seem to be focusing on me at all.
'How're your eyes?'

'Bad. How's your drinking?'
'Fine. Better. Getting better all the time.'
'Liar.'
'Okay – it's not so good.'
'So stop. Unlike me, you have a choice in what's happening to you.'
'I will stop. I want to. But I know that I could do it if I had a reason to stop – like to be with you. Please take me back, Lucinda. I need you.'
'What? To help you stop drinking? Is that your only reason?'
'No! Of course not. Lucinda Lou-Lou, Lucinda Llewellyn. My life's empty without you.'
'Well, you shouldn't have walked out.'
'I made a stupid mistake.'
'So?'
'So, what?'
'So, it's not that simple.'
I snapped into my backup plan.
'Let me take you on a holiday. Holiday from the Old English, holy day.'
'A holy day won't fix anything.'
'What about three holy days? Or fourteen holy days. As many holy days as you want. A lifetime of holy days. I'll take time off work. I'll organise everything. It'll be good for you to get out of the house.'
'I have a regular routine,' she replied. 'And it's not good for me to disrupt it. I have appointments I need to keep.'
'Appointments with whom?'
'A volunteer from The Society.'
'What's his name?'
'His name is Trent.'
'Trent? He sounds like an arsehole.'
She smiled.
'He's been training my guide dog.' She hesitated. 'My *bikkja*. His name's Wilbur.'
'Wilbur?'
'Yes.'
'Three days, Lucinda. Three holy days. Please.'
'I need to think about it.'
'I'll pick you up Friday morning, then?'

'You don't have a car.'
'I'll hire one.'
'What about my appointments.'
'Cancel them.'
'If I do decide to go, there will be a sobriety test before we leave.'
'Good, so, it's settled then?'
She nodded and tried to smile.

I booked a cottage in the Grampians and a Mazda 323 to get us there. I chose the Grampians so that Lucinda would be more inclined to cling to me amongst all those precipitous mountain ledges. And I chose a Mazda because they're named after the Persian god of light and creator of 486,000 lucky stars, Ahura Mazda.

Friday morning was freezing. I caught the tram to the depot, picked up the car, and drove it back to my house to pack. I was so excited on the way to Lucinda's that I started singing along to 'Like a Virgin'. I was blowing on my hands and steering with my knees when a cyclist came out of nowhere. I grabbed the wheel and swerved, lost control and veered towards a telephone pole. There was a crunch and squeal of metal, and a sharp pain shooting up my back, then nothing.

I was lying in the hospital bed, staring at the ceiling, when a nurse led Lucinda in by her arm. She sat carefully on the edge of the bed, gently ran her hand over my face, then let it fall to her side.

'You feel terrible,' she said. 'Are you okay?'
I squeezed the morphine button.
'Just whiplash and a broken leg.'
She touched my arm but drew it away when she felt the needle.
'And the car?'
'Damaged beyond repair.'
'Did you take out insurance?'
I shook my head. 'There were meant to be almost half a million lucky stars watching over me.'
'So, how did you crash with all those stars watching over you? Perhaps you were a little benumbed?'
'*Klummsen?*'
'Were you?'
'It was a cold morning, so I was slightly *klummsen*. But that wasn't the problem. There was a cyclist—'
'Dwayne?'

'Mmm?'

'Were you drunk when you crashed?'

I didn't answer and she repeated the question. When I finally told her the truth, she let out a disappointed sigh and fell silent.

'I'm sorry about the holiday,' I said.

She shrugged.

'I didn't think it would work out.'

'It could have.'

'But it didn't.'

'I'm going to start attending AA meetings.'

'I'll believe it when I see it… hear it.'

'You want to hear it right now?'

'Okay.'

'Okay. My name is Dwayne Strang, and I'm an alcoholic.'

'Finally.'

I hit the morphine button again.

'I've been thinking.'

'God, what now?'

'Remember you said that good things come out of bad things. I was thinking maybe it's like the way a bit of sand gets inside an oyster and irritates away until it becomes a pearl.'

'I don't think the alcohol is making any pearls inside you, if that's what you're getting at.'

'No, that's not what I'm getting at.'

'Well, I hope you're not implying that you're the piece of sand that's got into my shell and that you're making pearls inside me. I mean, it's true that you irritate me, but I doubt you're making pearls.'

'Okay, forget the oyster thing. What I'm saying is…'

And I stopped. I didn't know what I was saying, and what I wanted to say. Lucinda sighed.

'Just speak plainly.'

'I know my love is *klummsen*, but you make me warm and you give me light. I want to try and do the same for you.'

'That's sweet, Dwayne.'

'I know you think you don't need me now that you've got your dog—'

'Wilbur.'

'Yes but, do you really think you can replace me with a dog?'

'Well, he is much more reliable than you.'

'I thought you'd come to cheer me up.'

'Not necessarily.' She smiled. 'You're not jealous of a dog, are you?'

'No, of course not. Has a nice reading voice, does he? A good conversationalist? Fluent in Latin, Greek and Sanskrit? Riffs on word origins like Jimi Hendrix? Cooks and cleans for you? I'm sure he's a wonderful replacement.'

'Actually, he's pretty good.'

'Jesus, Lucinda, you need me, I know you do.'

'Maybe you need me more than I need you.'

'Okay, fine. Maybe I do. Look at me, I'm a mess.'

'Oh, stop feeling sorry for yourself. It's not very attractive.'

'Okay, sorry.'

She fell silent for a moment.

'I've decided something.'

'What?'

'I've decided to let you come and read to me for an hour every night for two weeks. On a trial basis. And if you smell of alcohol, or if you slur a single word, that's it, you're out.'

'And what if I pass the two weeks?'

'If you pass the two weeks, I'll consider letting you cook dinner for me – and Wilbur.'

'Hey, I don't want Wilbur sleeping in our bed.'

'Who said anything about you coming anywhere near my bed?'

I nodded; it was going to be a battle by inches.

'So, your new dog-lover, what does his name mean?'

'It means: wall fortification.'

'Hmm. How depressing.'

'Not if you take it as meaning strength.' She hesitated. 'I've also decided to give him a middle name and surname, something to give him some room to grow.'

'What?'

'Wilbur Adonis Strang,' she said, trying not to smile. 'And yes, he's very muscular and profoundly beautiful.'

She stood beside me.

'So it's settled then? You'll come and read to me?'

And I nodded, knowing that she didn't need to hear me because she already knew the answer. She ran her fingertips over my face, and carefully made her way out of the room.

Hell is Other Parents

Jo Case

Vanessa and I collide at the school gate, in a tangle of dog leads and frantic barking. Her dog is a waist-high German shepherd with a glossy coat and a fractious nature. Privately, I nickname him Kujo. I have two easily excitable terriers. The Good One throws herself at everyone she meets, hysterical with lust for their affection. She rubs her fluffy white locks on their legs, barking urgently in a demand for love, or at least a pat. The Evil One throws himself at everyone he meets, hysterical in his desire to show them who's boss. Short dog syndrome.

'Um, I saw Felix baring his bottom by the monkey bars just then,' says Vanessa. 'I told him that it was dirty and to pull his pants up, but I thought I should let you know.'

'Thanks,' I mumble, quickly changing the subject. 'So, I'm still picking Angus up tonight?'

'That'll be great. I've got a big essay to write and I've hardly done *anything*. See you at six?'

I'll need to tell Santa that there are no Bionicles for Christmas.

Angus pounces joyfully as I approach his classroom. He is bouncing on the spot with excitement, clouds of blue dust billowing at his feet and settling on his black lace-up school shoes.

'My mum said I have to tell you every time Felix says something rude!' he announces.

Rewind to two days ago. 'You're early,' Vanessa greeted me. 'Are you okay? You look terrible.' She pulled me into the 'good' sitting room – the one they don't actually use – to tell me about her afternoon.

Apparently, she overheard Felix saying something about sucking a woman's breast on the way home and told him that if she ever hears anything like that again, he is *no longer welcome* at their house.

'I like Felix,' she said, in a tone that screamed the opposite. 'But Angus is innocent, and Hank and I would like to keep him that way. I don't mean to judge, but I don't know where Felix has picked that up from. Do you? He's a very advanced reader, so maybe he read it somewhere?'

Yeah, I thought sourly, like all those *Playboy* magazines I keep in my bottom drawer. I apologised and assured her I would investigate and give my son a thorough talking-to.

'I mean, it was one thing when he told Angus how babies are made,' she continued. 'I didn't really mind that. I mean, I didn't really want him to know about it yet, but what can you do? I did have to put up with him saying "penis" and "vagina" all weekend, but… but that was okay, I guess.'

'What exactly did you say?' I growled, as soon as we were out of the house.

'I said that *Supergirl* was the stupidest movie I'd ever seen and Angus said Supergirl was beautiful. So I asked him if he wanted to suck Supergirl's breast.'

'Where did you get that from?'

'From when you get born. You know, breastfeeding!'

His stepmother is breastfeeding. I breathed a sigh of relief and told him never to say anything like that again.

Six-year-old boys love to dob on each other. I have a magic formula that I recite to all visiting children. I don't want to hear about it unless someone is hurt, someone is in danger or about to get hurt, or something is being wrecked. I fill the gaps by keeping my ears tuned while they play, pouncing on bad words when they least expect it.

Vanessa has overridden my formula.

'He keeps doing it because it makes the other kids laugh,' says the vice-principal. 'But they don't laugh so much anymore. They think it's weird.'

We're sitting in her office with the door shut, discussing the pants-pulling-down behaviour, which has become Felix's speciality. Outside, in the corridor, Felix and Angus are providing a thudding, squealing soundtrack to our conversation. It's an effort to keep in the tears. I nod and agree, apologising for what seems like the thousandth time.

'Felix is a great kid,' she says. 'He's come so far this year. We've told him we're really proud of him. He's incredibly smart. Sometimes, perhaps, that causes problems. But we love having him around.'

'Really? You do?'

The vice-principal hands me a tissue.

'Of course we do.'

As we walk home through the park, I remind Felix about the message to Santa. And if he pulls his pants down in the schoolyard again, I warn, I will give all his Bionicles to his cousin, Jacob. The sky is dark with smoke from distant bushfires. I push through the heat and smog towards our street. Felix points to the wall of a nearby power station as we pass.

'That's graffiti,' he says. 'Sam says that when he grows up, he wants to write graffiti.'

The boys lean into each other, giggling. Felix whispers something.

'Excuse me,' says Angus. 'Felix says that when he grows up, he wants to sniff vaginas.'

'WHAT?' I interrogate the boys. It turns out that Felix said he wants to sniff bums. Which is bad, but Andy Griffiths rather than Hugh Hefner territory. Angus just wanted to say "vagina". I growl at them both. My throat hurts, my eyes sting, the backs of my knees are sticky with sweat.

As I unhook the picket fence and push open the gate, Angus taps my arm.

'Excuse me. Felix said that daisy is stupid.' He points into the grass.

I look at him.

'And stupid is a bad word?'

He nods.

'Okay,' I say, and determinedly busy myself with locking my bike to the veranda post. Head down, I fantasise about killing

Vanessa, who has clearly condemned me to a long and painful afternoon.

I am cutting up honey toast and Granny Smith apples at the kitchen table. Angus wanders in to fetch his carton of Ribena, and stays to watch.

'So, if Felix is rude again, his cousin will get all his Bionicles?'

'Yes.'

'Oh. You know, you could give them to me.'

'That's an interesting idea, but I don't think so.'

'Oh.' He takes a slice of apple from one of the plates. 'You could give half to me, half to his cousin?'

'No.'

'Maybe I could have just *one*?'

I snap.

'Angus, if I was to give you Felix's Bionicles if he was rude, you'd tell me he was rude, wouldn't you? So, I don't think it's a good idea. They'll go to his cousin.' Pause. 'And hopefully, Felix will be good.'

'I won't say he's rude—'

'No.'

By 6.10 p.m., I have a headache with trying to work out who is really being rude, who is making up stories, who actually deserves to be told off, and how to explain that I don't really care if someone said 'bloody'. There are just as many complaints and rude words from 'innocent' Angus as Felix. Next week, I plan to revert to my dobbing guidelines.

Vanessa arrives at 6.30 p.m., breezily. She has, as usual, brought Angus's brother Tom with her. The three boys shoot out into the backyard for a light sabre duel. My husband, Tony, shoots her a look and disappears. He is furious, as is Felix's father, about all her fussing. They think she is a prude. Felix's father actually came out with a killer of a line when I told him how upset she was about the 'where babies come from' chat. 'What would she prefer?' he said, icily. 'That Angus goes around saying "prick" and "cunt"?'

Vanessa deals with the frosty atmosphere by settling in for the long haul, to show that we are friends and everything is okay. She talks and talks. She follows the boys out the back and comments on the progress of the light sabre duels. She tells me about a meal she made recently and gives me the recipe. She tells me how nice the lemon tree is, and about her lemon tree, and about her friend's lemon tree, and what her friend does with lemons, and how her mother propagates fruit trees, and how she herself does it. It is 7 p.m. She asks me, finally, about the sucking breasts thing. I tell her about the breastfeeding and she is surprised and relieved. She tells me – again – that she wishes Angus hadn't been told the facts of life. She tells me – again – that he's been saying *vagina*. That she was doing the ironing and he said, 'Mum, you have a vagina, don't you?'

At 7.30 p.m., she finally leaves, with a green shopping bag full of lemons. At the door, she grabs my arm and asks, 'Are you doing anything right now?'

I need to cook dinner, serve dinner, bath Felix, get him into his pyjamas, put him to bed and read a story. All within the next hour. And then I need to research and write an article.

'Why?'

'Angus is missing his bike,' she says. He left it here last week. 'Can you walk him to the park so he can ride it through to our street? I'll drive the car around and meet him on the other side of the park.'

'Okay.' As we trudge to the edge of the driveway, Vanessa grabs my arm again.

'Hey!' she says. 'Come *here*!' And she grabs me in a hug. I smile weakly and wave goodbye as she and Tom get into the car and prepare to drive home.

'Why does Felix like Bionicles so much?' asks Angus.

'I don't know.' I try to be upbeat and friendly, overcompensating. 'I guess he just does!'

'I don't,' says Angus. 'I like superheroes.' And with that, he climbs onto his bike and pedals off down the hill towards the park, me jogging behind.

It's my birthday. After the early morning festivities, I drop Felix at Vanessa's house, warning him to *treat her with respect* and *do exactly as she says*.

At the end of the day, I arrive to pick him up, after a blissful day of eating, shopping and lazing about. Vanessa greets me at the door with the pinched look I've come to dread, yet expect.

'Did you have a good day?'

'Fantastic.'

'That's great!'

She leads me into the kitchen, where smoke is streaming from the griller. Felix and Tom are nestled quietly under a sleeping bag on the carpet, eyes fixed on the television. Angus is nowhere in sight.

Vanessa makes me a latte as she scrapes the blackened toast into the bin and puts two fresh slices of bread under the grill. As she froths the milk, she tells me about her day. Angus had a screaming tantrum when Felix wanted to play with his new toys. Tried to kick him out of his bedroom. Said he didn't want him to touch anything of his. Now, he is asleep in Vanessa's bed. They'd had an afternoon nap together while Felix and Tom watched a *Batman* DVD.

'It's been a tough day,' she sighs. 'They've been talking about sex again. They were teasing each other, saying they wanted to have sex with a girl at school. And they said something about boobs.'

I apologise, wishing the ground would swallow me up.

She places a hand on my arm and leans in close, her face just centimetres from mine.

'Why do you think Felix is so obsessed with sex?'

My mind whirrs. Last time they were at my house, Angus was just as bad as Felix on the subject. I wonder whether to mention this.

'They were all talking about it a bit on Wednesday,' I venture.

'Mmmm. It starts, and then it just goes round in a circle, doesn't it?'

'I think it's about having just learned how babies are made and getting their heads around it.'

'I think it's his reading,' she continues, as if I hadn't spoken. 'Like that book he brought over.'

She gestures to Andy Griffiths's *The Bad Book*, which is lying, confiscated, on the counter. 'It is totally inappropriate and very rude. It's all about bums and things.'

I am momentarily floored. I didn't really think when I put that book in his bag, but it is suddenly obvious that I've made a bad decision.

'Hank brought home some Marvel comics the other day,' she continues. 'They were aimed at eight-year-olds, I think, but we couldn't believe it. There was some *very suggestive stuff* between Peter Parker and Mary Jane. Not explicit, but, you know, *implied*. Felix must read that stuff. That must be where he's getting it.'

I reiterate that I thought the 'subversive' reading material was *Where Did I Come From*, but once again, it's as if I haven't spoken.

Then she says, 'I think Felix's problem is his personality,' and it takes every ounce of self-control I have not to punch her. I call Felix, briskly, and track down his shoes. Vanessa makes small talk as I tie his laces, but all I can hear is a furious buzzing in my head. I have had enough. Vanessa wishes me a happy birthday. At the front door, she hugs me and hands me a plate of homemade biscuits.

On the ride home, I lecture Felix about respect and lack of it and furiously interrogate him about his day.

'Angus wouldn't let me play with any of his toys,' he complains. 'He was angry that I was in his room, so he said, "You want to sex with Cherie".'

'And what did you say?'

'I said *he* wanted to sex with her.'

I flick the switch on the talk about how, 'it's for adults' and, 'just because he said it, doesn't mean you should'. I tell him that Vanessa thinks he's a rude child now and that I'm not sure if he'll be welcome there again. I tell him that his behaviour is not a nice birthday present for me. On the back of my bike, he starts to cry.

Tony greets us at the door. I fill him in, confused. I don't know quite who I should be angry with and to what degree.

'That's fucked,' he says. 'What a bitch.' He takes Felix by the shoulders. 'Mate, no matter what Vanessa says, you're a great kid. We think you're great.' He hugs him.

'Your behaviour today was not great,' I add. 'But you are.'

I'm certain I haven't handled this situation well.

Fuck it. It's my birthday.

We all go out to dinner, to Felix's favourite local restaurant, where he orders a lemon chicken, roti and rice, and pushes unsuccessfully for a blue heaven milkshake. I read to him from *The*

Bad Book, while we wait for our meals, holding him very close on my lap.

'Oh GOD,' huffs Vanessa as she arrives at her front gate to let me in. She grabs at Kujo, who is hurling himself at the fence, lurching his great black head through the bars to gnash his teeth at me and my two small dogs.

I have been standing here for minutes already, shouting, 'Felix! I'm here!' accompanied by a chorus of barks: Kujo's deep sandpaper growl accompanied by the piercing yaps of my dogs.

'I called you as soon as I got home,' she says, strongarming Kujo through the security screen and into the hallway. 'I wanted to say "I'm sorry, I can't do this," and ask you to pick him up. But…'

I'd been settled on the couch with a book and a mug of coffee when the phone rang. I let it go to the answering machine, but whoever it was had hung up.

'… you obviously weren't home yet.'

'No. Sorry. What happened?'

'Well… it wasn't *really* his fault…' It turns out that Angus had offered Felix his bike to ride home, then changed his mind, screamed all the way home, and told Felix he couldn't play with any of his toys once they got there.

'I think,' says Vanessa, 'that we should not have Felix over any more, until further notice. You know, to punish Angus.'

'Okay.' I stalk off down the footpath, collecting Felix at the end of the driveway, the dogs straining at their leashes and the two brothers following us on their scooters.

We are on the train from Yarraville to the city, on our way to Readings Carlton to meet Andy Griffiths and Terry Denton. Felix reads Andy and Terry's *Just* series (*Just Kidding*, *Just Annoying*, *Just Stupid*) so often that the books have the appearance of ancient texts: creased covers, deeply cracked spines, dog-eared pages yellowed with unidentified stains. He reads them on the train, in bed, at cafes and in the toilet. More often than I'd like, an hour after bedtime, I'll open the door to the bathroom and there he is: pants around his ankles, goose bumps on his bare legs, frowning intently at a *Just* book.

It's been two months since Felix was banned from Angus and Tom's house. He hasn't been invited back… until now, for Angus's birthday party tomorrow.

'Maybe we could get Angus's present at Readings?' I suggest, as the blue-striped stations of the underground City Loop streak past our window.

'Yes!' cries Felix, head snapping up from his lap. 'Do you know that they don't have *any books*? Really, Mum. Their bookshelves are full of toys. Toys! We *must* get Angus a book and get him into reading.'

As a lazy woman embarking on a lazy Saturday, I am pleased that we can kill two birds at one bookshop.

'But we can't get him any Andy Griffiths,' says Felix. 'Vanessa hates Andy Griffiths. She told me he's inappropriate.'

'True.'

'We can get him *Maxx Rumble*. Angus is into footy, so he'll like that. And Terry illustrated it, so he can sign it!'

'Good idea.'

'Do you know they don't even get bedtime stories?' Felix is puffed up with seven-year-old scorn. 'They just get bedtime *toys*!'

'I'm sure that's not true. I'm sure they have books. Maybe they just keep them somewhere other than their rooms.'

'They don't! I've seen their whole house!'

I doubt it. Vanessa is a crazy bitch, but I know she reads.

At Readings, clusters of awestruck children are already gathering in front of the raised area that serves as a stage, some of them creeping close to the microphone and the signing table. Felix takes a seat between two older boys, who look around ten or eleven. One of the boys clutches a rainbow-striped stack of *Just* books.

'Oh. I have them,' says Felix.

'I love the *Just* books,' says the kid. 'I have the whole series.'

'Not *Just Shocking*,' corrects Felix. 'That's not out yet. You can't have that.'

'I *know*,' breathes the boy. 'I have the whole series except that one. I *have* to get it as *soon* as it comes out. If I don't get *Just Shocking*, I will *die*. My life *will not* be worth living.'

Felix gazes at him in solemn admiration.

'Me too.'

The two boys begin an animated discussion about the bumosaurs in the new book and the characters in the *Just* series. I leave them to it and buy the new book and the *Maxx Rumble* at the counter.

When I get back, Andy and Terry have arrived. Felix shows all the signs of growing up to become one of those really annoying people at writers' festivals. The ones who just want to demonstrate how clever they are. The ones who make a statement instead of asking a question.

'I was wondering, the other day I made a new comic about Bum Man. And his power is earthquake farts.'

'And your question?' says Terry.

'Well, Andy, I wondered if you would write a story about him in *Just Shocking*?'

When the kids are asked to demonstrate farts, his is the grossest. He suggests that Terry add poo to his butcher paper drawing of a bumosaur.

When Felix's turn comes to have his book signed, Andy greets him by name, without even having to consult the Post-It note stuck to the title page of his book. Next, Felix moves on to Terry with his *Maxx Rumble* book.

'Hi Felix.'

'Terry, my friend's mum is *not impressed* with Andy.'

Terry laughs. A lot.

'Why is that?'

'She thinks his books are *inappropriate*.'

Terry laughs some more.

'Tell Andy. Hey. Andy!' Terry plucks at Andy's sleeve. 'Andy! Felix here has something to tell you.'

Felix repeats his statement. Andy splutters with laughter.

'I think *she's* inappropriate!' He gathers himself. 'No, really, she's absolutely right. My books *are* inappropriate.'

Felix goes home happy. So do I.

I tell him many times NOT to tell Vanessa what Andy Griffiths said about her. I tell him as we leave Readings, as we board the tram for home, as we walk in the front door and when he goes to bed.

I can tell he is dying to do it.

Sunday morning, as we cross the park, Felix recalls the incident in loving detail, relishing the words on his tongue. I remind him not to tell Vanessa. I do it again as we approach the front gate.

'Yes Mum.'

I remind him that there always seems to be trouble here and that he must behave.

'Yes Mum.'

Another parent is lingering at the gate, watching Kujo throw himself at the bars in a frenzy. We make small talk while we wait for Vanessa to come and rescue us. She wrestles the dog inside the house and out the back door, returning to unlock the gate and let us in.

'Hi!'

'Hi,' says Felix. 'I went to see Andy Griffiths yesterday!'

Vanessa looks at me and rolls her eyes, then turns to Felix and makes a disgusted face, looking back to me, as if for support. It's as if he told her he went to Sexpo yesterday.

'Oh *did* you?' she says wryly. 'And was he *rude*?'

Felix runs past her down the hallway, thrusting his present at Angus, who greets him with a delighted shriek. Crisis averted. For now.

At 3 p.m., Kujo is nowhere to be seen, so I am able to ring the doorbell instead of shouting from the footpath. Vanessa sweeps me down the hallway, past the table of iced cakes and chocolate crackles, to where a huddle of small boys in football jumpers are watching television. But no Felix. The boys swing to look at me.

'Felix said a bad word,' says Angus.

'Right.'

I give Vanessa a questioning look.

'I think he might be upstairs. In Angus's room?'

I nod crisply and climb the stairs. The door is locked. I knock. No answer. I call his name. Vanessa is close behind me. She pokes a wire into the lock and gives it a deft twist. It seems she's done this before. Felix is glowering behind the door, arms crossed.

'I have had *the worst day* in my entire life.'

'What's wrong, Felix?' asks Vanessa, bending so her eyes are level with his and putting a comforting hand on his arm. 'Don't exaggerate, now.'

'I don't want to talk about it.'

'We'll talk on the way home,' I decide, grabbing his hand and leading him downstairs. He grunts out a goodbye to Angus, under duress. Angus waves cheerily as Vanessa gives Felix his lolly bag and follows us down the hallway and to the gate, waving us down the footpath.

They had a fight over footy cards. Angus said his were lame. He said they weren't. They bickered.

'And you said a rude word?'

'No.'

'What did you say?'

'I said Angus was an idiot.'

'And that was the rude word?'

'Yeah.'

'Did you get sent to time-out?'

'Yeah.'

'Vanessa shut you up in Angus's room?'

'Yeah.'

'What did she say to you?'

'She told me never to use that word again.'

Since she banned Felix from play dates 'to punish Angus', Vanessa has avoided us after school. Today, she runs across the schoolyard to catch up with us, greeting us with white-hot charm. She launches into a monologue about a headache and her annoying mother and reading George Monbiot. I focus all my conscious attention on not being rude. Which translates into curt nods and lots of 'yes' and 'really?'

'Have you recovered from yesterday, Felix?'

'Yes.'

As we near the end of the cul-de-sac, she turns her attention to our dogs. The Evil One lurches at her, barking. Felix looks her in the eye.

'He doesn't like you,' he says.

To Childhood

Todd Hearon

Moth-eaten faith, old flame (old shame) I have sworn
You off. Again. To furtively return –
Bourbon I stashed in the basement mattress where
My uncle whoops it up with country whores:

>   You are no good to me
>   If I continue to abuse you.
>   Why can't I let you die?
>   You've done your chores.

Your fishbowl full of formaldehyde,
Your toy box rupturing with foreign wars –
No one believes you, childhood.
Let alone my poems.

>   But at night the lost limb itches.

I follow you down my Florida of the mind,
Poor Ponce de León, after his beloved,
Syphilitic guide.

Attack of the Tiny Miracles

Max Barry

On ultrasound it was a teddy bear in space. This was at the beginning, when there was only one. A tiny, bold spacebear explorer, floating through the great galaxy Uterus.

Not looking away from the screen, Mehline groped for my hand. I was too slow: she got it. Tears formed in my eyes.

'Amazing, isn't it?' said the nurse. 'Did you know?'

I didn't say anything. 'I knew,' Mehline said.

We climbed into the car. I reached for the ignition. Mehline put her hand on my arm. 'You're not happy.'

'I'm happy,' I said. 'I'm just, you know, a little overwhelmed and all that.'

She looked out the window. We were in the maternity ward car park. A steady flow of pregnant women tottered by, some assailed by children, tugging at their arms, running in front of cars, crying because they didn't want to go home, or did. 'You said you were ready.'

'I know. I did. I am.' But by the time I got to *am*, my throat closed over. Mehline took back her hand. 'Ready to *start trying*. Because no one gets pregnant right away. Like Philip and Jacqui, nine months at least. And the Owens, that was, what, three years? That's how everyone says it is: all those years of being terrified you're going to get pregnant, then when you want to, nothing. Like waiting for a bus.'

'This is not a bus,' Mehline said.

'I know! It's a foetus, and we only *just* agreed to maybe start trying and suddenly we have a *foetus*, and that's a little fast, don't you think?'

'We did not agree to *maybe* start trying.'

'We… okay. You're right.'

'And stop saying foetus,' Mehline said. 'Say baby.'

I took a breath. Outside the car, a planet-sized woman with one hand in the small of her back yelled that if Samantha didn't hurry up, she was going to get one hell of a smack, she wasn't joking. 'I'm happy. I'm happy. I just need a little time. Because it's really freaking sudden, you know? You know?'

'No,' Mehline said, so quiet I could barely hear.

* * *

'Back again!' said the nurse. She was pretending to be friendly. One thing I had discovered about maternity nurses: they thought you didn't deserve a baby. They didn't say it, but it was clear enough. They probably saw a lot of losers; you deal with enough pregnant morons and you'd begin to despair for the future of the human race. Around them I always found myself straightening my posture, trying to look reliable.

Mehline lay back on the examination table. The nurse switched off the main light. LCD striations across her face, Mehline said: 'It's just… a few days ago, I started feeling… not pregnant.'

'I'm sure it's nothing.' The nurse flipped up Mehline's shirt to expose her belly. I gazed at it. It was beautiful. I should commit it to memory while I still could.

The nurse squirted clear jelly around Mehline's navel and pressed the scanner into place. From the machine came otherworldly ultra-sounds: *whoa, whoa, whoa*. Good advice, I thought. But too late.

'There,' said the nurse. 'Live and kicking.'

Mehline sighed, relaxing. Until then I hadn't realised she was clenching her entire body.

The nurse leaned forward. 'In fact…'

'Look at me,' Mehline said. I couldn't do it; I gripped my coffee. We were in the hospital cafe; I'd made it that far. 'Look at me.'

'It's just so *unlucky*.'

'It is not. It is the opposite of that.'

'You know what I mean. What are the odds?'

'It is not so uncommon.'

'For *test-tube babies*. For people who jam six embryos up the duff because it's twenty thousand dollars and they're forty-five and it's their last chance to raise something that doesn't have a tail. Not for *normal people*. For normal people, it *is* uncommon. It's astronomical.'

'It's a double blessing,' Mehline said.

I sucked at the coffee. I didn't know why I was drinking it; I was already shaking. 'I was just getting my head around *one*.'

* * *

Next time we visited was for the eighteen-week scan. We had a different nurse, a girl with freckles and a ponytail. 'I hear last time you got a surprise.' Her eyes shone. We had passed muster, then: been judged fit potential parents. Or maybe this nurse was too young to have become jaded.

'We did,' said Mehline.

The nurse laughed, reaching for the light switch. 'Twins can be sneaky. One hides behind the other.'

I thought about this as she lubricated Mehline's stomach. It made sense. Mehline and the twins: they revealed themselves strategically. First you agreed to go out for drinks because she was cute and funny and why wouldn't you? You had nothing to lose. And then you were spending so much time together, she might as well move in; it just made sense. And you did love her, of course you did. That's why you married her. A formalisation of the relationship you already had, that's all that was; you can't keep dating forever. And married people have babies, so naturally you try for one. Suddenly you realise your wife is shopping for jeans that expand around the middle and it's all slipping away: the sex on demand, the late-night computer games while she sleeps, the easy, ad hoc beers with friends, the pulling on of sneakers for a run just because you feel like it. All of it is ending. You sit there staring at the medical gel that glistens like a translucent turd on her distended, once-beautiful belly, and you think: *When did I agree to this?* The only answer I could think of was: when we met for drinks. That was my only chance to stop this. The rest was a landslide.

The nurse pursed her lips. She looked at Mehline, me, then back at the screen. 'Ah...'

'What is it?' Without moving, Mehline had become a solid object, a granite sculpture of tension.

'It's…' The nurse reached for our folder. 'I'm sorry, how many are you expecting?'

I didn't understand the question. 'Both of them.'

'Two,' Mehline said.

The nurse looked at the screen again. 'I'm seeing three.'

I stood. They looked at me. Mehline, her voice high and artificial, said, 'Honey, where are you going?'

I gestured to the door, frowning. 'I have to… I'll just be…' Then I was sitting in the waiting room with three nurses and the receptionist peering at me, snapping their fingers before my face.

'Mr Halsham?' A nurse took a cup from the receptionist. 'Drink this.'

I sipped. It was sweet, like ignorance.

'Mr Halsham, you lost consciousness. How many fingers am I holding up?'

'Three,' I said.

That night I lay in the bed, staring at the ceiling, while Mehline moved about the room, undressing and tidying things. Finally she lifted the covers and slipped in beside me. I could hear her breathing. 'Do you want to talk about it?'

'No,' I said. 'I'm good.'

Eventually, she rolled over and turned off her lamp. I lay awake for a long time.

* * *

Our obstetrician was called Dr Bane. Her first name was Jane. Doctor Jane Bane. She was small and old and gave you the feeling it was her baby; you were just incubating it for her. She phoned us to request another scan. She wanted to see this for herself. Those were her words. Usually an appointment with Dr Bane meant sitting around waiting for her to return from delivering a baby, or to deal with all the patients backed up from when, earlier that day, she had been delivering a baby, but today when we pushed open the smoked glass door to ultrasound services, there she was, one arm on the reception counter, chatting to two nurses. Their heads turned toward us simultaneously.

'Ah, here they are,' Dr Bane smiled. 'Hello, Mehline! Jack!' I had never seen her smile before. Back when we just had the one, she couldn't say my name without glancing at our folder. Apparently this was quite exciting for Dr Bane: a challenge, something to sink her teeth into. 'Let's go straight through, shall we?'

All three nurses followed us into the examination room, chatting animatedly. It was no wonder nurses didn't think adults deserved babies, I thought to myself: they didn't have to take them home. For them, babies were precious miracles who disappeared from sight shortly following birth. I, on the other hand, had to find them somewhere to sleep, clothe them, wash them, get up to them in the night, teach them to not pull their pants down in public, pay for their education, and it costs half a million dollars to raise a child, did you know that? They didn't make that number up. There was a study.

I took my place against the wall as Mehline climbed onto the table. She was quieter than before, overwhelmed. She had been reading: at home, all her books were open or dog-eared at 'Multiple Pregnancies'. These were not happy pages: they were thick with back pain and mortality rates and selective reduction.

The room darkened. A hand closed on my arm. 'If you feel faint, let me know.' It was a nurse, the older one. Beside her, the others smiled. It was funny to them, of course.

'Let's see these alleged triplets,' said Dr Bane. She folded her hands behind her back, watching the screen.

'There's the first,' said the nurse with the scanner, as a grainy ghost passed across the screen.

I said, 'Did you say *alleged* triplets?'

Dr Bane didn't look at me. Her spectacles were solid with light, reflecting the monitor. 'Easy to double count, when there's more than one.'

The nurse pointed at something on screen. It resembled a giant squid lurking in the ocean depths. 'That's the second. Posterior presentation, see?'

'Yes, yes,' said Dr Bane.

I said, 'Double count?'

'They move,' the older nurse explained. 'We can only see a section of the womb at a time.'

They moved. Of course they did. They were in a sac eight inches wide, being prodded with a scanner; they shifted. There was margin for error. I felt hope burst within me, bright and wild.

'That's the third. Smaller, you see?'

'Yes...' said Dr Bane. 'You're right.' I stared at her. She was a despicable person. 'But what's... Go back. No, to the right. There.'

The nurses sucked in their breath simultaneously. I closed my eyes. Still, I heard it: the exhalation of the nurse beside me, the single, elongated syllable: '*Four.*'

Mehline and I sat in Dr Bane's examination room, gripping hands. Dr Bane was not there; she was using the phone. She was calling somebody about our case and did not want us to hear what she said. The room was filled with diplomas, photos of babies, and gushing notes of thanks. The public display of these notes annoyed me. It suggested that my own gushing note would be expected in due course. I would gush if and when I pleased.

The door opened and Dr Bane entered. 'Well. What a day!' She perched on the edge of her chair.

I leaned forward. I had thought about this. I would be calm and reasonable, but I had something to say, and I would say it. 'One hiding behind the other... I can see how that might happen. But then there were three. Where did it come from? And now... now four? How is that possible?'

'It's an inexact science,' Dr Bane said. 'Like counting cats in the dark.'

I took a breath. 'Are they multiplying?' Mehline looked at me. 'I mean... could they be?'

Dr Bane shook her head. 'No. Not this late.'

'I think they must be.'

'Mr Halsham, your wife is eighteen weeks. A second trimester foetus can't divide any more than you can.'

'You know what this is like?' I lowered my voice. 'A virus.'

Mehline took back her hand.

'Generally speaking,' said Dr Bane, 'we don't consider children a virus.'

'I'm not saying they *are* a virus. Just like one.' I gestured. 'You're a scientist. You know what I mean.'

'*Shut up!*' Mehline's face was deep, mottled red. '*Shut up!*'

My mouth dropped. 'I just mean—'

'I don't care! I can't hear any more of this!'
Wounded, I said, 'Honey…'
Four, she said, and then she leaned forward and covered her face with her hands. Her shoulders shook.

Outside the clinic, I went to put my arm around her, but she shrugged it off. I stopped; she kept walking. She wasn't even heading for the car; she was going the wrong way. I said, 'Mehline!' She didn't turn. I waited in the car for an hour. Each time I called her mobile, it rang three or four times, then dropped. Eventually I drove home. I ate, slept, alone.

* * *

I woke to the phone ringing. It was eight or nine in the morning, late. 'Mehline?'
It was the receptionist from the clinic. 'Dr Bane would like you and Mehline to come in for another scan.'
'We already did. We had a scan yesterday.' My head was still thick with *Not Mehline*; I didn't understand what she was talking about.
'Dr Bane isn't happy with yesterday's scan.' After a while, she said, 'Hello?'
'What's wrong with yesterday's scan?'
'You'll really need to ask Dr Bane. Can you come in this morning?'
'Yes,' I said. 'No. I can. But Mehline's not here. You'll need to call her.'
There was a pause. She knew. 'Okay.'

I was there on time, but it was already over, Mehline emerging from the examination room, her face thin with worry. She had rescheduled to miss me. When she saw me, her eyes jerked away. I said, 'What's happened?'
The nurses exchanged tight-lipped glances. Then Dr Bane spoke. I hadn't even realised she was there; I had been preoccupied with Mehline. 'Operator error.' Her voice was unforgiving.
'What's operator error?'
'There are only three,' said a nurse, the young one. She looked frightened. 'We miscounted.'
'They move.' This was the older nurse, her arms folded tightly

across her chest. She threw a defiant glance into the examination room. 'It happens.'

'Three...' I felt wonder. I had just saved five hundred thousand dollars. Then I looked at Mehline and saw her watching me; she was reading my expression. Before I could open my mouth, she pushed past me, out of the clinic.

I caught her in the car park. She was crying, her face red and puffy. When I put my hand on her arm, she threw it off like I was contagious. She looked, I realised, like a woman who had lost a child. 'Get away from me!'

'Please. Mehline. I'm sorry. I'm so sorry.'

'You... you *son of a bitch!*'

'I know. Mehline, please, forgive me.'

'You are a heartless, selfish pig!'

A pregnant couple snuck by, avoiding eye contact.

'I am. I know. I see that now.' I got my arms around her, and this time she didn't push me away.

'I always knew you could be self-absorbed. But this...' She wiped at her face. 'You must never, ever be like that again.'

'I promise. It was the shock. I'm over it. I swear.' I kissed her face.

We stood there a while.

'If you ever, even once, utter one single complaint about our three babies, I will leave you.'

'Okay,' I said.

* * *

The next four weeks were wonderful. It was like discovering each other again, like falling in love. We looked at baby furniture. We redecorated. I moved my computer into the bedroom, and filled my study with boxes of cots, prams, change tables. Mehline moved through the house like an angel, like a burgeoning fertility goddess.

We didn't talk about the next scan. But we knew it was coming. The day before, as we cleared away plates, Mehline said, 'You don't need to come. It won't be anything special.' Her voice was carefully neutral.

'I'll come if you want.'

'No,' she said. 'It won't be anything special.'

My phone rang at 10.45 a.m. There were great, hitching sobs. I said, 'Mehline?'

'I cannot apologise enough,' said the nurse. 'I mean, it's just unprecedented. We're checking everything. Maybe the equipment... whatever it is, I am just so sorry.'

'Just tell me there's two. That there's definitely two.'

She hesitated. 'This morning's scan shows two. But... I have to say, at this juncture, I'm not confident we know what's going on.'

I stared at her.

'As soon as I know anything,' she said. 'I will let you know.'

I turned and walked out, to the car, to Mehline, curled up in the back seat.

The receptionist called four hours later. There was something wrong with her voice: it was thin and strained, almost frightened. 'We'd like you to come in again.'

'Did you find the problem?'

'It's possible that...' In the background, I heard someone say: *Ssst!* 'It's better if you just come in.'

Mehline was shaking. I stood beside her, gripping her hand, as she lay back and rolled up her shirt. Once again, all three nurses accompanied us into the examination room, but there was no sign of Dr Bane. I had the feeling that Dr Bane was not absent by choice – that rather, Dr Bane did not know we were here.

The eldest nurse pressed the scanner into the halo of gel around Mehline's belly button. I stared at it for a minute before realising why it had caught my attention. 'Different.'

The nurse looked at me. 'I'm sorry?'

'The scanner. It's new.'

Her lips tightened. 'Yes.' *Whoa, whoa, whoa, whoa.* Alien shapes flitted across the monitor. 'It's possible...'

'What's possible?' She didn't answer. 'What's possible?'

She put down the scanner. 'Oh, God.'

Mehline said, 'Please, what is it?'

'This... really, this is just humiliating.'

'Tell us,' I said.

'The old sonogram equipment was ghosting.'

Ghosts, I thought. *Her womb is full of ghosts.*
Mehline began to cry. 'What does that mean?'
'You have one,' said the nurse. 'One wonderful, healthy baby. You always have.'

When we arrived home, there were two large boxes by the front door, a delivery. They were car seats. Mehline pressed into me. 'I'll take care of it,' I said. I took her into the lounge room and sat her on the sofa. But even there wasn't safe: the double-width pram lay half-assembled on the floor, and on the coffee table a parenting magazine was open to an article on twins. I covered Mehline with a blanket and went through the house, cleansing it. When I was finished, the car was full of boxes. I had no idea where I would take them.

* * *

Two days passed. When the phone rang again, it was Dr Bane. She was frothing with outrage; she swore she would never use those people again. 'It's not just unprofessional,' she said. 'It's unforgivable.'

'It is.' I was pleased by her anger; it was an emotion I couldn't feel any more.

'I want you to come to a new clinic. It's cross-town, unfortunately. But after what's happened, I think we need to start this whole process again, establish a baseline we know we can rely on. Can you do tomorrow morning?'

'Tomorrow morning?'

'For a scan,' Dr Bane said.

When I put down the phone, Mehline was in the doorway. Her eyes were huge and wild. 'No. No.'

'It's a new place. They—'

'I don't want to. No.' She began to back away. Her face was white; she looked ill.

'Mehline, you're pregnant. You're obviously pregnant. Nothing's going to happen.'

'They'll take it.' She wrapped her arms around her belly.

'They won't. They can't. You're thinking crazy. Mehline.'

Since the last scan, she cried silently, without warning; it was like she had exhausted her inner reservoir of grief, but couldn't stop. 'Just leave me one. Please. Just one.'

* * *

The new clinic was in the base of an office building, flanked by a newsagent and a gift shop that sold posters and balloons. When we stepped through the sliding glass doors, the receptionist knew who we were; seconds later, two nurses were with us, cooing over Mehline and holding her hand. 'You poor dear,' said one. 'I can't imagine. I simply can't.'

The examination room was larger, one wall dominated by a photo of a dozen giggling, nappy-clad babies, all in a line. Mehline began to cry as soon as she saw the table, and there was nothing anyone could do: she was beyond consolation. Her face was waxy, her hairline thick with sweat. I held her and tried to kiss her hair while the nurse eased her back. Mehline sought out and found my hand, pulled me closer until our faces were pressed together and we could see nothing but each other. Heat poured from her. 'I love you,' I whispered. I heard: *whoa, whoa, whoa.*

The nurse said, 'One healthy baby. Everything looks fine.'

Mehline began to shudder. It took me a while to realise that she was laughing. She was gripping me like a world champion wrestler, drenched in sweat, laughing. I was the opposite: suddenly I couldn't stop crying. 'I'm just so happy,' I said.

Missing

Kalinda Ashton

He goes to the local market after work to collect fresh goat's cheese and the grainy bread she likes, which is dense and peppered with caraway seeds. The Greek woman at the deli smiles at him; clucks, 'Where's your wife? At home?' even as she turns away to wrap the loaf in unbleached brown paper and shuffle it into a bag. He tastes the stuffed olive she hands him on a thin toothpick, 'Try, try,' and licks the salty brine from his lips, handing over a fistful of coins, with the note, that clatter almost rhythmically onto the glass counter top.

He hates olives but he can't refuse something for nothing, a meanness so long ingrained in him he doesn't try to resist it, and he likes the deli assistant who has dark smoky eyes and a round midriff. Manda would have chided him for this reluctance. She can say no without grief. She'd shake her head, tell them 'nthanks' or, if pressed, claim to be allergic.

When he gets outside he sees the streetlights have come on and while it's dry now, the air smells of rain and there are puddles underfoot. He hugs the groceries to him with one arm and digs in his jacket pocket for the keys. *Jesus.* He was gone about eight minutes and already they've given him a fine. He pulls the ticket off the front window and looks around. The parking attendant is chalking tyres at the other end of the lot. He's never noticed before the special paper they use for the infringement slips: silicone or some other synthetic substance, covered in a slick shiny coating and thus protected from rain or sun. It's his third in a month and he's been hiding them from Mandy. He's meant to be the frugal one. She's generous, at least in a fashion, but there's a hierarchy. She hands over change to homeless people, to buskers. She gives to

Greenpeace but never the Christians, not even the Salvation Army and last time World Vision knocked she quizzed them for so long the man with the clipboard began to wilt and cast impolite, wistful glances back at the street behind him.

He swings out of the market and drives fast, nodding his head to an old Cure song on the radio, forgetting he's forty-two, reliving the years he spent trying to get along with the surfie boys on the coast as a teenager, pretending to love afternoons spent sprawled on the bluff of the cliffs sucking down spliffs and tossing beer cans into the sea or onto the heads of people walking along the path. He had caught the train into Perth on his own and picked his way through the second-hand record stores, making spidery lists of independent must-haves, and then he'd bought himself McDonald's and listened to mainstream cassettes at the megastores until they chucked him out. Music for him was like pornography was for other fifteen-year-olds: to be consumed privately, obtained on the sly, and he felt like this until he went to university and realised his secret was everyone else's.

Mandy's music motif had been bleak, anarchic and predictable when she met him: Joy Division, Public Enemy, The Clash, nothing gracefully tracked down or discovered   and coveted. He had picked it at thirty paces. A few years later she'd had her first re-invention and started listening to jazz at bars he could never locate. Then later it was dance music and shoes with heels, her lean muscular arms wrapped in shiny tops, instead of all that black clothing she'd clung to. The purply-red viscous lipstick that used to come off on her teeth and smudge as the hours passed so that eventually it gave her a faded cheer as if she'd been sucking on a child's icy pole. She could do that, though – come home one day wanting to be someone else. That's what had happened with Miaow Miaow. 'I hate cats' had turned into 'I want a cat' with hardly a breath or changing of skins in between. She was trying to make the cat learn a new name now, hissing practise alternative titles to her while she ladled out food and tried to make up her mind what she wanted the cat to be called. She liked to give the cat pornographic titles like Miss Furry Chalice or Delectable Diva Does Puss in Boots so that he could look appalled.

One of the neighbours has taken his usual spot so he parks around the corner and walks back, sheltering the limp bread bag from the latest downpour with his jacket. Mandy had forgotten to turn off the front light again and it gleams over the uneven wooden slats of the porch.

He can't see her bright little blue car in the driveway, the one that would crumple in a crash like a Coke can squashed underfoot. Either she isn't home, or she's round the corner at Katya's, sulking. He parks in a tight spot next to the pub, a block down from their house. She'd driven a dark, dun-coloured VW Bug when they were dating, before they got married. The first night he had come home with her he'd had to duck to avoid getting knocked in the face with bits of cardboard. She'd pegged up some string across the back seat and dangled cut-up photographs of her friends going to a dress-up party, and news captions across the string, each peg waving another disconnected image. 'Are these people terrorists?' the news headline asked, across the painted faces of her friends, dazzling but also dazed, eye make-up slipping in the flash's glare, mouths too soft. He held up some of the photos and admired the oceanic green of a mermaid's slippery tail, flicked past the multiple fractured dress-up costumes people had worn. 'But how do people sit in the back?' he'd asked and she'd answered, 'They don't.' He hadn't wanted to be boring so he didn't ask whether she could see properly in the rear view mirror or if the swishing sounds of the photos swinging, and occasionally falling, distracted her while she was driving.

'Shit.'

Some of the goat's cheese has leaked out, and oil sinks into his work clothes and runs down his arm. He loves the sharp aroma but it won't impress people at his job if the smell lingers amongst his things. He locks the car, waves indifferently to the man across the road and lugs his groceries to the front door. When they'd moved in, this house had been a shell, a weatherboard without real insulation on a block of tangled weeds. There had been musty clumpy carpet and no heating, so the place was chilled and inhospitable during winter. Manda had inherited it from her father who had been renting it out before he died. They'd scrubbed the floorboards to rid the place of the warm, sweet stench of mice and the putrid rot of damp, and he'd started installing proper heating.

Manda's begun the garden too, this month. Though when he squints to see the progress, he realises the Australian natives she potted on the front porch are gone. She must have taken them around the back to prune and fertilise.

He's whistling as he climbs the steps until he notices their beautiful stone Balinese statue is missing from its usual home under the magnolia. Some of the terracotta pots have gone, too. This has long been a neighbourhood that regularly turns up in the local newspaper for kids attacking the bus stops, or carving swear words and abuse into the trunks of trees in the scrubby parks. Now it's getting gentrified but he'd been nervous about putting expensive plants out the front.

Manda had argued with him. 'Maybe if they take things it means they really need them, more than we do.'

'Nobody *needs* plants.'

'We all do,' she said piously, 'just to breathe,' and then she'd turned away.

He turns his key in the lock and pushes open the door. It might be that she's just rearranging the ornaments, changing the orientation. It would be just like Katya to suggest feng shui to clear the air after an argument. For all he knows, she's convinced Manda it was the small citrus tree on the paving that caused their problems in the first place. If Manda knew what he was thinking she'd put her hand under her chin and watch him carefully. *I'm not stupid. Actually.*

The hallway's very light. He hoists his bags down onto the floor. The wooden slat blind's missing from the front bedroom. When he looks around, other things are gone. They've been robbed. He sees all the gaps in the room, goes to check for her jewellery but finds the antique box that contains it is gone. He rushes towards the front door again as if the burglars might be right outside and then he stops, foolish and shaky.

Half of the paintings have been taken off the walls too – they must have been interrupted – and he's stumbling into the kitchen when he realises how strange it is. They've left the DVD player but chosen the giant and out-of-date box TV. They've swept half the curtains (*'Curtains'*, he hisses to himself, unbelieving) from the windows. Cushions are gone. The bevelled oak side table. But when he puts his head into the spare room his laptop is there and so is the book he was reading this morning, sitting splayed down on the desk. The desk lamp's not.

The desk lamp is Manda's, a pretty antique glass ornament she found in a dusty St Vinnie's store after looking in one of those kitschy country gift shops in Ballarat for something just like it and finding only dolls made of twigs and lavender-painted baskets that had made her pretend to put her finger down her throat. The op shop was next door. It had been his idea to go in.

None of her clothes are left on the rack or in the dresser. The many pairs of shoes that once lined up against the bedroom wall – heels and boots, flats and sandals – are gone. He plunges his hand into the drawer she kept her underwear in and his knuckles hit the wood, which reverberates with a hollow thud.

He goes to the kitchen to get a glass of water and slow his breathing. He steadies himself by placing his fingertips lightly on the bench and leaning back into his heels. His shopping – ingredients for a penitent luxurious apology dinner – lies dropped in the hall. It seems more definitive when he looks again. She's taken the armchair a friend upholstered in buttery leather for her, and her books from the shelves. He'd never realised how widely she read before but the gaps speak to him. She'd owned essays from renowned female photographers and armfuls of gardening and cooking manuals wedged next to literary memoirs and an unhealthy number of Jeffrey Archers, which she hid when her mother came to visit, for fear of a lecture about Thatcher's cronies. The thick glossy fashion magazines are gone too and the albums, although he doesn't realise this until much later.

And here they all are, in the pauses on his shelves, where his own books fall to the side and slouch into one another, their sudden roominess placing them at a jaunty, diffident angle.

He rings her mobile. Again. Again. He is almost sobbing as he repeats 'please, no,' like a mantra. It rings out. She has turned her voicemail off. He remembers how to hide his number and rings again. Nothing.

When he calls an hour later, fingers chilled, hand cupped around a glass of whiskey, the phone's been switched off. He texts her. *Please darling. Talk to me.* Then later: *I'm sorry I didn't realise you were so unhappy.* She could have left a note. By 9 p.m. he hates her. She must have found her own place to rent, booked a moving van, been gradually packing her things away for weeks to orchestrate this. Whenever she decided to go, it had nothing to do with the last fight. He's not an especially angry person, or a controlling one. Why couldn't she have told him in person, or at least on the phone? They had slept together last week. Last week she would have been applying for apartments.

He will have to call her mother but his head throbs. It can wait. His hand trembles. He punches in draft after draft in the keypad of his phone, as if the right phrase in 160 characters might dissolve the whole nightmare. She's long been the superstitious one, he the practical, but he's imagining if he says the right thing now that it could still all be undone, revealed as a thoughtless joke, or overcomplicated surprise: at the very least a break, counselling, addressing their problems. By eleven, he's so drunk that his lunch rises in his throat. He puts his hand over his mouth and gags. The messages proliferate but they all come back to: *I love you. Don't leave me* or, *I hate you. Fuck off for good.*

He makes himself a sandwich with the goat's cheese, thin slices of red onion, and some of the truss tomatoes. He uses the white sandwich bread he stashes at the back of the cupboard, the stuff she says tastes like plastic or pillow stuffing. His only moment of triumph is to fling her twelve-grain loaf at the wall. 'I don't have to eat this fucking bread anymore.' No one witnesses his newfound freedom in baked goods.

He decides to take an inventory. Even her garage junk – the folders of assignments from when she was studying journalism, the abandoned poems, her HSC certificate – has disappeared without a trace. At first he thinks she has been scrupulous and cruel at the same time. Nothing that he owns is gone: his special mug that he's owned for a decade; the extra-long couch he bought when he got his first bonus at work; his snazzy racing bike; his expensive knife set, which he brought into the marriage – all these remain. She had said it was too soon to marry but he'd been forty when they met and wanted it all signed off and behind him. She was fourteen years younger than him. She had never wanted to open a joint account but he claimed it was the only sensible way to pay for shared expenses. When he goes to look at the latest statement, the paperwork they allow to build up in the first drawer of the desk is all gone.

She has taken more than her things, she has taken all of their things, the objects they co-owned, the pleasures and accumulations they possessed together.

That night he rings his oldest, dearest friend. Graham's recovering from prostate cancer and often sleeps during the day and paces at night.

'Umm. Hello?'

'It's me.'

'Oh.' But the sigh is gentle. 'What's going on?'

'Manda's left me.'

'Which Manda?'

'*My* Manda. Amanda. Who do you think?'

'Amanda who?'

'Very funny.'

'It's 5 a.m. Max.'

'Sorry.'

'I've got a meeting at eight. Look I'll ring you tomorrow and figure this out.'

Max lets the phone slip from his grasp and then leaves it off the hook.

Later, he can't find their wedding photo or the card and wrapped present they'd planned to give to his sister on her birthday. He searches in vain for hours for a single sign of her: a wedding ring left behind, the photo of the two of them in Mexico they'd kept stuck to the fridge, her perfumes and jars in the bathroom cabinet. But there is nothing. She must have put the goofy college photo of Max and his buddy Graham up instead. Even the cotton sheets on their bed don't smell of her. He sniffs and there is the faded scent of eucalyptus washing detergent. He can't bring himself to run his hands over the pillowslip for strands of her hair.

He sleeps all through the next day and into the night, getting up only to piss. In the afternoon he walks out in his underpants to find a snack, furtively, rapidly carting it back to bed. He wakes thirsty, sleeping on bits of crisp and toast crumbs. When he finally gets up, the room feels as if it's shrunk. Without all her stuff it's oddly smaller, not roomier. It only takes two paces to reach the door.

He emails his boss to say he's had a family crisis and he will be working from home. He helps out with online content for a travel company, in the correspondence and complaints department. He masturbates idly, forlornly, then gives up and posts some of the copy on Hamilton Island, allowing himself a slug of whiskey each time he strikes 'paradise' or 'dream holiday' in the text.

He spends the next few days drinking, working furiously and watching *Dr Phil*. Today there is a woman who is compulsively cheating on her husband. She keeps getting pregnant during her affairs with different men, and giving birth to children and then giving them up to foster care. Her surviving children hate her because she keeps tossing their siblings out like old clothes. The extramarital kids hate her for giving them away at the ages of six, four and two. The husband is a big beefy man, emanating some powerful force-field of denial, who blinks, perplexed at his wife's uncanny capacity for ruin and deception. Max can't stop watching. He begins to whistle. The healing power of other people's misery is extraordinary and he is dizzy, light. He doesn't check the machine for messages or stay alert for the sound of her car.

With his feet up on the couch, as the clock ticks on, he lists the advantages. It's hard to be nostalgic when all the reminders, the concrete visual symbols, for nostalgia are gone. He can't put on the 'My Bloody Valentine' track they first fucked to, because it is no longer here. There are, apparently, no longer any photos of her in the house so he cannot weep over them, or tear them up and chuck them in the air and then fling himself on the scraps, scraping the torn fragments together on the carpet in instant regret.

For days he finds things missing. Rummaging for the silver tea strainer in the drawer and realising he can no longer see the matching milk jug they got from Katya upon their engagement. When he reaches into the top cupboard for cornflakes he understands that she has not only taken Miaow Miaow, but all the tiny tins of decadent cat food that *he* bought. The photo albums documenting their entire time together are gone.

On day four he dresses for work and picks up the phone to call her mother. He wants to know if she's in Melbourne, if she ever plans to face him, what he should do with her mail when it arrives, or the various bills they're bound to receive. Really, he wants to know if she's there, if she's so disappointed in him and her life, so irritated and bored ('done with him', she would say) that hiding out at her mother's is even an option. The machine blinks but it's only Graham.

'*Sorry if I said the wrong thing the other night. Didn't mean to be insensitive but it's in my nature. Anyway, whoever she is, it's only a girl, right? Ha.'*

Max presses the delete button. He dials Manda's mum. She answers curtly, already suspicious. He isn't paranoid. She always sounds as if she's experiencing some vast disruption or an interrogation. 'This is Max Walker.'

'Yes?'

'I really want to talk to you about what's happened.'

He could hear her muttering to someone in the background. 'What did you say your name was?'

'Please let me speak to her.'

He's left with a dial tone.

On day five he dresses, gags as he brushes his teeth, and goes back to his job. He works without any investment, with his head down and a clenched jaw, until twelve. At lunch he accepts a cigarette from Nick, who ushers him into a cafe and orders a strong coffee. 'So what's the crisis?'

'Huh?'

'Jack told me. Your family crisis. Hangover? Hot chick?' It's not always easy to tell when Nick is parodying himself and when he is just being himself. This may be why he is such a terrific copywriter and jingles man.

'You're kidding me, right? Manda's left me. My wife.'

Nick puts his hand in the air, his palm a stop sign. 'Come on mate. In Second Life maybe. Unless you got hitched in the last twenty-four hours you're still a sad single loser like the rest of us.'

Max puts his head in his hands. 'Is this a joke?'

Nick pats him on the shoulder and lights his own smoke. 'It's cool.'

'It's not *cool*. How could it be cool? Why won't people admit they know her? So, okay: you never met but you knew I was living with someone.'

'Ah, fantasy. Maybe it's all that dreaming.'

'What?'

'Perhaps you've been reading upstairs's copy of *The Power of Positive Thinking*.' Management's various attempts to reform the workplace culture included placing copies of paperback books that lived on the monstrous line between corporate achievement and self-help in the staff tearoom to 'promote goodwill and encourage excellence'.

'I would never borrow something like that.'

'Suit yourself.' A shrug.

They eat in silence but after Max had forced himself to swallow a Greek salad, Nick grabs his hand. 'Where's your wedding ring then?'

'Here.' But when he looks down there isn't even a faded band of skin. 'I don't know…' Nick's getting up to leave but still he utters the rest of his sentence. 'I didn't want a ring but she said if that was the case then I couldn't expect her to wear one. It was both or none. So we went both.'

'Carn, Maxie.' Nick's breath smells. 'Bachelor boys, that's us.' His grin is garish.

Why has he never noticed what a poky cave their bedroom is? He carries the cordless into the room but when he pushes open the door it bashes into the bed. In the end he crouches into a small ball between the door and the bed, his knees huddling near his chin. Graham is advising a few Valium and a trip to the GP.

'She's not "some girl". You were our best man. I can show you. I've got a photo in my wallet.'

Graham waits.

When Max scrabbles at the clear plastic window next to his drivers licence there's a picture of his niece and an unfamiliar mobile number scratched in pencil across a Metcard. The image of him and Manda, their grinning heads wedged together in a black-and-white photo booth moment captured at Spencer Street station, is gone.

'Bitch. She's taken that too.'

'Yeah? From your wallet?'

'Why would she do that?'

'She didn't. I thought she left while you were at work?'

'She did.'

Max thinks of how Manda always talked through the movies to the chagrin of fellow audience members. He remembers her putting up her thick black hair in a ponytail, taking the band from her wrist, pouting at the mirror. She used to read the newspaper on the loo, assume a deep voice unselfconsciously during sex, and complete Sudoku puzzles within three minutes. The memories are like movie frames fast-forwarded; they leave impressions but no narrative. They don't contain any time; they're elastic, adjustable, full of juxtapositions that would be ridiculous if their ironies weren't infused with pain.

'She's fucking left me with nothing.'

Graham's begun to speak with the careful diffidence he saves for disasters and emergencies. 'I can offer you calming painkillers – one of the few cancer-related perks – and a bonus unwanted reality check. That's it. What are you expecting me to say?'

'That you knew her.'

'I can't. No one knew her, Max.'

'That you get how horrific this is for me after all these years and *no explanation*.'

Graham pauses. Max imagines him signalling to his girlfriend, *one minute*, and acting out silent representations of Max being utterly crazy. 'I'm sure it feels real.'

On the morning of his sister's birthday he wakes with his head pressed into the wall. The room's too small and he cannot imagine now how they ever fitted Manda's furniture in here. Indeed, he realises that the double bed is far too large for the room. He drags himself out of bed and his feet immediately kick into the wall. So, straight after he has stretched, his joints popping in protest, he unpacks the single mattress and base they'd kept for guests. He dismantles the big bed, heaves the mattress onto the street, sweat gathering under his arms. He carries out the base and leans the two together while the neighbour watches from behind his lemon tree.

He props up a sign and writes in capital letters, forcing his script into carefree abandon: FREE. UNWANTED. PLEASE TAKE.

At the party he stuffs pavlova into his mouth and then cream buns, and drinks low-carb beer, the only alcohol on offer, until he's afraid. 'You met her, Trace. Manda. You remember her?'

His sister cradles her baby and swiftly snatches a cake knife from her older daughter's grasp. 'Was she the one with the mohawk?'

When she has been gone for exactly a week, the afternoon following his sister's celebration, he finds he cannot enter the front bedroom. Their room, his room, has become a kennel. He cannot lie full-length in it, and the only way to access it is to crawl in on his hands and knees. He can't remember if Manda wore perfume or if she bought bras with underwiring or padding. He can't recall if they were going to have children. Since the house resists him, he finds himself walking the streets, refusing the not unwelcome offers of smoke and speed from those who recognise the calibre of his desperation.

Instead, he makes his way to the Melbourne Museum and breathes easier once he is meandering through a contained space. He hears his feet tap purposefully on the gleaming floor, his gait blend in with the other groups and families. At the Science and Life exhibition, which carries a sedate warning about nudity and sexuality for parents of small children, he stares intently at a photograph of a naked man of forty, who is lit up from behind. The man carries less flab than Max, although his penis falls slightly to the left, and flops recalcitrant against his thighs. Max has more hair but the man in the photo looks smug, knowing.

As Max is leaving, he sees a boy of about five leaning forward to touch the dinosaur display in the children's section. The child's mother is glancing around, poised to restrain him if an authority figure appears. The boy has glossy hair and crooked teeth. When he sees Max watching, he reaches out his hand to him.

'This is stegosaurus,' he announces and he waves and reaches. The boy's mother catches his hand.

'Uh uh. Leave the nice man alone. We're going to see the bugs now.'

After they have gone, Max stands but does not weep and reads panels about how old the bones are, and competing theories of extinction.

The Teaspoon and the Tolling Bell

Imogen Melgaard

A peculiar collection has been thrust upon me. It is a collection of events. I call them events because, through repeated coincidence, I can only see them as a choreographed dance. Floating around in a sea of possibilities, they waltz into my life with the pretence of something quite ordinary. They are simple happenings. In the population of a metropolis it seems certain that they should occur. But what is less certain is why I have been asked to participate, witnessing one event and being rewarded with another, a moment of bizarre discovery, which has coerced my mind into perceiving a benign household object as a souvenir of catastrophe.

The meaning of these events is elusive and, while I have explored possibilities, I have arrived at no definitive reason for their happening. I rehearse them as memories, rewrite them as stories, imagine more endings; I can't get them out of my mind. Still, at night, as I lie in bed, they hum in my ears, a melodic ringing, the tolling of a bell. They are coincidences, I tell myself, for reassurance. But, packed as tightly as they have been into the space of a few weeks, they feel sinister and bizarre. I have begun questioning things, I have been wondering about design. It scares me; sometimes it excites me. What is coming? For, surely, if I am to understand this as a choreographed dance, there is to be a grand finale.

First it was a woman. She dropped into my life when she was spat off the treadmill beside me, convulsing with a cardiac event. I was the first one on the scene. I got to her side, took her hand, and asked, like an idiot, if she was okay. She was not, her face told me. A blue-purple began blooming beneath her make-up.

We started CPR, a gym instructor and I. Paramedics arrived

and I was asked to continue with compressions, now though with my hands splayed out over her naked chest, my finger resting on her right nipple, my upper body force bending then breaking her ribs. More paramedics arrived. I was asked to stand clear as the defibrillator charged the woman's body. I found it hard to let go. I stepped back and wandered out of the gym. I walked home with the memory of the woman's breasts still in my hands. The next day was Valentine's Day. Hearts were everywhere. It was a strange coincidence that I searched, through a habit of thinking, for meaning.

I was plagued by a silent film: the phone call to the woman's family. It showed me that moment, just as they were sitting down to tea, when everything would change. Everything changed for always – a path on life's map that took them from the ordinary instant and sent them off into unknown territory. The next day I found a teaspoon. Flattened by cars, it lay glinting on the road by my house. I picked it up. Why? I do not know. It seemed the right thing to do. Something in my hoarding nature would not let me walk past its glinting abandon. It sits now in the top drawer of my desk.

Next came a man, a family friend. I saw him in the morning. We talked about events. He has spent forty years on a psychiatric pension – he knows a lot about events. He gives me stories, clippings from the paper, various objects he has procured from his hard rubbish trawling, and poetic wisdom that seems to come from another world. All good for a hoarder; all good for a writer.

In the evening as I sat down to tea I got a call. Change in a sentence and life seems to shift. The conversation was simple, the ramifications complex.

'Hello?'

'... Yeah, it's me. What's news?'

'... Shit! But when? I just saw him this morning.'

He had a lunchtime heart attack.

The next day there was a flattened teaspoon outside my door.

Two is a coincidence. Two is company. These old adages rattled around my head as I grappled with this unlikely event. I picked up that spoon, too, although I had not yet correlated its discovery as a souvenir of catastrophe. It sits now alongside the original find. They look like two dolls. For some reason I am reminded of the elopement of the dish and the spoon. My two spoons, I decide, look like the happy couple perched on a cake.

These two incidents happened in such close proximity that I found it impossible to see them as separate events. Once again I found myself searching for meaning, a meaning that I could use to rationally explain away the haunting memory of the death snorts from the woman at the gym. It occurs to me that I am looking for something outside of simple happenings. It occurs to me that perhaps I am looking for coincidence.

I showed a friend the two spoons. We sat on the edge of my bed and discussed their meaning. We both searched their battered heads for clues but only saw our upside-down reflections. She was born a Catholic; I was born an atheist. She thinks God has sent me a challenge. I cannot agree. We called our friend who is nuts and thinks she was born a spirit, and she offers her advice. I am apparently to blame, although she doesn't say it in as many words.

She believes that I am manifesting these events. The universe holds infinite possibilities. Through the power of thought I have somehow attracted these events. She makes me feel like some kind of macabre force-field. I ask her why the spoons? She cannot answer but tells me instead of something called The Secret. On this night I can't sleep for all the whispering in my ears.

Bad luck comes in threes. Three is a crowd. I was on my way home from donating blood. Normally things are fine, but on this day my blood pressure dropped and I felt incapacitated by light-headedness.

I stayed for half an hour sucking on oranges, before I finally wobbled back home on my bike. Halfway home I found a girl in the street.

Her body was taut, her bag spilled open with a trail of books and pens rolling into the gutter. People had begun to gather. I stepped off my bike but was held back by dizziness. I watched as others began the process of reaching for mobiles, turning her on her side, holding her hand and searching for a response. The only response they got was the undignified animal snort that did not in any way match her neat appearance.

It was pointless to hang around. A crowd had circled the girl and the scene was turning into a circus. I wheeled my bike out of the crowd and made it home, where I promptly burst into tears. I could not stop thinking that at any minute a phone would ring somewhere, loaded like a gun, with news of the girl's fate. For her family, life would be set on different tracks in an instant. I was filled with an image of the city's phone lines buzzing with the coloured threads of conversations, and I wondered how many of these conversations were loaded like guns. I rang my friend and she offered me her company.

On the way to her house I found a teaspoon.

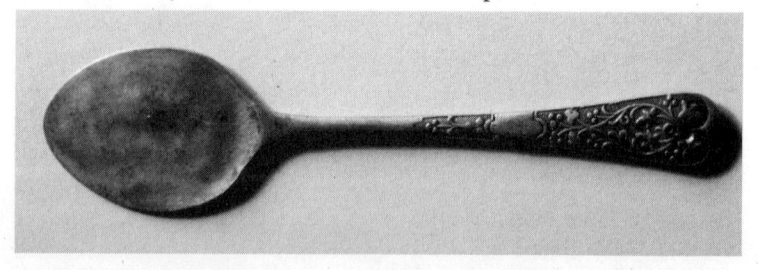

It is necessary for me to pick it up. I wrap it carefully in my hanky and nurse it in my bag. When I get to her house, her roof and bottles of wine are waiting. We swing out the window and onto the warm corrugated iron. I show her the spoon. She laughs. For her it is becoming funny. We ring our spiritual friend and she comes over to join us. I lie, sandwiched between the two of them, staring up at the stars. I think of taking this third spoon home and placing it in the drawer. My happy couple will now become a small platoon of silver soldiers, and I am reminded of a time when an egg and thin slices of toast were a battle and an army.

'What is coming next?' I ask.

'A bloody strange story,' they reply in unison.

I have trouble concentrating. I am trying to study, I am trying to read Foucault but all I can see is the word 'Fault'. My mind wanders to families I have never met and sits with them a while to watch possibilities unfold. I think of my own family, of the times they have sat around my hospital bed living that moment where the instant suddenly turns critical. I think of the parents of some kids I had once known who had been crushed in a car. On all the days they had woken up and assessed life's possibilities, they had never considered the death of their children as one of them.

I write the story. It sits in a file on my computer nursing the thoughts I have tried to leave. It gives me no meaning and yet it is out there written with words and meanings I have grabbed from the world, and this is a relief. Death should not be extraordinary; it happens every day. It is all over the news. It is a clinical term, but for me it always brings to mind the unassuming mountains of tissues that grow in the silent homes of the bereaved.

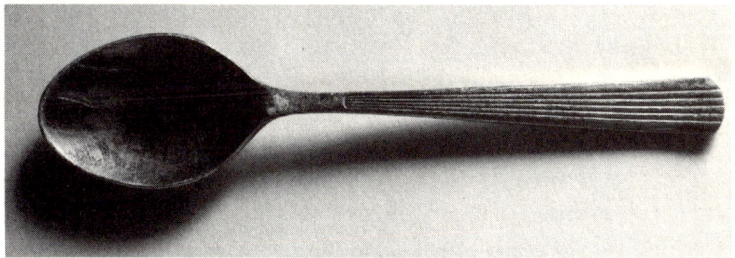

Four! I can think of no adages. I find the teaspoon first this time. I am at once wary, and pick it up as if it were a practical joke. As if it could happen again! But it does, and the next day at work a mountain of a man lies, for all to see, walking that thin precipice between the ordinary and the tragic. I am struck by the violence of that moment between life and death as hearts are pummelled and beaten, as ribs bend and break, as stomachs heave and convulse. Paramedics work for half an hour before a cover is pulled over the man's face, the curtain finally closed. Spectators wander away as if it were some kind of wrestling match, shaking their heads at the weight of the entertainment.

'Come home love,' my parents invite, their voices weaving into my city room.

I pack an overnight bag and head to the station, subconsciously scanning the footpath for flattened spoons. There is an amount of comical caution I have begun to assume in public. I block my ears with headphones and stare out at the dry landscape but bumps and hiccups in the carriages cause me to startle. I begin to laugh at my own hyper-awareness, at the absurdity of this situation. These coincidences have made me look too hard for catastrophe. Maybe my friend is right, maybe I am making these things happen, maybe there is something in me.

In the country I tell my parents the full story of the spoons. They laugh. We are in the kitchen chopping vegetables. It is preserving season and the house smells of onions and vinegar. My sister imitates my complicated coffee order: 'A decaf-soy-latte-one-sugar-no-teaspoon please.' Like a lot of things in my life this is becoming an elaborate joke. I laugh too; I don't know what else I can do. That night I flip through a thick file of old X-rays and search vaguely for a hint in the shadowy documents of my own body. Some years ago I had taken an ungraceful flight down a spiral staircase and smashed my head into the awaiting floor. In the weeks that followed, my brain was meticulously documented in the sliced images of various medical scans. Doctors were looking for damage; I am looking for my mind, for my memories, for the home of experience.

The next day my family are off to a street party. The new link in the transport artery from Melbourne to Bendigo has opened and our town, a small strip of shops set along the dip of the old highway, has now been bypassed. I'm not sure what there is to celebrate. How often we seem to laugh. Absurdity is the strangest humour.

There is music, a friend is playing his harp in the autumn light and people are singing. My mum and I are sitting outside the bakery, nursing coffees in our hands and dangling our feet into the deep, bluestone gutters.

'You could shoot a cannonball down this highway now,' she says to me.

I look out into the street at the dancing cluster of people caught in the afternoon light and then follow the stretch of highway up towards the horizon. There is a clatter and Mum swears. She has dropped her teaspoon into the gutter. I eye it off, stuck between two uneven stones glinting in the sunlight. It occurs to me that I will find neither rhyme nor reason for the events in a day. I leave this spoon. If the winter rains ever come it will be washed away for someone else to find on some other day.

Welcome to Romance Writing 1A

Rose Mulready

The advice everyone gives to first-time romance writers is this: don't talk down to your audience. They may read romance, but they're still intelligent women. They'll pick up the insincerity. They'll see right through you.

To which I say: crap.

If they're so intelligent, why aren't they reading Proust and TE Lawrence?

No, take it from me. You can totally dupe them. You can spend your evenings catting around drinking ouzo and smoking filterless Camels and doing guys with tattoos in the back of your car and then roll in to your garbage dump of a flat just as the birds are getting going, and tap out the last chapter with one eye closed because you can barely focus from so much booze, cackling all the while, wondering how anyone could ever fall for this shit – and they'll still eat it up. People will buy your books by the truckload and they'll write you letters saying how much they blah blah blah and you'll get awards.

Yes, you'll get awards. Three years in a row. Which, unfortunately, means you have to go to the ceremonies. Which would usually be a blast – what with the free grog and the canapés and the bowing and scraping and all – except you won't be able to enjoy it, because you'll be all trussed up in butter-wouldn't-melt taffeta and your hair will be in ringlets – *ringlets*, for God's sake – and you'll be simpering for four solid hours and all this on half a glass of champagne, because that's 'all I can have without getting a little giddy!'

And once on the podium, you'll have to lower your head reverently and clutch that cruddy trophy – it's a heart with a quill through it, believe it or not – and act all overcome for a second and then you'll cast your eyes up to the heavens and say something touching about the power of *loooooove*. Yes you will. If you know what's good for you. If you want to pay off the bank loan on that Maserati you totalled coming away from the User's Club last July. Not to mention the lawyer's fees.

But don't worry too much about it. Apart from the ceremonies, there's really only one other public exposure you'll have to endure, and that's the occasional nightmare session with a *New Idea* journalist. A tip for you here – don't let them come to your house. Spin them some bull about the ethereal vibrations of your writing space being very sensitive to intruders (it's okay to be a little nutty, they're expecting that). Make them meet you at the Windsor for high tea. Eat ribbon sandwiches and hold your teacup like it's a rare butterfly you've captured by one wing, and clutch at your throat a lot, breathlessly, girlishly, and talk about your penchant for eclairs. It's only for an hour – you can do it. Make sure they pay.

The rest of the time you can fairly much hang out at the flat, wearing an old pair of tiger-print knickers and a footy jumper, eating chicken nuggets and watching cable.

Which brings me to the writing bit. Yes, this is where you pick up your pen. That old ballpoint down the back of the couch will do. Scratch it around on the nugget box a bit to get it working. Important point here: you still have cable going. Because when it comes to saccharine, us book writers must bow to the TV guys. They're the kings. Pick out a few key phrases. Scribble them down. Even when you finally get off the couch and mosey over to the laptop (you can always have the laptop with you on the couch, it's true, but your chiropractor bills will be hell), keep the TV on. Keep switching around between telemovies and old mini series and re-runs of *Home and Away*. Let it bubble away in the background. We call it 'feeding the muse'.

Okay, you're basically going to need two things here. Let's call them 'the hero' and 'the heroine'. Now, your heroine's a feisty little thing. Yes she is, gosh darn it. This is the twenty-first century, people. She probably runs her own ceramics business. Single-handed. Or a b & b in a lonely little country town. And everyone loves her – the guy that sells her tomatoes, the old lady at the post office, her terribly wise and perceptive best friend – everyone, except for that guy that jilted her five years ago. Leaving her kind of wary and broken and thinking she'll never love again. Despite the fact that she's so lovely and vibrant and passionate and everyone says what a damn shame it is.

Right. Now your hero. Out-of-towner. Older guy. Not *too* old – just enough to have that kind of alpha-male weightiness and that air of seen-women-come, seen-women-go weariness and, of course, the wildly successful business. The one that brings him to this little town.

By now you're probably at about 10,000 words. Only thirty thou to go! Because, thankfully, these ladies that you're writing for? The ones that are only reading this to unwind between corporate takeovers and writing their PhDs? They're not in it for the long haul. You can write these in a week. Believe me, I've done it. In fact, *The Porcelain Heart* took me all of three days, and I was watching a test match for most of them.

Procrastinating – we'll get to that later. Whole other unit.

Sooo, hero and heroine meet. Preferably in some wild, elemental setting. Think banks of mighty river. Storm. Top of mountain. That kind of thing. Get her hair a bit mussed. (This is where you might like to have a can of Red Bull and a couple of Camels real quick, just to get that authentic chest-heaving, pulse-racing kind of feeling. We call this 'method writing'.) So, your heroine's all het-up. And she's strangely taken with this mysterious stranger, but he's so damn hell-sexy arrogant that…

Yada, yada, yada. Now's probably about the time you'll want to go have a shower. You're about halfway through now; you deserve a break. In fact, you deserve a shot of Stoli, don't you think? Have it while you're doing your face. Get out those boots, the ones with the spindly heels. And some fishnets. Now go the hell out and get tanked and laid. Don't forget to press 'save' on your way out. Really. Believe me. Don't forget that part. That's why *River Deep* took me a whole freakin' month.

And when you come back home? All juiced up and cavalier and cat-with-the-cream and to-hell-with-it? *This is not a good time to answer readers' letters.* Just don't.

What it's generally a good time for, I find, is the Shadow Book.

Now, the Shadow Book is an essential part of the romance writer's Sanity Kit. Along with hard liquor and gangsta rap. The

Shadow Book is where you'll pour out all of the little itchy feelings that rise up in you as you're spewing out this marshmallow hooey. You know, when you start to think, who am I, really? How did I get here? Is this it? I write *one* of these god damned things just to pay my way through photography school and suddenly the money's coming in and the publishers want four more and I'm dropping out before my final exams and I own three state-of-the-art cameras I haven't touched in years and my friends (so-called) never say so but I can see they think I've sold out – well I *have* sold out, I make no bones about that – but they're perfectly happy to crash in my spare room and let me pick up all the bar tabs and spot them the odd hundred here and there, oh yes, because they are the starving artists and I, clearly, am the whore. Those kinds of feelings. Here's where the Shadow Book can help.

It starts off pretty much the same as the other books. Heroine: just trying to get along in the world, thinks she's fine but isn't really, there's something *missing*, mane of auburn hair or whatever, enchanting smile dimpling the corners of her blossom mouth, etc. etc. Hero: tall; broad in the chest; hard, watchful eyes; sharp suit (or dusty boots and stockman's hat); thinks nothing of her, until…

And then it starts to turn. Ever so gently. Some details start to skew. We discover the hero's asthma condition, his fear of heights. The heroine's brewing moonshine in a still out the back of the b & b. And then (as the real book, the one you'll publish, gets closer to completion) it will kinda get out of control. The heroine will be feeding industrial chemicals into the town water supply, creating cancers and birth defects, and the hero will be sobbing into a handkerchief and wetting the bed at night, and new characters will come onto the scene, trick riders and dominatrixes and TV evangelists, and there'll be mad orgies and shoot-outs, and then there'll be a nuclear winter or something, and everyone will end up mad or cannibals, or both.

Yes, awfully cathartic. Ever so satisfying. Helps you through the night. But here's the thing. Pay attention now:

DELETE THEM.

Don't keep them on your computer, in a file entitled 'Shadow Books'. Don't show them to your (so-called) friends on long, crystal-meth-fuelled, chatty, revelatory evenings. No no no.

Because then? What will happen? Is this.

Welcome to Romance Writing 1A

One of your (so called) friends will get chatting to a journalist. Rather good-looking guy. Tall. Broad of chest. You'll meet this guy, out at a club one night, by 'accident'. And you'll fuck him in the toilets, but really you're thinking this could be something more, you like the way he moves and the offhand way he laughs, and so you'll actually give him your number and you'll spend all of the next week holed up with him in your flat, having mind-blowing sex, getting all kind of gooey and watermelon-grinny about him, until the point where your brain, by now a sort of mushed, ecstatic porridge, will think it's not suspicious but cute that you're having this arch pillow-talky chat about computer passwords, and he'll tell you his (or you'll think he does) and you, believe it or not, will tell him yours (which is, for the record, 'I'm with Cupid'). And you'll go to sleep. Smiling gently. And he'll go to work. With a USB stick. And although your fame, as a romance writer, will be really kind of limited, your fame as a romance writer who gets shickered and takes drugs and screws random guys in nightclubs and writes twisted, pornographic, nihilistic parodies of your bestsellers in your spare time and, to boot, keeps copies of your late-night replies to readers' letters – the replies you never send – in a file handily entitled 'Fuck you all', will be somewhat more extensive. The tabloids will love it. And there'll be a big fat advance to be paid back and no form of income to speak of and all the talkback radio guys will be going nuts, and the readers' letters? Slightly less adulatory.

Still. You know. All things considered… you'll really feel kind of relieved. Kind of strangely liberated. You'll be able to watch a couple kissing on the street without wanting to retch. Life won't be so bad. Even though you'll have no money and you'll have to start writing a fantasy book, under a pseudonym, one of those big fat books with elves in cloaks, and it'll take you ages – *ages* – and in the meantime you'll have to start teaching classes at the local TAFE to underdone kids and delusional housewives who think they can actually make it big in publishing from taking a summer course at this third-rate dump of a place – even given all that, at the end of the day, you won't feel so bad. Most of the time. In fact you might even get out that camera. The Leica, the one you'll have to sell next week so you can buy groceries. And you'll take a picture of yourself. In your tiger-print knickers. Grinning.

So. Any questions?

HAIKU ANGST

Steve's always tapping
At his new frickin' iPhone.
Gutters need doing.

I lost the receipt
For shoes I bought at Target
Geelong. Way too tight.

Wet towel again
Left on the bed. Rod is soooo
Dead when he gets home.

1.
Radio talk-back
About callers' dreams: I want
To rip my ears off.
2.
As a gift, mum gave
Me the vase I bought her in
Crete. Pre-Alzheimer's?

FURTHER HAIKU ANGST

Former fast bowler
Geoff Lawson once gave me the
Bird after a match.

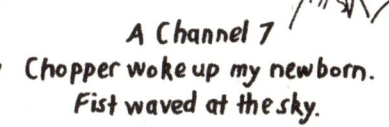

A Channel 7
Chopper woke up my newborn.
Fist waved at the sky.

Must pick up my kids
From the school dentist at five.
Free child-care, with pain.

1.
My subscription to
The Loungeroom Dancer expired.
Still, it's all online.

2.
Planted alfalfa
Too close to the BBQ.
Killed by spitting fat.

OSLO

Kieslowski's Unlikely Comedy

Patrick Cullen

In mid-February 1996, the Polish director Krzysztof Kieslowski telephoned Krzysztof Piesiewicz, the Solidarity-era lawyer who had been his co-scriptwriter for more than a decade. Kieslowski insisted that they meet immediately to talk about an idea that he had for a film.

'I am in the cafe across the square from the courthouse,' Kieslowski said. 'I have been here working on this idea all of the morning.'

'And I have much work ahead of me this afternoon,' Piesiewicz said, meaning that he was to review evidence put forth by the defence in the case he was prosecuting at the time.

'We both have much work ahead of us. That is why we must meet now. To begin.'

'No,' Piesiewicz pleaded. 'I have a case before the courts. I have no time for talk of films.'

Kieslowski fell silent as he often did when something was not going as he expected. Piesiewicz had collaborated with Kieslowski on his two greatest projects: the celebrated Three Colours trilogy and the lesser known, but no less significant, *Decalogue*. More recently they had been working on a new trilogy inspired by Dante's *Divine Comedy* and while they had already completed the script for *Heaven*, the remaining films existed only as treatments, and Piesiewicz knew that if this new idea of Kieslowski's took hold it would be years before they would return to *Hell* and *Purgatory*.

Piesiewicz leaned back in his chair until he could see out across the square to the cafe where Kieslowski was calling from. He imagined Kieslowski there, growing cantankerous: his eyes narrowing behind his horn-rimmed glasses, his forehead deeply creased over his thick eyebrows. Having worked with Kieslowski long enough to know that he always got his way, Piesiewicz relented. 'We will meet this afternoon, then,' he said, holding the telephone under his chin as he slid a wad of documents inside a manila envelope. He picked up his black leather briefcase off the floor beside his desk and placed the envelope inside. He would review the evidence after he'd finished with Kieslowski. 'We will meet this afternoon,' he said again, to himself as much as to Kieslowski. 'But you are on your own tonight.'

Kieslowski said nothing. It was not in his manner to express gratitude. Piesiewicz hung up, his hand resting heavily on the receiver, the creases of his knuckles forming an audience of frowns.

Kieslowski was recognisable from the doorway of the cafe. He was sitting across the room with his back turned toward the door. He was smoking, as usual, and the smoke settled heavily about him like a dense fog of which the day had yet to relieve itself. Piesiewicz moved between the crowded tables, holding his briefcase to his chest. He reached Kieslowski's table and placed a hand on his shoulder. Kieslowski flinched and stood abruptly, his hip catching the corner of the table, causing a smouldering cigarette to fall clear of the glass ashtray and roll across the table, leaving a trail of dark ash.

Piesiewicz sat opposite Kieslowski. Three empty cups sat in the centre of the small wooden table and in each lay the dark remnants of coffee. Beneath the cups a dozen or more broadsheets of paper were fanned out over the table. Piesiewicz had first seen such a rush of creation twelve years before, when they first collaborated on the screenplay for *No End*, their 1984 film which follows the ghost of a young lawyer observing the life his wife goes on to lead after his death. The sheets of paper on the table were covered with Kieslowski's distinctive handwriting: outlines of scenes, and sketches of sets with a series of detailed notes for direction. Piesiewicz held the edge of one of the pages and rotated it so that he could see something of what Kieslowski had done. He picked up more and more of the sheets of paper until he held them all in his hands. 'All of this just this morning?'

Kieslowski nodded enthusiastically.

Piesiewicz shuffled the paper, found something he recognised as a portion of the scene. 'What is this?' he asked.

Kieslowski leaned forward in his chair. Piesiewicz held the paper out in the space between them.

'That,' Kieslowski said emphatically, thrusting his forefinger on the topmost sheet of paper so that all the sheets slipped from Piesiewicz's grip. 'That is what I need to talk to you about.'

Piesiewicz picked up the page again to look more closely. He recognised the scene. It was from *Blue* and it began with Olivier and the lawyer entering the drawing room of Julie's house. After a brief discussion between the three, Olivier leaves and Julie then pours two glasses of wine. She hands one glass to the lawyer who opens his black leather briefcase and removes a wad of documents. The lawyer has come to discuss financial matters following the death of Julie's husband and begins describing what actions have already been taken but Julie stops him. She then asks how many digits there are in her bank account number and, when the lawyer indicates that there are nine, Julie sets about composing a nine-digit number from a series of random numbers. The lawyer's date of birth gives the first six digits; the age of his own daughter provides two. They have an eight-digit number. 'How many teeth have you got missing?' Julie asks. 'Five,' the lawyer says but, worried and surprised, he continues to count, moving his tongue in around inside his mouth, probing the voids. 'Sorry, six,' he says. 'I've got six teeth missing.'

Julie has what she is after. A nine-digit number – 270641196 – into which she asks the lawyer to pay all of the money from all of her bank accounts. The lawyer is dumbfounded. He searches for but is unable to find any logical argument with which to challenge Julie's request. He notes that he would need to know the owner's name to pay money into the account but Julie says simply, 'You'll find out.' She continues, indicating that all of their shares, her house and car, all of her possessions, are to be sold and the money is to go into that same account. 'That's millions,' the lawyer says with disbelief.

CUT TO:

EXT. EIFFEL TOWER. AFTERNOON
A young woman sits bored inside a booth selling postcards. We can see her behind the glass. Her

only link to the outside world is a small hole in the glass through which customers make their requests and hand their money. People come and go and the young woman smiles thinly during the exchanges. When customers depart, the young woman's face appears suspended behind glass, overlaid with the reflection of the Eiffel Tower.

CUT TO:

INT. LOUNGE ROOM OF TINY PARIS FLAT. EARLY EVENING
A young man lies across a couch watching a television in a darkened room. A glowing white light illuminates his face. On the television screen, a man digs in the snow with a small, brightly coloured plastic scraper used to remove ice from the windshield of a car. The man buries a large black case full of money and sticks the ice-scraper into the snow to mark the spot.

A key is heard in a lock. The young man pauses the film and lifts his head to look toward the door. The door opens and the young woman from the ticket booth steps in. She slams the door and storms into the lounge room. She slaps the young man across the face as he rises from the lounge.

> YOUNG WOMAN
> (In English)
> What the fuck have you done?

> YOUNG MAN
> (Pleading, in French)
> What? What? What have I done?

> YOUNG WOMAN
> (In French also)
> You tell me.

Kieslowski's Unlikely Comedy

>   (Then in English)
> You fucking tell me what you've done!

>   YOUNG MAN
>   (Voice-over in French)
> I knew she was angry. She was speaking English again. She only ever swears in English. Never in French. Never. It is, after all, (he speaks now in English with an exaggerated French accent) the language of love.

>   YOUNG WOMAN
>   (In French again)
> Look at this.

She holds out a slip of paper.

>   YOUNG MAN
> What's this?

He looks at her confused.

>   YOUNG WOMAN
> This is our bank account.

He takes the slip of paper and reads the account number. He nods.

>   YOUNG MAN
>   (In French)
> It is. It is...

>   YOUNG WOMAN
>   (In French)
> But...

She gestures at the balance of the account.

Young man sees the balance. It is millions.

                    YOUNG MAN
                  (In English)
    Fuck!

CUT TO:

Piesiewicz looked up from the page. Kieslowski was sitting with an unlit cigarette between his lips. He was about to light the cigarette but, when he saw that Piesiewicz had stopped reading, Kieslowski leaned back into his chair and raised his eyebrows inquisitively.

'What the fuck is this?' Piesiewicz said loudly, drawing the attention of everyone in the cafe, less for what he'd said than the fact that he said it in English. In an instant people recognised Kieslowski and turned away.

'This is my new idea,' Kieslowski said, as though the term 'new idea' itself was somehow worthy of absolute trust. 'You know I hate being stuck in a drawer and labelled.'

Piesiewicz nodded slowly, considering.

'I know people consider me an – how do they put it – austere filmmaker?'

Piesiewicz nodded again with increasing certainty.

'Or, as one might say, *cold* and *controlling*.'

Piesiewicz laughed awkwardly and averted his eyes from meeting Kieslowski's own gaze.

'I have had reason to think again of how I would like to be remembered. When I was at the film school in Lodz,' Kieslowski said, 'we had privileges; access to films normal Poles could never imagine existed. Films from Western Europe. Asia. America. Last night I went back to the school to speak with students. To talk about my films and such. But when I arrived I was met by the head of the school who apologised for not contacting me earlier. He said that I would no longer be able to speak. Instead the school was holding a screening, a preview, of an American film. The head of the school apologised again and again, saying that he hoped I would be able to return some other time. He invited me then to stay and watch the film with the students and perhaps speak with the directors of the film.'

'More than one?'

'Two,' Kieslowski said. 'They were brothers.'
'What was the film?'
Kieslowski shook his head. 'I do not know what it was called. I went late into the theatre. I was outside with a young woman who also wished to smoke and we shared her cigarettes and some of my thoughts. When we got into the theatre the film was already going. It is to be released next month in America. There were no subtitles so we all had to rely on our own English and even though it was in English there was something difficult about the way the characters spoke. "Yah", they would say. "Yah. Yah."

'Anyhow, in this film a man has some kind of trouble with money and he plans to have his wife kidnapped. He will pay the kidnappers – I don't think he knows them; someone else he knows has assisted in the arrangement. Anyhow, his plan is that his wife's rich father would put up the money for ransom, more than the kidnappers are asking for, and the husband will deliver the money himself, paying the kidnappers some of it, but keeping the remainder for himself. But – this is American – so it all, how do they say? Turns to shit?

'So this film is not a comedy but it is very funny. People laughed at the most horrible things. One of the kidnappers feeds the other into a woodchipping machine and all of the surrounding snow is turned pink with blood.

'It was an unusual film. There is a shifting protagonist: at first it seems to be the car dealer then it seems to be the policewoman, and she is pregnant. And the criminals are not usual. One is big and seems all the time sleepy and the other one, the smaller one, is,' Kieslowski paused while he sought out the words, 'funny-looking.'

'In what way?'

'I don't know,' Kieslowski shrugged. 'Just funny-looking.'

'Can you be any more specific?'

Kieslowski shook his head. 'No,' he said. 'I couldn't really say. But,' Kieslowski went on, 'the thing that got me thinking is that at the end of the film there is a large sum of money left buried in the snow. It is a loose end just like the money in *Blue*. And it made me think of this scene.' Kieslowski gestured at the sheet of paper in front of Piesiewicz's hands. 'I couldn't help but wonder: what did happen to the money?'

Piesiewicz held up his hands. 'Nothing happened to the money.

There is no money. It is just a film. Fiction.'

'Maybe so,' Kieslowski said, 'but it is a loose end. I cannot believe we missed it. We did so much to tie up all of our loose ends from all of the films. At the end of *Red* we have all of the characters – Julie and Olivier, Karol and Dominique, August and Valentine – coming out of the water after the sinking of the ferry. There are no loose ends from the trilogy *except*—' Kieslowski held out his hands as though to wrap his arms around the logic he was following, 'the money?'

Piesiewicz shook his head and looked around the room as though he hoped to find a jury prepared to convict Kieslowski, or else to find himself the victim of an American-style comedic stunt. What do they call that television program? *Candid Camera*?

'This film,' Kieslowski declared, 'is the one I will be remembered for.' People in the cafe turned toward the noise again. He went on undaunted. 'I must make this film.'

'Why?' Piesiewicz asked, his voice carrying signs of exhaustion.

Kieslowski admitted that he was still seething at a review of *Blue*, the first film of the Three Colours trilogy. The review suggested that that particular film, more than any other of his earlier films, demonstrated the almost fatal humourlessness that would always limit Kieslowski's audience to people who themselves were unfeeling. Kieslowski wanted to now demonstrate, 'what Americans call "range". I want to show the full scope of my humanity: humour and,' Kieslowski struggled to articulate his meaning, 'humourlessness.'

Piesiewicz stared at Kieslowski as though he was trying to put a name to his face.

'I have seen the way people watch my films. Some people cry. Some show no expression at all. But no one laughs. No one!'

'That's because you do not make comedy films,' Piesiewicz said.

'But now I will,' Kieslowski insisted. 'I must.'

Piesiewicz shook his head.

'What?' Kieslowski shrugged. 'Even I have had enough of my own moral anxieties.'

Piesiewicz leaned right forward over the table. He began his right of reply. He reminded Kieslowski of his previous commitment to his art. 'You are a director who spent a week finding a sugar cube that would absorb coffee in seven seconds—'

Kieslowski's Unlikely Comedy

'Five.'

'What?'

'It was five seconds. For that shot of Julie to be right, the cube had to absorb coffee in five seconds.'

'Whatever, it doesn't matter.'

'It matters,' Kieslowski said. 'It does. It had to be five. That's as much—'

'I know, I know,' Piesiewicz said, holding his palms up for Kieslowski to stop right there. '"That's as much as the audience can tolerate in a single shot." I know that, I have heard that all before. That's not what I'm talking about. *That* doesn't matter right now. What matters is that the film you're thinking of will undoubtedly be the biggest mistake of your career.'

Kieslowski thumped his fist down on the table. 'I will make this film, even if it is the last one I make.'

'And I think if you do make this film,' Piesiewicz said, 'it will in fact be the last one you ever make.'

'Do you really think so?'

Piesiewicz looked across at his good friend. He thought about all of the work that they had already done together, all they still had planned to do, and everything Kieslowski was capable of.

Kieslowski's gaze dropped to the sheets of paper on the table. 'Really?' he asked again, less certain now.

Piesiewicz nodded. 'Yah.'

Three weeks after calling Piesiewicz to the cafe to tell him about his plans for his unlikely comedy, Kieslowski went in for surgery to repair heart disease resulting from decades of heavy smoking. Having declined the opportunity to have his surgery completed in any number of hospitals in Paris or New York, Kieslowski instead declared his confidence in his local Warsaw Hospital.

Kieslowski never came out of the anaesthesia. It was rumoured, though never confirmed, that staff were not familiar with newly imported equipment used in the operation. Simple errors of judgement may have been made.

The Coen brothers' *Fargo* was released in America on the eighth of March, five days before Kieslowski's death. A year later, *Dialog* magazine printed the script for *Heaven*, the first film in Kieslowski's planned new trilogy. The Coen brothers immediately pitched themselves as directors. They went to meet the producers, telling them how they had always wanted to work with Kieslowski and how they'd even discussed the possibility when they met him at the Lodz film school, where Kieslowski himself had studied. There they had an opportunity to ask him about why he was not able to attend the screening of his film *No End* at the New York Festival.

'I think it was 1984 or 1985,' Joel had said to Kieslowski with slow deliberation. 'My brother and I had tickets passed on to us by a friend with whom I had studied film at the New York University back in the seventies. Ethan and I had already seen—'

'—And liked,' Ethan added.

'Yes,' Joel went on, 'we had already seen and liked *Blind Chance* and we were hoping we might get an opportunity to work with you at some point.'

Kieslowski was pleased by their enthusiasm for his work.

'But you never made it to the screening of your own film,' Ethan added.

'No,' Kieslowski said. 'You are wrong. I was just late,' he said sheepishly, drawing heavily on his cigarette. 'But there is certainly a story behind that.'

Ethan fidgeted. 'So, what's the story?'

'Well I had every intention of attending. It was my first screening in New York. I was hurrying to get there. I took a taxi from my hotel. The streets were thick with cars. It was raining. My taxi went through Central Park and the taxi driver hit a cyclist.'

'No way,' Ethan said.

'It is true,' Kieslowski nodded. 'All true. It was dusk, almost dark. And the taxi hit the cyclist, who fell, and the taxi driver ran over the bike. He had nowhere to go; the road is narrow there and your cars in America are terribly big and wide. But he did get out to help the cyclist. I got out too. We tried to help the cyclist up but he was in too much pain. His leg was bleeding. Broken, probably. Cars started sounding their horns. You could see a mile of cars lined up behind us, their headlights rippling in the rain. It was an enormous river of cars.'

Joel laughed his deep-throated laugh.

'No way,' Ethan said.

'It gets worse,' Kieslowski said. 'I had to be at the Lincoln Center in about five minutes. We were almost there. I asked the driver how much further and in which direction and he pointed down the road ahead. So I gave him the money I owed him, more even, and began running through the rain. And you might already be thinking what happened next. The taxi drivers coming up in the opposite direction saw a taxi standing and a man running quickly away from it.'

The Coen brothers groaned with the realisation. 'No way,' Ethan said again.

Kieslowski nodded. 'Of course they did. They thought I'd maybe killed the driver or something. I was dressed in my suit. It was raining. I was going to be late and wet if I did not run. So I ran. But all of these taxis were stopping and these guys with baseball bats were jumping out so I ran away from them. They chased me through Central Park with these great big baseball bats. You know,' Kieslowski held his cigarette between his lips and gripped an imaginary bat, 'those huge, long sticks.'

'Yeah. Yeah,' Ethan said. 'We know baseball.'

'Yah. Yah,' Kieslowski said and they all laughed.

A young German director, Tom Twyker, was chosen to direct *Heaven*. Twyker's first film, *Run Lola Run*, bore some resemblance to Kieslowski's own *Blind Chance*, which had posed three possible outcomes for a young man running after a train. When they found out that they missed out on directing *Heaven*, the Coen brothers set about writing a script based on Kieslowski's life. Their film was to be called *So-So*. (The title was taken from Kieslowski's usual response to the question, 'How are you?' 'So-so,' he would respond with characteristic pessimism, indicating that he was, at least, still alive.)

Rumour has it, from those who have read the complete script or talked at length with the Coen brothers about the film, that it is likely to be the Coens' first and last film without any laughs. It, like Kieslowski's final trilogy, has a structure inspired by Dante's *Divine Comedy*. The three *canticas* – *Inferno* (Hell), *Purgatorio* (Purgatory), and *Paradiso* (Paradise) – which represent Kieslowski's three films, behave as the three acts of the Coen brothers' film. The film is to be narrated in a corrupted version of Dante's original terza rima with the Soviet director Andrei Tarkovsky, whom Kielsowski admired greatly, performing Virgil's role of leading Kieslowski through Hell and Purgatory. Juliette Binoche, playing Beatrice, Dante's ideal woman, would lead Kieslowski through Heaven. The film ends with Kieslowski's death:

```
100.INT. OPERATING THEATRE. WARSAW HOSPITAL
In a brightly lit, white-tiled room, half a
dozen theatre staff in dark green gowns stand
at the head of an operating table. Behind them
a piece of equipment continues to alarm and, on
the floor, in the corner of the frame, an elec-
trical cord from another, newer machine, lies
unplugged. The lead was inadvertently pulled
free of the socket by a theatre nurse whose
younger, idealistic sister had, weeks before,
shared cigarettes with Kieslowski at the Lodz
film school [66] and then called her older sister
after midnight to tell her about it [67].

              JULIETTE BINOCHE
          (Voice-over in English)
   They stand about like gridlocked cars,
   caught there in some foreign land

The theatre staff are gathered around a manual
and it is clear that they are struggling to
make sense of it. Someone reaches out to turn
off the alarming machine. On the table a man
lies with his chest cut open. One of the nurses
breaks away from the group and stands alongside
the body. [In 67, the nurse's younger sister
has described Kieslowski as 'a warm and funny
man at heart', but the nurse did not share her
younger sister's enthusiasm. 'Kieslowski's films
leave me cold,' the elder sister had said that
night. 'I do not imagine that man has any kind
of heart.']
```

                    JULIETTE BINOCHE
                 (Voice-over in English)
           Until a lone woman moves to the body,
           touches a hand, finds it still warm
           and therein sensing the tragedy,

The nurse leans over and looks into the open
chest of the man on the table.

                    JULIETTE BINOCHE
                 (Voice-over in English)
           Seeks out the heart of a man, finds it there, still
           and as deeply moving, as unfathomable,
           as profound and immeasurable

           As a whole galaxy of distant stars

CLOSE-UP ON black, shining pupil of nurse. FIND
Kieslowski's face. The lids of his eyes are
taped shut and a tube runs from his mouth. HOLD
for one... two... three... four...

FADE TO BLACK

Disclaimer
With thanks and apologies to the Coen brothers, who never pitched themselves as replacement directors for Kieslowski's new trilogy nor wrote a screenplay based on the life of Kieslowski, to author's knowledge. The rest of this story is an imaginary account of an actual director (and his staunch collaborator Krzysztof Piesiewicz) who did direct the Three Colours trilogy and went some way to developing a new trilogy inspired by Dante's *Divine Comedy* before his untimely death.

A Dark Place

Brendan Ryan

Utes prowl the flatlands, high-beaming
piles of trees ready for burn-off.
Our spotties sweep ahead reclaiming the night
the darkness shadowed by wind.

We head into a paddock where the roos congregate
or so the stories suggest. We drink,
twitch at the glow of eyes scurrying away from the sights
tense at a heavier shadow bounding away
to the right. A 30/30 is loaded.
The driver flattens it
until we are surfing branches and rocks,
steadying our stubbies as the mob dives to the left.
One falls and we pull up.
Someone walks over to a Joey, blasts it.
I empty my .270 into a big Grey, yet he remains there
shaking his head, as if asking what are you doing?
With a guttural moan, he falls.
The pelt still warm, the vacant eyes,
I'm earning my keep with the stories that flow
long into the night. There is a quota
that must be observed, acknowledged
like peppering a red gum with a machine gun,
or watching the white posts merge
doing the ton. Somebody hands me a beer
and the tension between us becomes folklore,
a place from where nicknames are created.

There's another mob caught out near a boundary fence.
Our spotties frame them leaping head-first
into the wire mesh, again and again.

We Must Catch Up

Virginia Peters

I used to take a shortcut through this very road a few years ago when we lived in a little flat at the bay. I liked the semi-detached cottages, the way each half was finished in distinctly different colours despite being joined at the hip. I'd always look out for the clinic, slowed to observe its pillared entrance and the brooding pines that concealed it from the outside world. Back then, I thought a quiet street a strange location for such a place, although it makes perfect sense to me now. It belonged here, extending deep into the suburban block like an internal organ. 'The Fern Clinic, by appointment only', reads the small brass plaque as we bump over the metal grill.

We drive through a cavalcade of trees before coming into the light, lawn on either side, cut so short it resembles an undulating sea; and the car is a boat, its low vibration as we ride over the thick tar makes me feel seasick.

I lean my forehead against the cool glass and see my reflection in the side mirror. My face looks long. Long-ger. Not just an illusion, I think. It's all to do with the verb that underpins the human jaw, hinges it shut, tongue pressed flat to the palate. It's the French verb: to be. I am having trouble with my sense of being.

We arrive at a long, low building, blond brick. Park beneath a white structure that resembles the wingspan of an albatross. Seventies architecture. He looks at me before he opens his door to get out, and sighs as I look away.

I stand next to the boot, stilled by the drone of cicadas as he removes my case, my hands loose at my sides.

In reception it's cool. The walls are green. They tell him to wait while they take me straight through. I wasn't expecting it to be that quick. He rubs my back.

'Love you,' he says as I turn my head away, and I feel his kiss slide off my hair.

I walk with the nurse along a wide linoleum corridor.

'It reminds me of a maternity suite,' I tell her.

'Yes. I suppose it is a bit like that, isn't it,' she says, with matronly jolliness. I notice she walks lopsided with my case.

When we arrive at door 14, she says, 'This is you. You're in here with Sarah.'

Sarah?

'But, my husband booked me a private room.'

'Our private rooms are full,' she says, and as the door opens wide, a pool of sunlight spills into the corridor to claim me.

'Our Sarah's from South Africa, aren't you Sarah?'

I can see a blonde head sitting in an armchair by the window. The face looks up and smiles, gums pink and wet. They remind me of the false teeth you buy in joke shops.

Barely audible, I tell the nurse I want my own room.

'You'll be fine here. Sarah's quiet. She likes to read. You like to read too, don't you? A little bird told me you read the dictionary.'

It's true, but the little bird makes it sound ridiculous. My face prickles with heat.

'I don't read the dictionary,' I say. 'I study words.'

If I was to pinpoint a moment where it all began, I suppose it was at the park at the top of Prospect Road. I could so easily revere the moment I met her, with rambling paragraphs. But I must convey the normality.

We were pushing our children on the swings. It's hard to remain aloof when you're pushing a swing. I wanted to leave when she came and stood next to me. But Cynthia – knowing her as I do now – was aroused by the soft light of early spring, the scent of freshly mown grass. She would have been thinking, *Oh, isn't this just a lovely afternoon for making friends.*

As we pushed, we surged forward like a chorus line engaging in a dance step.

'I'm Cynthia by the way,' she said, with a wry smile, as though she too was noting the silliness of our movements.

She offered me her hand as the swings careered away from us. It was a soft, dry hand, and it surprised me with its strength.

'I live just up the road from you. Five doors up to be exact.' I looked at her closely. She had small onyx eyes, a lean face atop her elongated frame, and on her feet she wore pumps, long and white like a rabbit's hind legs.

'My daughter goes to the same school as your kids,' she said. 'You're new to the area aren't you? And you've got test paints around your front door.' She winked. 'I've been watching you.'

She grinned, for I must have looked astonished. Then I was reminded, guiltily, I was the type that never noticed anyone – but she didn't seem to care, for now she was telling me with wide eyes that I had an absolute eye for colour. I had a consultant choose my colour combinations, but instead of correcting her, I let a smile spread over my face.

I suppose if there was anything that should have put me on guard, it was in what she said next.

'What does your husband do?' A calculated question, so invalidating, yet at the same time, sadly enticing. So I told her what he did. She looked suitably pleased. And in the silence that followed, I gently queried, 'So what does yours do?'

She rolled her eyes as she answered, as though his success pained her, and she smiled knowingly at me, as though we were both in on the same joke.

> *__identity__ n. 1. the fact of being who or what a person or thing is > the characteristics determining this (whether they be yours or your husband's).

The psychologist's name is Ruth. If I could smell the name Ruth it would have the heavy odour of dark soil. No one tells you about social typecasting, I tell her; you just feel it, recoil from it and before you know it you become invisible with it. We spent all our time snootily ignoring one another, only to discover our exciting similarities in serendipitous chance meetings.

Cynthia had tulip shapes cut into the palings of her picket fence.

Her ironing board was sitting out on display like a piece of fifties art, a pile of glaring whites piled on one end in a plastic washing basket.

She had a large play centre in her backyard in hideous orange and yellow, and it looked particularly ugly beneath the beautiful old lemon tree. My youngest was inside this plastic contraption, sucking a red ice block.

'To keep her quiet,' she said with a wink.

I remember thinking there was something almost too wholesome in the chunkiness of her furniture, the dogged reappearance of tulips on her leadlight kitchen cupboards. I could easily imagine her lank front covered in the red checks of an apron.

Then I saw *The Sydney Morning Herald* spread out on the dining table.

'Do you get the paper delivered?' I asked.

She nodded. 'Can't live without it.'

'Neither can I,' I flung back, as though this was a bizarre coincidence.

She intimated another coffee with her cup, and as she went into the kitchen to make it, she kept talking, throwing her voice. I liked her tone; it was intelligent, opinionated. I found myself rubbing my chin, carefully composing my responses. We were enjoying ourselves so much; morning tea moved smoothly into lunch, our conversation slowing as we chewed on baguette.

Cynthia explained she was just a country girl and had followed a rather set path to being a schoolteacher. I made a little sound in an attempt to convey 'that's interesting', but she shrugged it off. Changed the subject to me.

I told her I'd wandered between jobs: trainee chef, bank teller and so forth, so forth, but I emphasised my last position as an assistant to a producer on a radio station – I felt as though that sounded the most interesting.

'You've had a much more exciting life than me,' she said, and I laughed this off, insisting I hadn't at all, but at the same time I believed she was right. I could see myself from her perspective, as someone less constrained, more open to possibilities. Her path had been rigid compared to my more serendipitous one. Cynthia had never left the classroom, except to marry, and I suspected that made me more worldly.

'We can hardly complain, can we?' I heard her saying, smiling in a way that revealed her narrow eyeteeth. 'Look. I just don't care what anyone else says. We're living in the most beautiful area of Sydney,' she said with a flourishing hand, 'we're married to men that love us' (that's an assumption, I thought, seeing as she was yet to meet mine) 'and I've been blessed with one child, and my God, you've got three.' She leaned across to rub my knee. 'How do you do it?'

I frowned. 'I don't really think about it, I guess. My kids have been incredibly easy.'

She shook her head as though I was underrating myself. 'Well, I think you're amazing.'

I smiled dubiously.

She came closer, tilting her head. 'I wanted more children,' I heard her say, 'but it hasn't happened.'

I wanted to reach out, touch her knee too, but it wasn't my way.

'I know I should be thinking about going back to work now. But I can't.' She went on: 'I just can't bring myself to do it – I love being a mother.'

I clenched my lips, resisted the dismissive cliché: it'll happen.

Walking down her hall that afternoon, she touched her palm to my back.

'It's so important we get to know each other.' She said it in a way that wrapped me in an aura of possibilities. It was as though she had a plan in mind – for us. I didn't. I just had a nice feeling that Cynthia liked me a lot, and I liked her, and although it seemed like an odd word to use, I also had a sense we were looking at each other with respect – it was something I hadn't felt in a long time.

> ***respect** n. a feeling of deep admiration for someone elicited by their qualities or achievements. Origin: Latin. *respectus*, from *respicere*: look back at, regard. We were two halves looking to feel whole.

On the third day my muscles ache from lack of use and I find myself wandering across the corridor to a door marked 'Lounge'. In here, I find a squat woman knitting in a tub chair. Her needles make a soft clack, and I cock my head to listen, finding it strange the way her elbows wriggle at her sides like stumps.

It was the same week I'd met Cynthia. A Friday. I'd been in the city and was running late by the time I arrived at the school. As I pulled up outside, I saw that the space where the children should have been was empty, a bubble almost filmy with translucency.

The woman with the Mediterranean accent in after-school care stood rubbing the skin stretched over her knuckles.

'I can't think, I just can't think what has happened,' she said. 'Maybe someone else collected them.'

'No,' I told her. 'Not possible. My husband is at work and there is no one else with any authority.'

'I cannot understand it. I cannot,' and her nails scratched through her hair. She would go to the office, she said, and talk with the supervisor about the procedure. Procedure was not a comforting word.

I ran to the children's toilets, flung open the doors, one after the other as though I expected to find their little bodies slumped in the far corners of a cubicle. Up the stairs, I checked another six or so toilets.

Coming back down, I saw the Mediterranean woman loping across the basketball court, a forearm clamped across her chest. Now I was jogging towards her, and a whirly of wind wrapped around us, wrenching at our clothes.

'Good news,' she breathed, her hands falling upon my shoulders. 'Mrs Martin has your children.'

'Who?'

'Mrs Martin.'

'Who's Mrs Martin?' I asked, shaking my head. 'I've never heard of her.'

Cynthia Martin stood on her doorstep. 'Look at you,' she said, with rueful affection. 'You look like you've been in the wars.'

'Oh, I'm alright.' I tried to smile. 'Hey, thanks for picking them up.' My lip trembled.

'Oh come here,' she crooned. I noticed the wash of red climbing up her neck as she stepped down onto the verandah. She put an arm around me and squeezed me to her. 'Next time, ring me,' she admonished. 'You know I'm here. Always,' she said, leading me inside. 'Nothing is ever too much trouble.'

I wanted to believe her. I wanted to believe I'd just been saved, not thwarted. It's all to do with perspective, I told myself, as I walked down Cynthia's oriental hall runner, past the hat stand, the row of decorative plates, botanical prints in crackled gold frames. In the family room I found my children sitting on an oversized sofa in front of a disproportionately large TV.

'Look who's here, children,' said Cynthia, in a contrived announcement. 'It's Mummy. Aren't you going to say hullo to Mummy?'

The volume of the TV was deafening, I reasoned, when they didn't bother to look up. Their eyes were glued to the set and their hands were rustling in fist-sized packets of biscuits – the sort of product I'd never buy.

'Come on,' she said, winking at me as her fingers gripped my arm. 'They're fine. And I know just what you need, my dear girl. An early drink.'

I smiled, weakly. 'Actually. You know. That's probably just what I need.'

*rely v. 1. depend on with full trust 2. be dependent on. Origin: Latin. *religare* from re-(expressing intense force) + *ligare*- 'bind'. Rely on me. Rely on me.

I was not aware of the Latin meaning of 'rely' at the time, but nonetheless I could feel its archaic root binding my arms to my sides as I followed her into the kitchen.

Ruth and I talk about marriage. It really is an institution. I tell her I didn't know I was about to be institutionalised. Like words, marriage has its own origins; it is root-bound and full of hidden meanings.

There's always something odd about meeting a friend's partner for the first time. I couldn't help but imagine them together, and my head became a light box of flickering images of intimacy. They didn't match. He had red hair and was at least half a head shorter with cheeky-boy freckles' and ears that looked too large and naked for his small face; with her towering over him he resembled a son more than a husband. I watched the way she moved around him – too carefully – blushing with her own stealth as she stooped to kiss his cheek, her long arm passing around his back like a serpent proffering a bottle of beer.

She introduced me to him as a future Australian author.

'Oh, please Cynthia. Don't.'

'Well I believe in you, even if you don't,' she said. 'She's very,

very clever,' she told him, 'but far too modest.'

The fact was, Cynthia had never read anything I'd written.

'She's exaggerating,' I told him, blushing. 'I'm just doing a course by correspondence. Postmodern Literature.'

'Well, good on you,' he said, with thorough admiration, then as an afterthought he added: 'Cynthia needs to do something like that.' I looked across to see if she'd heard him.

She hadn't. She was calling out, 'She's writing a book,' grinning at me as she poured wine into two cut-crystal glasses. 'I'm going to be her agent.'

It was the first I'd heard. I frowned a modest smile, and pondered on whether she had some sort of intuitive skill, a unique ability in divining talent that enabled her to see right through me to where my potential lay dormant, like a buried spring.

Later she told me her husband was very clever.

'But we just play along with them, don't we?' she said, her eyes conspiring with humour.

'We do,' I said, hoping I appeared just as complicit, but I suspected she was passive, completely in awe of her man. Perhaps even a little afraid of him, as I was of mine.

>*fear n. 1. an unpleasant emotion caused by threat or danger.
>Origin: OE *foer* 'danger', also 'revere' of Gmc origin.
>*revere v. 1. respect or admire deeply, from *veveri* 'to fear'.

The meanings are innate.

Well of course, I tell Ruth, we wanted our men to be clever, to do their best, we even wanted to fear them – anything less would have spoiled our illusions. And when our dependency became unbearable, cynicism was the best defence, followed by a flurry of guilty laughter.

Ruth lifts her eyebrow. 'Who are *we*?' she asks.

I look up, surprised. 'I'm speaking generically, of course.'

We were off to the town hall for the choral performance of Handel's *Messiah*. The four of us. We'd already had a couple of dinners together and this event signalled a change – Let's not just eat, let's do things!

Cynthia and her husband had been amused by our invitation. I suspect they thought a choral performance was stuffy and highbrow – we all did; and perhaps it's why we were suddenly very giddy when we saw each other in our very cultured, evening attire.

We sat together at the performance, between our husbands, on upright chairs like schoolgirls, giving each other sideways looks. On one occasion as the choir reached a crescendo, Cynthia closed her eyes and threw her head back and pretended to howl like a dog at the full moon, and then she winked at me. I was convulsing with silent laughter as she reached across and squeezed my hand, tight, to help me control myself. Then she left it there for a while on my lap, in a loose clasp. I was delirious with good fortune.

That night we walked the streets in pairs, all the way down to The Rocks. We could have caught a cab, but we felt like wandering, for it was a still night and after such haunting strains we needed the stars above us. It was nice to know the men followed behind us, their hands dug into their pants, a blazer flung over a shoulder, low chuckles; Cynthia and I in front, clip-clopping in our heels like mares. We stepped in rhythm, a contented sway in our lean hips. Then Cynthia hooked my arm in hers and pulled me closer. I did not resist, so she twisted her hand, and picking up mine, she linked our fingers together.

I laughed, and I said, 'People might wonder.'

'Let them,' she said.

I felt strange. I wanted to feel comfortable, but I couldn't, for my heart was beating ridiculously fast, and I was afraid my hand would begin to perspire.

'Are you okay?' she asked.

'I'm fine.'

'Guess what?' she said, leaning towards my cheek.

'What?' I asked, and she dipped her head even closer so that I could feel her breath hot in my ear.

'You look so beautiful in that dress.'

'Don't be stupid.'

'You do, you do,' and her 'do' growled against my cheek. Now I could feel each fine bone in her hand squeeze, clutching my bones between hers as she pulled me even closer. My face radiated a bright heat. It felt shameful. I had to put my head down as her eyes glanced across my face.

'You two a coupla lesos up there?' It was my husband calling out from behind.

'Too right we are.' Cynthia hollered. I saw a wink in the corner of my own eye, but it was her eye winking. Not mine. Wink wink…

*flatter v 1. lavish compliments on, especially in order to further one's own interests. Origin: ME from OFr. *flaterie*, from *flater* (stroke, flatter).

That night in bed – *You look beautiful in that dress. You look beautiful in that dress* – her words were floating in and out, piping softly with my breath, and I wondered if she was right, that perhaps I was beautiful and had lived all these years in complete ignorance.

One of the women explains she has a lithium deficiency, 'a clinical condition, not a personality disorder'. She makes 'clinical' sound bright and clean. 'Disorder', like an excuse – nothing more than a failure to keep things tidy.

'Well I'm just having a rest,' I tell her, making it sound as though I'd weighed up the clinic against a deckchair vacation in Fiji.

It was our ritual. Friday night. The oven on high, in a yellow kitchen light we basked in the warmth, throwing back wine while the children quietly watched re-runs of their favourite videos.

Cynthia crossed her legs and talked with her hands, using old-fashioned phrases such as 'waxing lyrical' and 'God love y'or!'

'I don't know what I'd do without you,' she said one night during a pause in conversation.

'Wow. That's the loveliest thing anyone has ever said to me,' I told her, feeling a tear bead in my eye.

She smiled warmly, put her hand on top of mine and feathered her fingers.

'I have to get back,' I groaned. 'He won't know where I am.'

'He'll survive.' She folded her arms, sat firm against the back of the kitchen chair. 'Let him manage on his own for five minutes. It'll do him good,' she said in a flat voice. 'They can be such selfish pricks, can't they?'

She grinned at my surprise.

I told her I still had dinner to cook yet. He'd be hungry. He'd be tired. So we bailed out the door, but somehow we ended up sitting again, on the steps this time, murmuring just beyond the halo of the streetlight, the children running relays up and down the pavement, racing against the sigh of the cars returning from the city.

'Look at them,' she said. 'Isn't it wonderful? These are probably the best days of our lives. Never go away, will you? Or if you do – please take me with you.'

I shivered as I made my promise to her, that I'd never leave her, and she pulled me to her, rubbed my arm as though I'd said I was cold, and it was then that the sweeping arc of a car came to land at the darkened kerb like a spaceship. Her husband's return.

The moment was extinguished with a sigh, and as I walked back up the road I wondered where it would all end. We were technically married to men, but emotionally, we were committed to each other. Did it have to end? Of course it didn't. It wasn't a love affair. There was no reason why she wouldn't be there forever.

> ***forever** adj. 1. for all future time – a very long time (used hyperbolically). Everything was hyperbolic, heightened, dramatised for maximum effect.

I'm beginning to enjoy myself here. I've started to take my meals in the main dining room with my room mate.

Today there is a new guest. She is dark skinned with glossy black hair, so long and thick it resembles the seaweed that washes up on the sand after a deep ocean storm. I'm immediately steeped in a hazy memory, a sort of briny vapour coming off a wide Sargasso Sea.

Cynthia picked up my three children now since my youngest started at school, mornings and afternoons. She was going past anyway – she might as well, she said.

'But I can do some runs. It's not fair on you,' I'd said.

'Pointless,' she insisted. She had to go anyway.

Cynthia was on several of the school committees, and she was also a volunteer on the school reading program. I had noticed she thrived on responsibility; still, it just didn't seem right that she do so much for me.

'Think of me as your benefactor. A benevolent supporter of the arts,' she said, as we sat at my kitchen table.

It was disorientating. I was beginning to feel I'd lost my bearings, and I complained the only way I knew how. 'Cynthia, my writing is just a folly. A hobby at best. I'm really not even any good,' I told her.

She turned her head slightly so that the whites of her eyes looked sharp. 'I know where that comes from,' she said.

I drew my chin in, and she took up the slack, leaning in to point her finger at me.

'Don't you let him tell you that. They'll take all your power if you let them, and you'll end up a shell. Sapped. Doing everything to please and nothing for yourself.' Her face was flush with blood and her eyebrows stood up like prickles. She clunked her mug down on the tabletop, took a breath and sighed it out her nose.

'I just don't want to see you undermined,' she said, almost wearily now.

'But he doesn't undermine me. At least, I don't think he does.'

She reached across and stroked my hand. 'No, I'm sure he doesn't,' she said, as though regretting any inference. I felt better on this familiar territory, and she looked at me warmly. 'I'm sure he really wants the best for you.'

I knew what that meant. It meant she wanted the best for me. My darling friend, she really cared for me, and for such little return. I could have leaned across and kissed her, right then.

I stopped going to the school. I can't say I missed the traffic snarl, or the stressful search for a park. Before long I'd even stopped reading the screwed-up newsletters and notes that came home in the children's bags. Cynthia filled me in on the details of what was happening, and I listened, with only half an ear. She found my poor recollection of details very amusing.

'One of the hazards of the artistic temperament,' she said, shaking her head.

Or, 'Nothing for you to worry about, toots.'

'Where's your purse? I'll take the money out for you.'

Or, 'Sign here,' handing me a pen.

'But what's it for, Cynth?' I'd ask.

'You're such a ditz,' she'd say, mussing my hair with the palm of her hand.

My head was filled with other things. Murder, sexual assault, infidelity, infanticide, all plot points for fiction that fast became dead ends as the fridge droned and the dryer tumbled and the clock ticked silently.

I would hear the children coming up the steps each afternoon, see their shadows through the stained glass of the front door – like little ghosts. Feel the sudden impact of them, a gale force funnelling down the hall, their hands greedily clutching treats – things I'd never buy them, expensive chocolate-coated ice-creams and bags of chips. Cynthia behind them, wearing an incorrigible grin, long legs in black, as sharp as shears scissoring down the hall, gold bracelets and silver keys jangling with life.

'You're only a child once,' she'd say, apologising for the treats.

'I suppose,' and I'd give her a rueful smile.

She began making her purchases in twos, because, 'well, I thought I may as well, while I was there.' A new cookbook for me, a bamboo steamer from Chinatown, a G-string, for a joke, because get with it! No one wore undies anymore.

I told him about the underwear.

'She fancies you,' he said.

'That's absurd.'

'I'm telling you, she does.'

I grinned. 'Do you really think so? I've never thought of that before.'

'Oh come on. Isn't it half obvious?'

Was it? I began to think.

I couldn't resist the way she'd call and say, 'It's me!'

'Hullo me,' I'd say. 'How am I today?'

She was just popping into Woolies or stopping at the park on her way home from school. Was it okay if she took my kids with her? Did I need her to pick something up for our dinner?

'Oh God, you're so good to me,' I'd sigh. 'What would I do without you?'

***depend** v. intransitive. to hang; to be sustained by; to rely on; to be contingent on; (law) to be awaiting final judgement.

'Of course I realised what was happening, Ruth. That's what made it so hard. I was powerless.'

The house was becoming a mess. A pigsty, he called it.

'There's more to life than keeping surfaces tidy.'

'But you have to have some semblance of order.'

'Order.' I slapped my knife down on the steel bench and swung round, diced carrot falling on the floor like polka dots. 'You're trying to suck the life out of me. I know it. I know exactly what you're trying to do.'

'What the hell's got into you? You're mad.'

'You're right. I'm mad as hell.'

'You've lost the plot,' he said with disgust.

'Plot? You're right,' I told him. 'My life has no plot. You try doing this. Day after day. Nothing happens. I've lost all sense of meaning.'

'You have no idea how lucky you are.' His voice was scathing.

The next morning I caught the scent of Cynthia in my kitchen, and as I turned, felt the coolness of her moisturised skin as she pressed her cheek against mine.

'How are you, me,' she said.

'I'm okay,' I whispered in her ear.

'No you're not,' she whispered back. 'You're not okay.'

She came back after she'd dropped the kids at school. She brought me roses. Orange and yellow ones wrapped in white tissue. A burst of held-back tears and breath broke free as I put them to my nose, and she took the roses from me and held me in her arms.

'I'm wetting your shoulder,' I told her as she rubbed my back, saying it didn't matter.

We sat down at the kitchen table. She'd brought takeaway coffee, and I watched her lift a cup from the carry carton and hand it to me. We sat quietly for a while, almost shyly, sucking coffee through the plastic slots.

'You're not coping,' she said after a while.

'Is it that obvious?'

'Yes. It is,' she said. She pulled her lips across her teeth, and my eyes followed her as she got to her feet.

'Now, I'm going to clean up these breakfast things while you hop in the shower,' she said, looking down at me, her hands on her hips.

'But I don't feel like a shower.'

'Well, you need one. Now come on.' She turned on the sink tap and there was the sound of water beating against steel.

She was just finishing off my bed when I came out of the shower, turning back the cover so that it opened up like a white envelope.

'Righto,' she said. 'I've done all I can here.' She put her hands on her hips again, and breathed, 'How do you feel?'

'A little bit better,' I said, to please her. 'What's wrong with me, Cynth?'

'I think you're depressed. And I don't care what anyone says,' she said, stopping to stem a tear on my cheek with her little finger, 'but I really think it's high time you got some professional help. Oh don't look so crumpled. There's absolutely nothing to be ashamed of. It happens to the best of people.' She put her hand on my shoulder, her cool thumb moving back and forth over my bare skin. 'There's a clinic not far from here,' I heard her say, almost under her breath.

She pulled me to her. Shushing me. 'It's a good thing. It's a good thing. They'll help. I know other women who've been there and I know how good it will be for you. Here now,' she said, 'into bed.' And as she pulled away, my towel dropped. Ignoring my nakedness, like a nurse, she patted the mattress. 'Hop in. I've brought you a little sleeping pill. You'll feel better after a rest.'

'Oh God, Cynthia. A pill?'

'It's fine. You'll thank me for it. I promise you.'

She pulled back the cover, and feeling all the more pathetic in my nudity, I cowered and climbed into the opening she'd made.

I shrugged into the sheets, and when I'd settled, she sat down next to me and kissed my forehead.

'I'm just going to get you a glass of water. Okay?'

'Cynth?'

She stopped to look down, smiling at me gently.

'I feel terrible that I've never told you this before. I've been so… self-absorbed, but I want you to know—'

'Shhh. I know what you're going to say,' she said, stroking my hair. 'I know. You don't have to say it. I can feel it.'

***love** n. 1. an intense feeling of deep affection – a deep or romantic attachment to someone – a great interest or pleasure in something. Origin: Old English *lufu* of Germanic origin; related to leave (2).

*__leave__ (2) n. time when someone has permission to be absent from work or duty.

It seems the meanings of love and leave are quite synonymous. How fickle even words are.

I'm told he's waiting for me in the clinic's family room. Singular. I can't believe he's not brought the children.

Sitting before him on the edge of my chair, he tells me he didn't think it was wise for them to see me in here.

'It's not as though we're walking around in circles banging our foreheads,' I say. His smile is weak.

'Has anyone asked after me? Has anyone called?' And I watch his lip curl, exposing his teeth.

I rang Cynthia that afternoon to tell her I'd had a lovely sleep. I called her place several times, but all I got was her warm recorded voice telling me to leave my number and she'd get back as soon as she could. I rang the next day as well. This time I left a worried message – 'What's happened to you? I'm worried sick.' And the next, 'If you're not there Cynthia, could someone just please get back to me.' Other times I called and hung up before the message bank picked up.

The children didn't go to school that week. We didn't even leave the house. They watched videos while I dozed on and off, tried to read, but couldn't. I fed them the remains of the groceries in the fridge. Things like packaged pancakes spread with Vegemite, dry cornflakes mixed with peanut butter for lunch. We didn't shower. My five o'clock drink shifted to four o'clock, then I stopped bothering to check the time, and just poured a drink when a cloud, dull enough, passed over the house.

'Are these children going to school?' he asked me on the fourth day.

He called it a dereliction of duties. Selfish, deliberate. He was probably right, but knowing it only made things worse.

I had to see her. I would see her, and everything that had built up would melt away. Paranoia. Illusion. It was all in my head. We'd laugh tears of relief for what could only be a terrible misunderstanding.

I could see her shape through the coloured leadlight. I heard the click of her front door unlock.

'It's just me.' I waited for her to say *Hi me*. She didn't. Through the bars of the security grille I could see there were tiny pockets beneath the corners of her mouth.

'This is for you,' I said. 'It's a maidenhair fern.'

'Oh,' she said, and she opened the grille, and as the plant passed between us, the lobes shivered as though alive with nerves.

'I had an extra one and I thought—'

'Thanks. I'm sure we'll find a place for it.' Her friendly tone was automated, like her phone message.

'They wither really easily, so you've got to keep it indoors. And you've got to water them a lot. Regularly... but not too much.' I stopped, took a breath, for my voice had lost its wind; all that was left, a faint whisper, 'Can I come in?'

She jerked her head, indicating over her shoulder.

Code for something. I leaned in, eager to understand.

'I've got someone here,' she said under her breath, and I saw her blush.

Looking down the hall, as my eyes adjusted to the light, I distinguished long bare legs crossed over a barstool, blonde hair, the reflective chink of light caught on the curve of a wine glass.

'I'm sorry,' I said, pathetically.

'Don't be. It's okay. Really.' There was a touch of reassurance, and I grasped it like a twig.

'Is there anything wrong, Cynthia? Between us?'

'No.' Her brow puckered. 'Everything is fine,' and then as though she'd suddenly remembered the other day, she reached out and gripped my forearm. 'How have you been? I've been worried about you.'

'Okay,' I said, and I tried to smile.

She frowned. 'Look, I'm really sorry but I've got to get back. I'll call you, okay? Promise. You take care of yourself.' She nodded, anxiously.

And I nodded back, as though I believed her.

That afternoon I called my husband. I described what had happened, and I asked him what he thought.

'Oh look, I really don't have time for this. You do realise I'm under enormous pressure. And you're ringing and telling me about some blonde at bloody Cynthia's. She's a silly cow. Get over it.'

I hung up. I went upstairs and I looked out over the rooftops, over the orange tiles, the occasional mossy grey, row upon row; they reminded me of half-open books absorbing tales of family life. I could just see hers, the ridge of capping, the weathercock towards the street, the TV aerial at the back above the upstairs verandah and the parents' retreat. It looked so normal from here, nothing amiss. I could even see the top of the old lemon tree. I climbed out onto the sill. We were two storeys high. I imagined if I jumped, I'd break a bone at best.

> *estrange v. 1. cause to feel less close or friendly; alienate. Origin: C15 OFr. *estranger*, from Latin *extraneare* 'treat as a stranger'– from Latin *extraneus*-irrelevant. An abbreviation of estrange is strange.
>
> *strange adj. indefinably unwell.

'Three years together. It was bound to feel like a death,' I tell Ruth. The strange thing was there was no discernible end, unless a subtle facial expression can be counted as a last breath.

Finally he comes for me, and we drive away, our tyres peeling off the warm bitumen, the pleasing drape of lawn on either side gently squeezing us out like a pip.

We left the school. I hear Cynthia heads the P&C now. She's still with the blonde, an ex-air hostess apparently, with three children and another on the way. Cynthia will have her hands full there.

It's lonely without her, but I have a lot to thank her for. I have found my power in meaning. I take one word a day – like a pill – it calms me, grounds me in its roots.

Occasionally I bump into her, but only in the freezer section at Woolworths, quite coincidentally. We're savvy smilers, although I know we both sense the duck and weave of our eyes. On occasion we've forgotten ourselves and have glanced each other's cheek; we stand there, arms crossed, shivering with the buzz of the fridge freezers, blaming the brisk temperature for our need to depart hastily. The parting mantra, always – we must catch up. Yes, we really must catch up.

Panic in Year Zero

Vinnie Wilhelm

I'm alphabetising my mother's kitchen implements again (chafing dish, colander, decanter, egg slicer, egg timer, garlic press) when David calls from New York City. 'What are you doing?' he asks.

'Writing.'

David is walking down West Twelfth Street in the sun, carried along on the beauteous tide of fashion models in dark lipstick. Standing alone in a windowless room in Seattle, I can imagine the scene. He's off to meet Sidney, who will be grinning like a railroad tycoon through the blue haze of a $20 cigar, thinking poetically of capitalism, renewable energy, and the world to come. The two of them have just launched a consulting outfit that specialises in green development. They're planning their entry for an architecture competition soliciting ideas for blight removal and redevelopment in the decimated ghettos of Philadelphia. 'The key is sustainability,' David says. 'Sustainability is the linchpin of our plan.' In his black-frame glasses and Italian pants, he is smiling at the finely-ankled women of Greenwich Village, offering with his eyes to buy each of them a microbrew.

But I am thinking about Philadelphia. When I lived there I was twenty-two and made strange by the long sweep of my life stretching out before me like an endless story about nothing your uncle tells you on Thanksgiving when you're just trying to watch some football on TV. That gloomy fall of low-slung clouds in Philadelphia in the year 2000 I was rooming with a short sculptor, a man less than five feet tall. The two of us rented a third-floor apartment on Fabric Row, amid the cloth shops and carpet dealers of South Fourth Street, the outdated milliners and third-generation drapers, where at night a few thin young whores would sometimes wander through, checking their hair in the mirrors of the cars along the kerb, snapping at great wads of bubble gum.

On Friday evenings my room mate and I would usually drive out into the wastes of West Philly to see a lady friend he had over that way. Her name was Regina and she was an actual midget, whereas my room mate was just very short. Regina lived with her mother, who was of a normal size, and their basset hound in a crumbling row house on Fifty-Eighth Street – not far from where Wilt Chamberlain had grown up, as Regina's mother liked to point out. Their money came from alimony and I don't think either one of them went down to the street very often. Regina's father had taken off for Florida when he saw he had a midget daughter and made quite a fortune down there by fixing up a paddle-wheel steamboat and running dinner cruises along the St John's River in Jacksonville. Regina's mother kept a large photograph of him on her mantle. In the picture he stood on the deck of his steamboat in a white jacket with gold braid on the shoulders, one hand thrust between the front buttons like Napoleon posing on the battlefield at Austerlitz. Regina and her mother apparently still held him in high esteem, though he had abandoned them twenty years before and never returned for so much as a visit. The fact that he'd made out so well in the meantime seemed to justify everything, more or less. His cheque arrived like clockwork on the first of every month.

The four of us would have dinner, usually – Regina was a fine cook – and then play spades over beer and sweet sherry for Regina's mother. I was always paired with my room mate and we would always lose on account of his poor play. I never asked if he did it on purpose; I would like to think that he did. After the card game, Regina would take my room mate back to her bedroom, leaving me in the living room with her mother and the dog. I was surprised at first by the frankness of this arrangement. Regina's mother would sip sherry and tell me stories of interest from her life just as if there weren't a short sculptor fucking her midget daughter in the next room. 'You're a writer,' she liked to say, 'I will give you things to write about.'

I will cite, as a typical example of what she gave me, the story of Regina's mother's love affair with Frankie Avalon:

She was waiting tables at a diner on South Street, just an all-night greasy spoon but she rode the bus clear across town to get there, sitting by the window with a paperback romance, because she was eighteen and pretty and didn't know any better. This was 1960. She worked the graveyard, ten to six. No one else wanted to but for her it was the best shift, all the drunks coming in from the nightclubs on South Street, sharp-dressed and smelling like Aqua Velva, talking fast and smoking like the huge factories strung out along the Delaware. They paid attention to her. They told her jokes and asked her out and she liked it but never went with any of them. She lived alone with her father, who'd left a leg behind on the beach at Guadalcanal. Her mother was dead from meningitis. Then one night Frankie Avalon came into the diner. He just came right in like any other person and sat down in a booth with two other guys, all of them whooping and laughing. It was three o'clock in the morning and Frankie Avalon wore a checked sport shirt under a cream-coloured jacket; he wore black wool slacks and saddle shoes. Before he was famous he'd played trumpet at the CR Club on Christian Street – just a little moon-faced kid, twelve years old and blowing out dance tunes up on stage at the CR Club, next door to Palumbo's Restaurant. After that he played in Rocco and the Saints with Bobby Rydell. People in Philadelphia knew about Frankie Avalon from all the way back. Now he was a regular on *American Bandstand* and Regina's mother had seen him just a week before with Alan Ladd in *Guns of the Timberland*. He ordered ham on rye. Regina's mother wrote it down and said, 'Ham on rye for Frankie Avalon.'

Their eyes met.

He asked her name, and whether or not she liked to ride in convertibles. Of course she'd never ridden in a convertible before. His Thunderbird was right out front; he and his friends were driving to Atlantic City to have mimosas at dawn with Paul Anka in his suite at the Ambassador Hotel.

'Seems a little silly,' Regina's mother told them, 'driving all the way to Atlantic City for a glass of champagne.'

That made Frankie Avalon smile. He smiled with his *American Bandstand* teeth and said, 'Baby, that's just how you do it when you're Frankie Avalon.'

Regina's mother smiled too – in her living room forty years later she stopped talking and allowed a sly grin to break across her face.

'So did you go?' I asked.

'Of course not. I would have lost my job, my father would have killed me. I made him drive me around the block instead.'

She described the polished fenders of Frankie Avalon's Thunderbird and the two-tone paint job, red on white. She described the river wind in her hair as they rode around the block. He drove very slowly. The sidewalks were empty at that hour. Late September, the leaves had begun to drop and he insisted that she wear his jacket – camel hair, smelling like the smoke of a cigar. Back at the diner he kissed her softly on the cheek.

'There,' he said. 'Now you know how to ride in a convertible.'

This was before the surf craze took off, before the beach movies with Annette Funicello. Those stupid beach movies – nobody in Philadelphia knew how to surf. Frankie Avalon moved out to California, and Atlantic City fell into disrepair. But the cooks all came out from the kitchen on that night in 1960. They stood in the front window in their paper hats to watch Regina's mother drive back up in Frankie Avalon's red and white T-Bird.

'Wow,' I said.

'And to this day,' she said, 'I can't help but wonder how my life might have been different if I'd gone with him that night.'

We sat there in silence, mutually imagining the sunrise as it would have appeared from Paul Anka's suite at the Ambassador Hotel.

'Is that a true story?' I asked.

She turned and looked out the window. Outside, men were slumped in hooded sweatshirts up and down the block, talking on the corners and drinking on the stoops. The abandoned tenements with their faces boarded up, the sodium filaments buzzing where the streetlights worked, the trash swept into piles at the kerb by long gusts of wind. The night was thrumming beneath an orange sky, ambulance sirens in the distance, the Phillies had just finished last again.

I met my room mate by chance; I answered his ad in the newspaper. He was vague on the phone about why the guy before me had moved out, but I liked the idea of living with another artist. I imagined some sort of bond arising from our shared creative anguish, but this never happened, really; my room mate turned out to be boorish and bullying. He liked, for example, to fry eggs on my Salton Sandwich Maker and trim his body hair with my clippers – violations of my property that were intended, I felt sure, to let me know who was in charge. Still, we learned to get along in our way. He was tormented by the distance between our apartment and his studio, an obstacle that often kept him working at home for days at a time. It was only two miles but the buses didn't go there. You had to change twice and it sometimes took an hour, or so he claimed. He had no car. I had a car, however, and he was not above suggesting that I drive him over in the morning and pick him up in the afternoon, since I didn't usually seem to be doing much anyway. I suggested that he get a bike.

'I don't know how to ride a bike,' he said.

'How do you not know how to ride a bike?'

He shrugged. 'It never came up.'

We went together to a junk shop on Passayunk Avenue and bought a children's Huffy for $20 because the adult bikes were too big. The Huffy was black with yellow trim and lightning bolt decals on the frame, though time and hardship had exacted a price from the decals. My room mate was proud – men his size are often proud – and I knew he didn't like having to purchase the bicycle of a ten-year-old. That night I stood in the middle of South Fourth Street beneath the sizzling arc lights, holding the bike in place as he climbed aboard. He perched uncertainly on the yellow rubber wedge of seat. 'Don't let go,' he said. He was looking at me with great earnestness, the small round face behind the big round glasses. I'm sure it was humiliating to him: one more for the list. His sculptures were full of aggression and violence, nude men in various attitudes of rage. They expressed a monstrous frustration. He shaped the models in wax the colour of fresh blood. All over our small apartment, muscular wax men pounded the earth, tore their clothes, and strangled one another on the coffee table and windowsills, throwing terrible shadows against the fleur-de-lis wallpaper. 'Don't let go,' he said as he began to press his feet against the pedals.

I jogged alongside him down the centre of the empty street, holding the seat as a few scattered spectators looked on, the men loitering outside Hi-Time Liquor, the women folding clothes in the bright window of our laundromat. Up ahead, kids in vintage sweaters swapped wry smiles in the hipster joints of South Street, showing off their Zippo tricks, pale legs sheathed in artfully torn jeans. South Philly lay sprawling at our backs – down to the Vet, to the Walt Whitman Bridge, the steady cheesesteak lines at Pat's and Gino's, the Italian men playing pinochle in the bars. 'Don't let go,' my room mate yelled as we picked up speed.

He sailed out ahead when I released him.

His fluttering windbreaker gave an impression of wobbly flight, like a wino duck lighting out for Florida on the backside of a summer-long drunk. It took him half a block to realise I was gone. 'You son of a bitch!' he shouted. 'You son of a bitch!'

He wobbled left, turning accidentally onto Catherine Street, disappearing.

I went back upstairs to our apartment, where my novel waited like a deformed child I was too ashamed to let out in public. I sat down at my desk and re-read the paragraph I'd written that afternoon, in which, thrillingly, Jonas smokes another cigarette and considers the nature of loss. He was on the side of a dusty highway outside Amarillo, hitchhiking through a starkly beautiful landscape of emotions I knew nothing about, including love, courage, desperation, and especially loss. Plus I'd never been to Texas. I worked on the paragraph for half an hour, adding semicolons and taking semicolons away. The front door slammed and my room mate trudged up the stairs. His breath came heavily; his face was red, he was sweating. I asked him how things were going out there.

He said, 'I've pretty much got the riding part down.'

'Good,' I said. 'I told you it wasn't that hard.'

'Yeah.' He nodded, gasping. 'It's the stopping part I'm having trouble with.'

'You just squeeze the brakes.'

My room mate shook his head. 'I'm not comfortable with that.' He struck a pose not unlike the Heisman Trophy, with one arm straight out ahead of him, as if to ward off tacklers. 'I've just sort of been running into things and falling over.'

One night a few weeks later he came home in a red pick-up truck. I was standing outside our apartment with a cigarette, watching the girls of the South Philadelphia Bartending Academy arrive for their evening class across the street. That would have made it six o'clock. My room mate pulled up to the kerb and said, 'Get in. We're going to New Jersey.'

'Whose truck is that?'

'It's my friend's,' he said. 'Get in.'

My room mate had no friends, especially not the kind who would entrust him with a vehicle. He was not the type of person to whom you lent expensive things. I took a few slow drags on my cigarette to demonstrate that I didn't just get into red trucks and drive to New Jersey right when he said so. It was true, however, that my own plans for the evening involved a few more smoke breaks and hoping the phone would inexplicably ring. A couple of days before I had seriously considered impersonating a man named Hector in order to prolong my conversation with a wrong number.

'Why are we going to New Jersey?' I asked.

'We're going to my sister's house.'

'You don't have a sister.'

'I have a sister,' he said, 'in New Jersey.'

He drove furiously; he was a furious little man. His manner was graced by a recklessness that in a larger or more successful person might have seemed bold. We careened through the narrow streets of South Philadelphia at outrageous speed, chasing starved cats and ball-tossing children from our path, failing only by the fickle grace of luck to sideswipe the endless, dingy lines of parked cars. Hurtling across the Whitman Bridge, high above the corrugated grey waters of the Delaware, we beheld the dim continent of New Jersey spreading out before us.

My room mate stopped the truck before a complex of townhouse condominiums that backed up on a strip mall in Cherry Hill. He got out and stood looking up at the corner unit, which looked back with darkened windows.

'I don't think your sister's home,' I said.

'She's in Rome,' said my room mate.

'What's she doing in Rome?'

'I don't know. Sucking cock on the Spanish Steps.'

He walked briskly to the door and opened it with a silver key. I followed him inside. The foyer opened onto a spacious living room that floated murkily in the streetlight filtering through drawn venetian blinds.

'We're taking the couch,' said my room mate.

'Don't you think we should turn on a light?'

'No.'

'Now wait a minute,' I said.

'Don't judge me,' he said. 'You don't know anything.'

In our apartment we had no couch. We had the jump seat from a rust-eaten Chevy Astro van, circa 1990, picked up at a junkyard in Merchantville. This item had the advantage of seatbelts that came in handy on those rare occasions when I got stone drunk with my jaunty seafaring chum, Captain Morgan. Otherwise, it left a lot to be desired. My room mate and I were joined in the shadowy silence of the condominium's living room by this mutually acknowledged fact. Outside, crickets sang a dirge of New Jersey to the night.

Soaring back across the Whitman's river-conquering span, we rode high above the morality of furniture. Those were the old rules. The couch displayed its many-coloured floral print like royal plumage in the rear view mirror, overstuffed to the point of decadence, bulging obesely like the sofas given away on *The Price Is Right*. I allowed myself briefly to imagine that the hipster girls of South Street could feel its approach: the make-out venue they'd been waiting for was nigh. In the smoky bars and lounges, amid the skittering drum and bass, they would sense the quality of my couch in the cant of my shoulders, the confident way I held their eyes.

'It's a good couch,' said my room mate, nodding as we crossed back into Pennsylvania.

I believe these were the last words that passed between us that night. Two minutes later, the rain began. It was one of those cold, soaking autumn rains you get in the Northeast, with drops the size of hand grenades. There was nothing to be done. We left the couch in the middle of Jackson Street and drove home. I believe I heard my room mate crying behind the closed door of his bedroom sometime after 2 a.m. He hadn't sold a sculpture in months. He was almost thirty and living on credit, having spent the last of his money on casting fees at the foundry. Compared to him I'd only begun to fail. Tacitly we both agreed to never speak of the couch again.

I only ever saw one other picture of Regina's father, a photograph clipped from a newspaper. It had run beside an article describing the mayor of Jacksonville's public proposal of marriage to his secretary aboard a dinner cruise on Regina's father's steamboat. The mayor had apparently acted on a whim: he bought a diamond-sapphire ring with ten crisp hundred-dollar bills from a woman at the next table while his secretary was powdering her nose. When she returned, he rose and struck his wine glass with a knife to silence the room. The secretary had been named Ms Florida, 1992. The mayor, as I gathered from the article, was a man of legendary appetites. He rode a motorcycle to work at City Hall and had once nearly died in a parasailing accident; he claimed to have survived a shark attack while skin diving off Nassau by punching a twenty-foot Great White in the nose. When his secretary accepted, Regina's father was summoned to perform the ceremony on the spot. In the picture, he smiles in his white bolero dinner jacket with gold epaulettes on the shoulder. He has the ship's Bible in one hand and the other raised triumphantly in the air. His mouth is open; he is exclaiming. Before him, the mayor holds his new wife in a dashing embrace, bending her low to kiss in the style of Rudolph Valentino in the Jazz Age.

'They were married for seven weeks,' Regina's mother told me when I had finished reading. She smiled admiringly, as if this fact only added to the impossible glamour of these people.

I handed the article back to her. We were alone with the dog; my room mate had sabotaged me in the card game again and disappeared with Regina to her bedroom. I said, 'I guess that wedding was a tough act to follow.'

'That's right,' said Regina's mother. 'The mayor of Jacksonville, Florida.'

She sipped her sherry and I sipped my beer. The weather had turned; winter was pulling the clouds down on top of us, days so short you could sleep right through them. You could pull the covers up and roll over to face the wall and sleep right through them, bone-grey days full of long silences and stale air. I pictured Regina's mother walking down to the liquor store on Friday afternoons when my room mate and I were expected. I pictured her bundling into a heavy coat, a coat she'd been wearing since Watergate. She would slide her feet into brown rubber boots, ease down the stairs, watch the street for a while from behind the barred window on her building's front door. She would move down the sidewalk with her back held very straight, looking neither left nor right. One of the guys on the corner might say something to her, or one of the men in front of the liquor store. Probably no one would say anything. I pictured her opening the cooler to reach for a sixpack of Yuengling. The bills in her wallet would be crumpled; she would have to smooth them flat on the counter when she paid. Looking up from my beer, I could tell by her smile that she was thinking still of Florida, where it was still warm enough for shorts and sandals in the middle of November. Florida was everywhere that month, in everyone's ears and on the lips of every headline: Florida, Florida, Florida.

'Do you know who your husband voted for?' I asked.

'Oh,' Regina's mother said, 'I don't think the mayor was up for re-election this year.'

I didn't press the question.

The next Friday she surprised me by producing a tin of fatly rolled Turkish hash joints after Regina had taken my room mate away. I smoked one of the joints halfway down and the basset hound began speaking to me. The basset hound said, 'Naturally, I've had my share of disappointments. It's no mere jive talk to say that youth is wasted on the young. One imagines at a certain time in life that the world will forever remain a buffet of redolent fireplugs, that the frisbee will continue always to settle softly in one's jaws at the apex of one's leap. But age has its pleasures too, I believe – subtler pleasures, to be sure, but pleasures nonetheless. One's increased limitation is offset by a more refined sense of humour, for example, so that restrictions which might have seemed unbearable to a young dog become merely the basis for a good laugh. I don't mean to suggest that one begins to take one's self less seriously, but perhaps this is what it amounts to. One tempers one's expectations. One learns to take the long view. Simpler pleasures are experienced more acutely: the smell of wood smoke in autumn, the intricate markings on the wings of a butterfly. Of course the secret is that there is no secret, as they say. One discovers this and moves on. The breadth of possibilities we perceive early in our lives is a fallacy, mostly, albeit a pleasant one. Our convictions narrow but become more deeply held. Such is the process by which a dog may become either wise or defeated; I have chosen wisdom, or so I like to think. Ha ha. Listen to those midgets fuck.'

Of course I, lacking the ears of a dog, heard nothing.

On the way back to South Philadelphia, my room mate would give me the blow-by-blow: methods of foreplay, sequence of positions, the orgasmic tally – but also tastes and sounds, the briefest touches and passing visions. He always went into great detail; in fact, he had a genius for it. His erotic memory operated with tremendous precision. There was no experience in the history of my life I could have described so well as my room mate described his sex with Regina on those nights in the fall as we drove back across Philadelphia. That was really why he brought me along, I think: so he could tell me about everything afterwards in the car. It must have been like getting to do it all over again. My room mate was not in general a careful or even very observant person, nor was he particularly kind. When he got talking about making love to Regina, it was like a music box opening. It changed my idea of him. He never seemed to consider the possibility that I would find anything comical about the image of a very small man fucking a midget. Certainly it was not comical to him.

'Short people have the advantage in sex,' he told me once. 'The nerves are clustered, the territory is more compact. Rangy women lose track of themselves. The left hand's never sure what the right one's up to. Of course it takes a shorter man to notice.'

The truth is that I liked his sculptures very much. I admired, in a way, his willingness to struggle against forces that would obviously defeat him. This was the idea at the heart of his work, whether he knew it or not. He was very much inside his life, thrashing, in Philadelphia in the fall of 2000. The election smeared itself across the cable news like a car accident in slow motion; the writing was on the wall. I left Philadelphia in December and I wasn't coming back there ever. I was moving like Frankie Avalon and the long drift of history out to California. I was renting a studio apartment in Sacramento on a month-to-month lease, I was walking to work each day through the park where Squeaky Fromme once tried to assassinate Gerald Ford. Then summer fell like an axe on the Central Valley and I quit my job, moved to Berkeley, fell in love with an opera singer, managed for a while to forget the concrete blimp of my literary career. We watched the fireworks from Tilden as they went up over the Bay on the fourth of July; we made love in the back seat of her Saab. Cellular technology was on the rise and that was the last love affair of my life that would suffer to be quickened by the outmoded romance of payphones, piss-smelling payphones on the street corners of Berkeley and Oakland, in the noisy bars of the Mission and the Tenderloin, screaming into the receiver at the top of one's voice, weeping with one's head against the cold metal hutch. The problem with cell phones is that you can't slam them back onto the cradle like a barbarian smashing the head of a Roman soldier. She moved to New York at the end of August and I chased her, uninvited, superfluous and broke, limping with a battered suitcase across the dogshit-covered sidewalks of Fort Green. She was slumming in a fifth-floor walk-up on Dekalb Avenue with a guy named Living Room Johnson. I got there on the seventh of September.

The fall of the year 2000 in Philadelphia was full of things that hadn't happened yet. Five years later, in my mother's kitchen in Seattle, David is seeking to impose his despotic optimism through my cell phone. His gleaming, square-toothed smile bounces off a satellite and shines like a police interrogation lamp into my ear. It's two in the afternoon and I'm musky, unshowered, wearing a yellow bathrobe. Rain falls steadily on the state of Washington. My mother is out getting her moustache waxed. She has a date tonight with the waiter we met last week at Ivar's House of Clams, to which I say: Good luck, Mom, I too am convinced this one will be different. It's been a very wet fall here, even by local standards, which is kind of like a hot summer in hell. The standing water in my mother's basement is deep enough for drowning kittens. We do the laundry in rubber shoes. Last night I stood in a cold drizzle on the beach at Alki Point, thinking, as Kerouac might have, about the enormous continent rolling out behind me toward its colonial past, toward the Algonquin days of Mormon myth. Across the ocean came men in buckled hats, seeking religious freedom, vanquishing the natives with exotic germs, founding in their wisdom a nation that would come in time to shine like a beacon of liberty to the farthest corners of its own self-image. And now in this effulgent nation, stumbling through the onset of a calamitous century: me!

'Sustainability,' I say, repeating David's phrase to make him think I've been listening, although I haven't been listening at all. He's probably talking about something totally different now.

'Look,' he says, 'are you okay out there? We worry about you sometimes.'

'Who's we?'

'The royal we. How's the book coming?'

'Super,' I tell him. 'The book is coming super. It's practically coming on my face.'

In pale autumn sunshine, in the West Village, in the acquisitive sweep of David's gaze, the sleek Manhattan women are doing justice with their beauty to the high cost of their clothes. They are walking toward the great grey Hudson like monsters returning to the sea. They are walking away from the Hudson, chatting on their cell phones with wealthy, charming men. They are sifting through jewelled clutch bags, striding into the night on freshly shaved legs, backlit, with dancing-school-posture, the breeze taking tender liberties with the un-split ends of their hair.

'Buck up,' David says, 'it's a gorgeous day in New York City.'

Plus: he and Sidney have a plan for blight removal and redevelopment in the decimated ghettos of Philadelphia, across which I once chauffeured a small post coital sculptor on a scattered run of Friday nights in that doomed and fateful fall of the year 2000. We would pass by whole blocks standing abandoned in West Philadelphia, blocks in which every house had been left to rot – plywood in the windows, roofs collapsed, buildings you could see into like doll's houses because one side had fallen away – and the burned-out husks of insurance fires. We passed by them in the dark, cocooned in the safety of my 89 Sentra, as my room mate enumerated the glories of love. Above us the sky glowed orange. Around us the city spilled out in every direction, rotting from the inside. The traffic lights had no censors. We sat at deserted intersections, watching their slow routines unfold. A green light is a lonely thing staring down a long, empty street at three in the morning. Sometimes I still feel, as I did then, that it's out there somewhere, it's coming, whatever it is.

My room mate's voice was soothing to me. It rose and fell steadily as we drove. Sometimes I would put in with a question or add some observation of my own, and then he would go on. He would talk until the thing was exhausted. And then we were quiet; we kept moving; we were gone.

'I knew a bitch once – this was many years ago. She had a tawny shade I admired, very expressive eyes: a corgi. I suppose we were in love. We would escape from our houses and meet behind a Chinese restaurant on Market Street. She could put away lo mein like a St

Bernard; she was, in general, a dog unashamed of her appetites, and we plundered garbage cans from the university to City Line Avenue, flouting risk, chasing down old tabby cats. I felt for a time as if we owned this neighbourhood, as if perhaps the two of us had dreamed it up for one another. I suppose in a way that we had. The burger joint over on Locust, Crown Chicken on 52nd; the smell of rotting meat, summer nights on the Schuylkill. Once we found the hindquarters of a pony-sized raccoon by the railroad tracks in Fairmount Park, and how well I recall the face of my corgi as we indulged ourselves beside the moonlit rails. There are moments in one's life when all of one's desires seem suddenly to be of a piece. The world assumes a fearsome congruity; one feels passion to be incontrovertible. Everything falls before it. We lived like bandits in those months, daring each other onward with conspiratorial smiles. I suppose in the end that love itself is a kind of theft. She had a restless heart, a reckless soul, and these were the very things that drew me to her, so I should hardly have been surprised that day out back of Main Garden when she failed to make our rendezvous. But I went looking for her all the same. Perhaps I never should have, but then again, it could not have been otherwise. I found her in an alley off Peach Street, being mounted by a golden retriever. A golden retriever! She wasn't even in heat. I ran to the Girard Avenue Bridge and stared down into the face of the river. How slowly it moved, beckoning me – the gentle current of death, whispering its endless promise. I stood there for hours, I could hardly tell you how many. The sun came up, the sun went down. Oh it's such a tired old story, isn't it? In the end I simply turned and walked home in the dark; I just turned and walked away. I thought for weeks that the pain would kill me but it never did. Happiness leaves a bitter aftertaste, but of course this fades with time. We are left in the end with the pleasure of our memories. In the end this will be our great reward. Pass me that smoke, friend, let me tell you about loss. Whatever you have will be gone tomorrow, I can promise you that. This is our blessing as well as our curse. Pass that smoke over here. Listen. Your friend may not be tall, but listen – I daresay he fucks like the dickens.'

The Honeyeaters

Myron Lysenko

i get off the bus and run
towards the station looking forward
to lunch with my new love

on the platform
a sign reads: boring passengers
please make way for exciting passengers

i hum a song
and i'm the closest thing
to an excited passenger here

clouds tuck themselves
into the corners of the sky
as a flock of shadows flies past

a wattle bird darts
from tree to tracks
with a stick in its beak

i can't believe
that it's making a nest
up against the railway line

men pick stones
off the tracks and throw them
against the end of the platform

i watch them for a long time
then yell: where's my train
they reply: it's not here

i say: i know it's not here
it's late and it's making me
late for my date

they smile
while they work and glance at me
as if i'm lost

i ask:
will the train still be able
to arrive through all this mess

the youngest man
says: it's not a mess
it's progress

the men keep working
and i pace the platform
thinking that i need a taxi

i run to the phone box up the road
but when i reach for the receiver
it's a huge nest of bark and twigs

i rush back
to the station and notice
that everything has changed

a block of apartments
has gone up along the tracks
completely blocking my train

i ask a young couple if they have
a mobile phone
but they say they're out of credit

The Honeyeaters

a pop star is about to open
a new shopping centre which has appeared
on the platform and i sing out:

hey! i need the train
and she says: yes, everyone's watching
reality TV

i say: i'll be late for my date
but she shrugs and continues to wait
for an audience to arrive

two honeyeaters
carrying hearts in their beaks
fly over me

they are headed
in the direction of my love
and they are singing

so i jump off the platform
and run after them
as i puff along the track

they fly into the canopy
of a tall flowering tree
and their beaks meet like a kiss

i run along the tracks like a train
except now i'm an express
not stopping at any stations

until i reach the end of the line
where my love stands in the middle
of the station smiling at me

The Love Quiz

Rosemary Jones

Every night after dinner they played the Love Quiz. They cleared away the dishes, piled them in the sink in a froth of suds, and waited for the coffee to steep. They took it in turns to be the compere. The question that inspired the game in the first place was: what is love? Each time the compere asked – what is love? – the other one pressed the buzzer fast. Actually it was a tea towel, and they flicked it, hard like a rodeo whip – snap. You might think that was a little violent for a love quiz, but it meant they could wipe a plate and answer a question at the same time, though sometimes one of them got out a bell from the cats' basket of toys and tinkled that instead. If they were in a bad mood the Love Quiz could lift them out of it. Or it could plummet them down even further, into a black, uneven place where neither of them gave a toss about love anymore. When it ended badly they swore off the game for a couple of weeks. But they always came back to it. It was a diversion, an end of the day/beginning of the night demarcation line. It was a little piece of insanity in the kitchen. A fantasy. A safe harbour. It rivalled *Jeopardy*, and if they had been the entrepreneurial kind they would have marketed it and made quite a sizeable fortune.

The man – we'll call him Eric – said love was one of the greatest forces in the world that made sense, but only as long as you didn't try to nail it down. If you did, it was another story.

The woman said she couldn't find a definition for love if she tried. Nancy – Eric called her Fancy Nancy when she flicked the tea towel with that confident snap ('Yes! It's Fancy Nancy,' he announced to the kitchen walls and the cats if they happened to walk by) – didn't know if love even existed, except that if anything happened to Eric, she would want to die on the spot. Instantaneous self-combustion. No grieving widow outfit for her, thank you. But that was a long way in the distance, because maybe they'd stay married and healthy for forty, even fifty, years and celebrate one of those gold wedding anniversaries. Some people did, though on a national scale the odds were against them. Unless they moved to another country where the statistics weren't so gloomy. Somewhere warm and balmy. Not too hot. Beside the sea in a Mediterranean climate.

The first question in the Love Quiz was always the same, of course. What is love? Then the compere, either Fancy Nancy, or Eric, would pause. The contestant didn't have to answer that question (they could practise snapping their tea towels instead). It was more rhetorical. Like the follow-up question: is love infinite? Is love forever (as in moonlight and diamonds and other much-loved love clichés)? And then the question of questions, which deserved a drum roll and a clang of cymbals: is love a trope?

Eric liked the trope question best. If he was the contestant he'd flick the tea towel, preferably the Irish linen, and twirl around in his imaginary contestant's booth. 'Yes!' he'd cry and brush his hands through his hair very quickly. If he thought about it too much, there was nothing more to say. Love was left out there, a trope, the very best of tropes, hanging over the centuries.

So they quickly moved on to the next question, usually a finish-this-song-line question. 'My love is deeper than the blank blank blank.' Or poem lines. 'Thou art more blank than blank.'

There was never a prize, or an end to the game. It was one or two questions, every night, and then, like they do on all good quiz shows, they beamed at each other and shook hands, though really, because it was a love quiz, they drew up close and kissed. A Love Quiz kiss. A kiss-for-the-cameras kiss.

Sometimes Nancy wrote questions down, which was against the rules. The unspoken rules. There were no rules: it was a love quiz after all (though not a *free* love quiz). She might remember something during the day that she'd scribble on a tiny scrap of paper and stuff into her bureau drawer where Eric would never find it. Then she'd pull it out and rehearse it before dinner. In the rules (the unspoken rules), they weren't meant to go looking in the book of quotations; they were meant to get their questions from the stuff of life itself, from bits and pieces heard or read or played on the radio, but you couldn't go looking. You couldn't go looking for love. But she did. She went to that book of quotations and her questions got harder and smarter, though not much funnier.

'I think you're cheating,' Eric said.

'You can't cheat at the Love Quiz,' Nancy said.

'Oh yes you can,' he said.

She pulled out the scraps of paper she'd been saving in the bureau drawer. Lines of sonnets. Elizabeth Barrett Browning. 'If thou must love me, let it be for nought / Except for love's sake only.' Edna St Vincent Millay. 'What lips my lips have kissed, and where, and why / I have forgotten.' Gerard Manley Hopkins. 'Nothing is so beautiful as spring – When weeds, in wheels, shoot long and lovely and lush.'

'Do you really think this is cheating?' she said.

'Ah, well,' he said with a furrowed brow, caving in. 'I suppose it's expanding our love horizons. It makes me think that love is in the air,' he said and suddenly swung her round the kitchen. 'Besides, it's spring, and nothing is...'

'So beautiful as spring,' she said.

She and Eric were meant for each other. If they hadn't made up the Love Quiz they should have met on a quiz show. Or a blind date. They had met in the local public library instead, which wasn't very romantic at first glance. On the red couch beside the magazines. Near the photocopier. As soon as she'd seen him her eyes lit up. Christmas lights. It had taken him a while to notice. He needed new glasses.

Eric had a friend. A cross between a friend and an acquaintance, married with three children. One summer evening they came to visit and the children ran round and round under the dying dogwood tree and ate barbecued prawns, and chicken marinated in honey and spices. Everyone seemed to be getting along just fine. The husband and the wife, that is. And the children. They were triplets, and if you looked carefully you could tell the difference. Eric could tell if he had his glasses on.

The husband was hard to talk to. He blinked his eyes at Nancy, as if he was bewildered. But he seemed devoted and caring, and manoeuvred the chicken off the kebab sticks for his boys. The wife was nice, full of talk of the children – with the triplets lying inside of you side by side for months, and then to see them darting around alive and well, you would tend to have them on your mind. She said they carried the habits of the womb into the outside world, the way they dipped a head this way, extended a hand that way – it was all there, on the ultrasound, or in a kick or a punch in her belly. She would have passed the Love Quiz, Nancy thought – not that you passed it exactly, but that she would have had a question, or an answer, up her sleeve.

Two seasons later (that's *all*), the husband left the wife and the triplets. He had a love connection on the side. He wasn't fulfilled in his marriage, he said. He made up all kinds of excuses. He grew his hair long – like it was when she first met him, his wife-about-to-be-*ex*-wife said – and wore polished wooden beads around his neck. He was doing what happened in one out of three marriages. It wasn't working, and now he'd found somebody else. He was, at last, being true to himself, he said. He asked his wife for a divorce; he would have liked one from an ATM, or a drive-in fast food window, or some other modern American as-fast-as-you-can device. Because he felt guilty, he said, making love to someone else while he was still married.

There wasn't a song about adultery on the Love Quiz. But it put a dampener on things. Nancy and Eric worried what might happen to them, out of the blue, in a shift of seasons.

And then Frank Sinatra died. A heart attack, on the West Coast one night, some time after they'd finished doing the dishes. That week they made the counter top into a late-night bar, poured a small glass of whiskey each and draped tea towels despondently around their necks. Nancy played compere and reeled off the first phrases.

'When somebody loves you…'

'It's no good unless he loves you,' said Eric, whipping the tea towel into action and using the counter top as a piano.

'Love and marriage, love and marriage…'

'Too easy,' said Eric. 'They go together like a horse and carriage.'

'I'll be seeing you…'

'In all the old, familiar places. My turn,' Eric said. 'Make it one for my baby…'

'And one for the road,' Nancy said, sipping the whiskey, finding that sad-eyed lonesome thrum to go with the words.

'And the final question for the night, one that all our contestants should be able to answer. Fly me to the moon…'

Nancy cracked the tea towel. Then she stopped. She placed the whiskey on the counter top, and threw up her hands. 'I can't remember,' she wailed.

'Perhaps the contestant would like to sing it,' the compere said patiently.

'No she wouldn't,' Nancy said. But she tried. She sang that lyrical fly-me-to-the-moon phrase, then could only go – da da de da.

'It's no good,' she said. 'This is a bad omen.'

'We still have to kiss,' Eric said. 'It's in the rules.'

'I'm not kissing on a bad omen,' she said. 'And there are no rules.'

'It's only a bad omen if you imagine it.'

'But it is, it's like breaking a mirror, not being able to remember a Sinatra classic.'

'Can I give you a clue?' Eric said. 'Can I whisper the answer into your shell-like ear?'

'This is how marriages begin to crumble,' Nancy said. 'Over disagreements and misinterpretations.'

'Who said our marriage was crumbling?'

'No one. But it could, especially if there's a bad omen.'

Eric folded the tea towels and put the dishes away.

'I think you're being unreasonable,' he said.

He never said things like that. Not usually. Nancy's head shot around 180 degrees to look at him. 'Do you?' she said.

'This quiz isn't for real,' he said calmly, though still in his best compere's voice. 'It's only a game.'

'I thought it was,' she said. 'A game is a game is real life,' she said.

'Oh okay,' he said, giving in again, though Nancy wouldn't have minded if he'd argued the point a little more. 'In which case, we really have to kiss. We can't pretend to kiss. We can't pretend to end the game for the evening. We have to really do it.'

'Oh,' she said, and tilted her head on one side and fluttered her eyelids.

'You know,' he smiled. 'Just kiss first.'

'Fly me to the moon,' she said, and kissed him and then the phrase came shooting out of her mouth and into his, 'and let me play among the stars.'

'There,' he said. 'You did it. Though in real life,' he said to prove a point, 'you wouldn't get to kiss the compere.'

Because it was a sad Sinatra week, they played the Love Quiz again. Fancy Nancy snapped the tea towel, Eric twirled around in his contestant's booth, they both crooned to each other across the counter top, and later, after it was over (they named it the Sinatra Memorial Quiz Night), the compere and the contestant danced up the stairs, and fell asleep dreaming of romantic scenes with lakes and moonbeams and forests and starry Sinatra nights. They dreamed the contestant and the compere really did fall in love on television, and that they made the front cover of a TV magazine – with the headline, 'Is Love a Trope?' – that they stuck above the counter top to remind them of what love was all about.

Months after Sinatra's death, Eric phoned one evening to say he'd be late home, that he couldn't attend quiz night. *You can imagine what that means, though you shouldn't leap to conclusions*, Nancy heard the compere say. 'I shouldn't leap to conclusions,' Nancy said, snapping the tea towel at the cats.

'Miao,' went the larger of the two cats, as though it were the compere.

'Miao,' went the smaller cat, not to be out-miaoed. It circled her with its tail erect as if to say – don't make any false moves.

Nancy left the dishes to soak and went upstairs. She looked in all of Eric's coat pockets. There was no evidence of anything. What had she expected? And then in a blue blazer he hadn't worn for a couple of weeks her fingers fumbled over a hard, tiny, folded scrap of paper stuck against the pocket seam. She sat on their bed to unfold it – surely it was nothing. But there were the familiar words, not in his handwriting, but in a curly scrawl as if the letters were all wearing tutus – *love is a trope*, it said.

Fancy Nancy took the note downstairs and slapped it onto the detergent bottle by the sink, taping it over the Palmolive letters. She wanted to be certain that when he got home, he knew that she knew a third contestant had been added to the game; she expected him to announce the new woman's name, with a proper compere's introduction. Then the contest would begin in earnest. She glared at the cats, folded the tea towel, and sat in the dark by the sink to wait for him.

Pink

Leanne Hall

When I arrive at work in the morning the first thing I do is turn my computer on, make a cup of tea and check my email. I like to arrive early, when the office is dark and quiet, so that I can clear my inbox and plan my day. I do my best thinking at this hour, when there are still neat lines mown into the carpet by the cleaner.

The first item in my inbox today is from Mark Whistle, my boss. He's adding another work to the show with only two weeks until opening. There's no question about it, because this is what he wants. The email was sent at 3 a.m. and is riddled with spelling mistakes. There was a time when this email would have sent me into a panic, but I'm beyond that now. I swallow the panic before it rises. I'm already thinking: how can we do this? Rather than: why the fuck am I being asked to do this?

Kristy is the next to arrive, then Lena. Kristy wears a black miniskirt and a thin veil of cigarette smoke; Lena carries dinner leftovers in a Tupperware dish. I know Lena has read Mark's email when she groans. Seconds later Kristy snorts derisively.

'Do you think it's legal?' Kristy asks. 'To buy stolen tellies and exhibit them?'

'Every time I see Mark's name in my inbox, this muscle in my neck goes twang,' complains Lena, rubbing her hands over her face. She bangs her head against her desk. I think this means she doesn't know or, if she does, she doesn't want to think about it.

That's not the bit I'm worried about. 'How are we going to get a six-metre-tall replica missile into the gallery?' There are two ways into the basement gallery. An average-sized goods lift, or two steep flights of stairs.

Kristy slides her top drawer open and picks a pill bottle from her extensive collection. She rattles it as if it's a maraca. Between the head-banging and the pill-rattling, we could start a decent orchestra in here.

'Would you like a beta-blocker? I take them whenever I'm feeling a little anxious. They really do work.'

There's a bellow from behind the partition that separates us from the finance department. Lena calls the thin wall The Great Cultural Divide.

'Beta-blockers? You're an idiot! I take those for my heart!'

Kristy kneels on her desk and thrusts her head over the partition, giving me an eyeful of her undies.

'We weren't aware you had one, Bruce!' she spits, before bouncing back into her chair.

Lena is calm, as always. Only her hands, clutching the glass edge of the table whitely, betray her.

'I'm just saying, Mark, that we're partially government-funded, and as such, we need to be really careful about how we spend our money. Going to Cash Converters, or out the back of the Leinster Arms to buy stolen tellies with taxpayers' money is not going to look good.'

Mark Whistle insists on meeting in the boardroom, which resembles a designer igloo and is far too cavernous for our purposes. There are only four of us at a table the size of a small landing strip: Mark Whistle, Kristy, Lena, myself. The creative, the publicist, the legal, and me. My official title is Exhibition Co-ordinator, but Shit-kicker would be a more accurate term. My job description is filled with words such as communicate, liaise and co-ordinate. The words they forgot to include are: beg, conjure, weep and blackmail.

I shuffle my papers. If I have something in my hands I'm less likely to leap over the table and sock it to Mark Whistle. 'How am I going to transport a missile from California, and clear customs, in less than two weeks?'

'I have some names.' Mark looks like he hasn't been to bed yet. He lifts his head and sniffs. I'm pretty sure he's trying to inhale some of Kristy's second-hand smoke.

'You have *names*?' Kristy says in an impressed tone. 'Do you have money as well? Whose budget is this coming out of?'

Most people make the mistake of underestimating Kristy. They only see the blonde hair, the wide blue eyes and the baby-doll voice, and don't realise that she's actually a velociraptor in the guise of a poodle. Mark looks down at my calculator intently like it might tell him the answer.

'How much did you promise—' I have to glance at his email again to get it right, 'The Post-Ironic Art Collective?'

He throws his hands up. 'We'll worry about that later. For now we just have to think rockets, yeah? Stolen tellies, right? Relevant social comment, yeah? You see where I'm coming from?'

I don't, but that's nothing new. I pick up a file at random from my stack of papers. Five minutes before the meeting Kristy told me that she had only received about fifty per cent of the information she needed to plug the show.

'KomodoKodomo,' I say. 'Tell me about it.'

Mark shifts in his seat, peering warily at me with his chin balanced on his clasped hands.

'What do you want to know?'

I open the file. There are only three sheets of paper inside. 'How is Kristy supposed to put together a press release if we don't know anything about these people?'

'I don't know,' says Mark irritably, drumming his fingers against the table. 'They're Japanese.'

'Mark,' chimes in Kristy. 'The rocket people describe themselves as "tactical media practitioners". I thought we showed artists.'

I hold my breath and wait for it. Mark pushes on the table and tips his chair back on two legs and looks at the ceiling in despair. Here it comes now. Kristy and I can high-five each other later, in private.

'You're supposed to be my support team,' he whines. 'Why do you make everything so difficult? I'm under a lot of pressure, yeah? I don't know if you guys appreciate that.'

He clatters back down to earth and puts his head in his hands.

'I feel like shit today. I feel like my head is full of – what's that stuff? Lint! I feel like my head is full of lint.' He looks at Kristy with wild brumby eyes, and then whispers, 'You got something?'

My phone beeps as I walk through my front door. I kick the mail further into the hallway and dump my shopping bags on the kitchen bench. I wrestle my phone from my pocket and flip it open.

'What are you doing?'

'I just got back from work.'

'I'm making jaffles for dinner if you want some.'

I use my free hand to flick the fridge door open and toss the groceries in. I've never understood why fridges are lit to look so warm and inviting. I wonder how many kids die per year from crawling into fridges.

'Maybe.'

I shut the fridge and pick up my letters from the floor. Bills and letters for people who lived here ten years ago. I get sent an unusual amount of plus-size catalogues.

'Come over.'

I sigh. I just bought everything I needed for a stir-fry. But I can never, never say no to him. If I say no to one single thing, it's possible I may never hear from him again. I say 'no', but when it comes out my mouth it sounds like 'yes'.

'Okay. Can we put something green in them so that I can fool myself I'm eating something healthy?'

'Nope. Come now.'

The phone beeps. Conversation over.

I never used to watch TV until I met Ty. Now it seems it's all we do, lie on his couch bathing in television glow. Tonight we watch one of those medical miracle shows that should be crap, but which is actually quite gripping. This week the program follows a baby girl from Egypt, who has a second head. The second head grows from her crown, and looks like a warped version of the first head, except that below the neck there is nothing more than a fleshy stump. The doctor refers to the second head as a 'parasitic twin'. A twin embryo failed to fully separate in the womb – one of the twins continued to develop normally and the other did not. I waver between distaste and tenderness when I look at the second head. Both heads are beautiful in their own way. The parasitic twin has its own brain and breathes and blinks and sometimes smiles, but it can never have a life of its own. It puts an unbearable strain on its sister's heart. With the second head there she will never be able to crawl or sit. The parents and the doctors make a decision to separate, which will result in certain death for the parasitic twin. I look at the funny, stretched-out face of the second head and I feel inexplicably sad. I'm lying with my head on

Ty's tummy, rising and falling as he breathes, but I feel completely alone in my sadness. It runs deeper than I can understand.

Two girls are putting on make-up in the staff toilets when I enter. New interns. They glance up briefly as the door swings open, and then turn their attention back to the mirror above the sink. I'm not high enough up in the hierarchy to warrant a greeting. I take comfort in the fact that I am responsible for much of their misery, and they don't even realise it. If I really don't want to do something, photocopying or envelope stuffing, I suggest to Mark that it would be excellent experience for an intern. We have a healthy, disposable army of them – art students desperate to get experience with a prestigious organisation. They get to boast to their friends about where they work; in return we get free, non-unionised labour.

I lock the cubicle door and sit down. It takes me a while to pee. I hold my breath and try to relax. I've never liked anyone listening to me go the toilet. Ty, on the other hand, doesn't even bother shutting the door when he goes. Finally I manage a trickle that turns into relief.

One intern talks while the other makes lipstick-y mumbles of assent.

'I saw this pattern, this really strange pattern, almost like honeycomb, but softer and rounder. It took me a few minutes to realise, but when I did, it was obvious. It was a pomegranate, like being inside a giant pomegranate.'

'That's not what I saw at all.' The other intern smacks her lips together loudly. 'I saw cupcakes. A whole field of them, all with pink cream cheese icing. And raspberries perched on top, exactly like nipples.'

They laugh.

'But seriously,' says one. 'It was kind of… you know, sexy, wasn't it?'

The atrium is crowded with dim black figures, crammed in shoulder to shoulder. A DJ plays records on a makeshift stage at the far end of the room. I shoulder my way to a quiet corner, picking up a miniature bottle of champagne from a waiter on the way through. I take my phone out of my bag and dial Ty's number. The line clicks immediately, without ringing.

You've called Ty. Leave a message.

I don't. He's out to dinner with his ex-girlfriend and is supposed to join me at the opening afterwards. It's eleven o'clock and his phone is turned off, which only means one thing. We started going out, or whatever you call this thing, before he'd technically broken up with his ex. She's a model, of all things, and travels constantly. She's only in town until the weekend.

I pour half a bottle of champagne down my throat. The bubbles attach themselves to my boots and carry me through the throng. I find an island of potted palms, and balance precariously on the rim of a pot, wishing I were just a little bit taller. There's no sign of Kristy and Lena. Below me a group of women dressed like deconstructed parrots prattle on, their hands waving, their conversation riding on a wave of free chardy. Several of the women have asymmetrical haircuts that are supposed to make them look chic, but instead make them look as if they are afflicted with some sort of palsy.

I finally spot Kristy on the far side of the room, near the entrance. She's talking with a politician of some note, a lumpy man with a mashed potato face. Her head is tipped winsomely to the side and her eyes say: *you are the most fascinating man I have ever met*. I know that she's already calculating his place in a complex matrix of money, influence and power. Lena is nowhere to be seen. I wouldn't be surprised if she showed early and made sure Mark saw her, then left as soon as she could.

Our CEO taps the microphone on stage as I nudge my way back to the outskirts of the atrium, like I'm part of a rotating penguin huddle. I escape through the side door into the main building.

The way to the exhibition is a narrow tunnel that ends in two flights of suspended stairs. The gallery is a long subterranean room that used to be a subway train platform. The walls are dark, the air musty, the space separated into shadowy alcoves by movable walls. Projectors balanced high on the outer walls shoot solid beams of light. I walk along the length of the room. Mark's rocket stands in the middle of the room, surrounded by a nest of flickering TV screens. We compromised by buying the TVs second-hand from op shops.

In true opening fashion, very few people are actually looking at the artwork. A couple sit quietly on a leather couch, watching a woman hula hoop on the screen in front of them. In the far corner someone's kids sit in the games pod with controls in their hand. My feet barely make a sound on the carpet. After months of working on the exhibition, I don't have much interest in actually experiencing it. I stop at the entrance to a small room and read the white panel describing the artwork.

The Box
KomodoKodomo
Digital video
Biological components

Underneath the name and the artist, where there's supposed to be a written explanation of the work, there's nothing. Warm pink light oozes through the doorway, melting through the strips of white fabric curtaining the entrance. I lean forward, intending to poke my head through the curtain, when I'm struck in the chest so hard I fall backwards onto my arse. My empty champagne bottle rolls into the shadows, forgotten.

A pair of hands grasps my upper arms and hauls me to my feet. I brush my hair off my face and look into the eyes of a man somewhere in his fifties. They're strange eyes; the pupils almost entirely cover the iris, leaving just a thin circle of green around the edges. He has an expensive gold watch on one wrist.

'I am so sorry,' he says, but he doesn't release his grip on my arms. Very slowly, and without breaking his gaze, he slides his hands up to my shoulders and then runs his palms down my back. For some reason, the champagne perhaps, I let him. When his hands reach the small of my back, they move north again and linger around the side of my breasts. I don't move. I'm not in the slightest bit aroused, but my breath is short and shallow.

His eyes flicker down to the badge pinned to my chest.
'You work here?' he asks rhetorically. 'I know the CEO.'
I don't reply. On second glance I'd say he's closer to sixty.
'I've just been to see the show.' He says this with significance that's lost on me. If I didn't know any better, I'd say he was on drugs, or under some sort of spell. He hasn't blinked once yet. I watch him as he moves closer, slowly, as if I'm a small, furry animal that might bolt at any second.

'Are you...?' he asks.
'Wet?' I offer. 'Nope.' I just want to get out of here, out of the

gallery, out of the whole building.

'Oh.' He looks crestfallen for a second, before his face recomposes itself.

'I have to pee,' I say, and make my exit.

I walk back up the stairs and along the tunnel. I grab another mini bottle of champagne on my way out and stash it under my coat. I drink it while I wait for a taxi, hailing with my bottle as they zoom past, all of them with their lights already on. I spill a slosh of bubbly on the concrete when I unlock my phone and dial Ty. I feel my dignity fizzing away on the concrete. If I was drunker, or more melodramatic in nature, I might just lie down here, with my head on the footpath.

You've called Ty…

This time I leave a message. I have so many things to say, it's hard to pick just one.

'I adore you,' I say as a taxi finally brakes and puts its indicator on. 'And you have a heart of stone, you dumb fuck.'

I have a cruel dream, of when Ty and I first met. We're standing outside the Old Bar and we're going our separate ways – he home, me to a gig – which makes what happens happen. He has his hands on either side of my face and he's kissing me, small, soft kisses. There's no urgency because we know we're not spending the night together. We kiss until the bouncer sighs loudly and says, 'This is all very cute guys, but do you mind moving a bit further away from the door?' We laugh and move a few metres away but the moment has gone.

We meet for breakfast early the next morning. I would rather be doing my laundry or reading the newspaper, but I have difficulty saying this to him. I don't feel embarrassed about dialling under the influence. It's not the first time it's happened and it certainly won't be the last.

'You didn't make it last night.' I keep my voice flat and stir my coffee a few too many times. We don't talk much over breakfast as a rule. It either shows that we're comfortable with silence or just plain bored with each other. A man cycles past, leaning back on his seat with his arms crossed smugly, like he's in the comfort of his own home, and not balanced atop a moving vehicle.

'I think they're a bunch of wankers,' says Ty, stabbing his French toast with a fork. 'And all art is a waste of time.'

I don't defend myself, or my job. I've been thinking the same thing lately. I wonder if this job is making me into a bad person, a mean person who takes pleasure in other people's discomfort and pain. I have to constantly do things that don't feel right to me.

Ty has bags under his eyes like he's been up all night. I clench my hands under the table but in the end I don't ask.

The gallery buzzes with school groups and pensioners and young mums with strollers. The computer games are popular as usual, but the longest queue starts at The Box and snakes along the entire length of the gallery.

I pick up an exhibition guide and flick through the pages until I get to the section on The Box. There's an indistinct photo of a shadowy head and a hazy pink halo. *We bring happy seduction to make true knowledge of principled action. See the joy number!*

'Have you been inside?'

I jump, but it's just Kristy at my shoulder. She has a lit cigarette wedged between two fingers and waves it around as she talks. I glance nervously at the sprinklers overhead and shake my head.

'I heard… I've heard some good things,' I offer tentatively.

Kristy snorts.

'I had a go yesterday. It reminded me of childbirth. There was something claustrophobic and sticky about it. I don't know what all the fuss is about.' She points at the queue for The Box with her cigarette. There is an unusually high proportion of men in suits waiting impatiently in line, the sort of men who wouldn't normally make time in their busy work days to look at art. 'Look at that. Sometimes I think they just want to crawl back up there and forget the world.'

'Lena says that Mark isn't happy with the numbers.'

'The numbers are fine. Mark's just annoyed that every reporter he talks to wants to talk about The Box.'

'He'd rather talk about his rocket?'

Kristy stubs the cigarette out on the sole of her shoe, seasoning the carpet with ash. 'You got it,' she says.

After work I go to Myer and buy lavender hand cream I'll never use, and a red lipstick I'll never wear. An iron band of tension pulls tightly against my eyes and forehead. The cosmetics department is lit like a nuclear reactor. Shopping in an overheated department store is masochistic at the best of times, but I just can't seem to make the decision to go home.

I skirt around the aftershave counters and all of a sudden the man from the exhibition opening, the geriatric groper, is in front of me. I turn to walk away but I've been spotted. To my horror the groper waves and walks towards me. He's wearing a polo shirt and a stripy knit slung casually around his shoulders. I thought people only did that in ads.

'Hello,' he says, sounding completely unsurprised. He's one of those rare people who look better in the daytime. I can see money and confidence in his tanned face.

'Fancy seeing you here,' I mumble like a gauche teenager, hitting the toe of one of my shoes with the heel of the other.

'I was at your work again today. I wanted to see the exhibition again, properly. It's always difficult at openings.'

'Really?' I try to sound interested.

'Actually, I just wanted to see The Box again.' He has the decency to look mildly sheepish. 'Have you been to see it yet?'

I shake my head. My cheeks are starting to heat up.

'I was just about to go for a coffee. Would you like to join me?'

I'm pretty sure I'm going to say, *go away, you creep,* but when I open my mouth, all I say is, 'Sure, why not?'

I sit with my back to the footpath at the GPO cafe, hoping that I won't see anyone I know. As soon as we are seated I regret my decision. The groper leans forward, offering his hand.

'I'm Julian, by the way.'

I take his hand, briefly. 'Pan.'

'Like the mythical half-goat, half-man creature?'

'No. Like Pandora.'

Julian chuckles, a low, rolling burble. It's the most attractive thing about him yet.

'You really have to go look at that exhibition,' he laughs.

I open my mouth to make my usual explanation, *my dad is a professor of Classics,* but then I can't be bothered.

'You spend a lot of time in the city then?'

'I live very close by, in the Majorca Building.' There's no trace of suggestion in this statement. 'I sold my house and bought a small apartment when my wife left me.'

'I'm sorry to hear that,' I say. I hope I'm not about to become a stand-in therapist.

'Don't be. I had an affair. She was right to leave me. I wasn't cut out for marriage.'

'It's a pity you didn't know that before you got married.'

'I thought that I was cut out for marriage, until something strange and unexpected happened. I ran my own architecture firm for almost twenty years. A few years ago I was asked to teach at the university, part-time. It was good timing because I was looking at stepping back from my business. One of my students was worried about her marks and made an appointment to see me. When she arrived she closed the door, quite deliberately. We're supposed to leave it open, for all students. She sat down and put her feet up on my desk. Her skirt fell down over her thighs—'

'I get the idea,' I interrupt. I wonder if this ever happened to my dad. I shake that particular thought off before I start dry retching.

'That's how it started. I realised I could get younger women, girls almost, and with little effort.'

I must have been raising my eyebrows.

'Who wouldn't? Tell me, any man in my position, who wouldn't?'

'Does that explain the other night?'

Julian shakes his head.

'You're a little out of my usual range.'

'Ouch!' I wince. 'Washed up at thirty.'

Julian smiles, with perfect white tombstone teeth.

'That was something different. I was in a strange mood that night. I felt… not my usual self.'

Our coffees have arrived. I'm going to be awake all night if I drink mine, but I sip from it anyway. Julian drinks his long black without sugar.

'And what about you, Pandora? No ring on your finger. Are you married to your job?'

I tell him about Ty, or attempt to. I've never had the words to describe what we have. Julian attempts a clinical summary.

'So, you're together, almost every day, but you don't really call it a relationship. And you're theoretically allowed to be with other people, but neither of you really takes that option.'

I nod. It's close enough.

'It sounds like a whole lot of love and dependence in the complete absence of commitment,' says Julian. 'A recipe for disaster in other words.'

'Maybe I like disaster.'

'Maybe that's bullshit.'

'And you're telling me that the girls you're involved with never get hurt?'

'I'm honest. I always state from the start what I can and can't give.'

'But still,' I say, 'people get hurt.'

He nods, reluctantly. 'People get hurt.'

I call Ty and he tells me to come over. When I get to his house the door is ajar and he is lying on the couch, watching telly. He doesn't take his eyes off the screen as I squeeze onto the couch, lying alongside him. I unbutton my dress just enough so that he can get to my breasts. He starts to touch me, almost absentmindedly. I straddle him and he throws his head to the side, his eyes shut. He looks boyish, with his T-shirt and messy hair and expression of concentration. After I come I collapse forward, resting my face in my usual place in the crook of his neck. He moves me with his hands on my arse and then finally it's over for him as well. These are the moments that work for us.

Ty goes to the kitchen for a beer and when he returns he sits in the armchair, rather than next to me on the couch. This is his signal that I won't be sleeping over tonight. I find my undies on the floor and button my dress up. I lean my head against the back of the couch with my eyes closed, and wish I could will myself to sleep. Anything to stop thinking. I'm wired on caffeine.

'I'm sick of this,' I say. I don't want to speak, but my mouth doesn't listen. It moves against my will.

'Sick of what?'

'This.' I cave in on myself while I'm talking; I fall forward until my head rests on my thighs and I address the floor. 'I'm sick of us never discussing anything, sick of no kissing, sick of you only touching me when you want sex, sick of you never giving me compliments, of you looking at every woman on the street, sick of hearing about all the other women you've ever been with…' I lose momentum somehow, even though I should be able to go on for hours. 'I'll leave and you won't do anything about it. You'll let the whole thing go, just like that.'

Ty doesn't reply, but everything about him, the thin set of his mouth, his unmoving shoulders, tells me he doesn't care. I'm not playing by the rules. He hasn't looked me straight in the eye since I arrived. I pull myself together until I'm standing, swaying. I haven't said what I wanted to say. What I really want to say is this: *you're the parasitic twin growing out of the side of my head.* But I don't. I just leave.

I arrive at work early, but instead of going to the first-level offices I catch the lift down to the basement. The gallery is dark. At the far end a woman pushes an industrial-strength vacuum cleaner in decreasing circles. I walk straight past Mark Whistle's rocket and only halt when I come to The Box. The door to The Box pulses with rosy light, even though none of the other exhibits are switched on. I brush my hand through the gauzy curtain and a gust of warm air blows in my face. I wish that I could wash myself of this, this feeling. I wish that I could wash off everything in my life and start over, clean and new. I touch the curtain again, gently; I walk through.

Samuel Bartlett

Letter from Edinburgh Writers' Festival

Russell McGilton

Lou Lou,

I've been to the writer's festival here and guess who I saw: CHUCK PALAHNIUK!

Amazing presenter. Really took the stage – to the point that the host was just some useless appendage to the evening. He started his talk by throwing out blow-up dolls (both male and female) to the audience. 'The first person to blow one up gets a book.' By the end there were hundreds of blow-up dolls being blown up and flying around the room.

Aside from that, he's just a great storyteller. I don't know if you've read any of his stuff but he tells this story of a friend who had just finished college and is working at the Seattle airport as a baggage handler in the basement. You have to wear gloves because the conveyor belt has holes in it and can catch your finger and rip it off. But his friend was desperate to see the world and had this college debt and remembered that he was part of the union, which had a rule that if you lose a finger you get $20,000. So he takes off the gloves and, sure enough, his finger is whipped off. And as he's soaked in his own cold sweat, looking at the missing index finger, he's thinking 'I'm gonna get my twenty thousand' – when he turns his hand around and sees that it's still attached.

Rather than rush off to emergency he starts yanking at his finger. White tendons are stretching as he's pulling at it, pain shooting up his arm, when security, seeing all the blood on the bags, storms in. As Chuck finished the story, a woman cried out, 'WHAT HAPPENED?!' Well, his friend didn't get the $20,000 but now has his finger sewed back on and an arm full of ruptured tendons.

Awesome, eh?

Edinburgh fest a blast. Having sell-out shows here. Hope your world is groovy.

Russss xx

off-white

*Grace
Yee*

this is where:

I
the chubby italian with the sapphire stud in his ear
destroyed
the vietnamese family tree
      on account of an overhanging branch

the podiatrist goes to work
in a rusty hyundai
so his wife can be seen
      driving the kids to school in a mercedes suv

the mothers of the grade three boys
sincerely believe
that their sons are too nice to urinate
      on the soap in the school toilets

the dentist
is trying to talk
her eight-year-old daughter out
      of being gay

the only mother who stays home
is a fish

II
backyard swimmers wouldn't be seen dead
with kidneys
    [rectangular pools are]
    [the fashion darling]

III
the most popular interior paint colour
    is off-white

IV
you could wedge a four-inch thick sheet
of polystyrene
between a person's smile and that thing
that beats in his / her chest
and there'd be room to spare
                    for a feature wall statement

The Hungry Grass

Aaron Mannion

Whenever you go back somewhere, somewhere that's important to you, the light's always wrong. Today it's too bright. Not glary, just a diffused, even, mid-morning kind of brightness. It isn't how I remember it. Mostly I think of it as twilight, the time of day where, as a boy, you realised you should probably already be at home. Or I think of dark, glittering days where your skin goes the chemical pink of a redhead's lips from being scalded by the rain, or of the piercing sunlight that left us all squinting in the photos from my First Holy Communion. Or I remember the time when my mother and I rode home in the pitch black of night; me on my bike and her on her horse, Camiri. The mare had been at the stallion and we'd been delayed. At first my father had driven in front of us, giving us light, but he'd been sent on to feed the animals and we kept on in the dark, waking unseen cattle whose surprise frightened the horse, until slowly our eyes became accustomed and the world appeared in grey and blue and mushroom-white.

'We'd better get going, David. We can stop again on the way back.'

'Yeah, course.'

We are standing on the road outside our old house, which I haven't seen since we left it eleven years ago. My father's wearing a black suit and a black tie because we are on our way to my grandmother's viewing. I've dressed as sombrely as I could, but I worry about the tie, which is dark purple and red, and reminds me of the colours in those flickering Sacred Heart of Jesus pictures.

We get back in the car and continue on down the Mount Talbot Road. I remember all the roads and landmarks clearly. On the right is Bolgen Hill with the tall beech trees on top, behind which I'd once taken off my clothes and rolled across the fawny green grass. I'd come up in hives all over. For a week at school I'd looked like a leper.

I predict the appearance of the lonely pump house from behind Buckley's corner, but I'm surprised by the large, modern bungalow which has been built just ten yards in front of Gleason's cottage. My father sees it too.

'Well, Gleasons have done well for themselves.'

'South Fork. You'd think they'd have built it away from the old place.'

'Maybe the parents are still in it and one of the kids is in the new place.'

'Maybe.'

I look over at my father. His eyes are off up the road, a good five seconds in front of us. He's quiet now. Since we left his house forty miles away in Athlone he's talked, off and on, of his mother. He'll glance over at me, and then wait a few moments, and then he'll tell me something about her. I feel like there's something he doesn't think I've understood. He wouldn't put it like that though. It's her childhood he's been talking about, how she was an orphan taken in by the O'Hanlons and about how poor she was. My father has only one picture of his mother as a girl. She's about nine or ten and she's standing in front of a cottage in an old tatter of a dress. He once got a friend of mine, an art student, to do a sketch from the photograph, but he asked that she put his mother in something pretty. I think it was his way of doing something for her.

I've never had anyone close to me die. I've tried to imagine it, but usually it's just words in my head and my next thought's of Chelsea or lunch or something. It just doesn't register. Once though, once I got it in my head that my mother was going to die. I mean really got it in. It shattered me. Gone, just gone. The whole world would be like that feeling you get in an elevator, when your guts aren't where they're supposed to be. I'd never see her again. It seemed to mean that I'd always be alone, that I'd always been alone. It frightened the shite out of me to be honest.

I hadn't known my grandmother well and I feel no grief now, but I try to understand what it means for my father.

We're already at the Ballymahon crossroads. The countryside

here is foreign, though familiar. The nation of my childhood ended a few miles back. After you pass the turn-off to Rossmartin, you start moving into lowlands. It's flat and scrubby, and for the next ten or fifteen miles the fields are smaller and are bounded by hedges and bits of wire and even the occasional car body. Off to the west is Clanfergus Bog. The rest is wet, mucky land, not really good for anything much and it's mostly used to hold a few cattle or, after you cross the River Suck, for forestry.

Around our old house it was different; the land was buckled by glaciers into hills and folds and plains, broken up here and there by patches of gorse and stones. In the lower fields, people kept cattle or cut silage, but on the hills and in among the crops of stones it was sheep. The fields were generally bigger and were edged in narrow stone walls three or four feet high. Aside from the ones around orchards, or some of the ones backing onto roads, they were all dry-stone walls, which means that there's no cement or mortar used of any kind. Instead the stones are chosen and fitted, each into the other. In country like ours, where the stones were as often square as round, the walls could be thinner and even the best dry-stone waller left skinny triangular gaps through which you could spy Indians or cops or enemy troops as they came towards you. Out in the fields there was little cover. Sometimes you'd be lucky and you'd come across a hump or a hollow that would hide you, but for the most part there was only the grass, cropped smooth and close by the gnawing sheep, like baize on a pool table, and interrupted only by sentinel thistles. You either had to keep low, in by the walls, or do away with stealth and make a long, raw run across the open spaces.

'That's where your second cousin, Aileen Gregan, lives.'

My father points out a house on a small plot carved out of the pine forest behind. It looks like a house lost in a dark fairy-tale.

'Is it?'

I feel guilty for not keeping the conversation going.

'Who was that guy that used to give me chocolate? He lived around here. Jenny was friends with him.'

'Joyce was it? Michael Joyce. He used to keep a mare or two.'

'I think so. Down that road to the left. The last one before Granny's house.'

'That's him.'

We're nearly at my grandmother's house now. I'm not looking

forward to it. The last funeral I was at I was only eight or nine, and I don't know what it is I'm supposed to do.

'How's your mother?'

'She's fine. She sends her condolences. I told you that, didn't I?'

'You did.'

'So does Zoë.'

'When did you see her?'

'Last week. We met up in London.'

'How was that?'

'Awful. I got too drunk. I can't leave it alone. I know there's no going back, but I can't accept it's over.'

'There's other girls out there for you.' He looks over at me. 'It doesn't mean it wasn't important, but you'll find someone else.'

I don't want to talk about it and I think of turning on the radio. I stop myself. I'm not going to be rude.

We don't pull in at my grandmother's house as I'd supposed. My father says we're meeting in Ahascragh and then going up to the nursing home to look at the body. We pass by the house. It looks smaller than last time I saw it. The pebble-dash is mottled in black lichen and black-green moss. Nobody's lived in the place for almost a year now, though apparently my uncle, who lives next door, has kept a fire going over the winter to keep it dry. They'll have to decide now what's to be done with it.

In Ahascragh we stop at a pub called Dolan's. I've never been inside it before, though I remember dropping my grandfather off there after mass on a Sunday. I'd always imagined it'd be dreary in here, but there's a jukebox playing and it seems open and friendly.

We walk through the public bar, which is empty apart from two old men in the corner, into the lounge where the family have gathered. I recognise my uncles and aunts and the older cousins. Some of the kids though I don't think I've seen before. I'd never visited my relatives. My mother and I would be off with the horses every weekend and there was never time.

Everyone's smiling and saying hello. My aunt Mary asks how I'm doing in university and what am I studying. I tell her English and she asks me am I going to be a school teacher. I watch my father talking to his older brother, who's just flown over from Australia. No, I'm not sure what I'll do, get into the theatre if I can.

I go over to my father and uncle.

'Is this your young fella?'
'It is. He's bigger than the last time you saw him.'
'He is. So, are you still going with the horses?'
'No. I gave that up.'
'He's over at Oxford University in England.'
'He is. Charlie said something about that alright. Well done. You'll be a professor soon no doubt.'
'I'd better get the degree first.'
A small old man in a suit jacket and royal blue jumper places a hand on my father's elbow. 'I'm sorry for your troubles. She was a great woman. It's a great loss to ye.'
He shakes each of our hands in turn and then moves on.
My father looks at his brother.
'Was that, what's his name again? Rory, Rory Quigley isn't it?'
'No, no. He's a Quigley alright though. Seamus, I think.'
'Is he now? You know his daughter is a real estate agent in Ballinasloe.'
I look over to the bar. The publican is standing at the end of the counter, talking to some of the family. Halfway along the bar there's a doorway through to the other room and I can see some of my cousins clustered around a video game.
'Can I get anyone a drink?'
'No thanks. This'll do me.'
'No. We have to drive in a minute.' I walk over, but my father calls me back. 'Actually, could you get me a Lucozade?'
'Will do.'
'Do you need any money?'
'No. I'm fine.'
I get my father his drink and buy myself a lager. He's over with his sister, talking, so I sit and watch the racing on the telly. I left my cigarettes in the car.
The cousins come back in from the video game. Among them is a pretty, dark-haired girl with sharp blue eyes. They gather at the far end of the room. My eyes flash up and I catch her glance as she leans against the wall, surrounded by cousins, like courtiers. I taste the beer in my mouth, hopsey and tanging like summer and short skirts. The flush of blood wakes my appetite for nicotine and I find my hand tapping my pockets in false hope. She's probably a relation for fuck's sake.

Zoë left me because I'd cheated on her. We'd gotten back together since that, but it'd always been there. I think in a way it had made me love her more, thinking I could lose her any minute. I'd see a smile or a laugh and it'd feel like they, and every other memory I held of her, were about to be ripped out of me. She said she couldn't trust me. I'd tried to change her mind. I said it was like the little bit of sand that starts the pearl on its way. She wasn't having any of it.

I ask my father for the keys and go back to the car to smoke.

The wind's risen and blown the brightness out of the day, spreading a thin, high cloud across the sky like margarine. The nursing home is a dark grey, stone building. Someone said it used to be a convent. It doesn't have the look of an institution to me, though neither does it look like the work of the gentry, and only they could have had a house that size. It's too grim for them, too penitential, and it lacks the spare grace of Anglican architecture.

We don't go in. Instead a man comes out and leads us up to a small building at the back. He unlocks the double doors, folds them back and then leaves. I had thought a priest would be here. I'm standing towards the rear when the family starts to file in slowly. I can see a few chairs around the walls and I check to see how my father's taking it. His hands are clasped in front of him. His head's bowed, like he is at mass.

I still can't see properly inside and I look off behind, over the small wall and onto the fields. A hill spills steeply down to what looks like it'd be a small river or drain, but it's occluded by the fat roll of bank in front of it. Off to the right is a tight little copse, twenty yards square at most. I'd prefer to be over there, chasing my childhood and staining my trousers bright green.

We're at the door now and I see my grandmother laid out in her coffin on a table in the centre of the room. I've never seen a real dead body before. It looks too normal. It should be spooky or upsetting, but it's just there, as still and quiet as the chairs standing by the wall. She's wearing a white lacy dress. Is it hers or is it something bought especially? Her hair is almost purely white and is set in curls. It looks thinner than I remember it. The skin too is white, hinting at pink and maybe yellow.

There is only one person in front of me now and I don't know if I'm meant to kiss the corpse or not. The man in front isn't family and he merely touches her hand and pauses, closing his eyes briefly. I've probably seen what I'm supposed to do, but I can't get it clear. My father's behind me and I step up to the body. I place my hand on hers and close my eyes and say the words of a prayer in my head.

As I leave, I try to glance over my shoulder at my father. Someone walks in the way and I don't see whether he kissed her or not. People are talking quietly in groups and I sit on the wall, listening and wanting to smoke.

'David Mallone.'

I look to the voice and see a cousin of mine. He's albino with ghost white skin and hair, and eyes rimmed with empathetic pink, and I know him instantly. I can't be sure of his name though. I think it's Diarmuid, but I could be wrong.

'How are you?'

'Do you remember me? Diarmuid Black.'

'Of course I do. How's it going down in Wexford?'

'Ah, not bad. There's no point complaining at any rate.'

We shake hands and he sits down, propping his gammy leg out in front of him. When he was little, shortly after we'd arrived over from Australia, he'd been hit by a car. I was too young to hear much about it. I know that he'd nearly died and that there was talk of brain damage. I have images too, but I don't know where from. If I think of his father, I see a man gone bald early, a man who wouldn't rush out of the rain, who'd sort of just accept it. I see him as vulnerable and resigned, like the varnish that protects most of us from the world was cracked on him and he knew it. I don't know where I got that from. I probably just absorbed it from the talk surrounding the family. There were stories too of Diarmuid as a boy, flying into rages and smashing the fish tank and the television. Beside me now, he's cheery, not exactly joking, but with a look like one of us is about to amuse the other. He makes me feel friendly or something.

I ask him what he's doing and he asks me the same. I fancy a cigarette. Nobody else is smoking though and I wait. I find myself a bit stuck for something to say.

'Do you know what this building used to be?'

'No. Before it was a nursing home you mean?'

'Yeah. Do you think it was a convent?'
'I don't know. I suppose it might have been.'
'It doesn't look right for that. It's a bit higgledy-piggledy.'
'Maybe it was some landlord's house.'
'I don't know. Wouldn't there be more stables and outhouses?'
'I suppose.'
'Also, it's too grey and…'
'And what?'
'I don't know.'

I don't go on. I don't say that it's too ugly to be Anglo–Irish. I'm too much of a West Briton in any case.

Everyone is moving back into the building. When I get there, the seats are taken. I find my father and stand beside him. A few of the women are holding rosary beads. Aunty Patty begins and in a few seconds we've fallen in behind. The prayers pass by quickly. I can't remember the ratio of Hail Marys to Our Fathers, so I keep the prayers under my breath and listen. Aunty Patty's thumb inches the beads through, counting off the prayers.

In the centre, the body just lies there. I wonder when it was brought in here. Did she lie there all night? Somehow, it seems even lonelier being alone when you're dead, lying there as still as the world before and after.

One of the babies starts to cry, but the prayers carry on. I try to remain interested. I once had a set of rosary beads, a white set. I'd thought they were sissy, all white and silver. I'd like to have them now. Something to keep track with, one bead, then the next. It seems reassuring.

We finish and everyone moves outside. There's a slow wandering to the cars. My father talks to Patty and I look at the nursing home. It extends out behind in a long wing. Two rows of windows, upstairs and down, let the light into what looks like corridors. It probably was a convent.

'David.'

Behind me is Diarmuid, together with a blond guy of my own age, a cousin I think, and the dark-haired girl from the pub.

'Diarmuid. How's it going?'
'David, you know Fergus and your cousin Sarah.'
'I know Fergus, alright. I'm not sure I've met you before, Sarah.'
'Or else we were too little to remember it.'

'David, we're getting together in Dolan's tonight, the young ones in the family. Come along if you can?'

'I will. I don't know if I can get over and back though. I'm staying over in Athlone with Peter.'

'Sure, just get a lift over and someone will put you up for the night.'

'I'll see what I can do. Thanks.'

I sit back into the passenger seat and light a cigarette. Someone's blocked us in and we sit waiting for them to move.

'You should try to give those up, David.'

'I know I should. What's the plan now?'

'Home. Do you want me to drop you off at Fergus's?'

'What do you mean?'

'Well, aren't you all going to the get-together?'

'Ah no. I'm not staying over. I hardly know them.'

'Are you sure? You'll get to know them.'

'No. I'm okay.'

'No problem.'

We sit there for a few minutes. I finish my cigarette and start another. Diarmuid and blue-eyed Sarah and a few other cousins pile into a car driven by Fergus. They're laughing and I feel envious.

'Where does Fergus live?'

'I think he's renting a house in Ballymahon with a few friends of his. We can stop in there if you want.'

'No, no. It's okay. I was just wondering.'

The car in front pulls off and we leave.

The day's settled now. The wind's dropped and the clouds have ground to a standstill in the sky. We're at the turn-off to our old house and my father asks me should we take it or cut down through Caltra to the main road.

'Let's have a look at it again.'

'We can stop in at Coyle's and have a drink and maybe a sandwich if you like?'

'That might be nice.'

We pass an orchard to the right. It was once attached to a big house that's now just a few old walls with trees growing up through them. I'd seen pictures. It was beautiful once, a big, clean Georgian house; three semicircular steps up to a gently classical front door, lawns and rose gardens and everything. It was abandoned in the thirties and the locals stole the lead from the roof and that was it. In a few years the roof had collapsed. It was ruined and they gutted it for timber and fittings. Finally, the Land Commission parcelled off the property for grazing.

I'd ridden my bike down here once with a boy from school, Paul something. We'd left our territory to come to rob the apples, though we couldn't tell you who we were stealing them from. It was a bit of an anticlimax in the end. There was no one about and the trees weren't tended and the apples were small and mingy.

Paul and I had stolen apples together all over the place. Before we'd set off we'd put on all the green clothes we had and sometimes we'd even each put a leg from a stolen pair of stockings over our heads and off we'd go through the fields, running, climbing trees for reconnaissance and throwing ourselves into ditches at the sound of a car. We'd come home stinking of sap and with carrier bags full of ripe and unripe apples.

We'd been friends, or schoolmates anyway. Once, I'd gone at night and stolen every apple and pear that was hanging from the young trees our teacher Mrs Talbot had planted beside the house. I couldn't wait to tell Paul the next day. But when I did, he didn't laugh. The teacher's son was in our class and Paul said he was going to tell him about it. I had to pay him five pounds to make him promise not to.

I'd left the school the next year. Mrs Talbot had caught me passing a note to a girl. It was signed 'Paul' and it had a picture of a house with an upstairs window marked 'My Bedroom'. She called me filthy and dirty, and made me stand in the corner for over two hours. I was still crying when my mother got home at four o'clock. When she heard, she moved me to a school in the next parish. The teacher came and apologised. My father and all the neighbours thought my mother should be satisfied with that. But she stuck to her guns and I didn't go back.

We cross a little stream. There's no bridge as such, just a bump as the road bulges up. If you don't know about it, you can hit it too fast and you bang your head on the roof. That's the border you cross to enter the parish.

I see my father arguing something beneath his face. I try to engage him.

'Do you remember Danny Coyle talking about the hungry grass?'

'I do.'

'Where was it meant to be again?'

'Didn't he say it was off to the right as you go down to Fahey's?'

'Beside the old quarry?'

'Yes. I think so.'

'Do you know does Danny still keep a few ponies?'

'No. He died, God bless him.'

Hungry grass is a pishrogue, an old wives' tale. It's cursed grass that, if you walk on it, will suck the strength out of you. To survive you need to have a bit of bread or sustenance on your person to eat. The grass is cursed because it grows on the unmarked graves of famine victims. After Danny told me about it, I'd spent hours searching, a couple of slices of white loaf in my pocket at all times. In the end, I'd get hungry and eat the bread, and then I'd be nervous as I traipsed over the fields on the way home.

We come to the crossroads that forms the village. It's half past one and there's a few cars outside the pub.

'Should we just go on to Athlone? We could have dinner in The Royal.'

'Ah, no. I'm happy to stop here, David.'

'I don't really fancy it.'

'Okay. I wouldn't mind getting home. Do you want me to swing by the old house?'

'No. Maybe we could stop at the top of the hill and have a look around.'

'Of course.'

We pass my old primary school. It's been extended and there's now a basketball court out the back. Beside it is the Talbots' big, two-storey house with the balcony that I'd never seen used. It's the same pale mustard colour now it's always been.

We get to the top of the hill and stop. I've watched the speedometer and I see that from the bump to here is only six miles. Six miles across. Six miles across a tract of land six childhood years long.

I walk along the grass verge back toward the village and then jump over the wall. There's a clutter of rocks and gorse down to the left, and I think I remember there being a little trickling rivulet in there somewhere. My father's on the verge, looking over at me. I go for a bit of a run and then stop, feeling foolish. I look down at the grass and then over at the stones and then at the gorse. The day's turned a bit cold now. It must have rained here earlier. My shoes are soaked and my trousers too. I see my father trying to find a spot to get down into the field.

'Don't bother.'

'What?'

'Don't bother, I said.'

'Are you sure? We can go for a walk if you'd like.'

'I can't be arsed. Come on, let's go and get something to eat.'

'Okay, then.'

'I've ruined my shoes coming in here.'

After a few minutes, we get out on the main road and leave behind the hungry grass and everything.

The wheels fart and sing on the rough tarmac and the wind whistles Dixie through a gap in the window. I light a cigarette and lay my eyes on short-lived patches of scenery. A field ploughed open to a flock of worm-thirsty seagulls. Here, now, and then gone. An old house with a dead tractor out the front stands beside a brand new shed: grey bricks and dappled grey galvanised iron, perfect except for a streak down the wall where the gutter leaks. Each picture offers itself up and then scoots to destruction behind my left shoulder.

I like sitting in the passenger seat with my father driving. Sometimes I feel almost weightless. It's best when it's all new. When all of you is inside and everything else is outside, just a passing world. Just me and my father and a glory of inaction. It's like the first few puffs of a cigarette break, when for a few seconds all the weight of the world is exhaled.

White Summer

Pierz Newton-John

James woke in pitch darkness and with a lurch of terror found that he did not know who or where he was. He sprang from the bed, hitting his head hard on something overhead. Light and pain flashed and he started to cry out, not 'Help! Help!' but *'Hilfe! Hilfe!'* Why was he speaking German? And then memory flooded back. A moment later the light switched on and Anja was standing in the doorway in a dressing gown.

'James, *was ist los?'* What's the matter?

He heard Karl, Anja's eight-year-old son, cry out. He had woken the whole house with his stupid yelling. He wanted to explain himself, but when he reached for the German, it wasn't there. He stared at her foolishly, his mouth opening and closing like a fish's. Finally he mumbled, *'Es tut mir Leid,'* I'm sorry, and sat back down on his bed miserably. Anja said something he didn't follow, then hit the light switch, plunging him back into darkness. Karl's wailing went on – *'Mutti! Mutti!'* – like an echo of his own cry, and he heard Anja's footsteps in the corridor as she went to comfort him.

His room was in a garret at the top of the house; he had hit his head on the ceiling where it sloped sharply over his bed. In the mornings he would open the blinds and look out on a landscape that could hardly have been more remote from Sydney's dry brilliance. Fat steeple-roofed houses clustered on the damp plain of the Ruhrgebiet under a low gunmetal sky. As days passed, erratic icy flurries gradually gave way to a thick, silent downpour that buried everything. For a time, before the whiteness wore out the eye, the pristine dunes of snow accomplished a miracle, transforming that prosaic scene into a fairytale tableau.

The cold had taken him completely by surprise; it was beyond anything he had encountered before, knifing straight through his warmest clothes. Even in the centrally heated house of his hosts, he felt persecuted by a constant chill. They believed that an overheated house hampered adjustment to the cold outside. He learnt a German word that encapsulated his experience: *trostlos*. Comfortless, hopeless – there is no perfect translation, but James understood the word exactly. It described an abject condition in which there is no respite from misery.

Anja's husband Dieter worked for a major pharmaceutical company. He was a big, thick-fingered man, almost the stereotype of the German executive, fattened on bratwurst and *Kartoffeln*. One evening he knocked on the door of James's room. He stood awkwardly in the small space looking flustered, his big hands fidgeting.

'I just vanted to... I vondered how are you going?' he said, using English for the first time since James had arrived. They had told him he would learn better if he were allowed to converse in German only.

James forced a smile. 'Fine. Thank you.'

Dieter sweated. 'Vee are vorried for you. You don't seem... heppy.' He blushed, apparently embarrassed by the word. 'Did you, did you vant to... talk?' His pained expression gave the impression he had fishbones caught in his throat. It was obvious he had been put up to this by his wife.

'No, no. I'm just... I'm just cold.'

'Oh cold!' Dieter's face beamed with relief. He had safely crossed the tightrope to secure ground. '*Ja*. It is cold this year. But in Shermany vee heff a saying: Who freezes is either poor or stupid.' He laughed and gave James's arm a hearty thump. 'Vell, let me know if...' He petered out. '*Gute Nacht!*' he said, and retreated.

There had been a day not long before he had left Australia when everything had fallen in on him.

Glen Thomas cornered him in the school toilet. 'Poofta!' he sneered – his usual taunt – then put him in a headlock and banged his head against the stinking metal of the urinal. 'Want a lolly?' he said, forcing James's face down towards the foul yellow blobs of soap in the piss-clogged gutter.

For an awful moment he thought he was actually going to be

forced to eat one, but then, as suddenly as it had begun, the attack was over. Glen released his neck from the vice of his arm, then stood indifferently at the urinal, pissing on the spot where he'd held James's head a moment before. Still in shock, James stood there stupidly, until Glen said,

'You checking out my dick? You really are a poofter aren't you?'

On the way home, Glen and two of his cronies were lounging against a wall, smoking and taking turns to spit on the footpath. He tried to ignore them, to look resolutely ahead, but as he passed, they made a sudden move towards him and he ran. He heard them laugh. It was too hot for them to bother with a chase.

'Run, faggot, run!' he heard one of them say.

Later that night, he ate dinner politely with his family. That was still in the time when nothing was said, when truths could not be named, but hung in the air, oppressive like the heat before the change. The time of silence and lies. His parents were still together, bonded by nothing more than the thin glue of routine, pretence and fear of change. When the ice-cream came for dessert, and James put the first spoonful into his mouth, he felt suddenly like a five-year-old child, and an awful sadness arose in him. He began to cry silently, tears sliding down and mixing saltily with the ice-cream he continued to spoon into his mouth. Everyone kept eating, and all that could be heard was the clinking of spoons on bowls and the suffocating sound of silence.

Later he went out into the garden, and in a sudden rage, kicked all the heads off the cabbages. Then he kicked the heads until they were all smashed and broken, debris all over the garden. But the aggression brought him no relief. There was pain in everything his mind touched. The garden had fallen into darkness and through the kitchen window he could see his parents washing up, his brother making a cup of tea. It was an unreal pantomime, and standing among the ruined cabbages, he felt as removed from the domestic normality of the scene as if he were watching a film of events a century in the past. He went to his room and fell on his bed, pain swarming over him like a cloud of bees. He bit down hard on his anguish – nobody must hear him – and the thought *I don't want to go* screamed in his head. But the ticket was booked, the arrangements made, there was no getting out of it.

Anja brought him an aerogram from his mother telling him that the summer had turned into a stinker. Three days over forty in a row. But here the nights fell to minus twenty. Along the road, the cars were stacked with snow, like wedding cakes. James helped the family cover a pine tree in the backyard with tinsel and baubles, and Karl danced around it, the magic of the snow merging in his mind with the enchantment of Christmas. But in spite of the familiar images of snow and Christmas trees, to James it seemed that summer had been abducted and buried beneath an arctic freeze. A white summer. He stood in his garret window, watching darkness fall at four o'clock, the twinkle of Christmas lights emerging everywhere, as if to replace the stars that remained hidden behind the permanent bank of cloud. To die of cold, he recalled, was supposed to be blissful, after a certain point. An overdose of snow, like heroin, death in a beautiful dream opiated by cold.

He was sitting in the living room studying the list of German vocab he'd made for the day, when he looked up to find a girl, a young woman, standing there. Under a crazy mass of black curls, her eyes regarded him with a warmth that startled him. It was a gaze that seemed to see through him, to laugh off his shame and self-doubt as if with a brush of her hand she could wipe it away like frost on a window. He stood, confused, and she came forward and reached out her hand.

'Hallo,' she said. '*Ich bin* Emilie. *Ich bin hier als Au-pair.*' He heard how the language was awkward to her, the way her French accent tried to soften it. Her handshake barely registered in his mind at the time, but years later he would realise he could still recall the sensation of it exactly, the warmth and inexplicable affection of it.

She was from Boulogne. She played the piano. Her German was bad – worse than James's – her English just a little better, so they conversed in a mix of the two languages, cutting out the English when their hosts were around. Her room was in the basement, next to the laundry where she did the family's washing and ironing. There was also a games room there with a pool table, a computer for Karl to play games on. They sat down there and played Uno, laughing at their linguistic mix-ups, at the strangeness of Germans, at everything. She laughed at the way he laughed.

'You 'ave a funny laugh,' she said.

'*Nein!*'
'*Ja!* You do.'
'*Was ist* so *komisch?*'
'I don't know. You sound like this.' She made an absurd whinnying sound.
'No I don't! I don't sound anything like that!' he laughed.
'There! You are doing it again!' She made the noise again.
'*Hör auf! Du klingst wie ein Pferd.*' Laughter was making his sides hurt, his head dizzy.
'It is *you* who sound like a 'orse.'
The laughter, her intoxicating proximity, made him suddenly brave. 'Do you have a boyfriend… in France?'
'*Nein.*'
'Are we in English or German?'
And they both laughed till they sobbed.

They were woken one morning while it was still dark, to go hunting in the Schwarzwald. Standing in the gloom of the garage Emilie looked as pale and dazed as he felt. The Mercedes sped along the autobahn in the icy fog, speedo steady on one-eighty, rapid-fire German on the radio reporting news he couldn't follow. The window was cold on his forehead as he watched the factories loom out of the grey. Behind concrete sound barriers, the hills were piled with the small, drab houses of the factory workers, hunkered down against the bitter weather. Then frozen fields and distant farmhouses half lost in the blur, lives he couldn't imagine.

The warmth of the car's heater, the engine's steady hum, lulled him. He dozed off, and for a time he was somewhere he belonged, some formless comforting place at the borders of nothingness. Then the engine noise cut out like a blanket pulled away to expose the hard silence beneath. He woke. Anja turned in the passenger seat. She smiled at him, a maternal smile he was familiar with. It told him she saw an unhappy child in him, she responded to a lost boy. But he was seventeen; childhood was locked and barred behind him now. In any case he did not love this stranger; he would not let her mother him. He looked away without returning the smile. Outside, in the drifting fog and snow, a fat man was gathering shotguns from the boot of his BMW.

When he opened the car door, the cold hit him in the face,

twined around his throat. He stood stamping the icy slush underfoot, clamping his hands in the warmth of his armpits. Dieter checked the barrel of his shotgun, sighted it at the sky that seemed to be collapsing onto their shoulders. Anja came over and gave James a slim metal box like a cigarette case. It was warm to the touch. She opened it to show him a coal smouldering inside in a woolly insulated bed. To keep his hands warm, she explained, pressing it into his coat pocket in that motherly way.

Of course, they didn't give him a gun. Instead he and Emilie joined the line of beaters who marched through the forest bashing the undergrowth with sticks to drive out the game. His feet went numb and the snow melted on his collar and trickled down his neck.

After a time the trees cleared and gave way to a field of dense scrub. Away from the shelter of the trees, the wind was sharp and bitter, snaking into his collar however tight he drew it. As they traversed the field, a small covey of grouse burst from the bushes. The hunters stood and fired. Stinging pellets of shot spat down onto James's upturned face, and he covered his head with his arms, almost crying out. One by one the birds fell, plummeted dead or dying out of the air. Only one kept rising for a time, defying the guns, heaving its body higher until it began to fade into the fog. And then finally, a puff of feathers and it, too, spiralled down. Dogs bounded forward to collect the kill.

With the limp, bloody grouse slung over their shoulders, the hunters were flushed with excitement and manly bonhomie. They slapped one another's backs and joked as they crossed the field and once again entered the silence of the Black Forest. The beaters spread out through the trees, growing further apart until it became hard to keep track of the line. He could see Emilie moving far to his right, every now and again striking at the scrub in a desultory fashion. In the near solitude, the beating felt meaningless and James let his arm drop and trudged on in silence. The silver case in his pocket kept the fingers of one hand warm while the rest of him shivered.

He heard a shout behind him. A man with a gun came running through the trees towards him. '*Was ist los mit dir?*' he shouted. '*Warum treibst du nicht? Schlag doch!*' It was the man he'd seen earlier taking his guns out of the BMW. His face was red, his jowls quivering. James could only make out half of what he was shouting at him. But he understood that he was being told to beat and half-heartedly whacked the bushes. To his amazement, there was a rustle and a startled hare bolted out of the undergrowth. A cry went up, blurts of excited German, as it shot terrified across the line of beaters. It jinked fast through the trees while the guns banged and the fat men shouted. *Go!* he thought.

The man raised his barrel. His eyes contracted to murderous points as he tracked the path of the dodging hare. The blast crashed against James's nerves, but the hare was still going.

'*Scheisse!*' the man swore, but he didn't lower his gun. There was a second barrel. The hare cut across a clearing towards the safety of a dense thicket. The man swung the gun to take aim, but now James was in his line of fire. He was staring into the shotgun's smoking muzzle.

'*Aus dem Weg!*' the man barked. But James didn't move. He stared back into the black hole of the gun, of the hunter's eyes. He had never thought of himself as having much in the way of courage, but somehow he found the ability to stand where he was, to paralyse himself, to stretch out the moment of defiance one second longer, one second longer. He saw ice in the hunter's moustache, the escalating rage on his face, watched as the thought of pulling the trigger, the easiness of it, the release of it, passed over the man's face. And then the barrel dropped.

'*Du* Idiot!' the man ranted, apoplectic. '*Bist du total blöd? Ich hätte dich erschiessen können!*' I could have shot you.

James looked down, letting the abuse wash over him. Snow had melted in his boots and his feet were freezing.

In the late afternoon the whole hunting expedition drove to a vast mansion owned by one of the hunters, a work colleague of Dieter's and a senior executive in the company. One room was decked out in medieval fashion, mounted stags' heads on the walls, and here they laid out their kill on a rough-hewn wooden table. The grouse, a couple of hares, and their prize quarry, a small doe. Its head lolled from the edge of the table, eyes dull, and a crimson slime trickled from its mouth to gloss the slate floor.

They threw logs into a huge fireplace, drank beer from enormous pewter steins, lit up pipes and cigars. The centuries seemed to vanish like a vapour. James sat on a bench in the corner, watching the spectacle of modern executives atavistically transformed into barbarians, Vikings roaring after the slaughter. And there *was* something intoxicating about it all: blood, beer, the heat of alcohol and fire after the snowy forest.

'I think they 'ave gone crazy.' Emilie had slipped onto the bench beside him.

'Wahnsinn,' agreed James.

They sat a moment contemplating the scene. Then suddenly she seized his hand, pulled him to his feet. 'Let's go.'

He followed her through a door into a long, silent corridor. 'We shouldn't be here,' he said, but keeping hold of his hand, she pulled him along the corridor.

'Look at this!' She gestured through an open door and, to James's amazement, he saw there was a huge indoor swimming pool there. On the far side of the darkened room he could make out the pine doors of what he assumed was a sauna. Through another door they saw a small cinema, then another room apparently set up as a disco. Other enormous rooms stood empty, as if the owners' imaginations had simply fallen short of their wealth. The money was beyond James's comprehension.

At the end of the corridor a door opened onto a snowy courtyard, lit by floodlights. It was silent apart from the muffled sound of discordant, raucous singing from the hunters at the other end of the house. Flakes fell and eddied like particles of light over the unbroken blanket of white. Where the lights ended the night was a perfect void, unfathomable as a pupil. In its darkness, the wind moved, stirring over the frozen forests of Germany. Emilie ran laughing out onto the pristine snow, her feet punching through it, leaving holes of blue shadow. She turned around, surrounded by a pale halo of iridescence cast by the lights in the icy air. She crouched to gather the snow in her hands and James, seeing what she was doing, ran forward and caught her around the waist, the snowball disintegrating over his back as she tried to throw it. He pinned her down on the snow, and suddenly her face was close, her breath a warm cloud on his cheeks. *'Du warst mutig heute,'* she said. You were brave today. And then they were kissing, her nose cold against his face, but her mouth hot and tasting of the mysteries of her body.

It was not a long kiss, by the standards of other kisses he would one day know. But it was long enough for her to take his cold hand inside her clothes, like a bird she was saving, taking home folded into her breast. Long enough for his hand to feel her heart beating in the soft, warm valley there, for his fingers to grow warm and spread over the swell of her, to feel her nipple rise under his palm.

Fifteen years later, he would wake in his bed in Sydney, with the same panicked moment of amnesia he had once known in Germany, and when the disorientation cleared, the knowledge struck his heart as if it had been a brass bell: *I am not at home.* But this place *was* his home. There was nowhere else to go back to. His mind floundered for a moment, seeking that emotional reference point and then, to his astonishment, it was Emilie's face he saw rising out of the obscurity of memory. For a while he lay on his back, tears making hot tracks to his ears, then sleep drifted over. And in the morning when he woke the memory was gone, the summer birds were singing, and he rolled over to kiss his wife's sleeping cheek.

Flight

Melissa Beit

Chase Holly puts me in the bag. All the Hollys are hot-blooded and Chase must've found out about me and Lani Rugg. Not much to find out, and I can't stop myself wishing he had real cause for vexation and I'd done what she'd asked me to after all. For ten minutes we've been standing round in the clearing while Chase stomps up and down and Rick and Trev hold my arms behind my back and breathe down my neck. Chong and Froggy've got their bums parked on either side of the ghost gum and so far they haven't been real keen to jump to my defence or even meet my eyes, but I can tell they're not enjoying the deja vu. We're all getting a bit old for this. For a long time I dunno what Chase has in mind, probably just a hiding, but then he turns to Froggy and snarls, 'Get the fucking bag.'

The first time Chase bashed me up was the last day of Grade 1. Mrs Garbutt made us line up round the classroom in order of where we came in the year, and there was me, right up the front rubbing shoulders with Lani Rugg, and there was Chase, red-faced and scowling, all the way round the other side of the room, over by the seaside posters, and the only person further south than him was poor old Frog. I felt pretty good for about one second and then Chase caught my eye and dropped his fist into his palm a few times. Being on the receiving end of a Holly flogging was an ordinary way to start the holidays, but the next day he came over and helped me get the cows in like usual and laughed at my black eye and things were back to normal, which was some relief to me. At the age of six and a half I already knew I needed Chase Holly.

Froggy clumps back to the car and for a minute or two all we can hear are sticks breaking under his thongs. Then a door slams and he crunches back into sight. He's carrying the sleeping bag, *my* sleeping bag, the one I took from that backpacker's tent two weeks back — a real flash number, red outside, black inside, reinforced zips and soft as a kitten. It's gotten pretty dirty since then from dragging round in the back of Chase's panno and keeping him and Lani Rugg warm at night, and even from here I can see it's covered in all kinds of stains.

It takes Chase a few minutes to do the thing up; he's about as agitated as I've ever seen him, face pink as fritz and all the muscles on his jaw twitching under the skin. He's had the bag unzipped like a doona, but when he finally gets the teeth to close and we all hear the whine of the zip, you can see it's no rectangle. It's shaped like a person, skinny down near the feet and wide round the shoulders, with a hood where the head goes.

I'm starting to not like the look of that bag, so I try again.

'Chase, mate, I didn't touch her. You can ask her. You know I never—' which is as far as I get before Chase lunges towards me. Rick and Trev've been holding me out in the sun for a while, so my wrists are slippery with all our sweat and I nearly get away, but then Chase collars me and forces the bag over my head. The horror hits before he's even finished dragging it down my body. It's hot in there, dark as a hole, and my arms are pinned to my sides. Straightaway I can't breathe.

He kicks my legs out from under me, pulls off my thongs, stuffs my feet in and cinches up the drawstring. There's just enough room inside that sleeping bag to lose my mind.

Chase is the only one who knows how my mum left because he saw it all from the branches of our pepper tree. He saw Mum and her new boyfriend pull up the driveway in the boyfriend's Datsun, and her grabbing stuff off the clothes line with one eye over her shoulder for the old man; and then he saw her helping me into the back seat and climbing in after me; and he saw the U-turn that stopped short in the face of my dad standing there with a shotgun pointing at the windscreen, and the almighty row that ended with nobody being shot but with me being pushed back out of the car onto the driveway, and the Datsun taking off in a cloud of orange dust.

Chase came back the next day to take me fishing and my dad let me go. He always trusted Chase, never me. Not after he saw me get into that car so willingly.

I'm sweating like a pig, and part of it is being wrapped in a nylon bag full of duck feathers in the middle of January, but most of it is terror. I waste a lot of effort and make myself scareder just kicking my feet and yelling for a while, but then I hear the panno start up and I lie still.

Everything outside the bag is muffled but I can hear Chase tearing through the gears as he heads up Paterlake Road, and then slowing down not very much as he pulls onto the highway a few minutes later. Then it's dead quiet and I wet myself and wish he'd just clobbered me.

Chase is twice my weight and a foot taller than me. He's got the Holly build. His folks look like the people in those ads on telly: eat less hamburgers or else you'll end up like this. His big brother Arky played front row for the Crows for thirteen years straight, from fourteen to twenty-seven, but then he got married and went to fat like the rest of them. Chase's big sisters Marnie and Jo-Rose've got bosoms on 'em like watermelons, and real accommodating arms, so the stories go, but my lasting memories of those two will be Marnie dakking me at the Barnes Cup Races in front of two thousand people, and Jo-Rose raking her fingernails over the roof of my mouth after I lipped her one time.

Chase is the youngest in the family, the smartest and best looking Holly in three generations, and this town adores him. When he takes his shirt off on the footy field, even the men suck their breaths in. He doesn't work out, but lifting hay bales and calves and fence posts has bulked him up instead of whittling him down like it did me. He started taking Sandra Keanes out just after his thirteenth birthday, and he reckons they did it on their first date. I dunno why he chose me to be his best mate, but I'm usually grateful.

I can see a tiny point of red light where the zip ends. My shoulders and arms are hugged tight to my body. I try to rip the material by biting it, but I just end up flossing my teeth; it's some kind of high-tech fabric they invented so people could sleep out on the top of Mount Everest, and it'd be easier to rip a piece of corro in half. The bag's a bit roomier round my feet, but I can't get down to them. When I try to bend over, the whole bag just bends with me in it. I remember that the bag felt cold the first time I touched it, grabbing it out of that girl's tent. It's not cold now.

I've been crying since the panno drove off and now the bag is wet and snotty round my face and clings to my nostrils with every breath. There're white spots in front of my eyes but when I blink them away it's just black again, with that one red dot. All over my body the sweat is running off into my clothes and I know I'm breathing it all in with each breath: piss, sweat, snot and the hot breaths I just let out. If I turn my head as far as I can the wet patch is on my cheek and the material doesn't suck at my face so bad. When that side gets sweaty and starts to cling, I turn my head to the other side. I count ten breaths on each side, and then I switch. The counting calms me down for a minute or two but then I start thinking and the bag hugs my chest like someone's sitting on it, and I look down on myself from above, a big red grub baking in the sun with air, air all around in a hot cup of sky, and then I lose it again.

When the chores are done on the weekend, Chase and I go down to the river. I chuck a line in, but Chase doesn't like fishing much. He doesn't have the patience – just stabs a worm on a hook, chucks it over and straightaway reels it back in again. Any fish dogging Chase's hook would have trouble keeping up with it. But he likes to talk. I sit there with the line in my fingers, occasionally bringing in a black bream or a cod, and listen to Chase talk.

Chase's dad is old school, a mean bastard nobody likes but everybody pretends to. In Chase's family the chicks do the cooking and cleaning and the blokes work the farm and drink beer on the verandah after dinner and call out for ice-cream or refills without a please or thankyou between them. In my own house Dad and I do for ourselves: if you mess it up, you clean it up; so the first time I ate at Chase's house I got out of my seat after dinner and commenced clearing the table to the struck-dumbest silence you ever heard. Chase laughed, gobsmacked, but his dad growled at me, 'Whadja think the sheilas're for?' and Chase shut his mouth fast.

I learned a long time ago that it was better not to mention the bruises and black eyes he sometimes shows up with, as Chase has a habit of passing them on. He reckons he can't ever remember crying, and I've never seen him blubber, not even that time he got his fingers jammed in the baler and just about sliced them off. But when he comes fishing with me, sitting out in the tinny with a beer or a smoke he's stolen from his old man, Chase unwinds like a roll of fencing wire and sends his dreams and fears and fancies spinning out over the water in a frail shining thread. He tells me stuff he doesn't even tell himself.

No one comes to rescue me. Rick and Trev do whatever Chase tells them to because they love him, probably even more than I do. I dunno the ins and outs of that story but Chong reckons Chase stopped their uncle mucking around with them when he lived with them back in Grade 3. Froggy and I both've got no old lady at home and we sort of bonded over that, but Frog doesn't have enough sense in his big orange head to spell out his own name (Francis Royston Ogilvie), and he'd never go against Chase. Chong would've been my best bet, but he's riled at me too. Chase's bagged him for years about his trouser-front feelings for Lani Rugg, often right in front of her, and it must've stung that she came at me the first night after Chase dumped her. My dad won't miss me until morning when he needs my help with the steers, but by then I'll be dead.

Something happens in the clearing, some shift I can't guess at, and the cicadas start up, so loud and shrill it hurts my head, even inside the bag. Our local variety're called Outback Screamers and one night last summer I watched one come out of its shell. Chase and I were out in the boat and the Screamers were so bad we'd stuffed bread into our ears. In the light of the full moon I could see Chase looking out over the water, his lips moving, his eyes half-closed, and realised what I had always suspected: he didn't need to be listened to; he just needed to talk and it didn't matter that I couldn't hear a word he said. Beside me on the gunwale a cicada had just started moulting. Chase always squashes them under his heel when he finds them, makes a big production of yelling at the corpses, 'I *told* you to shut the fuck up!', but I like seeing them around, knowing they've been hiding out underground for seven years. This one was doing it tough like normal, easing his behind out of the tiny slit at his back, pulsing and humping, resting and humping again. It looked like the worst kind of hard work, and part of me wanted to open up my pocket-knife and help things along a little, but I waited, and it waited, and ninety-three minutes later, that old insect was brand new, hanging upside down on top of its dried-up brown case, its pale clammy wings unfolding so slowly you couldn't see it happening until it'd already happened. Forty minutes later it was ready to go, wings like lolly wrappers and a giant orange M shining on its back, saying, *Made it!* or, *Man that was hard!* or, *Maybe I'll get eaten by a bat next!* It lit off the side of the boat and went buzzing away to the moon, and I picked up the empty case, hooked it to my fishing shirt and took it home.

In the sleeping bag I think of that cicada, and the tough brown case with the narrow slit still hanging on my flyscreen at home. I'm aching for a slit to appear in the bag, along my back or chest, so I can hump my way out and fly off into the cool dry air, and I wouldn't care if it took ninety-three minutes.

Then I realise there already is a slit.

Lani Rugg is small and wiry, with black curly hair cut short and sticking up fluffy all over her head. She's skinny, tough as a boot, with a straight, no-bullshit mouth, but eyes like a calf's: big and black behind eyelashes an inch long. She and I tied for dux in Grade 7, but she's beaten me every year since. Lani Rugg is going places; that's what she told me at the pub last night, after she backed me into the corner beside the jukebox. To the coast, to the city, to university, she reckons. She said she wants to be a journalist, a marine biologist, a national park ranger, a midwife. She wants to leave this shithole behind, with its local gods and its one-way decisions, and never come back; and even behind the bourbons she'd been sucking back through a three-inch straw, you could tell she was dead serious. She needed a ride, she said, and she needed to get out *now*, right now, tonight. She needed a ride with someone dependable, she said, and she nearly touched me – reached her hand out to my chest and held it an inch away for a long moment before letting it drop to her side again.

Flight

Chase Holly was in Blacktown last night, representing us in the footy finals, and if he hadn't dumped Lani yesterday lunchtime, she'd have been there watching him do his thing. I've been the third wheel in the Chase and Lani machine since they started going out four months ago, and I already knew her pretty well from school. She can spit further than any bloke I know, she loves cheese and mustard sandwiches, she snorts when she laughs, she can play the comb, and she cries at dumb movies. Last night she was beautiful and intense and scared-looking, and it was only with great difficulty that I fended her off and made it out to the ute in one piece.

This morning, when the crows woke me up one minute before the old man did and I staggered all over the verandah pulling my boots on, I was already kicking myself.

The opening is at my feet. I can't see it, but I know it's there. I can even feel it with my big toe, the cinched-up arsehole to the outside world. On the other side there's some kind of plastic knob that slides along the drawcord and keeps it tight, but a hole is a hole. I force my big toe through it. Chase ribbed me one time about my big toes, which're miles longer than my other toes, said I'd never be the dominant one in any relationship. On his own feet the second toes stick out a half-inch further than his big toes and he's always stubbing them. I'm grateful for my spineless big toes today; by pushing and pushing I get all my toes out, the ball of my foot, the whole damned foot.

I'm elated for about one second. My foot is out there, cool as a fish, and suddenly the rest of me starts to clamour for freedom. I have to swallow again and again to stop myself from vomiting. I imagine someone stumbling across me weeks from now, a swollen flyblown case of nylon with one mummified foot thrust out.

I force myself to think of the cicada, its slow, rhythmic pulse, its patience. I make myself wait ten breaths and then start the other foot working through the hole, worrying at that bit of plastic on the other side, working the cord through. When both my feet are out I make myself wait another ten breaths, lying still, and then kick around a bit to work the bag up to my shins. It's slow, hot work, all of it, and I keep taking breaks to keep myself together: rest, wriggle, rest, hump, rest, roll, rest, roll back. There comes a point when the bag is up around my thighs, still cinched tight, and my damp crotch suddenly feels cold from the outside air, and my hands can move around and grasp the zipper. It moves half an inch, then catches on the flaming material. I go back to wriggling and resting. When the bag is at my chest the light comes pouring in, white and painful, and I lose it completely; but it is the right time to lose it: with a wild flailing, my shoulders release and the bag comes off over my head.

I lie in the dirt with my eyes closed and the air is colder and sweeter than rain. I'm soaked all over and the dry breezes slide over my skin. When I open my eyes the sun has moved behind the trees and I'm starting to shiver. My tongue feels swollen up to the size of an orange. I roll over and get to my hands and knees.

Something clicks and I look up to see Chase Holly lighting up a smoke, propped up against a tree, watching me with wet eyes. He's cradling a plastic bottle of Coke, half empty, and he chucks it to me, a spin pass that of course I miss. I grab at the rolling bottle and fumble around with the lid and finally pour the stuff into my mouth. I spit it straight back out again. It's about half rum.

I take my time standing up but he doesn't move to stop me.

'I didn't touch her,' I say again, and my voice sounds whiny and high like a kid's, but this time he nods.

He sucks on the cigarette, half mull by the smell of it and the length of the drag. When he's finished coughing he says, 'I didn't dump Lani; she dumped me,' and spits onto the ground at his feet.

That explains her urgency, I think dimly, and I find myself wondering if she made it out of town last night or if she's trussed up in a sleeping bag somewhere.

I pick up the bag, wet and stinking the pair of us, and chuck it up into the branches of a tree. My arms are shaky, so it doesn't go up very high, but it snags on a broken branch and stays up there, dangling like a big filthy sock.

'Where's the panno?' I ask, and Chase wipes his eyes and stands up. He looks shaky too.

'I was gunna help you, if you couldn't get out,' he says, and I believe him.

'Where's the panno?'

'Dunno. I sent them cunts away. Wasn't their business. We gotta walk back.'

Wasn't my business either, but I nod and start across the clearing to Paterlake Road. It's five kilometres to town, but we have to go past the river, and I'll drink there.

I'm making plans. Get to the river, that deep bit under the bridge, drink till I'm full, even though that water's dodgy and nobody not dying of thirst would even consider it, cut through the Curry place to Hindmarsh Road and make it to my own farm just on dark. Shower, fresh clothes, grab the jar of dollar coins from the old man's dresser, climb into the ute. Drive out of town, heading east. Via the Rugg property.

Chase is recovering, dragging on the joint and sucking away at the bottle, and I know that pretty soon he's going to start to see the funny side of all this, start slamming his arm across my shoulders and mock-punching my chin, joking me round till he gets a smile. Tomorrow he'll show up at my front door with his fishing rod and a sixpack. He bumps past me and takes the lead as we walk up the long dirt road.

He doesn't even see my wings.

Grief

*Ian C
Smith*

(1)

His memory lapses, increasing now,
outline the fragility of sanity.
Trudging around the sheltered cove
where they loved, walked, swam, talked
he senses desolation, loss
as if lives had been ruined forever
and the settlement abandoned.
Homes seem shrouded in silence
the beach laid out before him
few bird cries, no bobbing boats
no laughing bikinis in the sun;
no sun, for that matter. Gone.
At last he finds someone he knew
learns of recent deaths and sadness
feeling like a visitor from the past
which he wryly realises he is.
Later, alone in a house with a view,
for seconds that take his breath away
he can't remember where home is.

(2)

Peering through binoculars
at a yacht rounding a wreck site

he sees a man step to the stern
then a woman emerges from below.
A silent theatre in the round.
He tries to imagine their conversation.
She could be a self-taught navigator,
her horizon limitless because
she doesn't want to linger alone,
regret mistakes, grow old, and worse.
Let's face it, all journeys must end.
She has brewed coffee in their cosy galley
and when they drop anchor tonight
she might rest her head on his shoulder.
He will smell her hair, light a cigarette,
lay his hand on her warm hip.
Lowering the binoculars he sees
a black cloud scudding their way,
shadowing the water which trembles.

(3)

Alone on the decking thinking of history
he stares at clouds which break apart
into ever changing shapes
driven fast as the past across their bay.
A woman bathing, a smiling child.
The sun has barely shown its face
behind the mountain they climbed.
He remembers reaching the summit
every muscle aching the following day
floating, laughing at their dream luck
watching Cape Barren Geese fly over,
wind gusting like a warning.
At last a boat, battling the waves
returning to safe harbour
where lights will appear like low-slung stars.
He feels her hand on the back of his neck
steps inside, with the mariners' charts of wrecks
slides the glass door shut with a click
that seems as final as death.

(4)

His thoughts a jostling mob, he jogs.
A lone cray fisherman pulls pots
beneath a single-engined plane
striving towards the bush airstrip
where a pilot made one error.
Those flyers leapt through flaming fuel
to show their scars, tell their amazing story.
Heart thumping hard now, he recalls
her face, pale with apprehension
when they bumped over the grassy tufts
before lifting above the crash site
to soar out across dark waves.
He thinks he might buy a crayfish
but eating it alone doesn't appeal.
Tiptoeing through scurrying sand crabs
he knows mistakes litter his own story,
considers alcohol as a meal option.
The beach is empty, the past crowded.
He stops, strains to hear the plane's engine.

(5)

Because a westerly rips relentlessly
across Bass Strait, he stays inside
reading *The Sound of One Hand Clapping*.
He thinks it fitting on this island,
wind beating at windows, roof
beating incessantly like his heart.
He swallows the book's sad grief
with whiskey he carries in a flask
on his own under a cold moon.
Last evening he caught leatherjackets
tearing their skins off, sickening
and satisfying himself at once,
preparing a meal to go with the book.
He thinks he might climb Mt Strzelecki

where a storm trapped a man for three days.
At the peak he would squat, still as stone,
where they huddled from the wind
leaning into each other, heads in the clouds
waiting for the rough patch to blow over.

(6)

Walking alone, wind buffeting the island
his own haphazard heart cast away
he sees Flinders' ship split the strait.
He picks up a paper nautilus, broken,
the gulls' cries familiar to both men.
Waves slap the reef in rhythm
as they speak of wonders taking place
during two hectic, insane centuries.
He regrets his dearth of knowledge
articulately describing great books
but awkward, stumbling with slang,
over the internal combustion engine,
finance, the internet, mobile phones.
Rocks and the horizon dwarf them.
To this brave Lincolnshire cartographer
whose love waits on the Earth's far side,
who understands about separation;
he suggests the consolation of rum
but is worried about personal details.

(7)

Near a deserted car park rubbish bin
guarded by a patrolling Pacific Gull
fixing him with a prosecutor's eye
he crouches like a forensics expert
to pick up several tarnished coins
dating back to pre-decimal days
while throwing out porn magazines

Grief

he didn't want to leave behind
with the books on sea creatures' evolution
in the beach rental where he sorrowed
over absent wives and girlfriends.
Stupidity and cowardice hover
like linked viruses in his thoughts.
Although he has only been crazy
about one woman, he believes
she would irritate him now
if she hasn't changed as he has
but he adapts, factoring in reasons.
The cold dawn smells like weary sex.

Agapanthus

SJ Finn

At the local graveyard I watch the boys hoick agapanthus from between the graves. They work in two groups of three: one with a pick, one with a spade and one walking armfuls of them to the trailer. The fertile ground opens easily, the tooth of the swinging tool digging and the spade spitting them to the surface. I lean on the vehicle, calculate that my place is a short detour between the burial ground and the next assignment. They'll look good, I think, blooming along my driveway.

It's been a long morning with the lucky crew – lucky to have their sentences commuted to community service, a get-out-of-jail-free-for-a-few-odd-jobs arrangement. Niggles from the boys: *bloody flies, fucking sun, bullshit tools, ruddy Corrections,* have burnt small craters into my frontal lobe. I've exerted a little of my own well-matched hard-speak to meet theirs: *you lot sound like a bunch of whinging cry-babies; problem is your pommy albino skin; it's because of those ten sets of thumbs you're sporting; come on, you're crims, Corrections is your peak body.* This last crack was pushing things, but I'm paid to volley their grumbles back and nine times out of ten the day finishes well enough, can even deliver a sense of satisfaction from completing a task or three.

Truth be known, this is my dream job. I get to be outdoors, use my skills for monkey-bar building, retaining-wall construction, BMX bike track planning and further on from that, there's something imaginative about this bunch. As much as they bitch and moan with boring brainless complaints, they're Rodgers and Hammerstein compared to the Catholic kids I took for woodwork a couple of years back, all trussed up and uncommunicative.

Besides, my view is that most of the boys in the crew have had a short suck on the old straw of life and there's a lot to be said for their mettle when their sorry stories come to light. There's only the occasional one that's got any real streak of nastiness, although, by the same token, few have any charm, which makes it easy to draw the line between them and me. Fraternising is out: clarity of roles is essential because the fence separating us is thin enough, standing, I would say (and have when pontificating on the subject), mainly on account of my having avoided the eye of the law.

And that brings up another sad distinction: most of them think everything's chipper. Blindly mistaken would be my take on that.

But perhaps that's where the boys and I are closer than I'd calculated, seeing, despite a flash of lucidity about a big mistake, I find myself hurtling up the driveway of my lifetime project, them leering at it from every available angle in the van with me. And, despite being cognisant of breaking a golden rule I've adhered to unwaveringly for the last five years – saying to myself, once won't matter – and whistling in that singalong way I know signals a number of things about my psychological state, I continue on. Certainly I should have known better, should never have considered lowering the barrier of my life so the boys could stretch themselves into it. But it's too late. My crew of petty crims and hard-muscled smart-arses, my crew who most of the time play easy ball and only take a little pulling into line, my crew who deserve some respect except from the people who have seen their charge sheets, which is me, are lusting, albeit with cool calm eyes, upon that which I hold most dear.

'Thought you didn't live here anymore?' Darrel Baxter is a sniff of a guy with greasy hair and a fetish for gym clothing. 'Thought you and ya missus split?'

'They did,' says Jimmy, who's sitting on the other side of Darrel.

I throw them a sly look.

'But have ya or have ya not?' Darrel says.

'Do ya, or do ya not?' Jimmy leans forward, guffaws across the dash, twisting his finger into another he's coined in a circle.

'Get a hold of yourself, Jimmy.' I pull the automatic gearstick into second to help the twelve-seater up the hill. 'Still *my* place. She's staying here till we work out a property settlement.'

And there it is, the mistake not only made, but carving an irreversible scar into me. In the rear view mirror, I check the boys in the back, wonder if they've heard. I can see Harvey Patton staring, projecting his boredom onto my temporarily dispossessed fields, and Collin Menace Jones beside him, trying to get something out of his nose with a very dirty index finger. I haven't known these guys long, and they're groovy boys, especially Harvey, more sophisticated than I'm used to amongst my crims.

My gaze slides forward, a careful realignment. It's one thing having Jimmy and Darrel know my business, quite another in regard to the rest. Matt and Adrian are out of range of hearing, sitting in the seats at the back of the vehicle. They like being separate, come from an even rarer breed than the trendy boys: the one-off, slip-up breed who won't be back for a second round with this crew.

When we come over the last rise of the driveway, Petal, Rachel's piebald bull terrier, is poised – not quite sitting on her haunches – in full view. I'm surprised the dog's here. Petal goes everywhere with Rachel like every bull terrier she's ever owned, so I'm suddenly thinking Rachel must be home, that she's taken the day off and might be scantily dressed somewhere amongst her cacti and roses.

Petal's tail begins to whip back and forth. I'm depending on the fact that Rachel's having one of her soup-bowl cups of coffee upstairs. Maybe even on the balcony I stumbled off eight years ago, breaking my nose on my knee as I landed, thank God, on an old trampoline we used to have set up in the yard.

'You guys unload the trailer.' I engage the handbrake. 'Put them on that side of the driveway.' I indicate the spot.

'Where ya going, Russ?' Jimmy says, a silly look on his face.

'Mind ya bum fluff. *Now come on!*' I bark, to remind the crew they're in the penal system and I'm not, which is, I keep telling myself, what I'm paid for: to keep some sort of upper hand, a slap-behind-the-ear hand.

They begin to get out of the vehicle as I go to find Rachel, to warn her I've got the crew here. I don't want to alarm her, don't want the flick of her anger-at-having-been-left tongue whipping over me in front of them. And then there's another consideration sidling into my mind: the she-won't-be-happy-I'm-here consideration. I start to cringe at my behaviour but I continue walking towards the house, perhaps because when it comes to my land I'm driven beyond any ability to censor myself. I know I should turn around, drive away, take the agapanthus to the tip, which was the original instruction from my supervisor, Ms Margaret Turner. But even as I'm considering it, I discard it.

At the house I peer through the kitchen windows. Rachel's at the table, steam rising from her cup, scarves circling her neck, her dark hair tacked up untidily. She always looks beautiful when she's pinned together in an untidy way. I comb a hand over my own mop before I realise what I'm doing, before I knock on the Tudor doors I pinched from a tiny disused church ten kays further along the road. She turns, looks over her shoulder and, without indicating whether she's pleased to see me, beckons me to come in.

'Rach.' Surprise ripens my voice. 'Didn't expect you to be here! Just dropping off some agapanthus I dug up with the boys.'

'Don't leave them here.' Her voice is curt.

'Why not? There's a whole load and I need the trailer this afternoon.'

Rachel stands, her lazy day-off clothes loose and flowing on her. 'This is my home, Russ, for the moment at least. You can't just rock up when you feel like it.'

'I've already got the boys unstacking them. I can't tell them to load up again.'

'Fine.' Rachel glides past me. '*I'll* tell them.'

I can tell by the way she sets her expression she won't be stopped. I even get the impression she's been ruminating on the less than gracious particulars of my character and the sight of me here without having told her I was coming is infuriating those ruminations, making her think I turn up whenever I like.

I follow her. Petal is watching the bad-boys move in an orchestra of unburdening the trailer.

'Hey!' she yells. 'You can pick them all back up again.'

There's a general hiatus of movement except in the case of Harvey Patton. Harvey, at the same pace he's been evacuating the bulbs, begins putting them back. There's not so much as a thought passing behind his eyes. Or, perhaps, too many thoughts.

Rachel shakes her head at the rest of them.

'Only accepting instructions from the *boss?* Well, if you don't pick them up I'll ring the cops. Maybe you'll listen to them.'

Petal stands like a piglet beside her. The cop thing, and, of course, my silence, clinches it. They scoop up the bulbs, dropping them back onto the tray of the trailer.

Rachel squares up to me then, her eyes rummaging over my face. When I can't maintain her gaze she simply walks past me, towards the house. Petal, sensing who's come out on top, trots off after her.

I can't arc up for obvious reasons, the biggest one being that Rachel and I are ugly to watch arguing, an ugliness that would give the boys something to mimic to their advantage. As it is there's plenty of gristle for them to chew open-mouthed on now. Already it's evident. The boys, working with an unusual skip in their step, have filled the trailer back up in no time. I catch Harvey's eye, his unfazed penetrating stare.

By the time the boys load themselves into the vehicle, I'm seething behind the steering wheel. I can feel the crew nudging and nodding towards my hard-worked house, built ground-up by unplugged guts, my guts. Laughs packed between his words, Darrel says, 'We're sorry, Russ.'

Then Jimmy pipes up. 'We feel for ya, mate.' And the two snicker in their usual underhanded sniggering way, surreptitious and ugly. I catch Menace smiling and know everyone's heard. Harvey's too Harvey and the boys at the back too pink-cheeked to laugh. That's the only reason they're not all doubled over with the joke of it.

I bite down. *Bastards*, I think, giving them nothing more to draw on. But that's when Harvey's voice carps up from the back seat.

'You sure she's gunna give you the place?'

I land a cool eye on his in the rear-vision mirror.

'Positive,' I say.

I go back to the house four days later when I see Rachel's car in town outside her workplace. In the trailer I have the agapanthus, saved, after all, from being dumped at the tip. Confirming her absence, Petal doesn't greet me and I drive to one of the back sheds, begin emptying the trailer in swift shovel-loads, certain she won't see the midden of bulbs. But as the last few tumble from the trailer's edge, bad-boy Harvey Patton, his smart-boy dandy jeans hanging loosely from his hips and his head cocked over in annoying passivity, appears.

'Harvey!' My voice slews off unreliably. 'What are you doing here?'

'Servicing the generator.' Harvey stands, wiping his greasy hands with a rag, a spanner somewhere between them. 'Saw Rachel in town. We got talking. Offered to come and take a look at it.'

I close the back of the trailer, acting as if I'm totally cool about this when in fact I feel like someone's got a vegetable peeler against my chest, removing the wispy hair that grows there by raking it back and forth. I look at him. 'Forgot you were a mechanic. Hope you know what you're doing.'

Harvey smiles, nods in a way that says *absolutely bloody right*.

I squirm.

'You want to leave a message?'

I stand there nodding, trying to think of what the right thing would be and it dawns on me that it won't be good if Rachel knows I've been here.

'Actually Harvey, I'd appreciate it if you didn't say anything about the agapanthus, or my being here. It's just between Rach and me after all.'

Harvey makes the smallest shrug and I move to the driver's door, pretending there's nothing eating me. I wave to Harvey and get in my car like I've got things to do. But as I'm pulling away, watching Harvey in my side mirror, I'm thinking Harvey's being here is Rachel's doing and that she's trying, trying and succeeding, to upset me beyond a decent limit with her employing one of the crew, having them *work* on the property. And she's not even here.

I want to ring her, but that's exactly what she'd expect and a demonstration of anger from me will only drive her closer to *him*. My mind pinions on this as I drive back to town. I'll wait. I see the boys again Saturday. As long as the blowfish doesn't squeal on me beforehand I'll say I learned that Harvey was at the property from Harvey. I shake my head. This is beyond the pail, beyond all decency; Rachel's lost all regard for the rules we laid down about mixing the personal with work.

In a town like Menence there's pity-little to do when it comes to entertainment. Routines become crucial and entrenched in this kind of place and traditionally I spend my Friday nights at the bar of the Terminus Hotel. I can have a sure bet who's going to be there and who's not. That's why I always feel it's a safe place to drink since, usually, I know exactly who I'll bump into. This is important, given drinking can severely interrupt an amnesty that might otherwise work well with any certain person. That's why I feel wary when Darrel and Jimmy walk through the door like they've come into a Wild West saloon and they're keen on being someone more than the Milkybar Kid. My plan, which consists of a relaxing session with my new woman, Kitty Holt, is to be foiled.

'Didn't know you two drank!' I say by way of hello. 'Thought you were purely yandi boys. Bong hogs.'

I sound dry-humoured, relaxed, while really there's a powerful rumble of foreboding in me.

'Russell.' They both nod, ignoring my goads, each pulling a stool up to the bar as if they're about to make a deal of some importance. Darrel leans forward, looks hungrily over the counter. But then Darrel, I think, always looks hungry.

I introduce Kitty, an unpleasant but necessary call seeing I'm not going to back down from my usual seat in my own local. Also, I'm thinking once the introductions are over nothing much will come in the way of chitchat. And, after the boys' eyes roam unabashed over the two of us, that's what happens. Everyone bunkers down in their own conversations.

Kitty tells me about her day, starting with the hygiene practices of fifteen intellectually handicapped adults she cooked relish and strawberry jam with at work.

'A lot of hair-twirling despite the surgical caps,' she says. 'A lot of ear-tweaking and nose-picking.'

When Kitty and I pause for a guzzle from our pots, Darrel leans forward.

'Russ, ya got some house out there.'

'Didn't know you had an eye for such things.'

It's a warning; one that's not picked up.

'Not as much of an eye as Harvey's got,' Jimmy squawks, laughing as if someone's using a mallet to hard pack the guffaws down in him, to sledgehammer them into his oesophagus.

'What are you on about Jimmy?'

'Harvey's seeing your place from the inside.'

'Bullseye.' Darrel tips his pot Jimmy's way.

I shake my head as if they've really lost it, try again to give the impression I don't approve of them blathering on about my life.

'Harvey's shaggin' ya ex, Russ,' Darrel persists. 'Living by ya pots and pans in the very kitchen ya built with ya own donkey-mule muster and blow.'

I frown, know Darrel's been rehearsing this. They crack up. Jimmy, his beer at his lips poised to swallow, is so busy crowing he can't take a sip.

'Fuck that!' I say, which is an understatement given the rage curdling in me.

'Ya better get out there 'cos Harvey's got a good mind to reinvest himself inta your property. He's a cunning one, the old Harve and well, your Rachel, maybe she's just tryna get one over you.'

'Alright Darrel.' I hate that he's just said what I myself have already thought. 'Got any real news about the state of the world?'

Darrel mocks disappointment but Jimmy can't wipe the smile from his face. They both tap the bar, can't hold it in.

'How bout a beer, Russ?' It's Jimmy.

'No thanks, we're off. Kit?' I say to her. 'Don't drink too much, lads, full day tomorrow.'

'We'll be in stripes.'

'I'll bring the dogs.'

When we get outside Kitty turns to me. 'You didn't take those guys out to your place, did you?'

I rub my hands, knead my palm with my thumb.

'Oh Christ,' she says. 'That's a moment not thought through.'

'It'll blow over. Don't worry. Let's buy some cider. Go home and get real happy.'

At work, the cider easing its way through my liver, making me heavy-limbed, there's a message in my pigeonhole. Harvey Patton will not be in attendance today.

With the bent postures of the boys smoking cigarettes, falling in sloping silhouettes across the pavement outside, I collect myself to portray impenetrable, upright, taking-of-no-bullshit. But the atmosphere is not as I expect. Without Harvey, there's an easy mood amongst us. It's clear I've been naive about him, about his quiet power, his ability to lead the group even if he doesn't appear to. It's that charismatic 'deeply cynical' thing, his quiet brooding demeanour. Probably the very trait that makes him attractive to Rachel. But despite that, I'm sceptical. Can't believe the thing between Rach and Harvey can be true. Boys have got me collared, I tell myself, they're having an almighty tug on my un-jailed legs. So I instruct myself to calm down. Besides, the only way I can deal with it is to hold it in, especially seeing *I'm* the one who left *her*, seeing *I've* already got myself a new beauty I adore.

And while I'm thinking this, while I'm watching the boys in DayGlo vests with long tongs and big rubbish bags, with rakes and wide-nosed shovels, cleaning up at the town's showgrounds, I'm settling on an idea, allowing it to fill my mind by adding peripheral plotting and fringe benefits for all those I manage to rope in. I make my first move and call to the crew.

'Down tools. Early lunch. Hot pies courtesy of Corrections Victoria.'

Keeping my promise, I drive the good bad-boys to the Perry, a wide chugging river that hugs its barren, chewed banks with a certain desperation. We sit at a picnic table by the edge of the water, squinting, our cold breath mixing with hot mince and pastry.

I tell them this lunch is in order to soften the blow, so they won't feel hard done by, won't be too pissed off with Harvey when they hear.

'Huh?' Darrel has his head cocked.

'Hear what?' Menace's brow is deep-furrowed.

'I thought he would have told *you*, Menace.'

Menace shakes his head.

'He's been excused from doing his hours.'

'*Really?*' Jimmy is frowning.

'It's not possible. Is it?' Darrel's hair is washed for once and it's knotted in a clump behind his right ear.

'Someone must have pulled strings. Found a loophole.'

'I saw him Thursday.' Menace's detestably dirty fingernails clamp his pie. 'Didn't say anything. Well, except for mentioning the view from your balcony.'

'Half his luck. Got everything going his way. Must be charm or something. I mean, I don't see it personally but he's got the gift. He's got the power.'

'Fuck that.' Darrel's thin, tracksuited leg is suddenly jigging up and down as if it's having its own private epileptic fit. 'Harvey's got another 200 hours or something. I've been here for weeks and nobody ever mentioned no loopholes to me.'

'You sure, Russ? You sure he's been excused?'

'Positive. There was a note at work not to expect him back.' (This is a white lie as far as I'm concerned and something I can recant later, plead misunderstanding of.) 'Meanwhile, he's shacked up with Rach, living the high life at my house and you sorry bastards are working your arses off. Don't understand how some people get away with shit like that.' I shake my head for effect. 'Wonder what argument he used.'

'Maybe the fact he's involved with the boss's ex.' Jimmy hisses and winds up his hammered-down giggle.

I scoff. 'If only! Nah, it's certainly not that. More likely he's made a complaint about the company he has to keep, claiming you blokes corrupt him. He's hot on himself, stuck up or something.'

I let it rest there; take my time.

'That's not right.'

'Should fucken kidnap the bastard, bring him out here.'

'Make him watch us for 200 hours.'

Darrel laughs as if he's taken a double dose of his dexamphetamines.

'Harder to watch than do the work.'

Jimmy's squawking causes a general rumble of mirth amongst the crew.

'Boredom's a killer.' Darrel's leg is pumping with the seizure again.

'Let's do it.' Jimmy jumps up, is pushing his fingers into the air like he's P Diddy Combs. 'Let's go get him from his love bed.'

I take in Menace's chiselled face, see he's considering things.

'We can tell him we miss him,' Jimmy sings, laughing so hard that good-boy Matt can't help but strike a laugh in contagion and the whole crew are writhing with hilarity.

'Let's go,' Darrel calls theatrically. 'Let's go get him.'

'You can't just go get him,' I say, wiping an eye.

'Bullshit. He should be suffering with the rest of us.'

'I'd be sacked and you'd end up in the slammer, some screw making your life hell. You'd have to do it at night with balaclavas.' They roar at this, at the overstated humour I've displayed.

'*Yeah*,' Darrel shouts. 'Drag him out for a dose of reality. Leave him *all* night.'

'Drive by my place and toot.' I wink at them, a clinching of the fact I can claim it was all a joke. 'I'd like to know he was suffering.'

During the afternoon they talk on and on about the idea, asserting it as their own at some point, turning the tide against Harvey. All I hope to do is upset the apple cart between Harvey and Rachel. She won't want them approaching Harvey at the house, or in the street. I'm pretty sure it'd be enough to put her off the cool Mr Patton for good; so I'm pleased, can't help but feel I've put in a decent day's effort with the crew, fixing the mess I made.

That night, cosy on the couch, Kitty wrapped around me, I've almost put Harvey and Rachel out of my mind. But, strangely, the lack of a car horn – as if I expected they'd really carry out the plan – germinates my curiosity and, typical of me, once the inkling of something is seeded it's an impossibly wide birth around it. The next thing I know I'm fighting off a great dread of Harvey and Rachel walking down the aisle and going straight from there to a solicitor's office so they can live on in the house she's got possession of.

I try to relax, concentrate on the devastation of an American town flattened by a monster tornado. But a far-off disaster distilled through a camera and onto the TV is not enough of a distraction, and agitation surfaces in me so that this time Kitty can't help but notice.

'Sorry, honey,' I say. 'Seem to have a pea in my subconscious. Need something to wipe out a few brain cells. How about I score us a smoke?'

'I'll come with you.' Her white teeth flash between full lips.

'No, I'll shoot round to Paul's. You know what he's like, no extras, no one waiting in the car. I'll only be half an hour.'

I kiss her on the head, know she's not happy. But I figure if I can see for myself that it's not true, that nothing's going on between Harvey and Rachel, I'll make it up to her, give her my undivided attention and, more importantly – in the fullness of time – she'll get to enjoy the house, my house, my wonderful house.

I scoot out the door, know I have to be quick to make it to my place and back in thirty minutes. I'm all energetic heart palpitations and speed along the road, my eyes peeled back in the fading light. If Harvey's there I'll get onto the lawyers, pressure them to speed up the process, push it through. I swing along the highway, make the right turn five kays out of town to head out to my property. And as I'm hurtling along the road, as the bitumen runs out and I feel gravel tickling the tyres, I get the sense something other than the heartbeats of Rachel, Petal and the fauna is cracking a rhythm. And then I notice a great glow mushrooming into the night.

Bonfire from hell.

The car lopes and scuds across the runnels of my driveway. My headlights kick up from the potholes. The glow seems to find centre directly ahead. And as I come over the final rise, I can't believe my eyes. My house is one great glowing tinderbox. I take it in: the huge oily flames leaping from the roof, the great flakes and fluttering embers swirling into the trees and across the sky.

I get out of the car, recognise the bad-boys standing around, their mouths gobbed open with surprise.

And as I scream for them to get buckets, as I start to rush around looking for the hose, Darrel comes towards me.

'What happened?' I call over the roar, seizing the hose nozzle and scrabbling at the tap.

Darrel's eyebrows cross furtively. 'Set fire to the compost. It burst into flames. Exploded actually. Spread to the house.'

'What? What the fuck were you doing lighting the compost?'

'Rachel asked us to. That's where she'd chucked the agapanthus. We had no idea the house would catch. Neither did Rach.'

I turn from the pathetic trickle coming from the hose, scowl at him.

'We were gunna take Harve out,' Darrel says, as if I've no right to be pissed off that my house is one curling ball of flame, 'string him up. But it's not true, Russ. We asked Harvey and he only missed today. He'll be back next Saturday.'

'*It was a joke!*' I scream in frustration at the hose, at Darrel, at the whole idiotic and unbelievably messed-up disaster. '*It was just a fucking joke!*'

'Sorry mate,' he murmurs, the wail of the Country Fire Authority registering in my mind as their truck makes its way along the road. Then, insanely hopeful I might nod in agreement, I hear through the roar, him again. 'I guess it would have been better to take the agapanthus straight to the tip.'

I fall to my knees at that moment, my folly a great huge weight pushing me down. And all I can envisage, all I can conjure in my mind, is the swollen bodies of agapanthus bulbs and the thought that I've never really liked the plants they turn into anyway.

The Brief Wondrous Lives of...

Kalinda Ashton
Kalinda has a love of soft cheeses and documentary films. When she is not consuming either, she writes. Her first novel, *The Danger Game*, will be published by Sleepers Publishing in 2009.

Max Barry
Max is the author of three novels: *Syrup*, listed by the *LA Times* as one of the Best Books of the Year in 1999; *Jennifer Government*, a *New York Times* Notable Book; and *Company*, a bestseller in the US and Australia. He lives in Melbourne. www.maxbarry.com

Samuel Bartlett
Samuel is a writer/cartoonist/animator who divides his time between Sydney and London.

Melissa Beit
Melissa has two small children so it is taking her a very long time to finish her novel. She writes short stories when they are asleep.

Tony Birch
Tony publishes short stories, essays and the occasional poem. His collection of stories, *Shadowboxing*, was published by Scribe in 2006.

Jo Bowers
Jo writes fiction and nonfiction and has been published in a number of anthologies, journals and magazines, including previous *Sleepers Almanacs* and *The Big Issue*.

Jo Case
Jo is books editor of *The Big Issue* and a regular book reviewer for Triple R's *Breakfasters*, *Australian Book Review* and various other outlets. She is stubbornly convinced that her own behaviour as a parent is beyond reproach.

Simon Cox
Simon was recently the young-writer-in-residence at the Katharine

Susannah Prichard Writers' Centre. Katharine Susannah Prichard was the first Australian novelist to gain international recognition. Simon likes grapefruit juice.

Patrick Cullen
Scribe will publish Patrick's first collection of stories in 2009.

Oslo Davis
Oslo does illustrations and cartoons for various publications, including the *Age*, *The New York Times* and *Meanjin*. He lives in Melbourne.

Daniel Ducrou
Daniel is a writer based in Northcote, Melbourne. His first novel manuscript, 'Conditions of Return', has been shortlisted for the Australian Vogel Literary Award and the Victorian Premier's Literary Prize.

Eleanor Elliott Thomas
Eleanor wears: muu-muu by Pol Pot; accessories by Benito Mussolini; hair by Kim Jong-Il. Calamitous terror of modern life, model's own.

SJ Finn
SJ Finn has had a happy dependence on words for many years. Getting them in the right order, though, not to mention in the written form, is another matter altogether. 'Agapanthus', luckily, is bound by rhythm, and words hardly come into it at all.

Leanne Hall
Leanne works in a bookshop, where she gets to talk about books all day long. She has had several short stories published and is currently working on a young adult novel.

Todd Hearon
Todd's recent poems have appeared in *Agni*, *Ploughshares*, *Poetry*, *Poetry London*, *Literary Imagination* and *Slate*. The recipient of a 2007 PEN New England 'Discovery' Award and the 2007 Friends of Literature Prize from *Poetry* magazine, he lives in Exeter, New Hampshire.

Ella Holcombe
Ella is twenty-six and lives in Brunswick. Her first collection of poetry, *Welcome, No Vacancy* was published by Five Islands Press in 2007.

Andrew Hutchinson
Andrew is the author of the award-winning novel, *Rohypnol* (Random House, 2007). His second novel will be released in 2009.

Rosemary Jones
Rosemary is a South Australian whose fiction has appeared in short story anthologies, literary magazines and on Radio Australia Writers Radio. She now lives and teaches in the US, where her work has been published or is forthcoming in *Cezanne's Carrot*, *The Mad Hatters' Review*, *Bent Pin*, *Salt River Review* and *Gargoyle*.

Richard Lawson
Richard lives in Sydney. When he isn't finding excuses for not writing, he coaches high school students in English.

Myron Lysenko
Myron is a poet and bookshop owner. Come and browse in Basho Bookshop, 139 Lygon Street, Brunswick East, Victoria.

Aaron Mannion
Aaron is still planning the perfect fallout shelter. He likes rain and dogs and some people. He feels embarrassed when people ask where he's from.

Russell McGilton
Russell is a writer, playwright, screenwriter and actor. He's written for publications including the *Age* and *The Big Issue*. He was a judge in the 2008 Bundoora Young Writers' Literary Awards. www.russellmcgilton.com.au

Imogen Melgaard
Imogen is a Melbourne writer who grew up in a paddock in central Victoria. Her writing blends her broad acre background with her urban student lifestyle.

Liza Monroy
Liza is the author of the novel, *Mexican High* (Ramdom House). She currently lives in Brooklyn, New York.

Rose Mulready
Rose is a lapsed romantic.

Peta Murray
Peta is a very slow playwright, and a reluctant teacher. She took baby steps in prose via the Professional Writing and Editing program at the CAE, where this story won the Cut Short Story Competition.

Pierz Newton-John
Pierz is an 'emerging' writer. He is stuck half-in and half-out of his chrysalis like a half-born caterpillar, occasionally excreting a literary work. He has won some prizes and been published places but he is not saying what or where, on the grounds that, if you aren't a writer, you don't care, and if you are, it will only make you feel bad about yourself, or superior, neither of which is good for you.

Ryan O'Neill
Ryan was born in Scotland, and now lives in Newcastle, NSW with his wife and two daughters.

Virginia Peters
Virginia lives in Coorabell, near Byron Bay. In between writing short stories she's working on a non-fiction novel.

JB Rawson
JB Rawson is a public servant who enjoys transport policy, kittens, and assurances that everything is going to be just fine. She has been published by Cardigan Press and Vignette Press *Mini Shots*.

Tim Richards
Tim is a Melbourne writer currently writing stories with the assistance of an Established Writer grant from the Australia Council.

Brendan Ryan
Brendan lives in Portarlington. His latest collections of poetry are *A Tight Circle* (Whitmore Press) and *A Paddock in His Head* (Five Islands Press).

Ian C Smith
Ian's latest book is *Memory Like Hunger* (Ginninderra).

Andrew Weldon
Andrew is a freelance cartoonist based in Melbourne. He has published two collections of his cartoons, the most recent being, *If You Weren't A Hedgehog... If I Weren't A Haemophiliac...* (Allen and Unwin).

Vinnie Wilhelm
Vinnie's fiction has been published or is upcoming in the *Virginia Quarterly Review*, the *Harvard Review*, the *Southern Review*, and elsewhere. He is currently living nomadically in America.

Grace Yee
Grace lives in Melbourne where she teaches English as a second language. She is a PhD candidate at the University of Melbourne.

THIS ALMANAC BELONGS TO

_____